SING SING NIGHTS

MR. KEELER *has also written:*

FIND THE CLOCK
THE VOICE OF THE SEVEN SPARROWS

SING SING NIGHTS

By HARRY STEPHEN KEELER

Author of

"Find the Clock," "The Voice of the Seven
Sparrows," etc.

WILDSIDE PRESS

First Printing........August, 1928
Second Printing....August, 1928
Third Printing......August, 1928
Fourth Printing....August, 1928
Fifth Printing ......August, 1928
Sixth Printing....*December,* 1928

To Hazel Goodwin Keeler

the charming helpmeet who sits across my breakfast table in Chicago, and who has done likewise in Limehouse, the *Quartier Latin,* New Orleans and even on Hudson Bay.

CONTENTS

Contents

Contents

SING SING NIGHTS

Sing Sing Nights

CHAPTER I

GENTLEMEN THREE

IN the large, square death-cell a sudden peculiar quiet had fallen upon four men of different nationalities. McCaigh, the American—he whom the newspapers, during the progress of the strange trial, had dignified with the appellation of "The Iron Man"— paced slowly up and down, his wide-set grey eyes roaming vacantly from the heavy oaken door, with its tiny barred window, to the solitary electric lamp which cast its shaded rays over a chamber fitted only with stout mission rockers, square mission table, couch and rug. A chamber it was which in its time had seen many a guest of high and low degree—a chamber which for years in Sing Sing prison had housed on their last nights those unfortunates who, formerly swinging off into all-engulfing blackness at the end of a hempen rope, were now more scientifically and expeditiously dispatched from an intricately wired chair connected to a 2,200-volt transformer.

Eastwood, the Englishman, the youngest of the four, sat back in his prison-made rocker uneasily drumming on his chair arm, and staring half-fascinatedly

at Shanahan, the red-haired guard, who was assigned
to sit with them and watch them on this, their last night
on earth. His delicately chiselled face, whitened from
over-confinement and the long rigours of a trial,
seemed even whiter than ever to-night in the rays of
the prison lamp; but in spite of its pallor it held an un-
mistakable handsomeness; in the eye gleamed forth the
light of fighting idealism.

Krenwicz, the one really foreign-looking man of the
three, lay on a long couch puffing away at a cigarette.
His was the lean, bearded, ascetic face of an intelligent
Russian of forty-five or less—the Russian suggesting
old Czarist days, now gone—and his eyes were eyes
which had seen trouble, had seen life in its shadows and
its high lights, and yet eyes in which shone forth the
smiling, dancing devils that proclaimed the incontro-
vertible philosophy of the tent-maker of Naishapur.
From where Krenwicz in his coarse homespun blue
prison suit lay, a passing glimpse through the crack
of the oaken door carried one's gaze far down a corridor to a large room, now lighted faintly by a tiny green
bulb, which housed a slightly raised platform bearing
a devilish-looking chair replete with nickel, copper,
leather and rubber fittings. But the sight of that
which on the morrow at dawn was to end the career of
him and his two companions, McCaigh the American,
and Eastwood the Englishman, evidently failed to
ruffle the composure of the lean man with the Russian
face, for he smiled and puffed away at his cigarette,
tossing the half-smoked paper tube into a brass cuspidor bolted to the cement floor.

Indeed, of all the four men there, Shanahan, the

death guard, the Irishman from County Cork, appeared to be the most ill at ease. His beefy, florid face looked troubled; he shifted his huge bulk back and forth in the heavy armchair; at times he mopped away at his flaming red pompadour with a mighty, muscular arm.

McCaigh, the man who was pacing the floor, was the first to break the silence that had descended upon the group.

"Well, gentlemen," he said, rather calmly, with that nonchalant smile which during the trial had given him the appellation of "The Iron Man," but which appeared forced in comparison to Krenwicz's quite spontaneous one, "we've got something like nine hours to live. What shall we do with ourselves on this glorious evening which the State of New York has so kindly consented that we spend in each other's company?"

"Most o' the boys w'at goes over th' line," put in Shanahan nervously, "plays car-rds." He paused. "There's a deck o' car-rds—chips, too—in that there table drawer."

He stopped, a little overawed by the air of calmness which hung over these three—to him—fine gentlemen of a higher stratum in life than that to which he was accustomed.

Again silence fell upon them. Eastwood, the young Englishman, rose from his chair, went over to the table and poured himself a stiff drink from the decanter with glasses which stood there. Swallowing it down, he turned his face to McCaigh.

"I'll jolly well say," he pronounced in finely modulated tones, "that your State of New York is certainly treating us like gentlemen on this, our last night."

Again silence. It was evident that conversation did not thrive. The mission clock on the stone wall ticked away, its ticks sounding like miniature rifle shots in a great forest. Finally Krenwicz spoke, flicking off the ashes of his eleventh cigarette on to the floor. His words bore not the slightest trace of an accent.

"Do any of you gentlemen anticipate a possible intervention by the governor?"

Shanahan spoke up.

"Boys, I don't want to disappoint yeze, but Governor Willets, when he does annything, does it quicker than th' lasth minut. I wish he'd help yeze out, for yezes is gentlemin, all right, all right; but whin it gets midnight th' night before the—before th' electicution—well, boys, don't raise anny false hopes in your hearts. I been in this j'int f'r eliven years now."

"Shanahan is doubtlessly correct," said Eastwood, dropping back into his chair. "We go." His voice grew hard. "And to me the going is all a pleasure. And furthermore, if it were all to be done over again I'd do it myself just exactly as I did."

"And I, by God!" muttered McCaigh.

"Gentlemen, and I," said Krenwicz, and his laughing eyes suddenly darkened into cruel shadows.

"And as soon as the old switch is pulled——" put in McCaigh, but stopped. Outside in the corridor were the sound of voices, the jangle of keys. A second later the oaken door swung open, and there stood revealed in the opening a blue-uniformed turnkey, accompanied by an elderly grey-haired man of around sixty years of age, finely clad in rich clothing of brown. Across his arm was a light overcoat. His face was keen, his eyes were grave, judicial.

Shanahan was the first to spring to his feet.

"It's—it's his Excellency—it's Governor Willets," he breathed.

An air of suffocating tenseness dropped like a mantle over the occupants.

With a glance at the oaken door, the governor stepped into the room, surveying the three condemned men curiously. The turnkey beckoned to Shanahan, the death watch.

"The governor wishes to speak to Eastwood, McCaigh, and Krenwicz in private."

Shanahan backed out into the corridor. The oaken door with its single square aperture swung to. Its bolts shot together with an ominous click. And the highest official in the State of New York was locked in the same room with three men condemned to be ferried by Charon across the dark river Styx within nine hours.

He gazed curiously, abstractedly about him. McCaigh, Eastwood, Krenwicz—who now sat on the couch —waited expectantly. The governor paused but a moment, then dropped into Shanahan's chair, nearest the door.

"Gentlemen," he broke the silence, "you know evidently that I am Governor Willets, Governor of the State of New York. You know, therefore, that I have the power of pardoning those who deserve pardon. Intervention has been sought for in your cases along many lines, wires—both political and diplomatic— have been pulled, levers have been worked along a number of angles. But, frankly, absolutely nothing has developed that has warranted my using my executive authority in the direction of clemency."

The faces of the three men reflected a variety of emotions. Krenwicz's, calm; Eastwood's, a half suggestion of keen disappointment; and McCaigh's, an elusive hope that somehow—some way—something was nevertheless to develop.

After a pause Governor Willets went on:

"Now, gentlemen, I am going to be brief. What I shall say I shall be able to say in five minutes. You, Eastwood; you, Krenwicz; you, McCaigh, are all going to pay the death-penalty at dawn in the morning for the murder of Howard Creynell on the night of June 11." Over the faces of the three hearers a look of strange, almost identical, bitter defiance went. The governor proceeded imperturbably.

"Let me review that case briefly," he said. "On the night of June the eleventh Howard Creynell, of the Authors and Artists Club of New York City, was shot and killed at his rooms in the Belgravia at eleven-fifteen in the evening, just after he opened the door of his apartment and snapped on the library lamp. A police patrol wagon returning from a vice raid in Upper Manhattan passed the Belgravia just in time for the officers to surround the place. You, McCaigh, a man bred and born to our laws and the penalties for their breaking, author of *The Riddle of the Onyx Hand*, *The Washington Square Enigma*, and others of our most intriguing and best-selling mystery novels, not to mention scores of novelettes in the better type of our magazines, were caught as you dropped from the fire-escape in the courtway at the bottom, your revolver still in your hand. At the trial, later, you admitted that you had been perched upon that fire-escape at the window of his library for hours."

Governor Willets turned to Eastwood.

"And you, Eastwood of London, at the first rush of the police were caught standing back of that huge Japanese screen; you, a man as well known in literary matters on this side of the water as in your own great home metropolis of England; author of over a thousand short stories so bizarre and odd that you have won fame from the very daring originality of your conceptions; a man whose stories have been printed on this side of the ocean as much as on your own side; a man who had the honor of winning the 5,000-guinea prize offered by the *Mercury* for the strangest short story of the year. You, Eastwood, had in your hand a revolver which held several discharged shells, as well as a skeleton or common pass-key with which you had gained access to those rooms, and back of which screen you must have stood for hours in the dark."

He turned to Krenwicz. "And you, Krenwicz, a man who came over to this country as a lad from darkest Russia in the steerage, a man who learned to speak our language so well that he was enabled to embark on a brilliant journalistic career that placed him on newspapers from coast to coast; a man who graduated from the journalistic field to accomplishing such a swift-moving novel as that one of yours which ran in the *Hearstmopolitan—The Jade Vase*—wasn't that the title of it?—a man who did one successful play, *The Daughter of Chow Chin,* and who was engaged before this trial to do another, this time for the promi-

nent and beautiful Chinese actress, Sara Ying of San
Francisco; you, Krenwicz"—he shook his head sadly
—"you, Krenwicz, who had achieved all that at the
comparatively youthful age of forty-five—you had
been sitting in a big armchair in the dark, facing the
lamp, where you could kill Howard Creynell the moment he should snap on the light. You did not know
that Eastwood sat back of that screen across the room
—that he had dozed off during the time that you had
entered through the kitchenette door; nor did you
know that McCaigh was perched upon the dark fire-
escape, waiting likewise for Howard Creynell to return
and snap on the lamp. You had told Parkins, Creynell's man, that you were Creynell's cousin from Syra-
cuse, and that you wanted to sit in the kitchenette and
smoke—to surprise Creynell when he returned home.
When Parkins left, you crept into the library and
into the big armchair. And you surprised Creynell
all right, all right! You gave yourself up immediately to the police that swarmed into the room, handing
over *your* revolver with its two or three chambers discharged."

The governor went on inexorably. "At the court
trial, which the Supreme Court of New York State has
decreed was free from technical error and the verdict
of which they have refused to set aside, something came
out why two of you murdered Creynell. Yes," he
added, looking oddly from face to face, "but two of
you did it, for there were only two bullet wounds in
Creynell's body. No bullet was found in the walls or
furniture of that room, no shots but two were heard
by the occupants of the Belgravia that night. No

third bullet escaped that night. There were but two
—and only two—fired. In the tense excitement, one
of you three thought he fired, but he did not. Two of
you, we definitely know, used revolvers which already
had not one but a number of used shells in their cham·
bers."

The governor paused and then changed his tack
suddenly. "At the trial it came out why two of America's, and one of England's, best and cleverest writers
tried to kill one of our leading club men, himself only
an amateur—a dilettante—in fiction and art. Creynell, while drunk that afternoon at the Authors and
Artists Club, and playing cards with the three of you,
had openly bragged that he had an assignation with
a woman—a mere girl—who had become madly infatu-
ated with him. He did not give her name, and possibly
—but not necessarily—that is why I presume it has
never come out at the trial. You three, however, testified at the trial that he had introduced this girl to
you the night before in the foyer of the New Amsterdam theater at the *première* of Krenwicz's play, *The
Daughter of Chow Chin.* She was young, innocent,
in the flower of maidenhood. Creynell, drunk in the
card game, told you all that he had promised to marry
her, but that he intended only to avail himself of her
mad infatuation for him at a Fifty-fifth Street house
of unsavory reputation. You three testified at the trial
that you knew he was already married, that he was
merely ruining her. You testified that to each of you
came the shock, the realization, that this viper—as
you termed him—must be killed to protect this girl
as well as others." He paused. "McCaigh, Creynell

once ruined a girl whom you loved. You cherished a smoldering hatred of him for that. As for you, Krenwicz, Creynell had dragged down a poor Russian girl from the Russian quarter. That girl was your cousin. You hated him for that. You, Eastwood, were simply a mad idealist who, as you said, wished to rid the earth of a viper. And each of you, unknown to the others, prepared to go to Creynell's rooms that night and end his career."

The governor paused and then went on. "You know, gentlemen, the result of the trial as well as I. Not one of you would admit that he was not the man who fired one of the two fatal shots. Stubborn, or idealistic, each of you is going to the chair because he will not claim absolution on that one score. You prejudiced the jury by refusing to divulge the identity of the girl in the case. You claimed that all of you had seen her, talked with her, but that Creynell had been careful not to give her name in the introduction. That is poppy-cock. Two of you murdered Creynell—yes, murdered, gentlemen, for you cannot take the law into your hands in this state while I am governor of it. No matter what Creynell was, it was up to you either to warn the girl and allow her then to do what she pleased in the matter, or to expose Creynell by some process of law. Not to kill him. Not to murder him. Not to shoot him down in cold blood.

"No, gentlemen, you can never, never secure a pardon from me. It was out-and-out murder—perhaps justified to you three, but certainly not to the law." He rose. He glanced at his watch. "I must go now." He took from the breast pocket of his brown suit a crisp folded document and tossed it on the table. "Mc-Caigh, Eastwood, Krenwicz—one of you failed to fire on the night of June the eleventh. That man, whoever he is, need not go to the chair if he will absolve himself. I have here a pardon, filled out—signed by myself. It is blank on the top line. That blank is for you three to fill in—to help you to decide which two among you fired, and which one did not. You three know. I do not. The law does not. The police do not. And the dead man, if he knows, cannot tell." He turned and pressed a button at the side of the oaken door. "In ten minutes I will have returned to your cell the death guard. On my way out I shall leave a sealed letter with the warden. That letter, which he will open a few minutes before the—er—electrocution, will apprise him of the fact that one of you has in the meantime received an official pardon and that the document is in the possession of its rightful recipient." He paused. "And in the next ten minutes, gentlemen, I would suggest that you realize you are facing destiny. Indeed, you had better come to a clean-cut decision of some sort instead of claiming glory." The governor's voice had grown bitingly sarcastic.

At the impact of the button, the turnkey's face appeared in the opening. A second later the door swung open.

"In ten minutes," said the governor authoritatively, "send in the death watch." The door closed behind him. The bolts shot into their sockets. His footsteps could be heard echoing down the cement corridor. The three men were alone.

McCaigh, the American, was the first to speak.

"Fight it out among you two," he said. "I don't know whether I fired or not. It's all hazy. But I intended to. So what's the difference? The damn snake! That girl—a goddess in embryo, if ever there was one. I'd kill Creynell over again if I had my wishes."

The lean Russian spoke. "I think I fired," he declared very slowly, "but I do not know for a certainty, due to the tension of the moment and the roar of shots so close to my ears. But even if I had not, I would go to the chair gladly for the extreme honor of having killed Creynell, the garter-snake of the snake tribe. I, personally, do not consider myself in the argument. I am finished."

And Eastwood, the idealist, the man whose home lay far across the seas, spoke, his words tumbling over each other. "I was back of that Japanese screen, yes. And I would have given him every chamber in the gun, gladly. I do not know whether I killed him, or even whether I fired—but I hope to God that I did. One thing is certain. It is an honor to be electrocuted for killing him, and I claim that honor. Fight it out, you chaps, among yourselves."

Silence.

Then McCaigh, the Iron Man, spoke. "Gentlemen, we have thrashed out this same irritating question to an appreciable extent at the trial, and to an exhausting extent before our lawyers. We could not then determine that two should take the blame of the two shots, and that one should escape. Yet here before us is a pardon. It means life for one of us. We cannot deliberately tear that thing up. Creynell is gone —the snake is crushed. And that was the end to be attained." He paused. "No one will ask that his name be filled out upon this document. But one must. The thing to be accomplished was accomplished. You, Krenwicz, or you, Eastwood, fill in your name."

Silence. Then Eastwood, the idealist, spoke.

"The ten minutes is nearly up," he said. "McCaigh is right. No need for all to die. Creynell is dead. Not one of us knows on account of the excited state of his mind that night and the rapid shots as the light went on, whether or no his own weapon responded fully to the pressure of finger against trigger—whether, in fact, he fired one of the two fatal shots." He paused again. "We might play your American game of draw-poker—we might even draw straws! But we three are not of the rabble. And so I have a wonderful contest to propose. In a few seconds Shanahan, ignorant prison guard, returns to the death watch. You, Krenwicz, have not only written many stories, but you are the author as well of a novel and a successful play. I doubt if there is a mystery writer in America or England who weaves into his plots a love story of such sheer fineness as do you. And you, McCaigh, while not a playwright, have proven yourself such an ingenious craftsman in the literary field that your future was assured, had—had all this not happened. As for me—well, I too have done something in my small way, perhaps, whether worth while or not I do not know, although I fear that my poor efforts have been vastly overrated by my indulgent critics. And so, because of all this, I propose that each of us do his mightiest story now, on his death night; that we spin our stories in words this time, instead of in ink; that our sole audience shall be ignorant Shanahan, death watch. **Let** us spin our three stories until morning, if needs be; till the coming of the grey dawn, and—and—the death chair. The story that most entertains Shanahan— that Shanahan votes is the best story—shall place its teller's name on the blank pardon, and the rest go to the electric chair."

A silence fell, while Eastwood's remarkable proposition filtered into the minds of his hearers.

Then it was broken by McCaigh, the Iron Man. "Eureka!" he cried. "A contest that is a gentlemen's contest."

"A game," said Krenwicz, "a splendid, absorbing game for three gentlemen on their last night on earth. A contest of wits, brilliancy, invention." He turned and surveyed the other two with a half-smile. "And if Eastwood, McCaigh and Krenwicz stick like cobblers to their lasts, it will be a strange joust that will be tilted out in the arena of a prison guard's mind—the Knights of Romance, of Mystery, of Love, of Fantasy, struggling to down each other!" He paused again. "Agreed, gentlemen? A fictional pantechnicon it shall be for—Shanahan?"

"Agreed," said the two others in unison. "The decision shall rest with Shanahan."

No sooner had they spoken than the burly prison guard himself inserted his key into the lock and entered. He carefully locked the door behind him, and looked puzzledly around the room. Krenwicz had already risen and had placed the pardon in the drawer of the table.

"Shanahan," he said slowly, twirling the decanter of

whiskey about on its base, "this—this is our last night. The governor has so decreed. And we have decided to entertain each other, if not Mr. Shanahan, by the subtle art of the fictionist. Get me, Shanahan? And to settle a little something between ourselves, we want you at dawn to announce which of the three has told what seems to you the most engaging story. Will you do it?"

"Will I do ut?" grunted Shanahan. "That will I, byes. 'Tis Shanahan w'at is a great story reader. 'Tis Shanahan w'at has rid ahl th' magazines an' buks he c'n get his hands ferninst." He dropped into a chair. "An' 'tis Shanahan what will tell yeze at dawn which wan of ye has spinned th' bistest yarn." He leaned back in his chair with a sigh of relief. "An' 'tis glad I am that yeze byes is goin' to spind your last night so calm. Yeze is dead game."

Eastwood spoke, a little hesitantly. "I trust, of course, gentlemen, that being a stranger to your shores, should I lay my story in London, that city which perchance I may never see again, that city so dear to my heart and so far away, and shall moreover weave into it as characters those who are my countrymen, I will in no way be violating the terms of our agreement"—he turned to Shanahan—"nor that I shall in any way confuse Mr. Shanahan?"

"By no manes," said that gentleman, smiling. "Did I not live in Lunnon when I hustled freight on th' East Indy Docks, a braw lad out o' County Cork? 'Tis the city I know like a buk mesilf."

"I think that answers your question, Eastwood," said Krenwicz kindly. "After all, what matters it

where a story is laid? Does not the true story-teller
—the artist—make alive the little spot on earth's surface where he lays his story? So lay *your* story, Eastwood, where your heart desires."

A pause followed the establishing of these preliminary understandings. Each man stepped to the table
in turn and poured himself out a small drink of the
fiery liquid. Eastwood looked at Shanahan as he sank
into the nearest chair.

"Will you select the first story-teller, Shanahan?"
He looked at the others curiously. "The best story,
gentlemen—think of it! It means love—happiness—
lights—life. How—how our art must exert itself to-
night!"

Shanahan gazed embarrassedly about him. "Well,
Misther McCaigh, sippose you till us the first yarn."

McCaigh, the American, bit his lips, then smiled
gamely. He surveyed Shanahan carefully from head
to foot. "Shanahan," he said slowly, "I think I can
tickle your fancy, and even mystify you a bit as well.
At least I shall try my best to do so. Like Eastwood,
I regret that I have not lingered long enough in your
great city of New York, nor yet lived in London, to
stage my story here among New York's sky-scrapers
or there among London's quaint streets. So I shall
therefore allow my little mystery drama to play itself
out on the boards of another London—that city of
America a thousand miles to the west of us, which has
so often been called the London of the West—where
I was born and reared. That city I see you have
already guessed is Chicago, great roaring metropolis
of millions of souls, with its four hundred and fifty

solid square miles of seething humanity and unseen melodrama always lurking around the corner." He paused. "Just what shall be the title of my tale in this peculiar Sing Sing nights entertainment I do not know, for it is a story that will never have to be named for an editor; and so I shall call it just 'The Strange Adventure of the Giant Moth.'" An attentive silence fell upon the little group. "And if you will now step forth with me to a quiet uptown corner in Chicago, far from the roar and clamor of its business section, I shall take the liberty of introducing you to one to whom I would hesitate ordinarily to introduce any gentleman —a quaint blade of half-Chinese parentage, by name 'Moonface' Eddy Chang, who will play an amusing part, if not an important one, in my little tale." Whereupon McCaigh, with that inscrutable smile of his, began:

THE STRANGE ADVENTURE OF THE GIANT MOTH

CHAPTER II

IN WHICH WE MEET MR. CHANG

MOONFACE EDDY CHANG, attired immaculately and twirling his cane with all the blasé composure of the typical idle youth about town, stopped short in his languid progress across the marble-tiled foyer of the Plaza Hotel. At the same moment his breath left him in a short gasp, and across his squat, semi-Chinese face flashed the look of the hunted. From where he stood rooted to the spot he studied carefully the corpulent, strongly-built man, obviously the house detective, who stood leaning on one elbow talking to the clerk.

Moonface always had possessed a more than keen recollection of human physiognomies. That face, that figure, his tingling memory warned him, belonged to no other than a former member of the Chicago police force. He paused no longer, but spun on the heel of his cloth-topped shoe and moved out of the hotel precipitately towards quiet Clark Street, filled at this point with unobtrusive shops.

Outside, in the street, he tucked his cane under his arm and mopped his forehead with a decidedly plebeian motion. "Damn!" he ejaculated. "Who'd expect to see one of the old-time bulls holding down the soft job of house detective in a hostelry 'way up here on the quiet North Side?" He ruminated on the matter, breaking into a brisk walk. "It's a small world, all right, all right."

By this time he was round the corner. Another entrance to the Plaza Hotel—a side entrance this time —loomed up. Across the way Lincoln Park gleamed vividly green in the morning sunlight; foliage waved in the breeze; children bounced gleefully on the soft turf. Moonface hesitated a moment, and then strolled towards the side entrance, looking warily inside from the corner of his eye.

Here, however, was visible only the polished brass gate of an elevator shaft, and a velvet couch for those who might wait for the car. The clerk's desk and the foyer containing that unpleasant-looking corpulent figure which smacked of the police and their tiresome meddling, was around a bend in the corridor, and hence not in sight. Moonface paused but a second; then, stifling an artificial yawn, he turned in quickly through the side entrance just in time to pop into the elevator car, piloted by a grey-clad conductor, as it reached the first floor to let out a handsomely gowned woman, flashing in silks and jewels.

As the car rose from the dangerous first floor, an inaudible sigh of relief oozed from Moonface, and he quickly consulted a slip of paper in his pocket. "Fifth floor," he said languidly, tucking away the paper in the pocket of his smart cut-away coat.

He strolled from the car at the fifth floor and

threaded his way along the rich damask carpet through gloomy halls until he came to a white-enamelled door bearing the number 555. Here he paused a moment, then knocked a peculiar knock: first a sharp blow and a wait, then two in succession, then a pause and another sharp blow.

The sound of a figure stirring from a chair inside was audible. The white-enamelled door swung back. In the opening stood a big pink-cheeked man dressed in fashionable clothes of brown, but just now in his shirt-sleeves only. A rich stick-pin gleamed in his silk tie. His age might have been around forty, although about him was a youthful air of alertness, springiness, wariness. His big blue eyes were cool and calculating. His neck was just a little thick and bullish. He was a handsome man, in spite of the fact that in his face lurked the suggestion that with him material ends justified all and any means whatsoever.

His countenance filled with a wolfish light as he beheld Moonface standing in the doorway. Silently he motioned back towards the interior of the splendidly-furnished room, with its striped upholstered pieces, its white-covered chiffonier gleaming with silver toilet articles, its windows looking out over the green, luxuriant park.

Moonface stepped in and the door closed behind him. He paused a moment to survey himself in a long pier-glass on the wall. He pivoted vainly in his well-cut suit, turning on his slender cane. He might have been handsome, were it not for the squat, round, half-Mongolian face tinged with saffron, with the piercing dark eyes that seemed even more piercing on account

of the expressionless field in which they were framed.
He turned to a chair as he heard the big man's voice:

"Sit down, Chang. I see my note to your old hang-
out reached you."

Moonface nodded. "And I nearly ran into a one-
time acquaintance of mine from the old Chicago police
force—house detective. My advice to you, old man, is
not to try to pull anything around here. I dodged out
just in time. Now I'm wondering how I'm going to get
out of this dump without passing him again. Chicago's
no place for me, that's certain." He paused. "Well,
what's the game, Gryce?"

"Not so loud." The man in the brown suit leaned
back in his chair and stuck his thumbs in the armholes
of his vest. He surveyed the trim, neat figure across
from him for a long while. He nodded his head slowly.
"You can do it, Eddy Chang, if you can cover up that
semi-Chink phiz of yours with enough grease paint.
There's the whole trick. Grease paint, as garish and
as thick and as colored as you can slap it on. Grease
paint'll get your moonface by."

"Grease paint!" ejaculated Moonface bewilderedly.
"Say," he added roughly, "what are you spouting
about? Grease paint—what is it I can do? What's the
game? I knew when I got your note that you had
something good up your sleeve. Come out with it,
Gryce! Spit it out! What's the trick?"

The big man drew his chair close to that occupied
by his visitor, and lowered his voice till it could hardly
reach beyond the edge of the rug.

"Moonface, it's absolutely the best thing ever. I'm
thinking that the Fates have been kind to me—and

you." He paused. "But here's the dope. First, before I go ahead, you've heard of Rufus Eldredge, the La Salle Street broker?"

Moonface wrinkled up his forehead. He pondered. "Yeah—I guess I have. Down on Chicago's Wall Street somewhere. The name has a familiar tang to it. But go ahead. What about Eldredge? Know him, do you?"

The big man nodded, smiling. "Know him? I rather think I do. Know him, his son, and his lovely daughter. Know the people they mix with. Been in their home. I'm in their set. Of course all this doesn't interest you—but——" He paused. "Moonface, there's absolutely the richest pickings of a lifetime waiting for me—and you. You know that my game isn't ordinary crookedness, and I——"

"I well know it," interrupted Moonface sourly. "You're what I call an international rogue, Gryce. You'd sell your country's soul for dollars. You've never spoken of where you sprang from, but I believe you're a man without any land on earth—except the one where you hang your hat at the time. You're out for the mon——"

"S-s-h!" The big man placed his fingers on his lips. "Not so loud, not so loud. Don't get wrought up over it. Have your own thoughts. All right. Now pay attention once more. Moonface, there's a man in this big, roaring city of Chi who has something of a most peculiar nature that to him is worth absolutely nothing—but that to me is worth just a hundred thousand dollars in cold cash. Never mind what his name is. He knows it's worth a lot to me—and he wants hard cash for it. He——"

"What is it?" interrupted Moonface hurriedly.

The big man's face clouded up. He coughed nervously. He ignored the question. "As I say, Eddy, he wants cash—hard cash only. And if I can get it from him I can turn it over for a hundred thousand cold in twenty-four hours. But he wants an even ten thousand dollars for it. There you are."

"Rats!" put in Moonface contemptuously. "Lift it from him." He reflected a second. "But, after all, why don't you buy it from him outright if you really can make nine hundred per cent?"

"As to your first question," said the man across from him, "he's smart enough to hide it. In all likelihood it's in a downtown safety box. Perhaps not. But you know, and I know, one can't steal anything when one doesn't know where it is. As to the second question ——" He fumbled down in his hip pocket and withdrew a leather bill fold. Opening it up, he displayed a number of crisp yellow bills. He counted them quickly over, some of them hundreds, in front of Moonface's avaricious eyes. "Three hundred—four hundred—five hundred—and—and sixty-three dollars, Moonface. That's all that's left of that consular trick we pulled off in Buenos Aires. Now, is it plain why I don't buy it from him?"

Moonface was silent. A glint of suspicion wavered in his eyes; then it disappeared. "Go on," he said at length.

"So there stands the situation," the big man resumed. "To make ninety thousand clear I have to raise ten thousand. And heavens only knows how I can do it—that is, until last night. Now, though, everything is changed. Moonface, come out of your dreams, man. You're just sitting down to a banquet where, if you handle your knife and fork right, there's going to be a hundred-thousand-dollar feast."

He rose from his chair and proceeded over to a writing-desk, where he reached into a pigeon-hole for something. When he returned to his seat his fingers held an envelope, crisp, bond, rich.

Moonface, quite fascinated by now, leaned forward in his own chair and watched the performance. On the wall a mahogany clock ticked ominously.

CHAPTER III

THE big man reached in the bond envelope and took from it two square bond cards. One he laid on Moonface's left knee; the other on Moonface's right knee. Each was a duplicate of the other. Each was expensively engraved. Each bore a coat-of-arms in its left-hand upper corner. Each read:

YOUR PRESENCE IS REQUESTED

EN MASQUE

AT A PRIVATE BALL

TO BE GIVEN AT THE HOME OF

MISS SHIRLEY ELDREDGE

ON HER TWENTY-THIRD BIRTHDAY

FRIDAY EVENING, JUNE SEVENTH

1400 LAKE SHORE DRIVE

This card signed by bearer,
to be left at doorway.

Moonface stared from one card to the other, puzzled. Then he looked up. "Two cards," he echoed faintly. "Two cards——"

"Two cards instead of one. Two cards in my envelope instead of one, by mistake," went on the other

27

sharply. "Ever hear of the winds tempering themselves to the shorn wolves, Moonface? Ever hear of
fate dipping down into the affairs of men? Ever hear
of luck, Moonface?" He paused. "Now, Eddy Chang,
pay close attention. I won't keep you on the rack any
longer.

"Eddy, Miss Shirley Eldredge has spoken of this
mask ball to me as far back as several weeks ago. Old
man Eldredge is a millionaire—got a splendid ballroom in his residence. According to what she has already let drop, there's going to be over three hundred
people present. You can guess the kind of females
that'll be there in full regalia: fat old dowagers with
diamond sunbursts swinging from their fat chests; silly
society girls with diamond rings and diamond brace-
lets from all along the Gold Coast between Lincoln
Park and the beach at Oak Street; thin, scrawny ma-
trons with diamond necklaces that sparkle and gleam
and scintillate; and last but not least"—his face took
on a peculiar look—"Shirley Eldredge herself with the
diamond necklace that belonged to old man Eldredge's
wife. I've seen it two or three times; I've touched it
when I've been dancing with her. And it's worth fifty
thousand dollars, Moonface, if it's worth a red cent!"

Moonface peered down at the two engraved cards on
his knee. Finally he looked up. "Light," he said im-
pressively, "is beginning to filter in on my obtuse mentality composed of one-fourth Chinese and three-
quarters white. I note particularly your pleasant mention of diamonds and more diamonds and then some.
I note also that either card gives entrance to the big
ball. And I——"

"And you, the boy with the cleverest pair of fingers in America or Australia, are to be there in a clown suit, with that phiz of yours smeared up thick with colored grease paints, and before the evening is over you're going to lift something that we can turn over to the nearest fence for ten thousand, buy in the thing I've broached to you, and which I'll tell you more about after we get the money to buy it in, and we split fifty thousand apiece. Now, Moonface, do you grasp the beautiful working of fate?"

Moonface was now all agog, sitting clear forward on the edge of his chair, his eyes agleam, his long, narrow fingers twitching at imaginary sparklers.

"Wait," he said eagerly, "I'm the man for the job, Gryce. Once I get in that hall and dancing around, I'll strip some fat dame of her rocks or forget that I've the cleverest pair of fingers this side o' Melbourne. But——" He pointed down at the engraved invitation. "But it says here it is to be signed and left at the doorway. Where does little Eddy Chang get off on that?"

The big man smiled. "Easy. I've been thinking, tossing, pondering, puzzling all night on that point. But now I've got it all fixed up. And here we are: Suppose you get away with the stunt all right, whether it's Shirley Eldredge's string or some fat dowager's. Suppose an alarm goes up. There's two explanations: either the jewels are lost or stolen. The first thing they do is to examine all the cards at the door, scrutinising every name written on them. Suppose they find that every name signed there is a bona-fide acquaintance of the family—an invited guest? Do you think

for a minute, Moonface, they can afford to unmask
and search every one of those three hundred guests?
Certainly not. Can't be done. The notoriety and the
confusion would be too great.

"If it were Shirley Eldredge's string," the big man
continued, "I know for a certainty that old man Eldredge would lose it before he'd have such a disgrace
as a public search come down on his function. So our
one big problem, therefore, is to provide a name for
that card—a name which won't be duplicated and
which at the same time will be one of the intimates of
the family.   Then an examination of the cards at
the door will reveal only the fact that whatever is missing has not been stolen but is probably lost, since no
wolves are in among the lambs."

Moonface, tense, absorbed, nodded. "You've hit the
problem all right, Gryce. The crucial moment is when
they examine those cards at the door just after the
alarm is given."

"Now, there are two people who are very close to the
Eldredge family circle," went on the big man imperturbably, "and to whom, at the same time, I have been
introduced. So close, in fact, are both, that from
what Shirley Eldredge has let drop in my presence,
both are certainly on the invitation list. One is Jack
Hennly, the millionaire polo player, a sort of idle
bachelor who lives like a butterfly. The other is Niccolo di Paoli, the famous violinist, who has been among
the gatherings in the library numerous times when I've
been there. So there are two people, you see, who are
undoubtedly to be on the guest list of this masquerade
ball. Suppose either the first or the second were not

to be present? And suppose he had not sent in written regrets? What would you think of that, Moonface?"

The slim figure stirred in the chair. "That would be too fine to be true," he commented uneasily. "But how do we know for sure that they both are on the guest list? And how do we know that either one isn't going to be there? And deesa guy, Neecolo di Paoli, who playa da violeen? I theenka as I could take his part, all righta, all righta, but dere be a deviluvva time eefa two dagos by sama name start to come in doorway, eh? What you tenka dat?"

The big man clapped his hands gleefully. "Bully, bully, Moonface. You always were there on dialects. But that's not the violinist at all. He doesn't talk like a Bowery peanut vendor. But you'll imitate him right, boy; you're there with the fine art; and you're all to the good but that face of yours."

He paused. "Well, I just got back to Chicago yesterday after being out of town on a hunting trip at an estate out near Elgin. Found the card—rather the two cards—waiting for me. After sending for you to talk things over, I began to concentrate my own wits on the thing. By morning I had doped out the tentative solution I've already given. First I called Jack Hennly's quarters—but no answer. The beggar probably sleeps all day and roams the white lights all night. If I'd got him I intended to impersonate Rufus Eldredge himself. However, to the story. Then I called the quarters of di Paoli. He answered the 'phone himself. I told him that I was Mr. Eldredge and asked him if he were coming to my daughter's mask ball to-morrow night.

"To my delight," the big man went on, "he apologized profusely—I could even see his hands waving over the 'phone—and told me that a sudden telegram coming in just that morning would make it necessary for him to leave within a few hours to stay over Sunday; and he asked the privilege of extending his verbal regrets to me in person instead of writing them to Miss Shirley. That was enough, Moonface. The Fates are with us. You, to-morrow night, are Niccolo di Paoli, appreciably the same build, weight, and height—but for God's sake cover up that squat face of yours with seven layers of thick grease paint." He paused. "Now, what's the answer?"

Moonface pocketed one of the engraved cards eagerly, almost as if he feared the donor might regret the rash gift. "Only one answer," he said eagerly, "and that is, I'm on! It looks to me to be the neatest thing that's come my direction within a year. It's the hand o' fate all right, Gryce. As Moonface Eddy Chang I'd have as much chance to stroll into one of those society diamond exhibitions as a snowball would have of existence down in hell—but, believe me, old man, once I get in there and dance with the ladies—and I'm some glider—we'll come out richer than we went in."

He looked at the card. "I'll be making my plans and figuring on them a little closer in the meantime. And while you're about it, Gryce, write out the spelling of this dago violin player. I don't want to sign wrong and crab the beautiful game." He paused. "I'll go as a clown, of course. That'll give me a chance for the grease paints. And how are you going to be masked?"

The big man went momentarily white under his pink skin. "For God's sake, Moonface, never mind me. Stay away from me the whole evening. I can't afford to take any chances. Never mind how I'm going to be masked." His voice rose. "Remember—remember—stay away from me. Don't try to find me out and talk to me. I don't want you near me. I tell you I can't afford to take chances."

"Oh—all right," returned Moonface frigidly. "As you like it. Pipe down. Pipe down."

The two men sat for a few minutes longer discussing some minor details of the plan, the bigger of the two describing in turn the girl, Shirley Eldredge; her father, Rufus Eldredge; and her brother, Malcolm Eldredge. Finally, Moonface, engraved card tucked snugly away in the breast pocket of his cutaway coat, his slender cane once more in his hand, arose.

"Then all's fixed," he said cheerfully. "All the scenes set for the big show. Where do I meet you the afternoon after the ball?"

"Come straight here," said the big man, "and bring the haul. Come through the side entrance, and in that way you won't have to pass through the foyer and meet your friend, your ex-Chicago cop." He dipped into his trousers pocket and fished up a steely-looking key. "Here's a duplicate key I made myself from the hotel one. Use this if I'm not here, and come inside and wait for me. These upper halls are deserted. If you haven't the nerve, call me by 'phone and let me know where to see you outside. We'll have to put the bigger deal through quick."

With a few parting words Moonface left the room. Once out of the elevator he slipped like a shadow from the hotel and boarded the first car on Clark Street. Inside of twenty minutes he was entering a dirty-looking curio shop on South Halsted Street, its window filled with brass andirons, faded paintings, and curious carvings. An old man with a long white beard and beady, shifty eyes, wearing a black silk skull-cap, came from the dark interior of the store and peered at his customer from behind the counter.

Moonface, evidently familiar with the place and the owner, inclined his head meaningly towards the back of the store, and then, slipping behind the counter, passed rearward into a dark little room fitted with a bed, a few dishes, and a gas-plate. The bearded shop-owner hobbled after him.

As soon as they were back of the partition that cut off the front of the store, Moonface asked in a low voice: "Krellwitz, are you in condition to pass over some cold cash Saturday morning for some sparklers— say a big sum this time?"

"Alvays retty, Moonvace," quavered the old man. "How mooch gash I neet haf on hant, eh?"

"How much are you paying per carat now?" queried the man with the cane.

"Shust as bevore. I bay feefty dollars per carat if dey ees a bure vite diamont."

"You dirty robber!" groaned the younger man bitterly. "Pure white perfect stones are worth two hundred and fifty per in the market." He paused, reflecting. "Krellwitz, have as much as ten thousand dollars in cold cash around you Saturday morning or afternoon. You'll see me again. That's all for to-day."

He left the shop, the old fence rubbing his hands and mumbling to himself. Outside in the clear bright sunlight of Halsted Street, Moonface stared up at the blue sky and smiled a broad, quizzical smile.

"Little Moonface to be the cat's-paw, eh?" he queried genially to himself. "To draw in the hot chestnuts for our friend in the Plaza on the strength of his phony yarn—turn over the stuff and then have him tell me the deal fell through? Does he think Eddy Chang was born yesterday, I wonder? Well, I guess not. We'll play his little game exactly up to the point where we get the stuff, then a visit to old Krellwitz and we're gone from this risky burg for good."

He bowed sardonically towards the Plaza Hotel, many miles to the north-east. "Thanks, thanks, kind, good friend of South American days, for the valuable little ticket to the Eldredge masquerade ball and the so painstaking arrangements for our identity and safe-conduct for to-morrow night. If it's the opportunity it looks to be, little Eddy'll be on his way to Australia by Saturday noon."

Inserting a cigarette into an expensive amber holder, he lit it and strolled down Halsted Street in the bright sunshine, smiling absently at the street gamins who wrestled back and forth along the dingy sidewalks.

CHAPTER IV

STRUGGLING before the chiffonier in his little room into an elaborate masquerade suit intended to represent a huge yellow moth, Wilk Casperson turned as he heard a sharp knock on the door.

"Come in," he said, working off the tinfoil on a stick of ochre grease paint.

The door of the room opened, and a youngish, alert fellow, perhaps twenty-five years of age, clad in a grey suit and carrying a cane, entered the room. He stood open-mouthed in the doorway.

"What the——" he ejaculated, and stopped.

The man in the elaborate costume smiled. "Don't get alarmed, Arthur. Come on in. Close the door behind you. I'm only getting ready for the big mask ball at the Eldredges' on Lake Shore Drive. To-night, through the courtesy of Miss Shirley Eldredge, I move in actual society!"

The man in the grey suit stepped inside, closed the door, and dropped into the nearest chair. He stared curiously towards the yellow-moth costume, and at Casperson enveloped in it; then toward the stick of grease paint. But he made no comment on that feature.

Wilk Casperson, smearing the stick across his

36

freshly-shaved cheek, spoke to the younger man, watching the latter's reflection in the mirror. "Well, Arthur Sennet, what do you think of our chances?" he asked. "As each day goes by, and the final hour of the judges' decision comes closer, I feel more and more cheerful. How do you feel about it?"

The younger man tapped nervously on the floor with his cane. "Wilk, I can't help but feel that we've copped the big prize. I've a terrific hunch that we're going to be the winners. And if we do, old man, the names of Arthur Sennet and Wilk Casperson are made along two lines of creative work—advertising and detective novels! It's tough to approach the ladder of literary fame by way of commercial lines, but the main thing is to get there. I was reading the carbon of the manuscript over again to-day—and, Wilk, I feel it's a pippin."

Casperson paused in front of the chiffonier. He turned and regarded the younger man across from him curiously. "How soon," he ventured tensely, "do you anticipate we would hear our fate—if we actually were the winners?"

"My hunch," admitted Sennet, "is that we would hear to-night—if—if it were really the case that we win. The decision is to be rendered by nine o'clock on Friday night, this day of the month and year. In fact Wilk, old boy, I've a feeling that I'm going to get a telegram at my old address—the one given on the manuscript—before midnight, telling us that we win the ten-thousand-dollar prize. I moved yesterday on account of my landlady needing the room for a relative of hers, but I've left orders with the house to forward any telegram immediately to my new quarters. And I, in turn, will call you up at once. Gosh, Wilk, wouldn't it be tremendous? I'm all a-tremble."

Casperson, adjusting the shoulder-straps of the yellow-moth suit, seized two cleverly concealed cloth-covered wooden armpieces from each of which was suspended a great yellow wing. He held them out, fluttering them with a slight motion of the wrists. "If we win," he said gravely, "my wings are flapping just as they are here—only visualize me as a rooster instead of a moth! And if we lose——"

"Don't say it." His visitor shivered.

The man in the moth-suit paused a moment. His face, marred by one stroke of the ochre grease paint, grew grave. He glanced towards the clock on his mantel. Its hands were pointing at eight-thirty in the evening.

"Arthur," he said slowly, "I've never told you how much it means to me if we win that prize. Aside from the fact that we're made, if we can continue to deliver such goods—and we can—that money means the most wonderful little girl in the world to me. It's Shirley Eldredge, Arthur, the only daughter of Rufus Eldredge, in whose home the mask ball is going to be held to-night."

"Great Scott!" exclaimed Sennet, peering at him. "And you never even breathed it before. And it's all settled, is it? How in the devil did you put it over? And what does the old man think of it? You—an ordinary advertising man—marrying the daughter of a La Salle Street millionaire broker. What does he say?"

Wilk Casperson looked blue. "I knew the moment that I met her, Arthur, that she was the only woman in the world for me. And the third time we met I told her so; told her that I could never marry her on a salary such as I had. And to my bewilderment she told me that she cared in just that same way; that she would rather marry me than anyone else in the world. Then, Arthur, I woke up to the fact that fate had been mighty good to me. And I woke up at the same time to the fact that I must have money—money at least to equip a home that should be all that she could want; not cheap furniture, but real artistic stuff; money to equip an office of my own to branch out. And——"

"And so that's why you were there with the steam on our big plan," interrupted the younger man, smiling. "That's why you worked like a Trojan. I was wondering, Wilk, what was putting the electricity in you. And you were simply playing all the time to make a stake to run away with a millionaire's daughter. Oh, you thief, you! And papa—you haven't told me what he says?"

Casperson shook his head dolefully. "Shirley says he will never agree. There's only one way for us to pull it off: we've simply got to walk off—be married—and then let him do as he pleases.

"You see, Arthur," he went on, "when I was with the National Advertising Agency, Eldredge was preparing to float a huge issue of stock of a company which afterward proved to be rotten through and through. It's a wonder how such a man as he got taken in on such a snide flotation. At any rate, his rivals, Bock & Co., across the way on La Salle Street, came to our agency and had us prepare a comprehensive booklet for prospective investors which ostensibly discussed stocks and bonds, but which in reality showed up the true speculative status of the business which Eldredge was going to float.

"They had me write the booklet," Casperson continued. "I was on salary and wrote simply along the lines laid down to me by the heads of the agency. I did the best I could. I sowed the seeds of distrust on the proposition. Bock & Co. had in some way secured the names of the entire list of picked investors which Eldredge & Co. counted on as clients—and which they already had circularized. One of these booklets was sent to every one. And I afterwards heard that it killed the proposition cold with the investors."

"And then what?" asked Sennet breathlessly.

"Simply this," replied Casperson: "Eldredge prepared to sue Bock & Co. and the National Advertising Agency for defamation and conspiracy to injure his business. That was what brought about our meeting. And through that meeting at his home I became acquainted with Shirley Eldredge. In the hour that she and I talked that day, while I waited for Eldredge to arrive and tell me what he wanted with me, I became a believer in the theory of love at first sight. However, no need to bore you with that.

"Eldredge arrived home," he went on. "He tried to induce me to agree to go on the witness stand and testify that my employers had requested me to cast discredit on his particular stock flotation instead of upon the general principles underlying it. I was in a quandary. Then what happened? The president of the company in question committed suicide and the treasurer skipped to Mexico. The books were found to be full of forgeries and in such shape that it was forced into bankruptcy in a jiffy. On top of that, half of its patents were found to be infringements.

"Eldredge doesn't seem to want to see it," Casperson continued, "but I saved the good name of his house by killing that stock flotation. And since then—well, he's as bitter as the devil against me, yet he doesn't try to interfere when Shirley invites me to their home for an evening chat."

Arthur Sennet heard him through. "Well, that's certainly some story, old man," he said, when his friend had finished. "You're obviously in Dutch with 'Wall Street'; but don't worry about it. Take the girl, and to the devil with the old man. I tell you, old boy, we've got to win that prize. Ours is the most original advertising scheme entered in the whole contest. I'll stake my life on that."

"Ye gods!" murmured Casperson fervently; "I sure hope so. If we win I'll take her quickly. But, if we lose, I don't know what I will do. I can't take her without a decent stake——and I've told her so. At any rate, notify me the minute you hear from the judges— if fate decrees that you are to hear."

He turned to the mirror again, and raised the grease paint to his cheek. "Don't go, Arthur. Stick around a while and I'll go on coloring up my face. I'm supposed to be a perfect imitation of a giant moth." He pointed to the bed, on which lay a brown, fuzzy cap with two long wiry projections on it. "There's my antennæ over there."

Sennet stared curiously at the finishing of the strange costume. Then he rose with a sigh of tension. "No; I'm going on, old man. Stepped in only for a moment. I'm under such a strain that I'm too restless to do more than walk up and down. We may hear something—we might hear nothing at all. But the most we can do is to wait. Good luck to you. Dance a dance with the little lady for me. And pray for good luck, old man, for both of us. It means five thousand dollars apiece—a new stake and a lease on life for each of us. I'll get in touch with you the minute anything develops."

He rose, and, with his hand on the knob of the door, nodded; then he passed out. Casperson finished the coloring of one side of his cheek and chin; then suddenly arrested the motion. He strode from the chiffonier to the door, where he peered out in the cheerless hall of his rooming-house. "Arthur," he called sharply.

No reply came from the lower landings. He hurried to the window of his room and stared down in the darkness of Dearborn Avenue, split by two rows of street lights. Farther up the street he caught sight of Sennet's jaunty figure swinging along. He returned to the dresser with a troubled look on his face.

"Confound my stupidity," he grumbled to himself. "Why didn't I remember to ask him, before he pulled out, what his new address was?" He fell to work again with the ochre stick. "But I daresay I can get it by 'phoning his old quarters."

For possibly fifteen minutes he worked feverishly with the grease paint stick. Then he stood up and

surveyed himself in the mirror. With the exception
of the black hair on his head, his whole body resembled
a giant specimen of the Lepidoptera, his face being
covered with grease paint of the same shade as the
suit and his eyes ringed with two purple spots similar
to those which had been sewn in silk on the wings.

He walked to the bed and donned the close-fitting
brown silk skull-cap with the long wire feelers projecting from it.

"Some costume," he congratulated himself. "It
ought to be the most original one there. If it is, the
five dollars rental was cheap."

He looked up as the clock on his mantel tinkled,
rousing him from his contemplation of himself. "And
now," he finished, "for a taxi—and society—and a
dance with the sweetest little girl in Chicago!"

CHAPTER V

STEPPING to the telephone on his wall, Casperson dropped into the slot one of several coins lying on the money-box. When he was connected with the number he asked for, he spoke rapidly:

"Hurry a taxi, please, to Number 842 North Dearborn Avenue. Casperson is the name. But I'll be waiting."

He hung up, and, taking from the corner of the room a new and expensive tan leather suit-case, opened it out on top of the white coverlid of the brass bed. In it he carefully laid a blue serge suit, a shirt, a collar and tie, a checked cap, two towels, and a round flat jar labelled "cold cream." To these articles he added a pair of shoes, each wrapped in newspaper. Then he snapped the suitcase shut and dropped into a chair by the window, watching the dark street for the appearance of two bright taxi headlights, and thinking of a certain slender, golden-haired girl on Lake Shore Drive.

Suddenly the two headlights appeared below, veered to the curbing, and stopped short in front of the dingy Dearborn Avenue boarding-house; there was a shriek of brakes, a honk-honk of the horn, whereupon Casperson seized his suit-case in his hand, pocketed a crisp

44

engraved invitation standing upright on the chiffonier, and sped down the dark inside stairway to the street. The chauffeur stared at him as he skipped hurriedly out across the sidewalk. "Fourteen hundred, Lake Shore Drive," he directed, and hopped quickly inside with his suit-case, where he became shielded from the curious glances of a passer-by and a trio of small boys armed with bean-blowers trudging down the street.

Up Dearborn Avenue, between two lines of lamp-posts, the taxi hummed, and turned eastward at Oak Street. Here it pursued its way for several blocks through a semi-fashionable residence section, and again turned northward on Lake Shore Drive with its undulating macadam road between the roaring lake on one side and green tree-covered grass-plots on the other. Speeding motor-cars, heavy, purring, massive, shot by the slower taxicab in both directions, and the light from the bright-flaming incandescents of Chicago's most fashionable thoroughfare flashed in and out of the machine where Wilk Casperson sat back snugly on the cushions. At length the cab slowed up before a great residence of cherry brownstone, with a tall ornamental iron fence hemming in the spacious grounds, a burnished metal gate pivoted across the smaller front entrance, and a driveway of cement winding around the side to a huge entrance from which bright light blazed out on the dark lawn. The cab turned sharply in here, slowing up presently on account of two limousines which were crawling along the private driveway in front of it. A negro footman in blue livery opened the door of each of the advance carriages in turn and helped out the occupants.

Arriving in front of the big side gate, Casperson got down from his cab and handed the chauffeur a two-dollar bill, waving back the change. The blue-clad negro footman stared at him, the taxi drove off, and he climbed the steps slowly. On the inside of the door a butler clad in grey, with side whiskers and phlegmatic, stolid face, stood guarding the door. From upstairs, access to which was given by a wide-carpeted stairway close by, came the sound of stringed instruments, of many voices, of gliding feet. Casperson handed his engraved invitation to the grey-clad figure, who immediately shoved forward to him a tiny bottle of ink and a gold pen which stood on a stand near by.

"If you please, sir. In case of emergency calls, you know, sir."

"All right, Brayley," said Casperson, smiling through the heavy grease paint. The butler peered at him, but the retainer's puzzled face showed no signs of recognition. He politely bent his attention to the signature.

"Mr. Casperson!" he exclaimed, staring down at the name just written on the card. "I'd never have known you, sir. Your costume is one of the best that has gone through here in the last half-hour. The dancing is on the floor above. Please have a dance card. You know the way, sir?"

Casperson nodded and took up the dance programme. He pointed down to the suit-case he had brought. "Yes, I know the way. However, Brayley, I'm going home in my own clothes to-night—after I get this confounded rig off. Where can I put my ordinary duds until the dancing is over?"

Brayley motioned to a little room off the inside hall. "There's the gentlemen's dressing-room, sir. Just place the suit-case in there, and it will be perfectly safe. I'll——" The entrance of a party of two ladies, dressed as Spanish dancing girls, and a man costumed as a bullfighter, caused him to break off his directions to Casperson and attend to the signing of the new cards.

Casperson deposited his suit-case in one corner of the improvised dressing-room, and, emerging, made his way slowly upstairs to the ballroom. Entering it, he paused a moment, struck by the vivid panorama of color and life there presented. The orchestra was playing a dreamy waltz; masked couples were gliding over the waxed floor—clowns, knights in clanking armor, Pilgrim Fathers, troubadours, Civil War soldiers, a convict in striped suit; Turkish dancing girls, resplendently blacked negroes, Hollanders, fat paunched, with tufts of yellow hair glued to their chins. A fat woman masked and garbed as a peasant girl was pirouetting with a slender man whose foppish moustache on his upper lip gave the lie to his assumed personality of a Robin Hood's fearless forester in Lincoln green.

For the rest of the dance Casperson remained standing on the edge of the floor, his own costume the cynosure of all passing eyes. His gaze roved around the huge ballroom, from the musicians back of their palms to the several entrances at the rear which led to the conservatory. Here and there—almost everywhere, it seemed—feminine vanity was displayed in the sparkle of jewels. A slim form in a domino was graced by a diamond bracelet that glittered in myriad electric lights; each of several women, fearfully and wonderfully garbed, wore a chain of the jewels on her neck; across the chest of one elderly woman, who waddled instead of danced, swung like a pendulum a veritable mine of colored fire in the shape of a pendant sunburst.

"Lord, but they must wear them and show them off," commented Casperson to himself; "no matter what else they do!"

The dance came to a close. Couples broke up. Some retired to the upholstered seats in the tiny wall pockets at the side of the ballroom. Some melted through the doors of the conservatory at the rear. Others merged into laughing, chatting groups on the center of the floor.

Casperson, followed by eyes everywhere, picked his way across the room, looking carefully at every woman, searching for a slim feminine figure which he had reason to know was to be garbed as a fairy princess, studying the tiny feet of several girls for a certain pair of gold slippers with jet buckles, scrutinizing their hair for the glint of yellow gold. A girl, detaching herself with a light laugh from the conversation of a tall Indian, a black silk mask over her eyes, turned just in time to stare at him. He came up to her. His eyes dropped from the flowing silk garment, banded by a single golden sash, to her feet, which were encased in gold slippers with jet buckles.

"Shirley!" he exclaimed. "Is it really you?"

"Wilk!" she returned. "Why, I'd never have known you. Oh, what an original costume. A giant moth!"

She drank in the details of the elaborate suit, then motioned towards the conservatory. He took her arm. Together they threaded their way from the ballroom into the more quiet place with its tall palms and trees. She led him to a sequestered seat back of a fountain whose water fell into a pool of bright goldfish.

When they had seated themselves, he took her hand and looked her over hungrily, from the gold slippers to the string of sparkling stones which hung about her neck and seemed to emit a stream of liquid fire. "Well, dear," he said, "I'm in no position to talk as a human being to-night—colored up as I am. But what did he say?"

The face of the fairy princess, even under its black silk mask, grew grave. "He—he was adamantine," she replied. "And not only that, but he flew into a fearful rage. He said that you deliberately and wilfully conspired to ruin the name of his brokerage firm —all the old accusations over again. And he even says now that he's going to put a stop to your coming here after to-night."

The man's face flushed, but it was not visible under the ochre grease paint.

"That's rough," he commented at length. "Then I wouldn't be able to see you. At least, it would mean that we'd have to meet clandestinely on the outside. Confound the luck! why wasn't I born with a million instead of with this cursed poverty? Why——"

"Wilk!" Her voice was reproachful. "Wilk, you know, dear, this thing"—she waved her hand about the room with its evidences of wealth—"these people are all nothing to me. You know that a four-room flat with you means more to me than a continuance of this supposably, but not really, desirable life. Please don't worry about what he says. Please don't say you wish you had a million dollars. What difference would that make?"

He laughed harshly. "It would mean only this: I could prepare a place to take you—a place worthy of these surroundings you've had. True, a big income isn't conducive to happiness if the right person shares your life with you—you and I are idealists enough to realize that—but the surroundings of that life must not be too crude."

For a moment he was silent. Then he turned to her again. They were quite alone. "Shirley, I'm going to tell you of the great plan which I'm praying will solve our problem for us. I had intended to keep the secret until I knew the outcome, one way or the other. But instead, I'm going to tell you to-night, so that, whether I win or lose, you will know that I tried mighty hard to blaze the way for our big adventure." He paused. "And here, little girl, is the plan in a nutshell. If it goes through then——" He stopped short, suddenly chilled by the thought of the converse of the proposition.

"Tell me," she whispered. "If it concerns our big adventure—then it concerns me. I'm waiting!"

CHAPTER VI

CASPERSON looked down at the eager face close to his own. Then he smiled, in spite of himself. "Well, here it is, Shirley. In the first place, one of the biggest commercial companies in the United States—a corporation that makes automobile tires, raincoats, and a hundred other articles of rubber—recently offered, through the columns of the advertising trade papers, a prize of ten thousand dollars to the advertising man who could construct the most striking publicity device for their products, whether it was merely a slogan, a design, a catchword, a sales scheme, or a general publicity plan of some sort. I have a young friend, Arthur Sennet, who is also an advertising man. He and I talked the thing over pro and con, and gradually evolved a tentative scheme—an advertising plan—which we believe is a world-beater for this particular case."

The fairy princess was interested, her red lips apart. "A plan," she echoed. "And what is it?"

"As follows," he replied. "You've read one or two of my old detective stories, written at a time when I had more leisure than I have now. Sennet, too, has done one or two short stories which have had real liter-

51

ary merit as well as decent publication. So our plan involved the following: the construction of a book-length detective novel, the plot to be laid in the plant and to center about the actual products of this rubber company; a novel which with paper cover could be printed to the extent of hundreds of thousands of copies at a few cents per copy; a book which could be given out with every purchase of any one of their products, whether the product sold at fifty cents or fifty dollars. Do you see what it would mean, Shirley, if it should go over? It would mean that our names as co-authors would pass ultimately into the hands of millions of purchasers; that the circulation of our piece of fiction work would reach a point far greater than any magazine or book publisher could ever give us. It would mean that future work of ours would be considered both in the fiction field and the advertising field—provided it were up to the standard of that first advertising-detective story." He paused for breath, carried away by his enthusiasm.

"And here was the problem," he went on. "The story itself must be so deeply interesting, gripping, and plausible that it could be enjoyed by either a news-boy or a clergyman. It must have the plot of plots, and yet a decent degree of literary style. But in the doing of it, it meant plainly that we must gamble our brains, our time, our energy on one proposition—for should it fail to win the big prize, then the novel would be absolutely unsalable anywhere else, since it centers about and involves only the plant of this firm and their products.

"Very well. Enough to say that we took this gamble.

We went down to Akron, Ohio, and got in touch with one of the minor officials, who took us through the plant —enough so that we got our ground data sufficiently. Back we came to Chicago. We studied their products, from auto tires to raincoats. We plotted and plotted and plotted—and often when we thought our plot was at the most ingenious point of its development we found some new twist or complexity, which we introduced. When we had reached the furthest point we could attain, we began on the writing of it. It grew and grew. Ultimately 'the great rubber-plant mystery' was completed, and we got the manuscript and the outline of its advertising possibilities off a few days before the contest closed.

"There's the status of the affair," he went on. "To-night at nine o'clock the judges were supposed to render the decision as to which of the advertising schemes submitted was the most novel and effective. The prize offered is ten thousand dollars. Arthur Sennet is out now, walking up and down the streets or sitting in his new quarters somewhere in Chicago trying to possess his soul in patience, hoping to receive a congratulatory telegram. As for me, I daren't even think about it myself. If we win—I win more than the five thousand. I figure that I win—you."

"And if you lose," said the girl sadly, "does that mean that we cannot take the big adventure? You know, dear boy, that such a prize will bring on dozens, if not hundreds, of competitors. None, perhaps, will submit anything so distinctive as what you've just described, but men will rack their brains to evolve plans that are equally striking."

"If I lose," he said lugubriously, "I don't see the
possibility of the big adventure for a long time yet.
I'm simply praying that our plan wins. I feel that
it's a wonderful mystery story. I have read the carbon
copy, and I actually wonder where it ever came from.
But, of course, it's simply the product of two enthusi-
astic brains, which partially accounts for it."

"Dear boy," she said, "you are all excited. If you
lose—and it's not at all certain that you will win, call
me a little pessimist if you will—you're going to be
terribly hard hit. I can see it in your voice, although
your face is no longer the face of Wilk Casperson with
all that grease paint. Please, please, Wilk, do not count
too much on the winning of it. If you should fail, the
blow will be too severe. Try to conceive of your losing
the prize as well." She paused. "Please be assured
that I will have my heart in my mouth—that I want
you to win it. And reason enough—a reason that I
have never told you. There is another man—one in
our circle, a clubman—who has made a profound impression upon father. This man cannot be anything
to me, especially since you've come into my world, but
the fact remains that father is just a little hypnotized
by his personality, that matters here will not be altogether pleasant for me if I fail to—well—respond. Indeed I want you to win it—for that will mean our big
adventure. But I feel for you if your castle tumbles
in. So try—please—to look at that contingency."

He shook his head. "I dare not," he said quietly.
"It means that I shall lose the only little girl that can
ever complete my happiness—lose her, at least, for an
indeterminate period. And as for the other man—I

have faith in you, yet that throws a new tension over our affair. We can't——"

He was interrupted by the approach of two figures. One of them was garbed as a comical clown in bright red silk, his face covered with white grease paint, his eyes ringed with two vivid loops of colors, his eyebrows grotesquely blackened. The other was a tall, slim, silk-hatted clergyman carrying a cane and wearing a long swallow-tail coat. His eyes, masked with a black silk band, wore huge horn-shell spectacles on the outside of the strip of cloth. The two figures came up arm in arm. Both the princess and Casperson looked up at them. Casperson recognized the supposed clergyman as Malcolm Eldredge, Shirley's brother, through the slim, youthful build and the horn-shell spectacles which the latter wore even when in ordinary dress. The clown, however, was a stranger to him. Young Eldredge was the first to speak.

"Hello, sis. Having a *tête-à-tête?*" He looked toward Casperson. "And you——"

"Hello, Malcolm," said the yellow moth. "This is Wilk Casperson. Didn't know me, did you?"

Malcolm stared down through his spectacles. "Great Scott, man, but that's some make-up you've got on. I wouldn't have known you in a thousand years." He turned to his sister and then pointed at the bright scarlet clown at his side. "Bet you can't guess who this is, sis."

Shirley Eldredge smiled blankly up at the clown, who grimaced down at her through his grease paint. "I give up," she said faintly. "The powder and color are too——"

"So you not know me, eh, Meesa Elderedge? I think if I have the fiddle with me you——"

"Mr. di Paoli!" she ejaculated.

"The same," said Malcolm with a smile, dropping down on the settee and removing his mask, then placing the horn-shell glasses back over his nose. "I found him tickling the vanity of Jack Hennly's rich maiden aunt over in the corner, and knew him at once. Sit down, di Paoli."

"I not like to interrupt," said the clown, grinning under his grease paint, "but I think I like leetle dance with Meesa Shirley as repayment for all the musica I have play in her library." He took from his huge clown pocket his dance program with its gold pencil suspended from it. "I may surely have the pleasure, Meesa Shirley?"

She glanced down at her own card. "The next dance is the fifth, Mr. di Paoli. And that one I have with Mr. Casperson here——" She turned to Casperson and gave him a knowing smile. "Wilk, you have never met Mr. di Paoli. This is Mr. Niccolo di Paoli, the well-known violinist." She turned to the clown. "And this is Mr. Wilk Casperson."

Casperson shook hands with the clown. "It is a great pleasure to meet you," the latter mumbled. "I do not remember to see you in Meesa Shirley's musicales."

"No," said Casperson, instinctively disliking this clown. "I'm a pretty busy man, and don't generally get around in the daytime." He turned to the girl. "But you were about to arrange a dance for Mr. di Paoli."

She looked at her card again. "The next—the fifth —I have with Wilk. The sixth is with Malcolm. My seventh is promised to Mr. Jack Hennly, and my eighth to a friend—to a friend of father's—who arranged for it last week. The tenth I've promised to keep for daddy. Will the ninth suit you, Mr. di Paoli?"

He bowed. "That is splendid, Meesa Shirley. I have *my* card all open so as not to mees having dance with you." He made a quick notation on his own card and bowed again. "Now I not interrupt any more." And he backed out of the conservatory, bowing all the way toward the open door. A moment later all three in the nook smiled in spite of themselves as they saw him, out on the waxed floor, tickling the neck of a fat woman from whose throat swung a glittering gem of red and white stones which flashed and splashed in the incandescents.

"A funny chap, that di Paoli," commented Malcolm frankly. "Like all his race, he just radiates politeness. But I've always liked him. And play the violin? He's a wonder at it, isn't he, sis?"

She nodded, smiling. The music outside suddenly struck up. She glanced at Casperson. "Wilk, I told a white fib when I said you and I had the next dance arranged for. I just took a chance that you had kept your card open. Shall we dance or sit it out?"

He rose and unloosed his brown-clad arms from the peculiar cloth bands which fastened them to the moth wings. "Let's dance it," he said enthusiastically. "I'd much rather."

So, with a parting nod toward Malcolm, he led her to the door of the conservatory. But at the door he stopped as her brother, replacing his black mask and his horn spectacles over it, called him back. "Casperson," the latter said sharply, "may I have a word with you before the dance?"

Casperson pressed the girl's arm. "Will you wait outside the door for me, Shirley? Malcolm wants to speak with me." And he left her, stepping back to the young man in the oldish, austere ecclesiastical garment. "What is it, Malcolm?"

The man, even under his•mask, was nervous. "Casperson, can you wait a few days longer for that two hundred? I'll—I'll swing the tide sure soon. I'm raising money fast. Let me tell you I'm desperate." He licked his lips. "You know I'm for you and sis—straight through. I've—I've a deal on—several in fact—and if my plans go through all right I'll be able to repay you most any day now. And I'll——"

Casperson put his hands on the young fellow's narrow shoulders. "Don't worry about that two hundred, Malcolm. The main thing is that the two-thousand-dollar hole in your father's accounts is plugged up and that he doesn't know what happened. The two hundred can't settle your sister's and my problem one way or the other. And, for Heaven's sake, don't try to pay back all those personal loans by any more rash speculation. If a certain deal of mine goes through, I'll help you out to the extent of a thousand more, so you can pay back Jack Hennly and some of those who stood by you. Remember, your father hates me, but I'm your friend." The music swelled suddenly in volume. He turned back toward the doorway. "Remember now —no more speculation. Stop it. You're safe at the office now if only your friends don't press you and give you away. So stay safe."

With a nod Casperson left the imitation clergyman, and soon he rejoined the princess who was waiting curiously outside the door. A second later he was out on the floor with her, swinging along in a one-step.

CHAPTER VII

FOR a complete turn of the floor neither the princess nor the giant moth spoke, revelling in the intoxication of the music and the rhythm. Then the princess, looking up at the moth, inclined her head toward him so that he could better hear her words.

"Malcolm seems awfully worried lately," she said, as they swung around a corner of the big ballroom. "I wonder if he's in any trouble?"

"I hope not," returned Casperson, turning her deftly. "I hardly think so." Down in his heart he knew that he had shaded the truth—that Malcolm Eldredge had indeed been in trouble—that the latter had been perilously close to a point which might have estranged him from his father forever.

The lights, the music, faded, and Casperson found himself recalling vividly the night, just a week before, when Malcolm Eldredge had appeared at the door of his room in the wee small hours and had blurted out the fact that, as cashier of his father's brokerage firm, he had speculated and had lost more than two thousand dollars of the firm's funds; how he had raised all but a few hundred of it through temporary loans from personal friends and professional money-lenders; how he had come in desperation to Casperson to see whether

60

the latter could help him to make up the remaining deficit and stem the tide that was threatening to engulf him. And Casperson, madly in love with Malcolm's wonderful sister, had drawn him a check for two hundred dollars, a sum which he had managed to save up.

The music, suddenly striking up more loudly, awoke Casperson from his abstraction, and quickly he turned the conversation into other channels, swinging the dainty, fairy-like feminine figure around in his arms, thrilled by the contact with the soft folds of her costume.

The dance over, they repaired again to the conservatory, where they sat talking during the intermission. Then came the music, and also Malcolm, who this time carried his sister off leaving Casperson to his own devices. The latter, remaining on the settee, and wondering whether to sit out that dance or to look up some lonely débutante and escort her out over the waxen floor, opened his eyes curiously as a blue-clad messenger boy trotted into the now deserted conservatory and ambled along the rows of rubber plants and dwarf trees. As he stopped in front of Casperson, the latter thought for a bare second that the urchin was some child guest in masquerade, but the wizened face and quick, keen, shifty eyes of the boy were never those of a child of the well-to-do. The boy stared at him; his eyes took in Casperson's costume.

"Mister, you're a yellow moth, ain't yer?"

Casperson gazed down at him. "Yes. That's correct; yellow moth. What about it?"

The boy held a white card in a grimy hand. "Den here's a message for yer. Dey le' me in to find yer, an'

w'en I was watchin' de couples goin' aroun' I spotted
yer over on de other end of de dance floor, and I seen
yer go into dis here greenhouse." He thrust out the
white card toward Casperson.

The latter seized it and studied it in the half-subdued
light. Pencilled across the left upper corner, as though
a notation for the boy's dubious memory, were the
words: "Yellow Moth." But the brief message across
the face of the card was in ink. The writing was odd,
even freakish. The "t's" bore each a double cross
rather than a single one; the periods consisted of tiny
irregular triangles; the "y" tail seemed to be tied into
a strange, unnatural knot of some sort; and the "e's"!
—they consisted of a peculiar distortion of the Greek
"epsilon," and stood out from the rest of the message
like currants in an angel cake. But one look at the
initials appended to the communication, and Casperson's heart gave a jump.

"From Arthur!" he said, half aloud. He looked
down at the boy. "Yes; it's for me." He fumbled in
a concealed pocket of the moth suit and found a coin,
which he gave to the boy. "All right, son. You can
go." The lad vanished out of the nearest entrance,
and a second later he was trudging round the edge of
the floor alive with dancing couples. At once Casperson
turned his attention to the text of the message. It read:

"W. C.: Unexpected developments in our affair.
Leave ball immediately if at all possible, and come
straight to 912 Ernst Court, for long talk. Outer
door of place left unlocked, so walk in. Come upstairs.
—A. S."

A long whistle escaped him. "It means either that we've won the prize or lost it," he said to himself. "I know Arthur well enough to realize that he's wrought up. But why in Heaven's name didn't he tell me more?" He pondered, puzzled for a second. "He wrote it out instead of typing it. That proves he must have been excited. Told me once that he had used the typewriter for so many years that his fingers had forgotten how to write." He studied again the example of the strangest of handwritings. "Hope the typewriter doesn't do that to my hand." He looked round the room, and then rose. "I'll have to go—that's certain. Too upset to remain after that. Thank goodness, I got one dance anyway with my little girl."

He picked his way from the conservatory and around the edge of the ballroom floor, now thronged with dancers in every degree of vivid costuming. Near the end he caught a glimpse of Shirley, dancing gracefully with Malcolm. He would have liked to wait and tell her of his being called away, but decided to telephone her first thing in the morning and explain the whole unusual matter. Down the broad stairway he picked his way, and into the gentlemen's dressing-room, where he found his suit-case, and quickly fell to changing back into street clothes.

First, however, he had to remove the ochre grease paint from his face; this he did in front of the big mirror which had been placed there for such purposes. He followed as well as he could the directions given him by the costume house which had rented him the yellow moth suit, but found that the removal of grease paint was not so easy as he had thought. He smeared on cold cream clumsily, but the more he smeared the worse mess he made of it. When he entered the room the clock on the wall had pointed to ten-fifteen; it had crept to ten-forty, when he got desperate and, smearing his whole face with the cold cream, wiped it off furiously, cream and paint together, with one of the two towels he had brought in the suit-case.

Scrutinizing himself, he found that he now held a bare semblance to a human being, in spite of the fact that there were still traces of the yellow coloring on his neck and ears; but he decided that he had experimented long enough. As dexterously as possible he wriggled out of the yellow moth suit, and changed over into his street clothing. Buttoning himself into a shirt and collar, he packed the jar of cream and the suit back into the suit-case and turned to leave the room. The clock on the wall struck eleven as he left the dressing-room and stepped back into the hallway. Mose, the negro footman, was now on duty at the inner door, and the old black servant stared, puzzled, at Casperson as the latter walked by him toward the grey stone steps.

"You is leavin' 'arly, sah?"

"Yes, Mose; got to go in a hurry," explained Casperson. "Sudden message. Unexpected. Will 'phone in my regrets to-morrow." He hurried down the stone steps into the night air; within a minute he was passing through the ornamental iron gateway at the end of the curved drive.

Outside, under an arc light, he consulted the card again. "Ernst Court," he repeated wonderingly. "It's somewhere over in that tangle around Walton Place and Delaware Place, but just where I can't——"

A Lincoln Park policeman passing him at that moment suggested possible information. So he stopped the bluecoat. "Officer, just where on the North Side is Ernst Court?" He shifted his suit-case in his hand.

The latter peered curiously at him in the street-light illumination. "Follow Lake Shore Drive clear around the bend of Oak Street up to Walton Place; turn west on Walton Place and follow that a half block till you come to a short, narrow street with one arc lamp at the mouth of it. That's Ernst Court."

Casperson thanked him and hurried on. Around the bend of Lake Shore Drive and past many handsome residences he wended his way. Turning at Walton Place, he found himself in a somewhat more plebeian neighborhood, with wooden and brick houses instead of brownstone mansions. He hurried west along Walton Place and presently stopped. He was at Ernst Court.

The latter thoroughfare, scarcely twelve feet wide, resembled nothing so much as a picture of a street in old London. One arc light, posted at the mouth of it, cast a sickly green illumination down its length, showing faintly its other opening on the street to the south. Low houses of old make fronted both sides of it, in the nearest of which white "for-sale" and "for-rent" signs showed plainly even from the mouth of the court. It was paved with old-fashioned cobble-stones, but a modern blue-enamelled sign riveted to the arc-light pole proclaimed "Ernst Court."

Casperson, pondering a moment, threaded his way down the narrow passage. The illuminated transom of a house showed the number 916. He trudged on a few steps farther. Odd locality to take a room, he reflected, thinking of Sennet's change of quarters made that day. He stopped before an old red brick, two-story house, with wooden steps. Both the windows of the first floor and those of the second were ablaze with light; the number, 912, showed plainly. This was undoubtedly the place. Up the steps he went. He pressed the bell button, and heard the ring. Quickly the door was opened. A blue-coated policeman stood in the doorway. Casperson drew his brows together into a puzzled frown. He paused a moment, then said:

"I'm looking for a Mr. Arthur Sennet. This is 912, isn't it?"

"This is 912 Ernst Court," the policeman growled; "but I guess it's nobody here you're lookin' for. If you are, he's lyin' upstairs dead. Go down to Chicago Avenue police station if you want any more information." And he closed the door softly in the inquirer's face, leaving him standing alone in the cool night air.

Casperson passed a hand feebly over his forehead. He stood on the porch, wondering. Had he stumbled on the wrong house and fallen into the thick of some tragedy? And yet—912, Ernst Court! That was the number on the card. "If you are, he's lyin' upstairs dead." The bluecoat's words buzzed in his ears. Who was dead? Could it be? That was hardly possible.

His ruminations were interrupted by the sound of gruff, masculine voices within; then the door was opened suddenly again and a man thrust his head outside. Casperson, standing in the blaze of light from the interior of the house, blinked his eyes, riveting them first on the room back of the door—a space fitted up like a reception room with wooden benches, chairs, and

a huge flat-top desk covered with a glass panel. Gradually his eyes took in the red thatch of the plain-clothes
man who stood peering out at him—his steely blue eyes,
his hard, brisk face—a typical policeman's physiog-
nomy. The officer continued to stare out for the frac-
tion of a minute. Then his keen face broke into a
broad smile of welcome.

"Come in, Casp—old Casp of the *Morning Sun*.
You're the first of the newspaper boys to get here. And
it's some dirty job, all right, all right. He was one of
the biggest moth collectors in the country. And he's
sitting up there now among all his moths with a bullet
through the spine—stone dead!"

CHAPTER VIII

A TANGLE IN THE THREADS

CASPERSON, standing on the low porch, gave a short, uneasy laugh. He felt, somehow, that this was all some strange dream. Here was he, ex-reporter of the *Morning Sun*, advertising man for the last three years, standing on the steps of a house to which he had come to see Arthur Sennet in response to the latter's note, facing Sandy MacTavish of the old Chicago Avenue police station; and the officer was telling him that "it's some dirty job, all right." And on top of that came something about moths. Moth! And he, Casperson, had himself been a yellow moth that evening.

He paused but a moment, giving up the puzzle as too bewildering, then passed inside like a man in a daze. MacTavish, smiling grimly, led the way up a narrow-carpeted stairway to a huge room at the top floor, evidently made by removing all the walls of that story. Casperson stood in the doorway on a narrow Persian rug, staring at the scene unfolded to his eyes.

Around the interior, from ceiling to floor, were flat glass boxes containing moths—gray, black, orange, purple, spotted, vari-colored; huge moths whose wings spanned five inches; tiny moths that were even smaller than the "millers" which swoop around gas-jets in tenement houses on summer nights. Under each specimen, fastened by a thumb tack to its layer of cork, was a tiny white card bearing letters painstakingly stamped in red ink with rubber type. And in each case those letters constituted some ponderous Latin name.

Along one side of the room was a long counter, filled with pins and thumb tacks, bottles, sheets of cork, empty boxes, white cards, and narrow strips of a thin white tissue paper. And in a straight-backed arm-chair at the counter, close to a desk 'phone, slumped a man's lifeless body, the head of which hung over to one side. Below the chair on the polished hardwood floor was a puddle of sticky liquid. A mirror, fastened to the wall at the rear of the counter, reflected the face to the two men standing in the doorway on the Persian rug; and it was the face of a man in the sixties, with tousled gray hair, seamed, wrinkled skin, and a strange, tumorous growth on the waxen left hand.

MacTavish looked at his companion. "What station did you come out from, Casperson? Had an idea you'd left the newspaper game long ago." He flicked his finger toward the ugly sight in the chair. "Got here just about ten or fifteen minutes ago after the old boy 'phoned he'd been shot. But he was dead as a doornail when we hit the place."

Casperson paused a moment before answering. "Sandy MacTavish," he said, "maybe I'm dreaming, but I stumbled in here to-night in response to a note from a friend of mine, one Arthur Sennet. It gave this number, Ernst Court. I had been half expecting some such call—and I was at a masquerade ball when it arrived. And here I am—and—well, what's it all about?

I'm not with the *Morning Sun* any more—been in the advertising game for the last three years."

The detective scratched his chin. "You don't know this old fellow in the chair at all, then?"

Casperson shook his head. "Never saw him in my life. Who is he?"

MacTavish frowned. "Then you're in the wrong place, Casp; that's all. Here's all there is to it. Got a 'phone message at Chicago Avenue station less than three-quarters of an hour ago. The voice speaking was so faint that the sergeant could hardly hear him. Says the voice: 'Send somebody to 912 Ernst Court at once—Professor Silvester—I've been shot by a burglar —bleeding to death.' And that was all the information. We jumped into the flivver, Murphy and I, and came here. The downstairs door was unlocked. We came upstairs. The old boy was dead. Didn't probably live a quarter of an hour after the shot entered his back." He pointed at the cloth back of the chair where a black round hole was visible; then at the pool of blood, which showed that the vital fluid had leaked from the man's back and down the hind legs of the chair in which he had been sitting.

Judging from the position of things, Casperson could easily deduce that the victim had never left his chair, even to telephone, for the instrument stood right at his elbow. Casperson's eyes roved from the ugly sight to the hundreds of glass boxes containing furry-headed moths that covered the walls.

"I'm certainly in the wrong place, MacTavish," he said, "for I don't know this man—nor his house—nor his moths. But, Great Scott! this is a night of coincidences. MacTavish, what would you say if I told you that I was masquerading as a moth myself to-night? On top of that I stumbled into the wrong house—and I meet you, old Sandy MacTavish of the old days." He shook his head. "And what are you going to do?"

MacTavish was scratching his chin. He gazed once toward the telephone. Already he had out a notebook and a pencil. "The first thing I'm going to do is to call the station and tell 'em it ain't no hoax like we thought it was at first. We know a little already about Silvester and his moths. Got acquainted with him when some sneak thief broke into this joint a few months ago." He paused. "As for you, Casp, you can help me out if you will. Will you go down the court and rout out some neighbor of this fellow? Then send him or bring him over here? I've got to get a little more light on things somehow." He turned to the 'phone.

Casperson turned toward the doorway. "I'll do it at once—gladly," he said, pleased at the opportunity of getting out of the place with its musty odor. With a parting look at the back of the dead man in the chair, and his white face reflected in the mirror in front of him, Casperson stumbled down the stairs and out into the night of Ernst Court, as the blue-coated policeman opened the door. The last he heard was MacTavish rattling the hook of the telephone.

He lost no time walking up the court to the house which had the illuminated transom. He rang the bell, and after a protracted pause a man in pajamas answered the door. "Will you kindly step down the court to Number 912?" said Casperson. "There's been a murder there, and the police are trying to get some line on the mystery." And as the man's face stared bewilderedly out at him, he added: "Do you happen to know if there's any boarding-house in Ernst Court?"

"A murder!" ejaculated the other. "A murder—in 912! Old Professor Silvester, I'll bet. Great guns! I'll be—— Wait—I'll be over at once." Leaving the door wide open, he turned toward an inner bedroom. He stopped, evidently realizing that Casperson had asked a second question. "Boarding-house?" he added. "No. This is the only house on Ernst Court, except old Silvester's, which is tenanted. Ain't no boarding-house around here. Only me and my wife and the professor in the row."

He disappeared, then came back in a surprisingly short time clad in trousers, coat, and leather slippers. Casperson accompanied him to the house of death, and, as MacTavish stuck his head out of the second-story window at the sound of their footsteps, he spoke:

"Here's a neighbor, Mac—the only one on Ernst Court. I guess he'll give you some facts."

"Come upstairs, both of you," called down Mac-Tavish, and he lowered the window. Presently Casperson, with his new companion, was standing once more in the room lined with glass boxes. He waited curiously, as did MacTavish, while the newcomer stared, horror-stricken, around the room. Then a low whistle escaped him.

"That's—that's him, all right. That's old Silvester."

MacTavish evidently had been consulting the telephone directory in the meantime, for it lay open on the wooden counter. His next question bore out that probability. "We know a little of this man at the station on account of his complaint some time ago that this place was broken into. But can you tell me one thing: there's two entries in the 'phone book; has he also got a place on St. Clair Street, a few blocks from here?"

The half-clad neighbor of the dead man nodded, still staring at the body huddled in the chair. "It's the old professor all right. Yes; he's got a home near on the North Side. Supposed to be one of the biggest specialists in the world on moths." His eyes roved over the glass boxes covering the walls. "At least, so the Jap has told me."

"The Jap!" broke in MacTavish. "What Jap?"

"Ushi, the Jap, he hired to live here and take care o' this laboratory. I've met him dozens o' times goin' up and down the court from the grocery store on Walton Place. He lives in the little back room on the first floor, and cooks his own meals."

"What's the Jap's full name?" broke in MacTavish quickly.

"Ushi—so far as I knew him. Ushi Yatsura, so my boy tells me, what works in the grocery store where he buys his provisions."

"Ushi Yatsura," snapped MacTavish. His eyes widened oddly. A look of keen satisfaction crept over his face. "Ushi Yatsura, eh? That's good." He paused. "Tell us all you know about Silvester. Then you can go. We won't bother you again till to-morrow."

The neighbor cleared his throat. "All I know is, as I says, that the professor's suposed to be one o' the biggest specialists in the world on moths—not butter-flies, but just moths. I got that straight from Ushi, the Jap. Seems that his spec'mens have been in museums all over the world, an' since he rented this here house he's been bringin' 'em all together from all over th' globe. Many a time in the last few months since Silvester took this here place, me and the wife have seen cabs with grey-bearded professors and wise, spectacled-lookin' men drive in th' court, and once or twice parties o' college students with their notebooks. Et—et—etymologists, I guess they call themselves. The Jap said the collection here is supposed to be worth a good many thousand dollars, but the old man's daughter over on St. Clair Street refused to have 'em in the same house with her. He ain't got no wife, Ushi says."

"I see," said MacTavish. He thought a moment. "That's all you know, eh?" The visitor nodded dazedly. "And your name, please?"

"Dolan. I live two numbers up Ernst Court from here."

"All right, Dolan. You can go. We'll want to see you to-morrow."

The man reluctantly turned in the doorway. A moment later he was thumping down the stairway and out to Ernst Court.

MacTavish turned to Casperson. "Now we'll go downstairs, Casp, and see the cage that held the flown Jap bird. I've been browsing around since you went out, and I've stumbled on something. Come!" He turned to the stairway.

Casperson followed the plain-clothes man down the

stairway. Murphy, on guard at the door, watched his superior silently. MacTavish strode to the back of another large room that looked as though it were intended to seat many persons—perhaps for a discussion, possibly for a lecture—and tried the handle of a narrow door. It opened easily, and he stepped inside, snapping on the single electric bulb that lighted it. The space was occupied by a single iron bed, a two-hole gas plate, a cupboard full of cheap dishes, a tiny ice-box, and a cheap bureau. The drawers of the bureau had been pulled out as though their contents had been removed in a hurry, and that this was true was substantiated by the fact that they were quite empty. Two or three quaint Japanese water-colors on the wall, and a small motto or inscription of some sort made of Japanese characters, testified that this was the room where Ushi, the caretaker, had slept and cooked his meals. But beyond this there was no sign of Ushi.

MacTavish gazed again about the room. "Of course he's gone," he said, turning to his companion. "Casp, do you recall the old murder case where millionaire Jameson managed to typewrite the name of his murderer before he slid off into the great Hereafter? You and I worked on that case together."

"Indeed, I do," said Casperson.

"Then come back upstairs," said MacTavish quietly. "Professor Silvester has gone the Jameson case one better!"

CHAPTER IX

CASPERSON stared at the detective, and Mac-
Tavish smiled an inscrutable smile. "Come," he
said, "and I'll show you something to arouse your old-
time newspaper blood." And he led the way upstairs
again to the room containing the lifeless man.

"Now," MacTavish began quietly, "I'm telling you
this because you say you're no longer a reporter. I'm
thinking this had better stay quiet for another twelve
hours—till headquarters cashes in on it. I discovered
it while you were up the court getting the fellow Dolan." He inclined his head down at the dead body,
then pointed at several white cards bearing red rubber-
stamped Latin names lying on a ledge, drying. "See
those cards the old boy had been preparing when the
shot took him?"

Casperson nodded. "But how do you know——" he
began, when the other interrupted him.

"Look down on the floor."

From the Persian rug in the doorway Casperson had
seen only the pool of blood where it had spread over
to the lighted part of the polished hardwood floor, but
now, in the deep shadow of the work counter, almost
at the dead man's feet, he saw an overturned flat, paste-
board box whose interior had been divided into small

compartments by rows of intersecting slips of paste-board, and a scattered heap of tiny bits of dark mate-rial. He leaned over and picked up two. He saw at once that they were rubber type from a font of stamp-ing type, and obviously from the set that had been used to mark the cards for new moth specimens. He glanced toward MacTavish; then, stooping over again, picked up one of several fine strips of very thin, al-most gauzy, tissue paper, each perhaps a half-inch wide and several inches long.

"Rubber type all right," he commented. "But these things—what are they?"

MacTavish pointed to a specimen of a medium-sized purple moth in an open box. An odor as of alcohol and formaldehyde seemed to emanate from it. It was apparently being dried into place, for over each outstretched, delicately colored wing was drawn tight a strip of the fine, gauzy tissue paper, pinned at each end. "Those strips," said the detective, "you can see for yourself, are used to hold down the wings till they dry in shape, the tissue paper being so soft that it don't hurt the fine coloring of the wings." He paused and reached over to a shelf on the wall and took down a tissue-paper strip similar to the one Casperson had just picked up. Then he went on talking:

"And this, Casp, is exactly what happened: the old boy was sitting here with the rubber type, making out cards for some new moth specimens. He had laid them all out on the window-sill over there to dry. He had returned to his chair and was sitting here when came the shot in the back from the doorway. Why, Heaven knows. From my examination of his back while you were gone it's plain that the bullet got him in the spine. That being the case, he was paralyzed from the waist down. He was able to draw over the 'phone that stood by his elbow and call for help. But while he was waiting for help, and didn't know that he was bleeding to death rapidly, he wanted to write out a message in case he should drop into unconsciousness. You can see there isn't pencil or paper or ink in sight; neither was I able to find paper or pencil in his pockets. What was there to write on or with? Nothing but one of these strips of white tissue paper, scattered all over the place, and the rubber type, and the stamping-pad there. Well, I am able to tell you that he typed out a brief message of fifteen letters, and that was the last thing he ever did except to tip over the whole set of type as he slumped back in his chair unconscious. And he bled to death while Murphy and I were cranking the stalled flivver over on Pearson Street. Now, you're getting puzzled, eh? All right. I found his message on the floor right under the chair." And with that statement he thrust out to Casperson the strip of tissue paper he had just removed from the wall shelf, and which he had been holding in his fingers as he talked.

Casperson studied the strange-looking communication. On the paper, in a vertical column, were four words, rubber-stamped, the stamping ink having soaked through the fine tissue paper so that the letters were visible from both sides, reading backward on one, forward on the other. He studied the backward reading for several seconds before he perceived that the ink had soaked through; then he turned over the strip quickly. Now he could comprehend the significance of the words. They read briefly:

FIND

USHI

HE

KNOWS

Casperson looked up from the paper. "And that settles the case nicely," he commented dryly. "Particularly since the Jap has flown!" He read the four brief words again, and then handed the precious slip back to MacTavish. "Find Ushi—and you've solved what little mystery there is."

MacTavish nodded absently, and within a second was back at the 'phone again, rattling the receiver hook. When he got his connection, he said hurriedly:

"Sergeant, this is MacTavish. You've got the details, but something new has come up. Will give it to you as soon as I get relieved from here. First, however, send out the word to all stations and depots to look for a Jap, name Ushi Yatsura, who may be trying to make a train out by this time. I can definitely say he either pulled the stunt or is badly mixed up in it."

After saying good-bye he hung up and turned from the instrument, looking quizzically at the younger man. "Snappy work, eh, Casp? But why the devil did the Jap kill the old boy? That's the question. Was it a row about something, I'm wondering?" He broke off, and gave an imitation of a detective thinking. Then he added:

"And in a little while comes the hysterics, when

yours truly will have to notify the daughter this fellow Dolan spoke about. That's the part about these things I don't enjoy a bit."

Casperson was silent a moment. "You've telephoned for detectives, haven't you, Mac?" The latter nodded. "Then I'm thinking I'd better get out of here. I'm no longer a newspaper man, so I'm not supposed to have any business with this affair. I'll have to call this the night of coincidences, considering the way I stumbled in on things." He turned in the doorway. "By morning I'll manage to get in touch with my friend Sennet and find out how he balled these addresses up. And I may drop in on you at the station for a minute to-morrow. Good luck, old man. Find your Jap, and your case is closed. So long."

As he left the house a distant church-bell was chiming midnight. Down Walton Place a blue patrol auto was lumbering along with a doleful clang toward Ernst Court. With his suit-case in hand, Casperson walked meditatively through the silent streets to his Dearborn Avenue boarding-house, whose white stone steps, situated in an interminable row of similar ones, suggested somehow the ghost of a former aristocracy.

He undressed and climbed into bed. For a long while he lay thinking, and then dropped off into an uneasy sleep in which the strange, waxy, white face of the lifeless man in the chair seemed to be flitting around in a huge ballroom where everyone was a fluttering moth with a shining pin stuck through the body.

When he first opened his eyes in the morning he had the peculiar sensation that the whole chain of events of the night before were part of the dream. Stepping to the door of his room, he reached out and got his morning paper. Over the headings he ran his eyes, looking for the word "murder" or "Ernst Court." Of a sudden his roving gaze stopped; his skin turned peculiarly cold; he stared and read and re-read. Then he passed a hand dazedly over his forehead. For the third time he read the article that had riveted his attention; then he sat back limp and speechless in his chair.

The article was quite long, and had a big head on the first page. It told in detail of something that had occurred at a society function the night before. A fifty-thousand-dollar diamond necklace that had been worn by the young hostess, and which had belonged to her mother before her, had disappeared from her neck. Its absence had been discovered by the hostess's father as he claimed the young lady for a dance. It was suspected immediately that there was a thief among the guests, and all the invitation cards given in at the door were examined, with the result that each one was found to bear the name of a bona-fide friend moving in the circle of this semi-exclusive family.

Coincident with the disappearance of the string of jewels, the article went on, a guest, who had just danced with the young hostess, had himself departed from the place in a hurry, not assigning any reason for his departure or notifying either his hostess or her people. The fact of his departure was established by the testimony of a negro footman who had been stationed at the carriage entrance to take charge of the door while the butler was downstairs superintending the preparation of the refreshments.

The necklace, it was stated further, had been seen on the young hostess's neck just prior to her talking and dancing with the departed guest; after that it was missing! The master of the house, the hostess's father, had gone immediately to the nearest police station to secure a warrant for the arrest of this guest, but had been informed there that he would have to appear before a magistrate in the morning in order to secure it. Whereupon he had altered his plans and had driven his machine away in the night toward the downtown section.

All in all, the article was not only interesting, but stirring, particularly to the pajama-clad reader. For the society function in question was the Eldredge mask ball; and the name of the departed guest, given out by the press, was Wilk Casperson, an advertising man.

CHAPTER X

CASPERSON dropped the paper to his knees and fell into a brown study. One thing was certain, staggering: Shirley's string of brilliants had disappeared *after* he had danced with her, for assuredly he himself had not stolen it. But what unkind destiny had made him the recipient of Sennet's note calling him from the ballroom at such a critical point, all unaware of what was to happen after his departure?

Vainly he cudgelled his brains to remember if he had seen the gems on her neck immediately at the close of his dance with her; but his recollection of the affair became hazy at this point. They might have been there; they might not have been. And in the latter case they might have dropped off and been picked up by some guest who yielded to a thieving instinct.

And now at him, Wilk Casperson, the finger of suspicion was pointing unwaveringly. He wondered why Eldredge, not very friendly to him at any time, had not persisted in having him arrested. His departure from the ball at such a point was about as damning as anything could be. But wondering, as he did, about the whole matter, he knew one thing for a certainty: and that was that he would go straight to the Eldredge

83

mansion and demand a hearing on such an infamous charge, warrant or no warrant.

But first he turned the pages of the newspaper again, his fingers now trembling the least bit, and shortly he came upon the article which he had first made a search for. It was on an inside page, and told little more than had developed the night before. It described the finding of the body of the aged entomologist, Professor Aloysius Silvester, at his Ernst Court laboratory, directly following his faintly telephoned message for help. It gave in detail the later findings at the morgue—which MacTavish had only broached—that the man had been shot squarely in the spine and had been paralyzed from the waist down. MacTavish, it appeared, had been unsuccessful in keeping the matter of the rubber-stamped dying message from the newspaper reporters, for the slip of tissue paper and its four words, "Find Ushi—he knows," were described and elaborated in full. The article did, however, contain one new development: it was that Ushi Yatsura had been apprehended at the Northwestern depot at one o'clock that morning and was now locked up safely at the Detective Bureau.

That was the extent of the information given out up to the time the morning papers went to press. Casperson read the story once more, then tossed the paper aside. They had caught the Jap, but the motive for the murder was still to be learned. The opening of the article drove his mind straight to the mystifying note he had received at the mask ball. Aloysius Silvester— Arthur Sennet! Initials in both cases "A. S."! Now matters held a new significance. Was that note really from Arthur Sennet, or could it have been a strange crossing of the wires?

He rose from his chair quickly and crossed to the hanger where his coat was suspended. Fumbling in the pockets, he withdrew the white card. His face was a puzzle—a pitiable puzzle—as he gazed down at it, turning it this way and that, studying both sides. With the exception of the pencilled words in the corner, "Yellow Moth," and one or two black finger-smudges made by the messenger boy who had delivered it, it was blank—on both sides!

What in Heaven's name did the whole thing indicate? Not a vestige of the original ink-written message to be found on it. Then but one thing loomed forth: whoever sent that card intended, through the use of some secret chemical, to have the last trace of its treacherous decoy message disappear from the sight of man.

In ten minutes Casperson was dressed. Without thinking of breakfast, he seized his hat and went out into the bright morning air of Dearborn Avenue. He did not know it, but a man—a keen-faced fellow—who had been standing on the opposite sidewalk, strolled casually after him, keeping a block behind. And when, after his brisk walk, Casperson strode up to the polished iron gate that covered the front door of No. 1400 Lake Shore Drive, and rang the bell, the keen-faced fellow dropped on to a bench facing the lake and lighted a cigar.

The door was opened by Brayley, his phlegmatic face showing pronounced traces of puzzlement.

"Mr. Eldredge in?"

"Come in, Casperson." The invitation came from Malcolm Eldredge himself; Casperson could glimpse him back of Brayley, in the dark hall.

The visitor entered, his lips trembling with angry questions. As Brayley closed the door quietly, Malcolm beckoned Casperson toward the upper floor. "Up to my room," he said. "Father has been expecting you. Wants to have it out up there."

He led the way upstairs to a cheery room on the second floor, in which stood a shining mahogany bed; the walls were covered with photographs of college boys in rowing and track suits, as well as with tennis rackets and oars. There he motioned to a wicker chair and closed the door.

"Great Scott, old man, you've—you've read in the morning papers about it?" Casperson nodded grimly. "I—I don't know what to say. The necklace has gone. It disappeared some time after you danced with sis. But I know you didn't take it." He paused. "And, Casperson, for Heaven's sake don't lose your temper with father and mention the money you lent me, or—or the money I—I took, will you?" He fumbled nervously in his pocket and drew forth a check which he had filled out. He tendered it to Casperson with a hand that shook a trifle, and Casperson took it curiously. It was made out for two hundred dollars and signed with the younger man's name. "That— that squares me, Casperson. My brokers telephoned me twenty minutes ago that a deal on margins in British rubber shares came my way—and now I can be all clear with the world again. Whew!—what a narrow escape." He paused, his hand on the door. "Casperson, you'll remember that, won't you? Please don't lose your head and bring me into it. And mail me my note marked paid as soon as convenient. And— and don't put the check through till late to-day."

He left the room. Casperson sat staring down at the check for two hundred dollars—the loan he had hardly dared hope would be repaid. So the boy had put over a deal in stocks and saved himself? Just as well, he reflected. He tucked the paper in his pocket and from his waistcoat drew a leather billfold from which he took a promissory note, signed "Malcolm Eldredge," and bearing the figures "90 days" and "$200."

Moving over to a tiny mahogany desk at the side of the room, he felt through his clothing for his fountain-pen, but discovered that he had removed it last evening when he had packed his things in his suit-case to take to the ball. Running his eye over the pigeon-holes of the desk, he found another pen and hurriedly wrote across the note "Paid in full," together with his name. Then he sealed the slip of paper in an envelope, which he withdrew from a pigeon-hole full of blank envelopes, and, writing Malcolm's name on it, placed it with its end just peeping out from the compartment.

His operations were interrupted by footsteps on the threshold. He turned in his chair, and waited as the door opened.

In the opening were Malcolm and an elderly man with silver-white, close-cropped hair, gold-rimmed eyeglasses on his nose, and a belligerent, sharp, business-like face. And at his shoulder in turn was Shirley, her yellow-gold hair set off by a charming morning gown of pink silk. But under her eyes were dark circles which seemed to indicate that the events of the past night had been perturbing, to say the least.

Rufus Eldredge stepped into the room, waited until the two younger people had followed him, then closed the door. He waited until Malcolm had seated himself on the bed, and the girl had dropped uneasily into a rocker. Then he stood with arms folded, his eyes riveted on Casperson. After some seconds of this ordeal for all concerned, he spoke:

"Casperson, did you mean it as a joke?"

The man accused gave a short, hard laugh. "Shirley's necklace may be gone," he said, "but it happens that I didn't take it. Be assured of that. What evidence did you have against me that I should be made the victim of all that newspaper notoriety? And why didn't you serve your warrant?"

"Because," snapped the broker in an obviously ugly mood, "I didn't want to soil our name with arrests, and cast discredit on any other social functions we may have in the future; because I didn't intend to give you a chance for a suit for false arrest; because I relied on your learning that you've been watched since three o'clock this morning, and that sooner or later you're going to be tripped up with my property unless you came here to square matters."

"Mr. Eldredge, I told you I haven't that necklace, and I will not sit here and be accused of stealing it." He turned to the girl. "Shirley, you don't think I took it, do you?"

She shook her head slowly, wearily. "No, I do not. Father, I don't care what the ugly circumstances may be—Wilk is not the one who stole it. I know——"

She stopped as Eldredge stepped to the wall and pressed a button. A pause ensued, and, presently, came a knock at the door. Eldredge himself opened it. Outside stood Brayley. "Get Mose, the footman, Brayley, and come upstairs, both of you."

The butler bowed and left. Within a minute he returned with the negro who had opened the carriage doors the night before. Eldredge admitted them both silently, then closed the door again.

"Brayley, you saw Mr. Casperson arrive last night? At what time?"

"He came, sir, roughly, around ten o'clock. I admitted him past the door, in his costume, not knowing him until he signed his name on the engraved card."

Eldredge turned to the negro. "Mose, you saw this same man leave here, did you? And he left in his street clothes, did he not?"

"Yassuh," returned the negro uneasily.

"What time?"

"Somethin' around eleven o'clock, sah."

Eldredge turned to the accused. "Casperson, you were absolutely the only guest at this ball of Shirley's to leave the place before it was over—let alone before the alarm was given. You danced that fifth number with Shirley—I've got her card myself—at around ten-fifteen. Those jewels were on her neck then— Malcolm remembers it—she herself remembers it—although now she's trying to stick up for you by getting undecided in her recollections. She——"

"I was called from the ballroom by a legitimate summons," returned Casperson, "and Shirley doesn't need to lie for me. I, too, can say that she had on the necklace at the time we started the dance."

"Very well," commented Rufus Eldredge. "She danced with you, with Malcolm, with Jack Hennly, with Mr. Cawthorne, with Mr. Niccolo di Paoli, the violinist, then with me. The necklace was missing after I took Shirley out on the floor. I called her attention to it at once. We made a quick search; then an investigation. And you had left the place twenty minutes before, without even the courtesy of giving your hostess a reason for going so early." He paused. "Casperson, I could have you locked up on the strength of those facts, but I have decided not to do so just yet. But mark my words: I'll wait until six o'clock to-night for the necklace to come back to me by messenger or in any way that you decide to send it. And, if it doesn't, I'll see that the law takes its course." He rose and threw open the door. "That's all. You may go."

Casperson stood up. On his tongue trembled angry words, but a look at the girl sitting so miserably across the room silenced the burst of rage that was threatening to come from him. Instead, his next words were calm enough, but icy:

"Thank you for the eight hours' respite, Mr. Eldredge. I'm not alarmed at the thought of arrest, for the simple reason that it will be impossible to convict me of this theft. That's more than certain." He paused, and turned to the girl. "Shirley, this means that our marriage is off, unless my name can be cleared." He turned back to Eldredge again, and his tongue grew bitter: "You didn't want your little girl to become my wife because I happened to be the innocent means of interfering with your stock flotation. And now you've got your wish. I'm hit hard, but not in the way you think."

He glanced at the two younger people and at the phlegmatic butler and the negro, who fidgeted uncomfortably on their feet. "Good-bye," he said, and strode from the room.

CHAPTER XI

USHI SPEAKS

CASPERSON, unaccompanied, made his way down the broad staircase, but before he had reached the big front door he heard behind him a tripping step and the flutter of silk. Shirley stood at his side, her hand on his arm.

"Oh, Wilk," she said, "of course you didn't take it." Her face was white. "What a dreadful tangle to happen—just when you knew that a little four-room flat would be paradise to me if you were there."

He seized her hand. "It's mean luck, all right," he groaned. "But, dear, that necklace will have to be found before you and I can come together. It's just a case of hard luck, that's all. Good-bye again. I'm too hazy to talk now. But I'll try to communicate with you later, so that we may meet over on the lake shore and talk."

He walked for a long while, quite unconscious of the fact that a block behind him a keen-faced man kept on his track. After he had partly worked off his internal discomfiture in this way, he turned eastward and was soon over in the tawdry region of the Chicago Avenue police station, which, strangely enough, covered both the district of Little Hell to the west and the Silk Stockinged area of the Lake Shore Drive to the

east. He went up the same old steps which he had
trod many a time in his newspaper days, and stepped
over to the sergeant's battered desk. A new face pre-
sided there, and in each direction he looked he saw
new faces.

"Is MacTavish in?" he asked.

"Right here," grunted somebody behind him, and,
turning, he caught sight of MacTavish standing in the
detectives' room. MacTavish beckoned him inside and
closed the door. They were alone. "Great Scott, man,
what the devil is all this muss about a diamond necklace last night? I just got down, and only finished
reading the paper ten minutes ago."

Casperson told him the story from beginning to end.
Then he took out the card which had drawn him from
the mask ball. "And here," he said, "is the message
that decoyed me from the ball, Mac. Read it if you
can. If I'd had sense enough to show it to you last
night, we'd——" He broke off. "But last night I
merely thought it was a mistake in the street number,
so I didn't even bother you with it."

The detective wrinkled his brow as he turned to both
sides of it and found, with the exception of the pencilled words "Yellow Moth," only blank white space.
"Blank!" he ejaculated. "Well, what do you know
about that? Funny business of some sort here. Casperson, can you recall that message word for word
now?"

It was no difficulty at all for Casperson to repeat
the message, almost verbatim. Whereupon MacTavish
slumped back in his swivel chair, drumming on the
desk with his fingers. Then he rose. "We'll have to

dig into the thing deeper than we have, Casp." He
fumbled in a compartment of his desk and took from
it a peculiar little contrivance—a fine steel wire with
twisted ends, bearing a single Yale key. The wire
bracelet, for such it undoubtedly was, had been cut
with a pliers. "Know where this came from?" he said.

The other shook his head gloomily. "No."

"I stopped in the morgue on my way down this
morning," went on the detective, "and had another
look at the body of Silvester. This improvised bracelet
is what they found on his arm, above the elbow. No
doubt, of course, that it's a key to something he's been
concealing. So I'm wondering if it was for this key, or
for what the key has locked up, that the Jap killed
him; for the Jap did it, that's obvious. Silvester's
rubber-stamp message and the Jap's flight fit together
beautifully." He glanced toward the clock. "I was
just about to start for the Detective Bureau to interview the Jap before they give him the third degree.
Come along, if you wish. It certainly looks as though
you are vitally mixed up somehow in this tangle."

"I'll go gladly," said Casperson, rising.

Together they left the place. Twenty minutes later
they were entering the gloomy old police building in
the downtown district, which housed the detective headquarters. MacTavish nodded toward the blue-clad sergeant at the desk. "Morning, O'Reilly. Want to have
a word and a look at this Ushi Yatsura you fellows
picked up early this morning on our tip."

O'Reilly jerked his thumb toward the basement
stairs. "Go right on down, Mac. Cell twenty-four."

Below, a turnkey unlocked the barred door to a

whitewashed corridor flanked on both sides with cells over each of which a solitary electric bulb burned. The whole interior presented a gloomy contrast to the sunlit streets above. MacTavish led the way down the corridor and stopped at cell twenty-four. Casperson, at his elbow, peered in curiously.

The prisoner was undersized, yellow, slant-eyed, and hardly more than twenty-six or twenty-seven years old. His face was a shrewder, more worldly-wise one than that borne by the usual Japanese house-boy, such as he had been, supposedly, in the professor's laboratory. He sat on the hard ledge, his face and chin in his hands; but he looked up as the two men pressed their faces to the iron bars.

"Come over here, Yatsura; want to speak to you a minute," said MacTavish.

The prisoner dragged himself slowly, almost reluctantly, over to the cell door.

"Whata you want weeth me?" he stammered.

"Ushi, MacTavish is my name. I'm from the Chicago Avenue station." He paused. "Ushi, what did you shoot old man Silvester for?"

The Oriental's voice held in it a trace of sullenness, of defiance. "Ushi nevair shoot old man Silvester, sair. Thata what they say w'en they peeck him up joos as he go f'um depot to tak' train back for Freesco. He knowa nothing about it all."

MacTavish studied the brown-skinned figure in front of him. "Ushi, why were you in the North-western depot when you were supposed to be taking care of the laboratory on Ernst Court?"

"Becooze me an' he have quarrel w'at all heez fault—

not mine. I speel bot'le o' ink on Pers'in rug in doorway o' lebbertory on secon' floor las' night—an' he
say Ushi got pay for new rug. Ushi don't not pay
f'r no rugs, nevair, to man w'at pay 'im only eight dollar a week. I say I not pay, an' he say he hol' back
my monee till it paid for." The Jap emitted a snarling laugh. "Old man Silvester not know Ushi got
monee enough save' to go back to Freesco, an' Ushi
queet on spot, leave las' week's pay go jus' like that"
—he snapped his fingers—"pack 'is suit-case an' slip
out. From there he went to depot an' bought ticket
for Freesco an' wait till train ready to go. An' they
peeck him up as he get on train. Thaz all he knows."

MacTavish held up in the light of the overhanging
bulb the wisp of wire with the Yale key twisted on it.
"Ushi, was this what you shot him for?"

The Jap's eyes took in the contrivance stolidly, un-
blinkingly. Finally he shook his head wearily. "I
nota keel him; thaz all I have say. I nota keel him—
I nota keel him at all. An' I don't not know nothing
about it."

MacTavish remained a moment longer in front of
the cell door. Then he turned to Casperson. "Come,
let's go," he said. "The old case of tight-mouth Ori-
entalism. Never saw a criminal from the East yet
who couldn't shut up beautifully whether matters concerned him or not. But they'll sweat him to a fare-
you-well up in the chief's office in a little while."

He led the way back upstairs. At the sergeant's
desk he paused. "What did you find in the Jap's suit-
case, O'Reilly?"

The sergeant took a black cigar from his mouth

with exasperating slowness. "Just shirts, collars, clothing, and a roll o' money—twenty or thirty bucks. Nothing out of the way; no gun, neither. He got rid o' that. Whatever he croaked him for, he probably didn't get. Likely revenge or anger. Chief's just arrived, and they're going to sweat him upstairs in a few minutes. Want to sit in?"

MacTavish shook his head. "I guess not. We'll go on." Outside he said to Casperson. "No doubt, of course, that Ushi's lying, and I'm wondering if a good old Chicago third degree can squeeze the truth out of a Jap prisoner. I'm a little doubtful about it." He motioned to a street car. "We'll mosey on to Ernst Court now, and see what this little key of ours fits—if it fits anything. The Jap had a look in his eyes that might have meant everything or nothing when I showed it to him."

Arriving a few minutes later at Ernst Court, they tramped down the cobble-stones between the close-set buildings and found a bluecoat sitting on the steps. With a nod MacTavish passed him by and led the way to the upper floor. There things were much as they had been the night before, except that the body was not in evidence.

The two men stood gazing about the room, and Casperson, his eyes roving along the work-bench, came to rest upon a stout steel drawer, painted black, built into its structure; near the top of the drawer gleamed a shiny nickel-plated lock. He stepped forward and tried it. It was locked tight and snug, not giving by so much as a millimeter. He turned to the detective, who was watching him. "Try your key on this, Mac."

MacTavish strode forward and inserted the key, hampered by its wisp of wire. It turned easily, smoothly. He pulled open the steel drawer. Inside were but two articles: a slip of blue pasteboard with rounded corners and a few words scrawled on it, and a huge glass-covered flat box, perhaps a foot long and seven inches wide. Like the many other boxes which covered the walls, its bottom, too, was lined with cork. Its contents were indeed safely enclosed, considering the tight glass, and it was obviously dust-proof, air-proof, insect-proof. Pinned by one stout steel pin, driven straight into the cork bottom, was an enormous gaudy moth, one whose vivid red-and-purple front wings cleared easily five inches each, or ten inches together; whose rear, or smaller wings, of a soft grey with several yellow spots on them, were perhaps not more than three inches across each. Fastened to the bottom of the cork panel by four thumb tacks was a tiny white label card, which bore red-stamped letters like those on the cards the professor had been making as death had overtaken him:

VERGITILLA PHYLEAS
(Giant Tropical Moth)
Habitat: Low Regions from Eastern Costa Rica to Western Colombia, South America.

"What a giant moth it is!" remarked Casperson, as he stared down at it. "And do you suppose, Mac, that thing could possibly be rare enough for——" He stopped as MacTavish drew forth the blue card with rounded corners which appeared to have been hastily

tossed into the drawer. He proceeded to read it over
the plain-clothes man's shoulder. Its few pencilled
words ran: "My address after Monday: Ontario
Hotel."

MacTavish turned it over. On the other side was
written in a fine hand, different from that of the
scrawled words:

"Rec'd ten dollars deposit on yellow-moth masquerade
suit. D."

A silence followed the discovery of the words on the
other side. It was broken by MacTavish, who thrust
the card forward at Casperson and spoke: "There,
my friend, is the beginning of light on your own unfortunate affairs. Who was the other yellow moth
that never showed up at the masquerade ball on Lake
Shore Drive?"

CHAPTER XII

A HUNT ABOUT TOWN

"THE other moth," Casperson repeated slowly. "The other yellow moth! Mac, I guess you've hit the nail on the head."

A moment of thought, and he stepped over to the 'phone on the counter, and raising the receiver, asked for a number. After a clicking had ensued, a woman's voice answered. Casperson asked:

"Mrs. Dolliver? Can you tell me where Mr. Arthur Sennet has moved to? Better—can you give me his new 'phone number?"

"Mr. Sennet's sitting on the front steps now," the woman answered, "waiting for a messenger boy or a mail-man or something. I'll call him."

Casperson waited impatiently, and presently he heard Sennet's youthful, familiar voice on the wire.

"Arthur," he asked, "you didn't send me any notes, or anything, since we talked last night, did you?"

"Not on your life," answered the other glumly. "Nothing developed. That's why."

"It's all right, then. Where can I get you on the 'phone if I need you? I forgot to get your new address. Last night may have been too late to expect to hear anything from the judges, so it doesn't mean particularly bad or good news, boy."

"Well, I'm sticking right here on the old steps," declared Sennet, "till the noon mail delivery; then you can get me at my new lodgings at 1062 La Salle Avenue; Superior 4449. That's all I've got to report."

Casperson, after noting the address and the 'phone number, hung up and turned from the 'phone. "Well, just as we ought to have suspected last night, Mac; the note didn't come from him at all. There was evidently another yellow moth supposed to have been at that mask ball last night, and he never showed up at all—or else he showed up after I left. If we find that individual we'll be able to get some light on our affair which the disappearing writing mentioned. And from there——"

He stopped, for MacTavish's attention was once more riveted to the great entomological specimen taken from the drawer, and its data at the bottom; whereupon Casperson changed the angle of his question.

"What do you think of it, Mac? Does it look to you as if it was worth stealing?" He came over again and looked down at it. "Reminds me of a moth dude, with its vivid wings and its funny little coat-tails."

"Coat-tails?" echoed MacTavish.

Casperson was looking around the walls. "Well, you'll see what I mean if you look at that top row on the wall there. Some have the lower wings rounded; others come into a sort of a point or peninsula like a coat-tail. I shouldn't wonder if that feature serves as a distinguishing characteristic of a couple of groups or so. At any rate, all those with the coat-tails somehow remind me of dudes, while the others don't."

MacTavish nodded. "I see what you mean." He

studied the specimen in front of him again, with its
many colors. "Casp, to you and me this thing ain't
worth a day's pay; but to a bug collector it might be
worth—well—murder! Who knows? One thing is
certain: this is the only thing in the room that seems
to be under lock and key." He ran his eyes along the
work-bench and the walls. "This is the only lock,
that's sure." He paused. "And if it wasn't for the
dying accusation against Ushi, I'd say it might possibly be the blue card they were after, for some strange
reason. And here's the third and most likely theory:
if this here *Vergitilla Phyleas* was wanted by some
crazy bugologist, who's the first person he'd hire to
steal it? Answer me that."

"Ushi Yatsura," replied the other quickly.

MacTavish gave a satisfied smile. "All right. That's
sufficient. And now, Mr. Vergitilla Phyleas—or is it
Mrs. Vergitilla Phyleas?—we'll put you back in your
steel mausoleum for the present." And replacing the
glass-covered box, he pushed the drawer shut and
locked it.

After another brief study of the room of moths
which provided nothing of interest, they left the place.
Outside MacTavish spoke:

"I'm going back to the Detective Bureau now, Casp,
to see whether they've got anything through sweating
the Jap. 'Find Ushi—he knows' means that Ushi
knows—but doesn't mean that Ushi tells." He paused.
"And where'll you be later this afternoon? I saw you
writing down the name of that moth, and I've a suspicion that you're going to look it up at the public library. If not, why not do it? And if so, I'd like to

run in this afternoon and see what scientific information you get." He looked at his watch. "It's near
noon-time now."

"To look up that *Vergitilla Phyleas* was exactly
my plan, Mac, and I'll copy what dope I get. As for
coming in on me, I'll be at my rooms, say at three
o'clock sharp. If anything vital concerning me develops, leave a message with my landlady. You'll find
me at 842 Dearborn Avenue, and I've a private 'phone
in my room with my name in the telephone book."

They parted at the dingy, narrow mouth of Ernst
Court, and Casperson took a car to the east which
would bring him to the costumers' near North Avenue and Clark Street, where he had rented his yellow
moth suit a couple of evenings before. Fifteen minutes later, as he waited at the counter in the eerie atmosphere of masked wax figures and costumes, a clerk
approached him.

"The other evening," Casperson said, "I rented a
costume here—an odd sort of thing, supposed to represent a huge yellow moth. Do you have any others
like that in stock? I'm trying to locate another mas-
querader who was dressed in just such a costume at
the same ball."

The clerk shook his head. "No, we have no others.
That suit was one we purchased from an old maker
over on West Monroe Street. His business is the de-
vising and making of peculiar costumes." He looked
into a worn ledger, which he withdrew from a desk
back of the counter. "His name is Adolph Stutz; his
number is 2440 West Monroe. I'm inclined to think
that it was his own design, and that he will probably

be able to tell you where he has placed other such suits."

Casperson thanked the clerk and straightway took a car to West Monroe Street. Here, in a district dirty and uncouth, with shabby houses and dirty-faced children, he soon found a basement with a little hunchbacked man sitting on a table cross-legged and working on a suit of scarlet silk. On the upper part of the window a sign in the last stages of dissolution announced: "Adolph Stutz, maker of masquerade suits."

Casperson went down a few steps and walked inside. The old man looked up at him. Casperson stated his errand. The old man stopped threading his needle and scratched his head, blinking through his steel-rimmed spectacles.

"I did mage four uf dose suids," he announced, "und I blace dem vun each in four masquerade houses." He rose ponderously. "But you say you like mooch to locate man vass vear vun, eh? Well, I shust dell you vere de four suids iss, and den you can look it up yourself."

He found some entries in a book made of yellow paper. As he called them off Casperson copied out with his pencil three of the addresses, the fourth being that of the costumer on whom he had already called. Then he thanked the old man, and, leaving him a half-dollar concealed under a piece of silk on the table, departed from the region.

The first house he called at was quite pretentious, and was situated farther out on Monroe Street, near a huge dance pavilion which advertised extensively in the street cars. The clerk in charge thought first that Casperson wanted to rent a yellow-moth suit, and brought out one which was very similar—almost identical with the one Casperson had worn the night before. The latter's queries, however, developed the fact that the suit had been there for several weeks; so that part of the chase was terminated. He was soon on the way to the other two addresses found in Stutz's book.

The second of the three, like the first, had the suit in stock. It had not been out for a week. But the third one, situated in the Loop, and with a bigger stock than any of the others, proved to have had such a suit. And it was gone!

"When did it go out?" he asked the girl clerk.

"Several nights ago," she replied.

"Is it your custom to write out a blue ticket, giving the deposit on a suit and signing it simply 'D'?"

She nodded. "Yes. 'D' is my last initial."

Again he told how he was trying to find the temporary holder of the suit, and she appeared glad to give him the only information she had.

"I rented it to a dark, handsome man, tall and a little corpulent, but very polished in his manner," she said. "I dimly recollect his saying that he had a friend who was a collector of moths, and he wondered why moths with their vivid coloring would not make unique subjects for masquerade suits. Of course I showed him the one we had and he rented it. I took his deposit, and, as usual in that case, did not bother with the name and address of the lessee." She paused. "That is all I can tell."

"It has not been returned?" Casperson asked.

She shook her head. "No."

He thanked her and left the place. Outside in the Loop, in the bright sunshine, Casperson paused to reflect on recent developments. He—or perhaps he with MacTavish's aid—had now brought to light that there was a man of a certain description who had rented a suit designed to represent a huge yellow moth. That was as far, at the present, as he could go. He was still bewildered, however. That he had received the note intended for the other yellow moth seemed somehow certain; the A. S. supposed to have been Arthur Sennet was really Aloysius Silvester. Who then, was W. C., who bore his own initials? And what connection was there between the human moth and the old moth-collector which caused an urgent note to go out from the latter to the former?

This set him on a new train of thought, and with the picture of the *Vergitilla Phyleas* in his mind, he wended his way over to the public library, where he got out an encyclopedia in the reading-room and found a good deal of dry reading about moths in general. He managed to hold his attention to the uninteresting material, however, discovering, at least, certain things he had not known before concerning the difference between moths and butterflies, and particularly a certain point of differentiation between the moths themselves. As he closed the huge volume he sat and looked off into space. "I never realized," he remarked to himself, "that there could be such a vast field of study in just the moth family itself."

He returned the book to the rack and went over to the call counter, where he asked for "Bertram, on

Moths," a book which he had seen mentioned at the end of the encyclopedia article as a popular work upon the subject. Soon it was brought to him in its bright gilt-and-red cover, and he dropped into the nearest chair and turned first to the index. There, as was to be expected, he came upon the words *Vergitilla Phyleas*, and found a short article devoted to that particular member of the great moth family. It read:

Vergitilla Phyleas: One of the so-called giant moths, and one, in fact, whose wings in a few specimens in museums have measured as much as twelve inches from tip to tip. It has been seen alive only during certain parts of the year and at twenty-one-year intervals in the low regions of the American continents, and never west of the eastern boundary of Costa Rica nor east of the western boundary of Colombia. Its span of existence seems to be in the vicinity of thirty days, after which time it expires or else passes through an intermediate stage till the expiration of the next twenty-one-years. At no latitude of Africa, Europe, or Asia has the Vergitilla ever been found. It is quite rare, not over fifty specimens being in existence, according to the author's investigations. Most of these are in museums. On account of the giantism of the Vergitilla it has been confused in numerous instances with the slightly smaller Oralia Purpura whose wing colors and markings are appreciably similar to those of the Vergitilla Phyleas. The Oralia Purpura, however, occurs in many lands and latitudes, and has a far longer span of existence than that of the Vergitilla, the two factors mentioned accounting for the extreme value of the last-named moth. A Vergitilla Phyleas sold at a London auction as high as eleven thousand dollars in American money. See the monograph of Professor Hans Schwenmauer, of the University of California, on the subject of tropical and semi-tropical moths.

For several minutes Casperson studied the article. Then fumbling in his pockets for paper and pencil, he discovered that he had left his pencil at the old

costume makers'; but on top of that he found that in
the excitement of Rufus Eldredge's entrance that morning, he had stuck into his own pocket Malcolm's fountain pen with which he had receipted the latter's promissory note. So on the blank pages of a letter he had
in his pocket he copied the article devoted by Bertram
to the *Vergitilla Phyleas*, and as soon as it had dried
he left the library.

Now he was quite decided as to what his next step
was to be. Something seemed to have come into him—
a strange tension—a realization that he was tumbling
upon something most queer, yet something which he
could not fully grasp. And so, after consulting a street
directory, he went straight to Professor Silvester's
residence in St. Clair Street, not very far from the
Ernst Court laboratory where the grey-haired entomologist had met his death.

CHAPTER XIII

ST. CLAIR STREET was a neat, trim thoroughfare with grass and trees along the sidewalk, and
"semi-aristocratic" houses that showed in their construction a past age of building artistry. The one
at which Casperson pressed the electric button was
set back from the street in a yard of large elms, and
the shades were all tightly drawn.

His ring was not answered; so he rang again, this
time much longer. Now one of the window shades was
drawn back slightly, and a very pale, girlish face
peered from the darkened house. A second later the
door was opened, and there stood looking out at him
a girl in a black dress, not more than twenty years
of age, dark-haired and with dark eyes under which
were circles of grief, and around which were the red
rims that meant weeping.

"Is this Miss Silvester, the daughter of Professor
Silvester?" Casperson asked, feeling like a brute for
intruding upon a person at such a time.

"Diana Silvester," she informed him, in a low voice.
She paused. "You are from the police station, too?"

He thought it best to ignore the question. "I realize
that the detectives have been bothering you a good

109

deal to-day, but I should like to ask a few questions—if possible."

She stood aside politely and motioned him in. He found himself in a darkened parlor that was tastefully and expensively arranged; here and there were glimpses of white statuary; over in a corner stood a grand piano. He waited until she had seated herself, then he dropped into a near-by chair.

"Miss Silvester, I regret very much the sad thing that has happened to your father. Have you any idea of the reason for his end?"

"There is no doubt in my mind," she said, in a low, melodious voice, "that the Japanese caretaker, Ushi Yatsura, killed him. My father had many enemies over the world—at least he has always said so. He once voiced the strange suspicion that Ushi, who answered his advertisement for a caretaker and houseboy, had been sent by some rival moth-collector in India whom he had made an enemy of, solely for the purpose of stealing his rarest specimens."

"Your father, I see, has travelled a good deal in his professional work. On the faculty of what university, may I ask, has he been?"

"My father," the girl replied, "as much as I know about him, was not an accredited professor. He had studied so deeply in his line that he was known to almost everyone as 'Professor Silvester.' As you just suggested, my father had been all over the world previous to the time he settled down in Chicago and was married to my mother, who died shortly after my birth. He has given numerous lectures upon moths, and has maintained something of a collection. But when he decided, a few months ago, to create his laboratory or private museum over on Ernst Court, he began to send all over the world for moth specimens which he had collected and prepared in bygone years and which had been lent for indefinite periods to foreign museums. Case by case they came by express, and gradually he and Ushi set them up in the Ernst Court place."

"Your father, I take it, had an income sufficient to allow him to devote his life to this specialty?"

She nodded. "Well—yes—apparently. But I have no way of knowing the size of his estate. He may be nearly penniless, for all I know just now. In former years we lived somewhat lavishly, but I have noticed that he had a tendency in recent years to curtail many expenditures."

Casperson nodded. He was getting peculiar information and yet it was bringing him nowhere. At length he broke the silence again. "Miss Silvester, do you know anything of a specimen known as the *Vergitilla Phyleas* which was not among those on the walls of his laboratory?"

"The giant tropical moth?" she queried, evidently comprehending.

He nodded.

"That is the one, then, which he got down between Costa Rica and Colombia somewhere. He spent about nine weeks hunting it, on his trip for the Johnsonian Institute, of Washington, D. C. He is an accredited member of that scientific society. He has not spoken much of the specimen, except to tell me that its appearances were about twenty-one years apart, and that its span of existence was but a few weeks. Also, he informed me that his quest was successful. Had it not been, he would never have lived long enough to make another attempt to secure it."

"When did he return from his last trip?" asked Casperson. "And when did he leave?" He paused. "And another question: has he been visited of late by a tall, well-groomed man with dark hair? Also, have there been any attempts, since he secured the *Vergitilla*, to break into this house or the Ernst Court laboratory?"

The girl paused, thinking over his four rapidly fired questions. Then she answered them in the order they were given. "Father returned from his last trip about a month or three weeks ago; he had been gone about six weeks, which places his departure around two and a half months previous to the present date." She stopped a moment, then went on: "As to a tall, well-groomed man, such a one has called here several times. I have shown him into father's study, and they have talked for long periods. One of his visits took place yesterday morning." Again she paused to reflect. "And as to the fourth question, I believe that the laboratory was once broken into by hoodlums in the neighborhood. We are not far, you know, from the so-called Geary Alley gang. But no attempts to break in here have ever been made. But last night——"
She stopped and made no effort to continue.

"And last night," said Casperson, leaning forward. "What happened?"

"Last night father started for the laboratory at around nine o'clock to work on some specimen cards. He returned to the house a minute or two later, all excited. He said he had seen a man well shrouded in a raincoat and wearing a felt hat watching this house from a point across the street; that the man had almost concealed himself back of an elm trunk, but father nevertheless had caught sight of him."

"And what did your father do?"

"He was nervous and excitable. He paced back and forth and went upstairs to my front room, probably to look out of the darkened windows. Later he snapped on the lights and still later came down. He stood about for a while, thinking, and finally, much worried, left the house. There's the whole incident."

Casperson reflected a moment. "Do you think the man was watching your father, Miss Silvester, or watching the house?"

She shook her head to both questions. "I believe that father had been under much tension of late, and exaggerated everything. As I told you before, I am certain that Ushi killed him. I have never liked the Jap boy, and believe, as father suggested, that he was connected with some of father's enemies."

Casperson did not press the peculiar matter further, but asked:

"Can you conceive of why the *Vergitilla* was locked up in a tight steel drawer instead of being hung upon the walls with the rest of the specimens? What would its value be?"

"As to its value, I cannot say," she replied, looking into his eyes. "Those things are invaluable to collectors, but to you and to me, perhaps, one would not be worth fifty dollars. I only know that of late father— poor father!—had been under the impresison that people were after him—were trying to get something from him. And he was going to discharge Ushi soon for the reason, as I told you, that he suspected more every day that Ushi was sent there by some certain rival collector in India to steal the *Vergitilla Phyleas*, for father had been publicly selected by the Johnsonian Institute, a full year before, as the man who should go to South America to capture the *Vergitilla* if it appeared at the end of its twenty-one-year cycle. And it hides, you know, under the leaves, and only comes out at night, when it is nearly invisible."

Casperson was interested. "That might account for why he kept it locked up, if he suspected Ushi. But Ushi didn't get away with it, although it certainly does appear that he killed his employer and fled."

For a while they sat there in the darkened parlor, neither speaking. The girl dabbed her eyes several times with her handkerchief, and finally Casperson, realizing that there was nothing more he wished to ask, rose from his chair, made his apologies, and went into the street.

He walked back to his Dearborn Avenue lodgings, still unaware of the fact that the keen-faced man with the bearing of a private detective clung to his footsteps, noting every turn of his course by the use of a pencil stub and a card in his coat pocket. Entering his room, Casperson sat an hour thinking on the two intersecting trains of incidents: the mystery of the *Vergitilla Phyleas*, and the unfortunate complication it had made in his own life through drawing him away from the Eldredge dance just as the fifty-thousand-dollar diamond necklace had disappeared.

Reflecting upon his own woes, for the time he forgot the mystery of the dead moth-collector. Again he recollected Rufus Eldredge's declaration that Shirley, after her dance with him, had danced in turn with Malcolm, with Jack Hennly, with a Mr. Cawthorne, with Niccolo di Paoli, and with her own father. It was obvious, then, that since the necklace had been stolen, the theft must have been perpetrated by one of the four people between himself and her father. Somehow the thought would not "down" that her father might have done the thing himself, in sheer rage at not being able to lower him, Casperson, in the eyes of his daughter, who had threatened to marry the man of her choice.

Taking pencil and paper, Casperson ruled off a column which he labelled "Dance numbers," a second which he labelled "Names," and a third which he labelled "Facts and Motives." For a few minutes he worked upon the problem. When he had finished he smiled wearily at his analytical work. It read:

Dance No.	Name.	Facts and Motives
5.	Wilk Casperson.	Supposed to have stolen necklace, but didn't.
6.	Malcolm Eldredge.	Hard to believe that her own brother could steal necklace, but . . . that unfortunate matter of the stolen money and the necessity of making it up . . . not looking very good.
7.	Jack Hennly.	Well-known millionaire clubman and polo player . . . plenty of rich relatives . . . wouldn't steal anything for the price of it, for he can't

		spend his own millions. But could he be a kleptomaniac?
8.	Mr. Cawthorne.	Don't know him, except having heard him mentioned at Eldredge's as a clubman. In all likelihood, no motive exists.
9.	Niccolo di Paoli.	Musician, very well known. Receives very high prices for public appearances. No motive.
10.	Rufus Eldredge.	Her father. Might have done it to throw me out of the running. Thinks I nearly ruined his good name, and he might retaliate. Funny world, and funny things happen.

For a long time Casperson lay on his bed, studying the analytical results which were shown by the paper he had just drawn up. At length he arose and took a seat in the window again. He smiled bitterly. In about three hours it would be six o'clock, and that was the hour at which Rufus Eldredge had stated that the necklace must be returned to his residence. The sight of the 'phone on his wall, however, made him think again of MacTavish, and in the doubts as to the latter's arrival at the appointed hour he decided to call the plain-clothes man up and read him the description of the *Vergitilla Phyleas* and tell him of the facts he had gleaned at Diana Silvester's. So he drew the scrap of paper from his pocket and stepped over to the 'phone.

But he stopped short in his progress across the room. To his amazement, the finer strokes of the pen had vanished completely—had faded into nothingness. In other words, the written description of the *Vergitilla Phyleas* was disappearing!

CHAPTER XIV

A VISITOR VIA ROOF-TOPS

ONE thing shot into Casperson's mind with startling force: the card handed him the night before at the ball had been written by no one else but Malcolm Eldredge, for from this same pen, accidentally carried off from the latter's room, had come the copy of the material concerning moths. This being so, it could mean but one thing: Malcolm had sent the decoy card in order to throw suspicion by getting him, Casperson, out of the place at the psychological moment.

With a new vividness there occurred to him the scene of that morning: Malcolm's nervous presentation of the check for the borrowed money he owed, and his request that it be not placed in the bank until late that afternoon. What else could it mean than that Malcolm had made off with the necklace and that very morning was intending to realize on it at some place he had arranged for?

Casperson drew out the check the other had given him. Here, though, no fading, magic, invisible ink had been used; indeed, the ink used was purple, instead of the light blue such as came from the fountain-pen. Here was the plain, even, bold handwriting of a business man, not the eccentric, disguised, erratic hand-

117

writing which had been deliberately used on the decoy card.

He shook his head with a sigh. Malcolm Eldredge must have been desperate indeed to decoy a man who had befriended him as he, Casperson, had done, with the intention of throwing suspicion upon him as soon as the theft of the necklace had actually been discovered. Yet Casperson feared that a man short in his accounts, inundated with debts to cover the shortage, with an irate, irascible father, unable to borrow the amount necessary to make good the loans that temporarily covered his defalcations, might not stop at throwing suspicion on a rank outsider to his own circle who was trying to marry one of its girls—in this instance Malcolm's own sister.

For a few unhappy minutes he sat staring down at the fading writing on the back of the envelope. Then a sudden peculiar idea struck him with force, and stepping to the telephone on the wall, he dropped a nickel and asked for Lake Drive 3339. He recognized the methodical voice of Brayley on the wire, and he lost no time in asking for Miss Eldredge.

"Who shall I say is calling?" asked the butler.

"Never mind the name, please," replied Casperson uneasily, wondering whether Brayley had had orders to cut him off if he called. "Just call her, Miss Eldredge."

A pause ensued, in which his heart pounded a bit, but soon he heard the voice that he longed for.

"Shirley, I want to ask you something. In the excitement of this morning I had no chance to ask you any questions at all; but now that things are cooling

down I am getting a better grip on the situation. No
sign of the necklace, I suppose?"

A pause followed his question. Then her words
came softly: "Wait a minute, please, till I look down
the hall." A moment of silence; then her voice again,
this time very low: "I was looking to see whether
father was in hearing distance; but he's locked in his
library at the end of the house. He has forbidden me
to talk to you on the 'phone of this house. As to the
necklace, Wilk, not a sign—yet."

"What does Malcolm think about this affair?"

"He's very cheerful about it. Says I look prettier
without the necklace; tells both father and me to forget it—that it's not worth a second thought, considering that we're rich, have our health and liberty, and
all that. Malcolm is the one person who seems to be
quite happy about it all."

"I see." Casperson paused. "Shirley, you recall
that I was made up as a yellow moth last night. Was
anyone else supposed to be there, so far as you know
from talking in advance to your friends, who was to
come garbed as a butterfly or a moth?"

"Yes, Wilk, there was. In fact, he came in the hall
at around ten-thirty, about in time to get the dance
he had arranged with me long ahead. I first thought
it was you, but when he got nearer I found that he
wore a yellow cloth bag over his head instead of grease
paint, as you did."

"No, it was not I, you may be sure," Casperson said.
"I was downstairs in the gentlemen's dressing-room
trying to get the grease paint off my face with cold
cream. But this other moth—who was he? I have

the best reason in the world for asking. I will tell you
in time what my reason is."

She answered him in the same low tone: "It was the
man whom I described to you in the conservatory—
the clubman to whom father is so partial that I'm sure
he is going to try to induce me to marry him: Mr.
Cawthorne—Mr. Wellington Cawthorne."

Casperson emitted a soft whistle. Wellington Cawthorne—W. C.; Aloysius Silvester—A. S. Yellow
Moth. It was plain beyond everything now. He
weighed another question, then put it:

"Shirley, did any member of your family know what
costume Mr. Cawthorne was to come in? And where
does he live? Please don't be alarmed. I'm not mixing him up at all with the diamond necklace, but I'm
trying to solve a perplexing riddle of circumstances."

She paused, evidently thinking. "Well, Wilk, as
to your first question, he and Malcolm, at the last
musicale, when Mr. di Paoli played, had an extended
discussion on the subject of novel masquerade suits.
It is quite probable that Malcolm was aware of how
Mr. Cawthorne intended to come costumed. He lives
at the Plaza Hotel, near Lincoln Park."

"Thank you. You've been a great help. Be patient,
dear. I'll tell you all in time. Before long I'll try
to speak to you again by 'phone. Good-bye."

He hung up, and, dropping back into his seat,
heaved a sigh of relief. Somehow, the thought that
Malcolm had been a thief—a thief of his own sister's
necklace—hadn't hurt Casperson so much, realizing as
he did the desperation of the young fellow; but the
fact that young Eldredge had conspired to draw down

suspicion on Casperson was the thrust that hurt. But a grim smile played on his face as the more comforting explanation and theory sifted into his consciousness.

And thus Casperson now reconstructed the affair: Malcolm, preparing to steal his sister's necklace at her birthday ball, had arranged his plan long ahead of time, using his knowledge of some connection existing between Wellington Cawthorne and Professor Aloysius Silvester. How he had known of that connection was doubtful at this point of the investigation. Had Cawthorne, at the Eldredge home, mentioned his acquaintance, or perhaps some impending deal with the famous moth-collector? However the knowledge was obtained, Malcolm's intentions were to get Cawthorne out of the hall at the time he stole the necklace, and thus clear the boards for him, Casperson, whom all the time he had seemed to favor. Unfortunately, Cawthorne had arrived late at the ball, Casperson had come garbed also as a yellow moth, and he had been the one to rush madly out of the place, interpreting the signature A. S. as that of Arthur Sennet. Oh, what a jumble of circumstances!

From this point Casperson's mind roved to the matter of the dead Silvester and the dying, rubber-stamped accusation he had left behind him: "Find Ushi—he knows." For several minutes he thought upon that message, wrinkling up his brows as though something —something which he could not ascertain—was troubling his inner consciousness. "It's actually getting on my nerves from hearing it so often," he said to himself. "And yet——"

He lapsed into silence again, still pondering on those few words. Finally he rose from his chair, and, going over to the bed, flung himself down backward; he placed his hands over his eyes, shutting out every object in the room. There he found he could think more clearly, and for a period of ten minutes he wandered around a strange Coney Island-like maze, in which the four words balked him, tangled him, and yet led him on to further intensive study of the past. Of a sudden he sprang to his feet.

"Eureka!" he cried. "Eureka! I've found it at last. The man was dying, weak. He was——"

He stopped. Out in the hall was the sound of footsteps followed by a sharp staccato tapping at the door. He looked in that direction and called, "Come in!"

The door opened, and a man in smart clothes, carrying a cane, looked hesitatingly in. His face riveted itself immediately upon the telephone on the wall close by the door, and he even glanced at the number plate carefully. He was clean and neat, his eyes held a sharp, ratlike look, with a pronounced suggestion of shiftiness in them. And his face! It was of a peculiar cast—flat, squat, almost Chinese.

He was the first to speak. "Am I addressing Mr. Wilk Casperson?" he asked.

CHAPTER XV

THE newcomer entered and closed the door carefully behind him. "Like to have a few words with you, Casperson, if you've a minute or so. Tried to get you on your 'phone many times to-day but wasn't successful."

"I see. Have a seat." Casperson pointed to a chair across the room. The stranger, however, ignored the proffered chair, and dropped into a hard, straight one directly between Casperson and the door. "What did you say your name was?"

The other placed his cane across his knees. "Name hardly matters," he replied pleasantly. He smiled, splitting his peculiar moonface so that it showed two rows of white, smooth, wolfish-looking teeth. He gazed about the room solicitously, then spoke in cold, level tones—so low that they could hardly penetrate the walls or the door.

"Casperson, I read about your stunt in the paper this morning. I must congratulate you. It was a master stroke. But may I ask one question: why did you lose your nerve and beat it? You should have stashed it somewhere in the place."

Casperson, aghast, stared at his visitor. "A master stroke. Should have stashed it," he repeated.

"Look here—who are you and what are you driving at?"

The visitor smiled again; into his eyes came a wolfish light. "I mean that if I had pulled the stunt off—if you hadn't got to it before me—I'd never have jumbled things by trying to make a get-away. You fool, don't you know that you've been followed all day by detectives, watching your every move?"

Casperson slid to the edge of the chair. "Say, what are you driving at? And once more, who are you? Are you a reporter? What do you mean by my 'making a get-away'? You're assuming out and out that I stole the necklace at the Eldredge ball last night."

The moon-faced man smiled. "Chuck it, Casperson, chuck it. It was a bully stunt. I had expected to turn the trick myself, but when I got to my dance with her young ladyship, it was gone. In other words, you beat me to it. And when I read about it in the papers this morning, I couldn't quite figure out whether you were my superior or my inferior, on account of your getting panic-stricken and trying to get out of the place."

It was on Casperson's lips to break out into some strong language, but he held himself together with all his might. He studied the fellow in front of him, trying to fathom what errand it was he had come on.

"Well, what is it you want, anyway?" he asked quietly.

"My dear boy, would it interest you to know that there's a man posted at the corner now, watching this room of yours like a hawk? Do you realize at all that you've as much chance of disposing of that necklace as a snowball in hell? Do you know how I got into this house? Do you know that I made the roof at the end of the block where the partly built flat-building stands, crossed the housetops, noted the terminals of the two sets of 'phone wires entering this house, came down the trapdoor in the top-floor bath-room, and found your room by inquiring from someone on the second floor, who thought I came in by the street door, admitted by the honorable landlady?"

"No." Casperson was lost in bewilderment.

"Do you know that the man watching this place, waiting, keeping you in the background until the minute you try to cash in on that necklace, doesn't even know that I'm here? Never mind who I am. If he had seen me come in he'd have pinched me sure— had the whole house raided, I guess. And you'd have picked ten years in the pen from the mess. However, all this bores you. Enough for me to say that I'm going out the same way I came in. And I'm going to retrace my path across the roofs. And I'm going to have that necklace with me when I leave. I'm going to place that string of sparklers quick for you, and for better money than you can realize on it alone. I'm going to clear you—put you in a position where they can dog your steps for the next year and get nothing on you. I'm going to charge you just half of what I turn it over for, as my bit for helping you out. Now do you see why I dropped in on you?"

Casperson gritted his teeth. He rose, stepped to the window, and looked up the street. There, leaning against a lamp-post and staring abstractedly down the street, was a solitary figure who had the undoubted bearing of a detective. And Casperson had seen enough of them in old newspaper days. He shook his head slowly. Thus far he hadn't even realized that he was being followed from place to place. But this man, this crook, was smarter than he.

He retraced his steps to his chair and looked toward the man across from him. "So there was a crook in costume at that ball. Which—which one were you?"

The flat-faced man laughed grimly. "It'll all come out in a few days or so when the wop comes back to Chicago. So you no remember me, eh, Meestair Caspairson? Di Paoli w'at playa da fina musica, eh?"

A grim shadow of a smile showed on Casperson's face. "Di Paoli!" he exclaimed. "And you were the clown in red silk?" He stared at the other with a trace of admiration in his face. "I am sorry to say," he went on, "that your little trip across the roofs isn't going to do you much good. It's evident that one crook at that ball failed to get what he was after, else he wouldn't make a roof-top trip to a man watched by detectives. No; I can't deal with you, and wouldn't if I could. In simpler language, I—did—not—get—that—necklace. Is that enough?"

The flat-faced man broke into a snarl. "No monkey business now. I told you I'd split half with you, and I'll do it. You fool, can't you see you'll trip yourself up trying to fence the thing? Can't you even guess the position you're in?"

"I have spoken," Casperson replied quietly. "So you had better go. You had——"

He stopped. The other had drawn from the pocket

of his coat a gleaming revolver. His face was now that of an animal, snarling, beastlike. "Cough up!" he snapped. "Cough up, and be quick about it! I didn't come across these roofs to monkey with you. Produce, I tell you!"

Casperson pointed to the window. "Suppose I go to that window and call for help. What then?"

The crook showed his teeth again. "Always the fool," he half snarled, half groaned. "When they find Moonface Eddy Chang in this room they'll give you ten years. I'll tell 'em you knew me from 'way back and called me here to get my help in disposing of that stolen necklace. I'll send you to the pen for ten years on the strength of that statement—and Moonface won't get a stretch of even a week out of it if he turns State's evidence. Now do you see where you get off?"

Casperson stroked his chin, still watching that villainous-looking revolver. He could see that he was in an ugly position. If the police knew that this crook sat in his room, if the latter should tell them the story he had just threatened to tell, where would he, Wilk Casperson, land, already suspected, through certain damning circumstances, of being the thief? Where would his chance be now with a jury? He was in a tight corner.

"Where did you get your ticket to the masquerade?" he asked desperately, sparring for a moment's delay in which he could think, could evolve some plan to get this man out of the place without any commotion.

"Don't worry your head about where I got that ticket," returned Moonface. "You'd know too much that wasn't good for you if I told you." He stood up and jerked back his coat-sleeve, pinning his finger upon the trigger of the weapon. "Now, you blighter, are you going to produce those sparklers or not? Are you——"

His words were sharply broken off. The clock on the mantel was chiming the hour of three. But that was not the cause of the interruption. The door back of Moonface had opened suddenly, and a red-haired man had leaped in on him, pinioning both of his arms behind him. Moonface was helpless. The revolver clattered to the floor from the impact of body against body. Then came the voice of MacTavish, speaking to Casperson:

"Got here on time, Casp; a little bit before, in fact." He looked down into the face of the snarling figure which he held with two brawny arms. "Thought you were down in South America, Moonface. Anyway, I'm glad to see you back again. What's the game up North this time? I heard your little story to Casperson—the last half of it, anyway; the keyhole leaked." He paused, getting his breath, which was coming fast, on account of the sharp struggle. Then, with a quick motion, he flung the crook to the floor. "Out with it! Tell us, and tell us quick, where you got your ticket to that Eldredge mask ball?"

CHAPTER XVI

"DOUBLE-CROSSED"

A DEATHLY silence followed MacTavish's gruff command, a silence in which the crook, lying on the floor, stared sullenly out in front of him. He rose clumsily to his knees, but, even as he did so, he peeped slightly toward the door. The plain-clothes man, however, with a low, hard chuckle, turned and snapped the key in the lock. Then he dropped it into his pocket, and turned as the slim fellow got to his feet.

"Come, Moonface," he said. "How about it? Going to talk or not?"

The crook frowned. He scratched his head. "What do you want to know, anyway?" he grumbled. "I didn't get that necklace. Would I have come here to demand it if I had?"

"Of course you didn't," said MacTavish. "That's plain. But I heard part of your little series of demands on Casperson, and I know now that you were at that ball trying to get your slippery fingers on that necklace."

"But you can't jug me for that," replied the crook. "Suppose I was there? I didn't get it, did I? And they can't prove I got it. I never beat it away from the place like this crook here." He pointed to Casperson.

129

MacTavish frowned. "Moonface, the Department at Chicago knows all about you. About a year ago a paper was stolen from the Consulate at Buenos Aires —a paper worth a good deal to some foreign Government. It wasn't a United States affair at all, but if that certain little South American Government knew that we had one of the two men known to have pulled that stunt—Eddy Chang, the quarter chink, and Cecil Gryce—they'd have requisition papers out in no time —for you, anyway. Say, Moonface, were you ever in a South American jail?"

The crook's lips trembled; he passed a hand over his forehead, to which beads of moisture had sprung. "Jeez'—a South American jug." He stiffened up. "Say, what do you want to know? Do I walk out of here free if I tell you what you want to know?"

"I'll promise you—Casperson here as witness—that you'll not be taken back to South America," said Mac-Tavish; "but we might not be done with you for several days or weeks." He paused. "Well, Moonface, who'd you get that engraved ticket from that you used to get into the ball?"

Moonface sank into a chair and drew up one knee in his hands. "It was given to me by Cecil Gryce," he announced reluctantly; "the fellow who was mixed up in that Buenos Aires theft. He's living in Chicago, at the Plaza Hotel, under the name of Wellington Cawthorne. He was invited to that ball, and accidentally got two tickets. Called me in—we've been in touch since we came back from South America—and he fixed it up with me to go to the ball and take the part of Niccolo di Paoli, one of the Eldredge circle. Since

he'd discovered that the Italian wasn't to be there, and
that the latter hadn't even sent regrets—he'd left Chicago so suddenly—I went made up as a clown, covered
with grease paint, and I signed di Paoli's name on the
card. It didn't take me long to figure the girl the
easiest of 'em all, on account of the looseness of the
string on her neck. I signed up for a dance as di
Paoli, but when I went to claim my dance the necklace
was gone and the little chicken never even knew it.
Someone ahead of me had lifted it. A while later
came the alarm. And to-day I found in the papers
about this guy." He indicated Casperson. "So I
decided to play him for the goods he got out of that
place. He's your man all right—unless you're in this
game yourself."

"Nix on that stuff," snapped MacTavish. "Now,
see here: why were you doing this stunt at the mask
ball? How much was this Gryce—or Wellington Cawthorne—to get out of it, since he paved the way for
the theft?"

Moonface cleared his throat. His face grew
troubled. "Here's all I know of it: Gryce, or Cawthorne—call him what you please—claims that someone in this burg had something that was worth a hundred thousand cold to him if he could get his fingers
on it. But he claimed that he couldn't steal it. He
says there was no way to get it but to cough up what
this someone wanted—ten grand in cold cash. He
showed me all that he had left from the Buenos Aires
robbery—a few hundred. He said this mask ball,
the two tickets, and my presence in the burg was the
hand of fate. I was to cop out a bunch of big sparklers

worth fifty thousand or more in one haul at the ball, hand 'em over to him so that he could raise the ten thousand from a fence, and he'd turn our money over again for ten·times the amount."

MacTavish gave vent to a sarcastic laugh. "And you would have turned them over to him? I know your kind, Moonface. I can tell from your tone that you haven't swallowed that story of your friend. If you'd got those sparklers you'd have mooched out of Chi on the first train, and let Gryce whistle for his money. One question, though: after you found the little lady had had her necklace lifted, why didn't you try your hand at some other set of jewels?"

"Why?" returned the crook. "For the simple reason that when it came out that a necklace had been lifted, my game at that ball was over for the night. I could hear the news going all round the place: Miss Eldredge's necklace has been lost or stolen. Every dame in the house had her eyes and her hands on every sparkler she possessed. I'd have been pinched in a minute if I'd tried to do any business then. I was shaking in my shoes, to be frank. All I wanted to do at that moment was to get out of the place; and I did it—as Niccolo di Paoli."

For a few minutes nothing was said. Then MacTavish spoke: "All right, Moonface. You've given the information we want. But now I'm going to make you do a little work. And remember—no monkey business! Get funny, and in stir you go in a minute and from there to South America; but work with us, and you'll probably slip out of Chi a sadder and wiser man." He went to the telephone and looked up a number. "Mr. Wellington Cawthorne in?" he asked when he had got it. "Not in? Thank you."

He hung up and turned from the instrument. "Thus far, so good. Get your hat on, Casp. We're going over to the Plaza to watch Moonface and Cawthorne accuse each other of all sorts of trickery."

"What the——" began Moonface, but a look from MacTavish silenced him effectively and quickly.

Then the three men started out toward Clark Street and North Avenue. As they moved along MacTavish laid down a few words and directions to the crook, who was pacing between him and Casperson, and Moonface not only meekly acquiesced, but produced a newly-made key, which he declared Cawthorne had given him so that he might wait in the latter's room at any hour of the day or night. Reaching the fashionable hostelry on the edge of Lincoln Park, they all went in, and MacTavish, his hand still on Moonface's arm, went up to the switchboard girl. "Will you ring Mr. Cawthorne's room, please?" he said to her.

She depressed a key, and repeated the motion several times. Finally she turned from the board with its flashing lights. "Not in yet."

MacTavish looked around the floor. "Where is your house detective?" he asked.

She pointed across the lobby. "That's him, standing near the pillar in front of the cigar counter."

MacTavish and the house detective fell to talking in a low voice some distance away from the nervous Moonface and the somewhat bewildered Casperson. After a while the detective took from his pocket a large copper key and led the way to the elevator, Casperson and the man at his side trailing along.

Upstairs the hotel officer unlocked the door of a splendidly furnished room on the fifth floor. The other three men stepped in. A second later the door was closed and locked behind them. MacTavish, with one look toward the near-by clothes closet, motioned to Moonface.

"Now, remember, my friend, no monkey business here. Remember what you're to do. You're supposed to have a key, which accounts for your waiting in here. And if any wink or significant sign takes place in here the house detective is waiting down the hall. Incidentally he'll follow you from here after you take Gryce out on some pretext, and rearrest you as soon as you've parted from him. You'll be locked up for a day or so—probably no more. That's all." He threw open the door of the closet. "Step in, Casp, and we'll wait for our friend, Mr. Wellington Cawthorne."

Inside the partly closed closet the outer room was visible through the long crack running up and down the side of the door which held the hinges. For a long, long time they waited. Casperson was beginning to get fidgety. At last the sound of footsteps came from the hall. Moonface half turned in his damask rocking-chair. The door opened.

Casperson, peering through the crack over Mac-Tavish's shoulder, was barely able to make out a huge, pink-skinned man with light hair and blue eyes, standing at the door. As he caught sight of Moonface he closed the door quickly and entered. Then Casperson had to change his position slightly in order to see what went on.

The newcomer was the first to speak: "Well, boy, I see you used the duplicate key I gave you. Let me compliment you on pulling the thing off to a T. But it was a tremendously lucky thing for us that this fellow named Casperson left the place; when he did. They're all on his heels; he's supposed to be the thief. It was good work, all the same. Shame to have to plunder the little lady, though. Her papa rather liked me, but she's too much of a little idealist to cotton to me. I rather think she sees through me. She——"

"Wait!" grumbled Moonface, interrupting the other babbling along. "Wait, Gryce, if you please. I came here to tell you that I never got that necklace. Somebody else got it—maybe this Casperson—maybe not. I have an idea, though, who did get it." He paused. "But I never got it."

"Never got it!" half screamed Cawthorne, rising from the chair he was just poised to drop into. "Why —why—you're crazy, man. Of course—say—what are you talking about? Kidding me, are you?"

"Nix, not kidding you at all," replied Moonface wearily. "I tell you somebody who danced with her ahead of me landed the necklace. It was gone when I came for my dance." He pointed to Cawthorne and his face became a thundercloud. "Old moth, with the yellow bag on your bean, did you think for a minute that I didn't know your paunch? You dirty dog, do you think I'm not next to your game?" Agitatedly, he rose from his chair and confronted the other, his squat face close to the boiled-beet countenance of the pseudo-clubman, who quailed visibly. "You copped that string yourself, Gryce, and your whole rotten scheme was to cast suspicion on me in some way, and make it show up that there was a police character in that room somewhere. They'd have pinched me, wiped off the grease paint from my phiz, and found I was Moonface Eddy Chang. And they'd have beat hell out of me down at the central office trying to make me show where in that hall I stashed it. You're a fine specimen of a side-kick—I mean snake."

CHAPTER XVII

CAWTHORNE, confronted by this amazing accusation, stood staring, his cold blue eyes popping from his head. At length his words came forth in a mighty explosion.

"You lie, you dog! You got that string of stones, and now you're trying to play me for the whole thing. But I'll fix you, you——"

"You'll do nothing," cut in Moonface coldly. "You'll do nothing at all, Gryce. I got out of that place only because suspicion happened to fall on a guest that had to leave early, for some reason. If the thing had gone the way you expected I'd have been in stir by to-day, and you'd have been out of town laughing at the man you double-crossed." Menacingly he advanced a step. "Gryce, either pry loose of five thousand bucks or I call in the police and spring the info that you're Cecil Gryce who worked with me down in Buenos Aires on that consular-paper theft. I'll do it, if I never do another thing in my life."

"You crazy fool!" snarled the other. "Are you looking for a sentence to the pen? Want to go back to that hell hole with its cockroach-infested dungeons?" He paused for breath. "Why—you can't prove I'm Gryce. I can call in the house detective and have you pinched for a sneak thief. Right now there's a duplicate pass-key on you—the one I gave you. They'd send you over the road. You can't make me out Gryce, you idiot."

"Now, listen," said Moonface wearily: "I'm no fool at all. If they once get it into their heads that you are Cecil Gryce, the guy that turned the Buenos Aires trick, and that you are in this hotel under a new name, they're going to hang tight till they jug you. That's certain. You can't prove up the identity of Wellington Cawthorne further back than a few months. You poor shrimp, where can you furnish a past life? Come out of it." He snapped his fingers. "You double-crossed me out of those sparklers—and we'll let that go. We'll forget it. Now cough up a few thousand, and I'll get out of here. Otherwise I call the house dick." He stepped over to the telephone and took down the receiver.

"Wait!" The voice of Cawthorne had in it that peculiar tone which a voice holds when its owner has been bluffed. "Wait—Moonface! Don't—don't ring!"

Casperson, inside the closet, felt MacTavish's grip on his arm. The quarrelling crooks now stood out of line with the crack in the door, so that neither man inside the closet could see them; but they could hear all that was said.

"Moonface," said Cawthorne, "I swear that I never got that necklace. Now, look me in the eyes. Moonface, didn't you get it?"

"I tell you no, Gryce. I didn't get it. Why, I'd

have been out of Chi, and on my way to New Orleans, if I had. Do you think I fell for your bunk story that morning? And now you cough up all the coin in your pocket. And cough quick."

A silence. Then came Cawthorne's voice, clear and cool, preceded by a hard half-laugh. "Moonface, I guess that proves it all right. You'd have double-crossed me if you had got that trinket. I ought to have known as much. You'd never have wasted time calling around here if you'd landed that string of sparklers." After a moment of silence, he went on: "Now, see here, Moonface, you and I had better be friends. No need for us to quarrel. I swear I didn't get it. Can't you tell by a man's voice if he's lying or not?—you're a fellow that's met men all his life."

Now Casperson could see him with his hands in the pockets of his smart brown suit as he paced the floor, across the line of vision, and back again.

"Moonface," Cawthorne went on eagerly, "here's the dope on the thing: my story to you was no lie. I tell you there *is* a man in this city who has—*had* is better—something that I can turn over for a hundred thousand dollars to the right men—and I know where those men are to be found. I know them, I tell you. All I needed was the—the thing. That man was Professor Aloysius Silvester, an erratic biologist who had a laboratory on Ernst Court—a specialist on moths." He paused a second or two. "Silvester was shot dead last night. A Jap that worked for him did it. And I'll bet that I'm the only man in Chicago who knows why the Jap croaked him. But the main thing I want to impress upon your mind is that the Jap didn't get what he killed him for; they haven't found anything in the Jap's suit-case but clothes."

"Where'd you meet this Silvester?" Moonface asked "And what's he got that you want?"

"Aloysius Silvester was no more his name," replied Cawthorne, "than Wellington Cawthorne is mine. Why, Moonface, that man and I grew up in a little town together—a place far, far from this—a little town with grass-paved streets, with green hedges and a quaint little church that used to chime over the hills at sundown; that—" His voice broke. "Oh, Moonface," he murmured, "why won't time turn back? How I wish to God I could go back even for a day and be a barefoot happy boy in that little town of the green hedges—far away from this roaring, fetid city. Why can't——"

"Lay off the sob stuff," said Moonface roughly, yet the other's words had interested him. "How did he come to take that moniker of Silvester? And how'd you get next to him here in Chi? And what's it all about, anyway?"

"Reason enough that he changed his name," declared Cawthorne, after a pause in which his voice grew calmer. "Silvester and his brother—I won't bother you with his real name—fell heir to a big country estate when their father died. I was just a kid then—a barefoot kid—in the little green-hedged town. And Silvester produced a will wherein his father had cut off the brother without a cent—and left him, Silvester, the whole thing. The estate was worth, probably, a hundred thousand dollars. The funny part was that the brother who was cut off didn't fight the thing at all, for he'd been estranged from the old man for several years, and the whole town had always predicted that he'd get cut off if the old man ever died suddenly. The court pronounced the will O.K., and Silvester got it all. He sold the whole estate inside of two weeks and left that part of the country. Then came a startling development.

"What?" Moonface was interested, beyond doubt.

"Some young clerk in the recording offices, when examining the will, found a commercial watermark in the paper. He took it into his head to look up the paper-mill record. And he found it to be the brand of a paper mill that hadn't started operation until just after the date on the paper. They called in handwriting experts, who found the will to be a forgery, and the man—we'll still call him Silvester—had decamped. The brother who would have been worth fifty thousand dollars was left holding the bag.

"That was all many years ago," went on Cawthorne. "I've been around the old globe a good bit since those barefoot days—since the one big sensation in my little home town. A few months ago, in Chicago, I was down in the Fine Arts Building going up to see a doctor, and I came across a card in the lobby bearing the notice of a lecture to be given in the Fine Arts Hall by Professor Aloysius Silvester, the famous specialist on moths. I studied the half-tone portrait of the old boy, but his grey hair and beard didn't indicate anything to me. But the mention of moths took me back to the little home town—to the man who swindled his brother—to the man who even as a boy was crazy on moths; who used to collect them, prepare them, trade them with the rest of us, buy them from the rest of us—who used to scour the fields all night with a home-made net to get new specimens. Something told me to go to this Silvester lecture. During the lecture it got very warm, and he took off a black silk glove that he had on his hand, and there was a tumorous growth on the flesh. Do you get it, Moonface?"

"I get it all right," said Moonface. "That tumorous growth had been there when he was a boy. So you had somebody to blackmail then? You went to him and told him you'd show him up for the forgery of thirty years ago—when you were both natives of the same home town. What then?"

Cawthorne grinned. "He finally admitted the accusation," said he. "How could he deny it? The growth on the hand and certain slight resemblances in his features were present. He'd changed his name, of course, as I told you. After he got the estate with the phony will, and sold it in a hurry, he roved round the world collecting moth specimens and loaning them to museums all over. Here in Chicago his rovings had stopped. He had married. Wife long dead, but had a daughter. Both living on St. Clair Street, where I used to call on the old boy. The days of the past, you see, were quite forgotten. So much for that. It ends the story, or at least as much as I see fit to give you right now.

"Now, listen to me: Silvester had something that he got especially for me, after I brought a little pressure to bear on him. He wanted ten thousand for it, and I was supposed to be trying to raise the balance of the money. Last night he was shot dead. The Jap did it. And, as I told you, I know why—exactly why. Some doubt in the police mind, but none in mine as to why the Jap pulled the stunt. But I'm certain the old boy had the thing hidden where the Jap couldn't touch it, or anyone else.

"Now, Moonface, keep your shirt on. Go easy! It's in the Ernst Court laboratory somewhere. As soon as this murder blows over, you and I will get into that place some night and with electric pocket lights search every square inch for it. When the time gets ripe I'll tell you exactly what we're looking for. And when we find it you'll get half of it—fifty thousand, Moonface—for I can turn it over in a minute for double that sum."

A silence ensued, broken at length by Moonface. "All right," he said. "I'll take your word for it for the present." The sound of him rising from the chair where he had dropped during the interview was audible to the watchers. "Well, suppose we slip downstairs and get a cigar and a drink of genuine Johnny Walker from an acquaintance of mine that's running a blind pig up the street. Might as well be friends. Then I'll leave you for to-day."

"I'm with you." The big man crossed the line of vision in the crack of the door and reappeared a second later with his hat in his hand. Then came the sound of the door closing, then the clang of the elevator going down. MacTavish, sweating and red-faced, flung open the closet door and Casperson followed him out into the cool air of the room. The plain-clothes man mopped his forehead.

"Let's get out of here in a hurry," he said. "O'Connor, the house detective, will pinch Moonface as soon as Cawthorne leaves him and gets out of sight." He opened the door, and locking it again with the pass-key which Moonface had meekly turned over to him a short time before, led the way down the stairs and through the main corridor to the street. Out on the sidewalk he smiled with satisfaction and said:

"Some mighty interesting information, eh, Casp, on the mystery of Ernst Court? Now——"

"Wait," interrupted Casperson, staring at a telegraph office where the clicking of many busy instruments sounded. "MacTavish, will you wait on the corner till I go into that office and send two messages —one to the Johnsonian Institute of Washington, D.C.; the other to Professor Hans Schwenmauer, of the University of California?"

MacTavish stared at him. "I don't get you, Casp; I don't get you at all. But I'll wait for you—if that's all you want. Is it connected with Silvester?"

"It is," said Casperson, "and, if certain answers come back, you'll have something interesting." With this cryptic remark, followed by a wink, Casperson entered the telegraph office.

CHAPTER XVIII

C ASPERSON wrote out two messages; the first was addressed to Professor Hans Schwenmauer, of the University of California, and read:

"Kindly telegraph undersigned at 842 North Dearborn Avenue, Chicago, collect, the following information: Does Vergitilla Phyleas belong to swallow-tail moths or the round-tail group? Very urgent. Please give answer to messenger.

"WILK CASPERSON."

The second telegram, addressed to the Johnsonian Institute, of Washington, D. C., was worded thus:

"Kindly telegraph undersigned at 842 North Dearborn Avenue, Chicago, collect, the following information: What report was issued by Professor Aloysius Silvester, of Chicago, with regard to his quest for the Vergitilla Phyleas in the tropics between Costa Rica and Colombia? Very urgent. Please hand answer to messenger.

"WILK CASPERSON."

He rejoined the bewildered-looking MacTavish out on the sidewalk. Together they went for a bite to eat, then moved on to Casperson's lodgings, where they dropped into chairs.

"Well, Casp, what do you think of those two crooks?" asked MacTavish. "It seems plain that Moonface didn't get what he was after; but did Cawthorne? Is he lying, or hasn't he got it? How do you make him out?"

Casperson, rocking back and forth, replied: "Mac, first take a look at this little paper I've drawn up." He handed the other the paper he had made out, showing each of those who might have stolen the necklace with possible motives or lack of motives. "Then I'll give you some more surprising dope."

MacTavish scrutinized the paper, then laid it on the arm of the chair with a frown of puzzlement on his forehead. Whereupon Casperson handed him the paper on which he had copied the matter concerning the *Vergitilla Phyleas*. Much of the writing had faded away; parts of certain words were gone completely. MacTavish stared at it dumbly. "What the——"

"That paper," said Casperson wearily, "was written by me with a fountain-pen that I accidentally carried away this morning from Malcolm Eldredge's room. I had written down some facts that I looked up at the library on the *Vergitilla*. Now——"

"The devil you say!" snapped MacTavish. "Secret writing ink. And——" He looked up, and emitted a whistle. "So it was Malcolm Eldredge that had a messenger boy bring that decoy card to you last night —and got you out of the place? He looked over again the analysis of the situation which Casperson had made. "And this reference to stolen money. What——"

Casperson nodded. "Yes, you may as well know about that now. Malcolm Eldredge has been in serious trouble. Lost nearly two thousand dollars—short in his accounts at his father's offices. Managed to borrow the amount from friends and professional money-lenders, and among them was myself. I lent him two hundred to wipe out the deficit entirely." He paused. "And this morning, Mac, he gave me back a check for two hundred, telling me his brokers had 'phoned him that some British rubber shares he had bought on margin had soared and he had cleaned up; but he told me not to put the check in till late to-day—to hold it unt——"

"Until he could turn over his sister's necklace at some crooked diamond dealer's where he had the thing all pre-arranged." MacTavish smiled grimly. "So the thief wasn't an outside man, after all." He glanced down at the sheet again. "And the entry here, 'Niccolo di Paoli, with no motive,' then, is all wrong; since Niccolo di Paoli was really Moonface smeared with grease paint and talking like an Italian."

Casperson nodded. "Yes, that's correct. I think we've got our man. The question, though, is what are we going to do? I want to marry that little girl; but I can't marry her so long as I'm under suspicion. But does it mean that I've got to incriminate her brother in order to clear myself? Besides, how is this theft to be fastened on Malcolm?"

"We can sweat a confession out of him in the chief's office," asserted MacTavish grimly. "Some third-degree stuff that'll knock the truth out of him and even bring out where he sold the necklace."

Casperson shuddered. "That's horrible, Mac. I've been present at some of your police third degrees. I'd hate to think that anybody I knew was locked up in a room with you fellows—and supposed to have some vital information." He reflected a moment, then said: "You see, I somehow appreciate how pressed to the wall Malcolm Eldredge was—how desperate. Then, too, Mac, I have to remember that, no matter what trouble he actually caused for me, he really tried to throw suspicion on Cawthorne—or Gryce, or whatever we call him—my rival for the hand of the only girl in the world. That fellow's a crook and I can't help but feel that it would have been the working out of poetic justice if he had received Malcolm's decoy note, left the place in response to schedule, and had all this suspicion landed on him."

"Well, could you bring yourself to believe," asked MacTavish after a pause, "that Malcolm and Cawthorne were in league for some reason? That Malcolm agreed to steal it—Cawthorne agreed to dispose of the thing to a fence, and that they both together agreed to get the laugh on Cawthorne's friend Moonface by inveigling him in there as di Paoli to steal it, and then tipping his identity up before the few Pinkertons present? According to your dance slip you've written out here, they both signed up early so that di Paoli—or Moonface—got his dance *after* they had their chance."

Casperson thought for a moment. "All sorts of strange things are possible in this tangle, Mac. There's no telling. Cawthorne might well have been in collusion with Malcolm, as you suggest. But if any such plans were in existence, the presence of a notorious po-

lice character at the ball would be just what they'd
need in case of alarm—someone to clear all the suspicion."

After a while MacTavish asked curiously: "And
those telegrams, Casp? What are you driving at?
Who are these two parties you wired to on the matter
of old man Silvester's death? Or was it the Eldredge
necklace?"

"No," replied the other. "They both concern the
Silvester murder. The first was to one of the biggest
specialists in the world on moths—beyond doubt even
a bigger man than Silvester was. The second was to the
Johnsonian Institute, the Federal scientific society under the auspices of which Silvester went down to hunt
the *Vergitilla Phyleas* a few months ago."

"The thing which Cawthorne says he can turn over
for a hundred thousand dollars, if he can get his hands
on it?"

Casperson shook his head. "No. I am convinced
that if Cawthorne actually knew where to find whatever it is he wants, he would use burglary or force to
get it. Indeed, he knows no more what he wants than
the man in the moon. He's driving in the dark." He
paused. "All this sounds mysterious, but I can't very
well discuss the matter further until at least I hear
from one of my——" He stopped. From the window
he caught sight of a messenger boy, who had just arrived at the curb and was dismounting from a bicycle.
"An answer may be coming now," he remarked.

Presently there was a knock at the door. In the
messenger's hand was not one, but two yellow envelopes. "Two wires, mister, fer Mr. Wilk Casperson.

Th' second one come jis' as I was gointer ride off."

Casperson signed for the two envelopes and slipped the boy a coin. Then, standing up, he tore open the first. It read:

"Professor Silvester reported that he had failed both to discover or to capture the Vergitilla Phyleas.
                    "JOHNSONIAN INSTITUTE."

He handed the yellow slip to MacTavish, and while the other read it he turned his attention to the second telegram. Its contents ran:

"Vergitilla Phyleas belongs to the round-tail group of moths. Absolutely.
            "PROFESSOR HANS SCHWENMAUER."

MacTavish looked up from the second telegram. "What does it mean?" he asked. "We know that Silvester captured the *Vergitilla Phyleas*—you and me both saw it, label, box, and all—yet he reported to the Johnsonian Institute, who employed him, that he failed in the hunt to see one or to capture one. Why did he conceal it?"

"Mac," said Casperson, ignoring the question, "can you shoot up to Ernst Court and get that specimen of the *Vergitilla Phyleas*, and then come straight to the Eldredge residence, where I'll be waiting? I think I'll be able to throw light on why the professor *might* have been murdered by the Jap, but why, at the same time, the Jap was not the one who did it or who knows anything about it!"

CHAPTER XIX

A T Casperson's statement the plain-clothes man stared at him. "Why the Jap might have—but didn't!" he exclaimed. "Then you mean that?"

Casperson moved to the bed and grasped his hat. His face was flushed. "That and nothing else." He glanced at his watch. "Will you go and get that and come—and ask no questions for the present, old scout? You shall have the credit of the whole thing if we untangle this snarl."

With a frown of perplexity, the detective got up. "I'll play the cards as you ask me, my boy; but I don't fathom what you're driving at. You want me to get the *Vergitilla* and then come straight to the Eldredge home? That's it?"

Casperson nodded. "Exactly. And right away." He fumbled in his pockets and withdrew a nickel. "And pardon me a second, Mac, till I 'phone a certain party."

Dropping his nickel in the slot of the instrument and consulting his notebook, he asked for Superior 4449. A woman's voice responded, whereupon he asked for Mr. Arthur Sennet. A moment later he was talking with the latter.

"Arthur, any news on the judges' decision?"

"None," was the dolorous answer. "I'm in touch with the old address where I lived."

"I see. Well, it occurred to me this afternoon that, if the decision had been rendered late last night, the congratulatory telegram—if there's to be any—might not be sent out to the winner—whoever the lucky chap may be—until some time to-day. In that case, if we still feel confident, and I do, something might come to-night. I'm leaving now for Number 1400 Lake Shore Drive, the Eldredge home, where I'm likely to be for several hours. If anything comes, you might send the news to me there, by boy, 'phone, telegraph, or wireless! Will you do that?"

"Gladly, Wilk. I'll come myself, jump through the front window, and let out a whoop like a wild Indian. Number 1400 Lake Shore Drive—the Eldredge's. O. K."

Casperson and MacTavish parted at Dearborn Avenue and Walton Place. Evening was dropping down over the city, and the low frosted globe lights along Dearborn Avenue were flaring into being when Casperson reached the Eldredge mansion and hurried up the steps. To Brayley, who answered the door, he said that he wished to see Rufus Eldredge himself.

"He was expecting you, Mr. Casperson," said the butler. "Come right in."

The butler led the way down the hall to the library, where he switched on a splendid table lamp, which cast a subdued glow over the rich leather furniture and the busts of bronze and marble. Leaving him alone, the servant went on to the dining-room. Presently Eldredge, at his elbow Malcolm and Shirley, her eyes wide open in surprise, appeared in the doorway.

The elder man paused a moment. Then a grim, sardonic smile spread over his lips. "Glad you reconsidered things, Casperson," he said. "Thought you'd realize, after you thought it over, that the whole thing was a hare-brained stunt."

Casperson looked at him coldly. "Mr. Eldredge," he said, "I have not come to make the confession you suppose. May I have the attention of all of you for a few minutes, or am I interrupting dinner? If so, I'll——"

"No," said Malcolm curiously, "we had just finished dessert and were talking over the death of Professor Silvester on the North Side last night. We were——"

The door-bell rang. A moment later Brayley appeared in the doorway of the library, at his shoulder MacTavish, bearing in his hand a stout paper parcel which showed plainly the square outlines of the glass box which housed the *Vergitilla Phyleas.*

"Oh, you are here, Mac," was Casperson's greeting to the detective. "Mr. Eldredge, Malcolm, and Shirley, let me present Mr. MacTavish, of the Chicago police department."

"How do you do, Mr. MacTavish? Hope you've come to throw some light on the matter of my daughter's necklace."

"No," said Casperson. "Mr. MacTavish hasn't come for that reason." He waited until all had seated themselves, including MacTavish. A pause of profound curiosity ensued before he spoke. "Last night," he began slowly, "I was called away from this place by a message written in the most erratic handwriting

I have ever seen, with instructions to go to a certain number on Ernst Court at once. Whether that handwriting was disguised, and whether the ink was of a vanishing kind, in order to cover up the matter afterward, is something that we must investigate here tonight before I leave. Enough to say that, when I got to Ernst Court, I found a dead man—Professor Silvester—who had been murdered in his studio by a shot in the back. And that calling away of me by that message has thrown upon me the suspicion of being a thief—a suspicion which thus far I haven't been able to remove."

He paused a moment, then looked about him at the circle of faces. Shirley was wide-eyed, curious, bewildered; Malcolm seemed uneasy—betrayed a mental disturbance; Rufus Eldredge leaned forward in his chair, his keen eyes half closed, yet scrutinizing the speaker from under his bushy eyebrows. MacTavish's face bore the same mystified frown it had carried when Casperson had sprung the initial bombshell in his room.

Casperson resumed his story. He retold in detail what he had just related, this time describing the decoy card to the last word, his peculiar costume, the fact that he, with initials W. C., held an important relationship with one whose initials were A. S. From there he went on to the murder, his later investigations of the day, his calling upon Diana Silvester, the visit of Moonface to his room, and his and MacTavish's trip over to the Plaza Hotel. He omitted not a detail of his movements since the preceding night, and, when he paused for the second time, the mutterings of Rufus

Eldredge under his breath were audible to everyone in the room.

"Great Heaven!" he speculated, "and I thought that Cawthorne was a gentleman, an upright man!" He shook his head wearily as Casperson outlined, word for word, the quarrel and later the conversation between the two crooks in Room 555 of the Plaza.

After waiting for all these facts to sink into the consciousness of his hearers, Casperson went on: "Now, there is no doubt from that conversation that Cawthorne was to receive something from Silvester—something he had arranged to have and which was to cost him around ten thousand dollars. And there is no doubt, either, that Cawthorne is what we call an international rogue; his theft of the consular paper in Buenos Aires shows the kind of work he does—the international kind. Cawthorne is no petty lifter of diamonds and trinkets such as the more dexterous Moonface is. Of all this we can be assured. But I am not yet certain in my mind as to whether or not Cawthorne stole that necklace and whether his quarrel with Moonface was a piece of rare acting.

"But two things have been brought out thus far in my investigations, particularly at Miss Diana Silvester's," Casperson continued. "First, that the professor was visited by a man of Cawthorne's description many times in his St. Clair Street home. In fact, we may say definitely that a visit was made yesterday morning, Miss Diana herself having stated as much. A mere description is not entire proof, so I am going to add this fact: Cawthorne came to that ball costumed as a yellow moth. He accidentally or carelessly

used the back of a round-cornered blue ticket to jot
down his next address for Silvester, the two evidently
feeling it necessary to keep in touch with each other
all the time for some reason. The words on the ticket
—MacTavish has seen them—run: 'My address after
Monday, Ontario Hotel.' The reverse side of the card
shows a receipt for a deposit on a yellow moth suit,
and I have located both the house and the clerk who
wrote it out. Professor Silvester, however, had placed
it in his private lock drawer with his *Vergitilla Phyleas*, his giant tropical moth; MacTavish and I found
it there. So is it all clear, the perfect chain? Remember, all this was my first indication that there was,
or might have been, another yellow moth at your ball
last night."

Casperson paused and gazed about him.

"The second thing brought out by my conversation
with Diana Silvester," Casperson went on, "was that
the professor had seen someone watching his St. Clair
Street house that night from behind a tree-trunk across
the way, and he had returned much agitated. He went
up to Diana's second-floor room and watched in the
darkness. After a while he snapped on the lights, and
in all probability the fellow fled. Anyway, after Silvester left his house for the second time he went to
Ernst Court, with his own plans now crystallized. If
that white card was not a decoy note in disguised handwriting, then it might be possible that Professor Silvester wrote a very erratic hand. He rang for a messenger
boy and sent that white card to Cawthorne at the ball
—Cawthorne, who had undoubtedly referred to this
masquerade ball, and whose costume the professor

either recalled from the conversation or else happened
to know from the front side of the blue card on which
Cawthorne had written, 'My address after Monday,
Ontario Hotel.' But the question would naturally remain: Why did he use invisible ink on the white card?"

No one proffered an answer, and Casperson resumed:
"Well, now that you have all the facts that I have,
what deductions can we make? There were narrow tissue-paper strips used in Silvester's laboratory for holding down the delicate coloured wings of drying-moth
specimens. And you've heard that the professor, paralyzed by his wound, rubber-stamped the message,
'Find Ushi—he knows.' And you know that Ushi
Yatsura, the Jap, was arrested at the depot boarding
a train for the West. He claims that he left Ernst
Court on account of a financial disagreement, and pre-
tends that he knows nothing of Silvester's death.
Whether we accept it or not, it need make no difference
just now as to why Silvester was killed.

"The main thing, of course, is to ascertain what
there was between Cawthorne and Professor Silvester
that Cawthorne hasn't even yet divulged to his pal,
Moonface. We know that Cawthorne had something
on the professor; that he knew Silvester came from
some 'little town with grass-paved streets and green
hedges and a little stone church that chimed over the
hills at sundown'; that under his right name he had
forged a will which had successfully swindled a brother
of his out of everything; that he had sold out the estate
and then disappeared to pursue his moth hobby under
another name and in every corner of the world. That
much gives us the source of any pressure which Caw-

thorne might have exerted on Silvester. Diana Silvester says that of late her father had been tight in money
matters—inclined to cut out many expenditures. Was
his stolen fortune of years back vanishing, threatening
to put an end to his expensive career of collecting
moths?

"We know," went on Casperson, "that there has
been but one important addition to the professor's big
collection during the last few months—that of the
Vergitilla Phyleas, the giant tropical moth. Under the
auspices of the Johnsonian Institute, of which he was
a member, but his trip under which was probably
financed by himself, he spent two months down in the
region between Costa Rica and Colombia hunting
around trying to get the famous nocturnal specimen
which appears but once in every twenty-one years or so,
and which was due at the time he arrived there."

Casperson drew two telegrams from his pocket.
"And yet I have two peculiar telegrams here—one
from the Johnsonian Institute saying that Silvester
reported failure on his quest, the second from Professor Hans Schwenmauer, an international expert on
Lepidoptera at the University of California, saying
that the *Vergitilla Phyleas* belongs to the round-tail
group of moths. But, as MacTavish will show you
when he unwraps that paper, Professor Silvester carried back to the United States, in a glass box, a splendid specimen of the true *Vergitilla Phyleas*. You may
read the red-stamped card at the bottom, if you doubt
it. What can we make of it? Why did he report to
the Johnsonian Institute that failure had crowned his
quest? Simply because he had not captured the *Vergi-*

tilla Phyleas, after all, and dared not present the giant moth he did capture to the Johnsonian Institute or exhibit it to any man who was an expert on moths. The telegram from Professor Hans Schwenmauer proves it." He turned to MacTavish. "Mac, open the box, and let us see the fateful moth."

CHAPTER XX

MacTAVISH stepped to the library table with the flat, square package he had kept on his knee throughout the discourse. There he unwrapped it, and exposed the glass-encased box with its flat cork bottom, the gorgeous, giant moth with wings outspread, and the white card below it giving its name and other scientific data. All in the library crowded around it, marvelling at its colors and its enormous size.

Casperson resumed his talk: "Let me say that I was fortunate enough to-day to extract from much scientific stuff in the encyclopedia that there are two groups of moths—those with the round hind wings and those with wings of the swallow-tail variety which come out in a well-defined tongue or finger like a coat-tail. Professor Schwenmauer, of the University of California, says in his telegram emphatically that the Vergitilla belongs to the round-tail group—yet this thing, labelled *Vergitilla Phyleas*, has a prominent swallow-tail on each wing. All we can deduce, therefore, with this authoritative information, is that this is some more common variety of rare moth which resembles it. And the one which resembles the Vergitilla most, in size and markings, according to Bertram,

160

who has written a treatise on moths, is the *Oralia Pur-pura*."

No one made any reply to this significant statement. Then Casperson took up once more the thread of his strange explanation.

"So, as I say, we can only see that this is a spurious *Vergitilla*; that only by pretending to have captured what he came after could Silvester get out of this particular region in Central America with what he went after—or better, with the side line he went for. For Aloysius Silvester, hard up in his finances and absolutely conscienceless so far as things external to his erratic profession went, had a side line in addition to capturing the *Vergitilla*—a commission to perform for one Wellington Cawthorne—a commission which was to net him ten thousand dollars profit, and the results of which Cawthorne, the international rogue, claims to be able to turn over for a hundred thousand dollars.

"And one last word: If you are not familiar with Central American geography you have not yet guessed that the region where this moth appears every twenty-one years—the habitat designated as 'The territory running from Eastern Costa Rica to Western Colombia'—is nothing else but the republic of Panama."

Picking up a metal paper-weight on the table, he leaned across that richly carved piece of furniture and made a sharp, quick blow which broke the glass over the gorgeous specimen. Picking up the sharp fragments from the box and laying them on a magazine, no one saying a word, so tense was the interest, he reached down and gingerly felt the huge front wings of the moth. Then taking hold of them carefully, one in each hand, he moved them back and forth till suddenly something surprising happened. They loosened —they came off, each bearing at the base what appeared to be a strip of beads of hardened glue, with some of the hairs of the body still adhering to them. With a half smile of satisfaction Casperson turned them over in his fingers and laid them out on the table.

The under sides were white. From the texture alone it could be seen easily that the wings were nothing but paper cut to shape and painted in various rich colors on the upper side. And all over the two white surfaces were fine black lines, equally fine red loops, diagrams, crosses of various shapes and proportions, conventional signs of different sorts, with undulating lines running back and forth. Here and there actual distances between points were given by tiny broken arrows; again, a minute compass scale showed the precise directional relation between two symbols. But what was most startling of all, not to mention enlightening, the very key to the strange tangle, was the tiny table meticulously lettered at the bottom of one of the wings, in letters no larger than diamond-point, which read:

⊕....heavy artillery guns.
☐....dry flat unwooded areas suitable for aeroplane landing-fields.
‡‡...past slides in canal, now repaired.
∴.....slides imminent. Can be precipitated.
♄....aeroplane guns.
O....gun emplacements, no guns.

♮....military posts.

‡‡‡‡....rail lines.

▥'....swamps.

↓....heavy woods and underbrush impassable to infantry.

|||....underbrush, low woods, can be cut away.

+....quicksand.

⇆....fortified.

★....radio stations.

A gasp ran over the group around the table. Casperson glanced up, his gaze travelling curiously from one face to the other. "And there you have it," he said calmly. "An up-to-the-minute detailed chart showing the vital points of strength and weakness of that whole strategic region; a chart by which—let us say, merely for a military example—Japan, for instance, planning an attack on Australia, could first demolish the Canal in a few hours, cutting off the main section of Great Britain's fleet entirely; or, as a further example, a chart by which this same Yellow Power could cut the United States' military capabilities squarely in half before attacking her; a chart for which Cawthorne in touch with international agents of many powers, not to mention Nippon herself, could get a neat fortune; yet a chart which only the old harmless professor, wandering up and down the region on both sides of the Panama Canal under the auspices of a nationally respected scientific institution, with his steel spectacles and his butterfly-net, his kit, and his camping outfit, could prepare and compile at his leisure almost under the very eyes of the soldiers and military guards. He——"

"Good God!" broke in Malcolm, whitening, "I—I—and I was to marry Diana Silvester—his daughter. I —I never——"

MacTavish turned on him sharply. "Then what about the vanishing ink? Quick! We're looking for information now. How about that secret ink in your fountain-pen?"

Malcolm Eldredge stared at the plain clothes man, dull-eyed. Then he said bitterly: "Yes, the secret ink. Diana and I both used it to write to each other; our letters haven't been getting the privacy they should have, in either one's home. She and I both had a supply. Hers was kept in the desk in her upstairs room. Mine I kept in a special fountain-pen. It fades out soon after it dries, but reappears if the paper is heated and kept hot. As to the mysterious man that was hanging around St. Clair Street last night, it was I. I was waiting to see Diana as soon as the old professor left the house. He refused to let her have any company in her home."

Casperson laughed. "That explains everything, MacTavish. Silvester got panic-stricken and thought that Malcolm, here, hiding in the darkness across the street, was some secret agent of the United States Government watching him. After peering out in the gloom and seeing that the watcher had moved away, he snapped on the lights, took a blank card, and wrote a message to Cawthorne to come to the laboratory at once. And, in doing so, he accidentally used Diana Silvester's bottle of vanishing ink. As to why he did it, he was frightened, as I said, and decided to get rid of the dangerous Panama Canal map that very night if he could get any money at all from Cawthorne."

A profound quiet filled the room. One by one those around the table raised their eyes from the overturned paper-moth wings which had been so cleverly affixed to a real moth. It was MacTavish who broke the silence:

"So that's why Ushi murdered the professor? Ushi was nothing else but a Japanese spy who saw a chance to get that chart of our latest preparations for the defense of the canal. Or else he learned in some way that Silvester had brought back from Panama more than a mere specimen of moth, and took a desperate chance of getting it back to his own country and reaping a huge money prize from the military authorities there?"

Casperson shook his head. "It might seem so, Mac. But you must recall that never before have Japan and Uncle Sam been linked in closer friendship. Your opinion is the one that Cawthorne, knowing only that Silvester had brought back such a thing from Panama but never dreaming how or where it was hidden, jumped at: namely, that Ushi Yatsura tried to get it. Cawthorne is an international rogue and could probably name the great value of that chart to the nation that would have most use for it. But, Mac, tell me why Ushi should necessarily have known anything about Silvester's secret mental workings, after all?" He looked about the room for a moment. "And this supposition about Ushi leads me to the big surprise of all —the queerest development in the whole Silvester murder case. And here it is:

"For several months I have been engaged with a man named Arthur Sennet—the one whose initials served to coincide with those of Aloysius Silvester—on a unique advertising device for which the prize offered was ten thousand dollars. That advertising device is connected with a huge rubber company in Akron, Ohio—a company which makes a hundred or more products, ranging from finger cots at five cents to automobile tires at a hundred dollars.

"Arthur Sennet and I studied every one of those products intensively when we were about to launch our device, for we had to know them from A to Z. For that reason the words, 'Find Ushi—he knows,' found printed on the strip of tissue paper at the foot of the dead man, have rung strangely familiar in my ears. 'Find Ushi—he knows.' I have racked my brain trying to fathom why those letters, left printed by the professor with his box of rubber type used for making specimen cards—the momentous clue to the murderer —should awaken any thought in my subconscious mind.

"For a long time I was deceived, believing simply that it was only a pseudo-remembrance, arising merely because the professor had used rubber type to print the dying message. But this afternoon, just before Moon-face called at my room by way of the roof-top, I flung myself back on my bed and thought and thought, following up every train that suggested itself from each of the four words in the message. And through that, and the fact that the external world was shut out from my mind, the solution came to me—came to me out of the clear sky. To me it was dazing, dumbfounding. And here it is, for what it is worth:

"The corporation for which Sennet and I worked out our commercial mystery novel was founded by one man, a pioneer in the industry, and over half of its stock is still owned by that man. Every product they turn out, no matter how small a thing it may be, bears a brand containing this man's name. Is it egotism? Or is it the spirit of advertising across the world? Whatever it is, I will say that every one of the thousands of rubber heels they turn out every day bears on the bottom, in raised letters, a slogan which, as in all other products, contains the founder's name.

"You will recall that Ushi's quarrel with Silvester centered about the Jap's spilling a bottle of ink on the Persian rug leading into the upstairs laboratory, and the professor's threat to make the Jap pay for it out of his wages. If a rubber heel bearing upraised letters were pressed to this ink-soaked portion, and later came in contact with the bottom of a narrow strip of tissue paper in such a way that only a portion of its slogan was printed, then——

"But why should I offer hypotheses? I claim outright that this is exactly what happened. Someone came up those stairs, shot Silvester from behind, stepped in to look at his victim's face as the victim sat dazed, and then turned and fled from the place now that the deed was done. I think I can prove that that rubber-heel slogan came in contact with the ink-moistened part of the rug, and then imprinted itself on one of the blank strips of tissue paper lying on the floor

with the overturned box of rubber type, where Mac-
Tavish picked it up later.

"The ink—writing ink, please, not stamping ink—
gave a reversed impression on the side where it struck,
but, soaking through the light tissue, gave a straight
left-to-right reading of that reversed impression. And
MacTavish and I, I'll admit, reasoned the whole operation backward."

Taking a piece of chalk from his pocket, Casperson
wrote the following letters on the mahogany table:

FIND
USHI
HE
KNOWS

He paused, chalk in hand, till all had seen the message. Then he added to what he had written, talking
as he worked. "Certain letters got lost in the shuffle,"
he explained; "due either to their having accumulated
some detritus from the intervening floor space, or more
likely due to their having failed to get inked on the
very irregular spot of ink in the Persian rug and its
transference more rapidly along certain fibers than
other fibers. I refer particularly to the letters L, E,
Y, and S, in the top line, the letters C, O, and N in the
second line, and letters E and L, in the third line. The
whole fifth and sixth lines were lost, if for no other reason then what impression we did get came at the bottom of the strip, and there was no room for lines five
and six." The diagram now read:

FINDLEYS
CUSHION
HEEL
KNOWS
NEITHER
JOLT NOR JAR

Casperson flung down the chalk. "Thus," he said wearily, "passes Ushi from the mystery of Ernst Court."

CHAPTER XXI

THE profound silence during Casperson's outlining of the connection—or better, non-connection—of Ushi with the message was finally broken by Mac-Tavish. "Then the problem," he said, with a grim smile, "is to find among the millions of people in Chicago the hundred thousands or so who wear Findley's rubber heels, and then in turn arrest the whole mass, and then——"

"No," Casperson interrupted, "the problem is not so hopeless as that. You remember—don't you?—Cawthorne's story told to Moonface that he grew up together with Silvester and the brother who had been swindled, in a little town with grass-paved streets, green hedges, and a little country church. You will not lose sight of the fact that since we know definitely the white card was sent by Silvester, that his writing was so eccentric, so erratic, so absolutely crazy, that——" He broke off and asked: "Mac, what do you know of forgers in general? Is the ability to forge a name coupled with the ability to write a graceful hand?"

MacTavish shook his head. "Not at all, for some peculiar reason. Some forgers I have seen couldn't write a legible hand of their own—yet they could easily duplicate any signature shown them."

179

Casperson turned to the others again. "I wish I could make you all see this card which Silvester wrote. The handwriting was—well—super-freakish, to say the least. The 't's bore each a double cross rather than the usual single one; the 'y' tail was tied into a strange, unnatural knot of some sort; the periods and dots over the 'i's were actually little triangles; and the 'e's!—they consisted of an abnormal distortion of the Greek 'epsilon.' And so, by what strange workings of fate, I wonder, was that card with the freak handwriting, that card which was never written by any but one man in the world, shoved under the nose of his penniless brother, who——"

A knock on the door interrupted him. Eldredge called, "Come in!" and Brayley appeared. "Telephone message for Mr. Casperson from a Mr. Sennet, who says to tell Mr. Casperson that a telegram has just arrived, and that they have won the big prize in some advertising contest."

"Thank you," said Casperson, while into the eyes of the girl came a light of joy. "And wait, Brayley, please. Brayley," he said, "you are an Englishman. I'll wager that you grew up in one of those hundreds of quaint little English country towns with grass-paved streets, green hedges, and with a tiny ancient church that chimes at sundown. And what did you think, Brayley—what did you do—when a blue-coated messenger boy last night showed you a white card which he wanted to get into the ballroom to deliver, when you recognized that writing as no other than that of the erratic brother who swindled you cruelly years ago? Can you prove by the servants in the basement that, while Mose, the negro footman, was taking your place at the inner door you were down with them overseeing the preparations for the refreshments? Or were you hurrying over in a raincoat to Ernst Court, where you rushed up the stairs of the number given on the card, looked in the big room, and saw sitting at the counter a man with a tumorous growth on his left hand? You knew then for sure, Brayley, that the threads of your life and his had crossed once more. But, Brayley, did you know that your rubber heel left its message behind?" He pointed down at the butler's shoes, where new rubber heels were plainly visible. "Come, Brayley, is it a Findley cushion heel that you're wearing? And can you bring up the servants to account for your whereabouts?"

The butler turned pale. He leaned against the door, weak, trembling. "Oh, God!" he sobbed, "it—it—it was me. Yes—yes. I saw blood. I went mad when I looked in that room and saw the left hand. I—I killed him—shot him when I knew for a certainty that it was him—Stanley—who swindled me out of my share of the pater's estate and made me a poor man for the rest of my life." He tottered forward into the library and collapsed into a chair, his staring face, fringed with its gray hair, low on his chest.

CHAPTER XXII

BUT WHO WAS THE THIEF?

A HALF-HOUR later Rufus Eldredge, Shirley, Malcolm, and Casperson sat silently in the library. Outside the click of a taxicab door heralded the departure of MacTavish and the shaking Brayley. As the vehicle drove away, Malcolm spoke:

"Poor old Brayley; I'm sorry for him. What will they do to him, Casperson?"

"It will be hard to get a jury to convict him, all the circumstances of the case considered," was Casperson's reply.

"But this doesn't solve the mystery of the theft of the necklace," Rufus Eldredge said bitterly. "Who was the traitor, the thief, after all?"

Shirley stood up resolutely, as if she had come to a momentous decision. She turned to the door. "Father, Malcolm, Wilk, will you come with me?" Wondering, they all arose and followed her from the room, upstairs along the richly-carpeted stairway, into the darkened ballroom, and across the polished floor into the conservatory. There she snapped on the shaded lights, and, walking straight to a secluded part of the great room, stopped in front of a big rubber plant that stood in a green wooden tub. Immediately she began prying up the earth at its base with her dainty fingers. Of

173

a sudden she dislodged something which, though soiled and damp, gleamed under the electrics of the ceiling.

She held it up and turned to face her father.

"Here is the necklace you are looking for," she said. "I would have had to tell the truth, for Wilk was suspected and always would have been. And I have been fighting the horrible facts all day." She turned impulsively to Casperson. "Oh, Wilk, you could not rid yourself of the idea that you must have money before you could make me your wife. And, oh, I didn't want that. But you were adamant. And in desperation I thought of the necklace—the jewels that my mother had said a dozen times should belong to me when she died. But there was—father; I believed that he would take everything away from me if I defied him—every jewel; he had threatened to do so many times—and I hid the thing here last night after my dance with Jack Hennly, never knowing that already you had been called away."

She placed the necklace in her father's hand. "I am the thief," she said; "the thief who stole what was hers by moral right and should have been by legal right. But take it back." She looked at Casperson again, and her eyes filled with tears. "Wilk," she sobbed, "take me away, please—no matter where."

On the face of Rufus Eldredge was a grim smile—one of pathos rather than victory; his voice trembled a bit as he spoke, holding forth the string of brilliants. "Wait, kidlets," he said kindly. "Wait—both of you. Don't be rash. Aren't you going to take your necklace with you to start housekeeping on? And—and—won't you even carry along your daddy's blessing?"

CHAPTER XXIII

A LONG silence followed McCaigh's story of the giant moth. Each man gazed curiously toward Shanahan, almost tensely. The first die had now been cast in a gentlemen's game for life, but the lone auditor was quite unconscious of the weight which was to attach itself to his decision. He spoke.

"Well, by gorry, Misther McCaigh, but that there story wur some story! It—it——" He wrinkled up his brows as though the exact depths of true literary criticism were beyond his intellect. "Yez had me figurin' har-rd in me mind, as ye spun it, as to who cud 'ave taken the necklace. 'Twas a game ye played with me—yez put ahl your car-rds on the table and yet ye had one up your sleeve all the time. Begorry, did I wonder, the more ye wint on, how does ye writer fellers make the hull t'ing wor-rk out jis' like a machine —every big wheel workin' in wid all th' other little wheels. 'Tis crazy I w'ud go did I ever thry and write a story."

McCaigh smiled at this naïve compliment to his constructive accomplishments, at least, if not his art.

"An' moreover," pursued the Irishman, "wheriver in th' divil did ye ever think up the thrick about the rubber-stamped message concernin' the yeller Jap boy,

175

Ushi? Begorry, where do you writer folks get them stunts?"

The Iron Man smiled grimly, perhaps because he saw he had made at least a profound impression on the one individual who was to judge the best story.

"My dear Shanahan, far be it from me to disillusionize too much one who is to be the judge to-night, but could you ever glimpse a professional writer's notebook you would see there the strangest assortment of still stranger observations that ever you rested your eyes upon. The pattern of the cracks in the glass of a window through which has passed a bullet—the putative locations of various objects of historical interest that are lost to mankind—the exact turn of a girl's lips when she purses them for a kiss—the unconscious wrinkle in a man's eyelids when he utters a barefaced lie—the distinctive creak of a wagon that carries but one new wheel—the exact smell of a vinegar factory in a small country town—Shanahan, you will find them all duly recorded there, a veritable pot-pourri, waiting their turn to be woven into the warp and woof of that tapestry which only writers spin." He smiled again.

Eastwood too smiled, although his was a wan smile —one quite unlike the hard devil-may-care smile of the Iron Man.

"That was an ingenious piece of plot construction, McCaigh," he said quietly; "as good as any of your longer things which I've seen in book form. I do protest vehemently against your American technique of making all your villains Englishmen, but outside of that minor point I liked your story immensely. I admire, too, your adroit psychology, for you baffled us

all, I think we agree, by providing motives and characters for the actual theft of the necklace, *participes
criminis*, so to speak—and yet we who are presumably
familiar with life and its motives could not guess." He
shook his head. "We who are familiar with life——"

Krenwicz laughed a harsh laugh. "Life? Why
should we three be discussing such abstruse subjects as
life? There is left to us but three times five hours—
no, two times." He looked at the mission clock, ticking
away on the stone wall. "One o'clock in the morning,
gentlemen. I move we proceed with the contest." He
looked inquiringly toward the Irishman. "And now,
Shanahan, who is next? Whom next do you wish to
listen to?"

"To you, Misther Krenwicz," said the death guard
quickly. "I have seen your play—'tis playin' t' packed
houses yet at th' New Amsterdam teayter—an' I liked
th' love——" —the big Irishman blushed rose-red—
"I liked th' love in it. I'll warrant it'll be a swate an'
strange love story that you'll be puttin' in *your* yarn."

"I thank you, Shanahan," returned Krenwicz dryly,
"for your appreciation of what poor abilities I may
possess in the depiction of tender sentiment—whether
this be compliment or criticism of my work." A long
pause followed. Finally he spoke, half reminiscently.

"It was, I think, Freud, the Viennese psychologist
and psycho-analyst, who first said that the stories
which writers spin are but rationalized and co-ordi-
nated dreams, and that dreams in turn are but the
symbolical realization of unfulfilled desires. Perhaps
some of the unfulfilled desires of my own mental cos-
mos are—well, for one, the biting disappointment—

the blind desire—to have done a play for Sara Ying of 'Frisco—that play which now, very likely, may never be done. And my mind too persists in straying back to those happiest days of my career, those exciting and colorful days—not these days spent in staring at a pen and a sheet of blank paper—but those days spent in journalistic work on papers from coast to coast. And it may well be that in this, my last story, my mind—through its inventive faculties—may indulge its fancies toward those unfulfilled desires."

He looked about him sadly.

"Like McCaigh over there, I think I too shall select Bagdad on the Lakes—Chicago—London of the West he calls it, for the site of my yarn, and will leave to Eastwood the real London! How well I remember Chicago—and particularly the vigorous quality of the journalism which prevails there, journalism unlike that of our effete and mechanized New York variety where a 'leg man' secures the facts of a news-story, 'phones it in, and a 're-write man' writes it up. For in Chicago, more than in all places, a journalist was expected by his own ingenuity, tenacity and pluck to force a latent news-story literally to unfold itself—to develop it, in other words. And when he had so done, he crystallized it himself, and not vicariously either, in words and phrases hammered out by his own brain and fingers. And that is journalism, as I see it, the most fascinating profession in the world." The speaker appeared lost a moment, like a man groping forth in space for the gossamer thread of a spider-web; and then suddenly he turned to McCaigh. "What, McCaigh, was the final outcome of the new Chinese monarchy that has supplanted the unstable republic over there? You, the Iron Man, seem to have been the only one of us who has had the fortitude to read the papers during these last dark days."

"The monarchy has been ratified by the last world power," said McCaigh coolly, "and peace, tranquillity and prosperity appear at last to have descended on China."

"I see," nodded Krenwicz slowly. "That, then, can supply me with still a further thread." He stared off into space. "Well, as long as I am chosen for the next honors—to play Scheherezade to Shanahan!—I'll smoke while I'm spinning. Toss me over those cigarettes." McCaigh tossed them over. Krenwicz lighted one and puffed upon it. "Suppose then I call my little extemporaneous mystery story 'The Strange Adventure of the Twelve Coins of Confucius'; and I will ask you all to step with me, as invisible comrades, into the city room of a large newspaper in Chicago, where you will meet young Mr. Jason Barton who, unknown to himself, occupies a somewhat unstable position on the editorial staff of the *Chicago Dispatch*, but whose ticklish position I hope, before I finish, to change either for better or worse. And that, too, through the politics of China herself!" Whereupon he began to relate, in a crisp, dramatic manner:

THE STRANGE ADVENTURE OF THE
TWELVE COINS OF CONFUCIUS

CHAPTER XXIV

IN WHICH MR. BARTON OF *The Dispatch* RECEIVES A
DIFFICULT ASSIGNMENT

"**B**ARTON, as soon as you've beautified your handsome self sufficiently, please step into my office!"
The crisp words, teeming with ill-concealed irony,
caused six reporters on the early editorial shift of the
Chicago Evening Dispatch to glance up from their
machines, their faces glaring with the light of sympathetic indignation.

Jason Barton, the seventh man, standing in front
of the cracked mirror before which he was smoothing
down a mop of rumpled brown hair that over-topped a
pair of steel-grey eyes, looked startled over his shoulder.
The hands of the big wooden clock ticking away at the
end of the *Dispatch* city room pointed to fourteen minutes of eight. The bright morning sun flooding the
long room showed most of the desks still arranged in
precise, almost geometrical, order; the worn wooden
floor, scrubbed and rubbed almost to whiteness by the
scrub-women in the night; one whole row of typewriters neatly covered with their rubber shrouds; and the
ground-glass cage at the further end which housed the

ogre of the *Dispatch*—that font of perpetual sarcasm —Frangenac, city editor!

Barton slipped his comb into his pocket, and, without a glance at the early men, strode down the long room whose lingering air of rigid cleanliness and mathematically accurate arrangement would be giving way to utter confusion by the time a dozen reporters should come stamping in on the big eight o'clock shift. Reaching the open door of the ground-glass cage, he walked in and stood at the desk.

"Something for me, Mr. Frangenac?" he inquired, with forced politeness.

Mr. Leon Frangenac, seated at the big flat-top desk, looked up, shears in hand. He was a powerful, strongly-built individual, indisputably French, although his English was without the trace of an accent, perhaps fifty years of age, with pale corpse-like cheeks that gleamed in vivid contrast to his short pointed black beard and his equally black moustache, waxed to a point on either side of his thin lips. His eyes, staring through Barton, were cold, beady, black, unfathomable.

"Close the door. Sit down." He flicked his thumb toward a chair. "And run your optics over this." He handed Barton a short clipping which the younger man saw at once was from the *Sun*, probably the most influential morning paper in the city, the paper which controlled the most mid-west senators and congressmen at Washington, and whose policy, run in a black line across the top of each and every issue, read: "*Cancel All European Debts to the U. S. A.; if not the whole Debt, then a proportionate part of each!*"

Closing the door behind him, Barton dropped into a chair and read the brief contents. They ran:

ONLY DAUGHTER OF EMPEROR OF CHINA ARRIVES IN CHICAGO

PRINCESS O LYRA SENG FINISHING EDUCATION BY TOUR AROUND WORLD WITH CHINESE PRIME MINISTER AND WIFE

Princess O Lyra Seng, the only daughter of Seng Hoang-Ti, Emperor of the new China, arrived in Chicago from New York yesterday on her tour around the world. The royal party, consisting of the Princess, her maid, Li Hwei Tsung, and Mrs. Li Hwei Tsung, are staying at the Hotel Rydenour. Yesterday afternoon was spent in a trip by carriage through the stockyards, viewing the meat-packing industry. It is said that the Princess O Lyra Seng is better educated than most American girls, and speaks several languages in addition to her own. She is twenty years of age, and is now completing her education by a circuit of the world, under the care of the Chinese Prime Minister and his wife. Mr. Tsung has conveyed to the American Press the regrettable information that the Princess will not give out any interviews because of diplomatic reasons. The royal party leaves for San Francisco the day after to-morrow, one week after their arrival in America from London, and from America's Pacific Coast gateway returns to Peking, after an absence of three months.

Prominent students of international politics now concede that China's latest reversion to a monarchial form of government will probably endure for at least a full century before the main mass of the Chinese people shall have reached the educational status that will make republicanism or democracy feasible; this permanency is also strengthened by two other important factors: one, that every warring faction in China has put its stamp of approval on the monarchy; and second, that Seng Hoang-Ti is the lineal descendant of the Seng line of rulers which ruled China for so many centuries. The advanced age of Seng Hoang-Ti, coupled with the fact that the Princess O Lyra Seng is his only offspring, indicates the extreme probability that the Princess will ultimately control the destinies of her 450,000,000 people.

Barton looked up from the clipping. "Very interesting," he commented dryly. "I note there was nothing doing in the interview line with her royal nibs. The *Sun* seems to have had to pad out with Chinese history to fill what space they did."

Mr. Leon Frangenac gazed absently out of the window toward the dingy buildings across from Newspaper Row. His pencil tapped rhythmically on a copy of last night's *Dispatch*, bearing across the top of its front page the rather startling statement of policy seeming like a gauntlet thrown directly into the face of its contemporary, the *Sun*: *Cancel France's debt to the U. S. A.; but make John Bull and all the rest pay up to the last farthing!* At length he spoke. "Barton," he said abruptly, bringing back his gaze to bear on the younger man, "paper is as high as it was ten years ago during the Big War. Last month's expense sheet, according to the frantic telegram from the Old Man in California, has a corn on it equal to the salary of one reporter. Your work hasn't scintillated particularly during the last few months, so far as I've noticed, and I've got to shave off that corn." He stroked his black beard. "Get me?"

"I gather somehow that I'm the corn," remarked Barton coolly. "But why all the Chinese literature? Anæsthetic before an operation in podiatrics?"

Frangenac leaned back in his swivel chair and laughed a mirthless laugh. "You're good, Barton. That was worthy of mine own tongue." He paused; the laugh faded; he was coming back to business again. "I met Howard Britton, owner of the *Sun*, last night at the Press Club. He was kind enough to advise me to save my time trying to get an interview out of O Lyra. Said the *Sun* tried out three men yesterday—and absolutely nothing doing. Also, I called up the Rydenour just before you came in. Clerk told me he had special instructions from her royal nibs through Li Hwei Tsung to tell reporters nothing doing; likewise to order the telephone operator to refuse connections to all parties trying to talk to the Princess by wire. It seems that they've got a complete suite on the fourteenth floor—and according to Britton they're very nicely isolated and quite protected. Now do you get me?"

"Light is beginning to filter in on me," remarked Barton uneasily. "I go out and get an interview with her ladyship, Princess Chow-Chow, and we avert the corn-shaving. In simpler language, I achieve the impossible—or else consider myself fired?"

"Tonight at six p. m.," said Frangenac coolly. "Sorry—but the corn must be shaved. Go out and get her ladyship to talk to your notebook—and I'll promise to fall on your neck—and find another corn to operate on, instead. Otherwise——" He stopped, listening. Through the ground-glass cage came the tramp of several reporters entering the city room on the eight o'clock shift. Frangenac's face took on its habitual sour look. "As to achieving the impossible," he grunted, "you Yankees give me a pain in the epigastrium. A Frenchman never squeals about impossibilities. A Frenchman has more enterprise, push and energy than two Poles, three Swedes, four Englishmen or four Americans. If it wasn't for my mechanical leg I'd go out and demonstrate to the whole crew of you how to fill up the pages of the *Dispatch* with real news stuff."

Barton flushed angrily to the roots of his hair. He himself was a Texas Yankee. His grandmother had been an English girl who, proselytized by Brigham Young's agents in England, had journeyed across the deserts of the West to join the colony of the Mormons, but who on learning all the facts of Brigham Young's religion, had happily-married a stalwart Texas trapper and reared a family without the shadow of a dozen other wives. And so with this mixed ancestry he continued to flush angrily. For the taunt he had just heard was Frangenac's old, moss-covered taunt to reporters. Always a Frenchman was equal to two Poles, three Swedes, four Englishmen or four Americans; sometimes it was five Englishmen and five Americans; sometimes six. And once, when Frangenac had been in a particularly nasty mood, it had risen to twenty of either. But it was known, not only from the *Dispatch's* frankly stated policy of cancelling the French debt to America and the French debt only, but from other facts that filtered into the newspaper world, that the *Dispatch* owner himself was of French descent on both sides of his family; and for that reason he loved Frangenac.

Almost as though he desired to emphasize the statement about his mechanical leg, Frangenac arose with difficulty from his chair and walked stiffly over to a cabinet at the side of the office. He returned with a bundle of papers, his right leg squeaking at every step like a thousand demons in purgatory. Then he dropped back to his desk.

"That's all, Barton. The Old Man wired me to lay off one man. Also, I don't feel that we're paying you enough for your brilliant work. I appreciate the fact that the *Dispatch* will probably collapse within a week after you leave us; so to retain your services and thus save the paper, I suggest that you go out and bring in a nice little interview with her royal nibs. I can conscientiously change the angle of fire then, and let out someone else whom I've had my eye on for a long time." He paused. "But if it's a case of too much mixed Yankee and Britisher blood in your veins, drop in at the cashier's office on your way out to-night. Your check will be ready."

Barton rose. His face was as red as a boiled beet. On the tip of his tongue trembled a fiery challenge to Frangenac to come out in the center of the city room and remove his coat. It was not the first time, however, that that challenge had trembled on the tip of a *Dispatch* reporter's tongue. But the obstacle that always prevented it from being framed into words was a simple one—Frangenac was a cripple.

A momentary impulse seized Barton to pour the vials of his pent-up wrath on the other's head, and quit on the spot; but a shred of cool common sense coming to his rescue told him that his triumph would be somewhat mild, since he was virtually discharged already. Instead, he leaned forward slightly and looked down at the other.

"Mr. Frangenac," he remarked, with all the suavity he could summon, "could you yourself get that interview with the Princess O Lyra Seng?"

"Me?" said the other, surprised. "I—well—that is to say——" He stopped in confusion.

"That's all I wanted to know," snapped Barton scornfully. "So you don't think it can be done, eh, Frangenac?" In his rapid speech he didn't notice that he had left off the "Mister." "But I'll do it." He shook one finger furiously at the other. "As for your confounded old equation—your contemptuous equation —it's nothing but an insult handed out because you're the high-muck-a-muck around here and the rest of us are the hirelings. It's possible only because you were lucky enough to be a Frenchman and to find an employer fifteen years ago who is so much French on both sides of his ancestry, so blinded to fairness in the matter of international finance, that all he can preach and talk of in his paper is to cancel his own mother-country's debt to America and yet at the same time try and expect every other country on the globe to pay up. Damn my soul, Frangenac, the Old Man is no more French in descent than Britton of the *Sun* is English descent, yet you don't hear the latter belly-aching around about cutting John Bull's debt and letting the rest stand. No, by Jumping Jupiter, he's fair—fairer in that particular matter than you and your employer. If it wasn't for Britton's cursed inflexible rule of employing no man who hasn't a straight record in the newspaper game of ten years' continuous employment, I'd go over to the *Sun*—that's—that's what I'd do. But about that interview. You've said I'm retained if I'm man enough—worth sufficient Poles and Swedes —to get it. I'll take you up on that. I'll just see whether you're a lying welcher as well as—as—as a Frenchman, and if you don't play fair I'll—I'll get in touch with the Old Man in California. Yes, by the

Lord, Frangenac, I'll—I'll get that interview. Remember that, I'll get it. I'll make you eat your words about mixed Yankee and British blood, if it's the last thing I ever do. That's all. I'll come back at noontime with it—even if it's only fifty words."

He spun on his heel and marched out of the office in a smoldering rage. He jerked down his hat from the hook near his typewriter and fumbled in the drawer of his desk for his notebook and pencil. Two reporters, just coming in, stared at him oddly. While he searched for the missing notebook, the telephone in the inner office rang sharply. Dimly he heard Frangenac answer it, speak for a minute and hang up. And as Barton marched down the aisle toward the door of the city room, he heard the door of the city editor's office open and the latter's sharp command.

"Barton! Wait a moment."

Barton spun in the doorway.

"I forgot," Frangenac was saying, "to express my appreciation for your oration, Barton. Indeed, it was a tonic for the day's work. It was funnier than Lincoln's Gettysburg speech or any of Disraeli's drivellings; and Mark Antony must have rolled over in his grave with jealousy. But isn't it rather early in the morning to be calling on royalty?" Several of the reporters pricked up their ears. From the look on their faces, however, an observer might have deduced that none of them had any love for Frangenac. "As long as you're specializing on the Orient this morning, here's a little stick for you to run out to first—before you grace the Rydenour with your presence. Sam Toy—Chinese laundryman—144 West Huron Street

—just found stabbed to death in his store by the policeman on the beat. Tong war stuff again. Run it down first, Mr. Barton, and if we're short of material we can slip it in for a filler. But of course," he taunted, his hand on the rapidly closing door, "we'll not be short to-night. We're going to press with a full first-page interview, captured by a wild and woolly Texas fire-eater whose English grandmother crossed the ocean blue!"

"I'll 'phone in on the Sam Toy stuff," replied Barton frigidly. "I'll see, also, that you get your interview, Frangenac."

And he was gone.

Outside on the steps of the old-fashioned building he paused, surveying the rumbling traffic of Market Street, his blood boiling in his veins.

"Of all the successful goat-getters the world ever knew," he fumed to himself, "that man Frangenac takes the gold medal! Lord knows I need his job, but I hate to burst a blood-vessel trying to get any story for a man like that. That impudent air of his and the squeak of his peg leg have got on my nerves till I guess I'm ready to part company with the *Dispatch* for good." He paused. "And confound his eternal running down of everybody but the French. If it's the last thing I ever do in this world, I've got to get that interview just for the satisfaction of showing him that a frog-eater can't rule over a news-sheet, published exactly five thousand miles from Paree, with a rod of sarcasm and a whip of irony. Yes, by the Lord Harry, I've got to do it. But how? There's the question!"

CHAPTER XXV

B ARTON did not remain stewing on the steps of the *Dispatch* office for very long. Already he was brightening up, for the sun was high over the dingy newspaper shops of Market Street. Likewise he was struck suddenly by the fact that Frangenac's second assignment was sending him in the very direction he wanted to go—on certain business of his own. As he tramped up Madison Street toward Wells, he established in his mind the approximate location of number 144 West Huron Street; then he consulted a letter in his breast pocket.

"Two birds with one stone," he commented to himself. "The Star Hotel must be within a few blocks from there."

He boarded a Wells Street car and, crossing the river, remained on it until he reached the 500's. There he dismounted on the dilapidated north side thoroughfare, strewn with pawnshops, second-hand tool stores and German apothecary shops, and walked slowly along, searching for number 550. He paused finally in front of a red-brick building with dirty windows that flaunted tattered yellow lace curtains, and a weatherbeaten door leading up a dark stairway. A painted wooden sign screwed to the door read simply:

190

> STAR HOTEL
> Rooms by day or week.

Up the dark inside steps he trudged, pausing for a moment at the second landing for the purpose of questioning a shirt-sleeved man who was seated in an office filled with rickety red plush furniture and a great rusty stove which had not even been taken down at the close of winter.

"In what room will I find Mr. Charles Fawcett?"

The shirt-sleeved man lazily squirted a jet of tobacco juice into a battered tin cuspidor.

"Rear room on third floor. Just go up and knock."

Up the uncarpeted stairs Barton went. At the rear of the dark third floor he knocked dubiously. When a voice replied "Come in," he entered.

A tall, broad-shouldered fellow of about thirty-five was lying back on a cheap iron bed, smoking a cigarette. His clothes were appreciably frayed, and his face showed that he had not shaved for a couple of days. The cheap, gaudy wallpaper of the room, reflecting the grey light from the closed court, showed a bulging suit-case of worn tan leather peeping from under the foot of the bed. Barton's quick gaze also took in a flask of moonshine from which the paper had not even been removed; instead it had been twisted off at the neck. The bottle stood upright on the bottom shelf of a rickety stand, and a sticky glass near by showed that within only a few hours some of its contents had been imbibed.

At Barton's entrance the man on the bed struggled to his feet, his gloomy face lighting up momentarily, showing features that were not unhandsome, barring the marked traces of dissipation. He pushed back the tangled dark hair from his eyes, and jerked out a chair from the wall.

"Jason!" His voice trembled with gladness. "I'm mighty glad to see you, old man. Excuse the surroundings—but—but—the exchequer is rather low. So you got my letter, eh?" He thrust out a hand that shook perceptibly.

Barton seized the outstretched hand silently, then dropped into a chair. He looked about him slowly, while the other took up a seat on the side of the bed. Then he spoke.

"Charlie, why didn't you let me know before that you've been in town for three days? I've been on the run all the time, but I'd have managed to get in to see you." He paused. "Your letter was terribly blue in tone, old man. So you couldn't land anything in this burg, eh?"

The other shook his head dolefully. "I never saw the beat of it, Jason," he retorted. "I canvassed every office in town for the first two days, but there's nothing doing anywhere. I'd have done better to have stayed in Omaha, but things were gone to pot there for me— so I blew out with my last few shekels."

Barton gazed at him rather strangely, but made no comment. Fawcett went on quickly:

"I—I was just thinking of going out this morning on the hunt, to make the circuit over again." He held up the sleeves of his coat. "But I'm wondering if I'm too frayed to land a newspaper job in this town. Do you think that's what's keeping me out of luck?"

Barton said nothing for a moment or two. Finally he spoke, a little sharply in tone, yet in a manner that a father might use to his son.

"Charlie, I'm afraid it's up to me to have to speak rather plainly with you. You and I went to college together—and I guess that Jason's one person who can take a chance on speaking straight from the shoulder, eh?" The other nodded emphatically. "You helped me in days that were terrible days for me, old man, and I haven't forgotten it. And that's why I hate to get personal. But as long as you and John Moonshine hobnob together, you're going to be what you call 'out of luck.' I'm telling you that straight. It may sting—but it's what you need. It beats the devil how a stranger in Chicago can always find a blind pig and get a half-pint for fifty cents, when the prohibition officials can't locate 'em to save their neck. However—John Moonshine—he's your enemy, Charlie. Yes, your suit is tacky-looking; likewise your features show the signs. Man alive, brace up! Stop it, I tell you. You're a crack newspaper man. You can give 'em all cards and spades when you want to. But paper is high; been high ever since Canada put her embargo on wood-pulp. And publishers are cutting down expenses to the last farthing. Until you brace up, and throw that bottle out of the window—oh yes, I spotted it when I came in!—you're going to be 'out of luck.' " He stopped. "There, I guess I've had my say. Now throw me out. The strong man of Nebraska University can easily do me up, if he goes for me."

The other gazed wearily toward. Barton. "Dear old Jason," he returned, "anything you want to say to me goes; do you hear that, old man? There's nobody but Charles Fawcett to blame for Charles Fawcett's luck. I'm a rotter all right. But I can give 'em cards and spades, just as you say. Why—boy—I'm better than you when I'm off the stuff for a few weeks." He held up his hand, studying it curiously. The fingers trembled visibly. "But now—well—I guess I couldn't run down a story of a tomcat fight in a back alley."

Barton tilted his chair back against the wall, studying the other intently. He had been Fawcett's most intimate friend at college when Fawcett had been strong man of the University and he himself had been only a green Freshman, picked upon and hazed by the older classmen. He remembered how Fawcett had saved him from an ice-cold ducking in the campus pond one bitter December night; also of the money the older man had loaned him at a time when money meant graduation. That money had long since been paid back— but the debt had not been discharged. A sudden wave of feeling swept over the younger man.

"The main question now," he observed pointedly, "is the condition of the exchequer in dollars and cents?"

"Jason," retorted the other grimly, "I'd hate to tell you. Ask it in cents—but not in dollars. It's low— veree low—so low——"

Barton fished down into his pockets, and withdrew a ten-dollar bill. "Here, Charlie," he said hastily, holding it out, "take this. Send out your suit and have it cleaned and pressed. If you haven't any clean linen buy a shirt and a few collars. Get a shine and a shave. Then march into every office in town as though you owned the place, and tell 'em you're the man who put over the Parkington scoop on the *Omaha Bee*. I'll venture you'll have a job inside of two days—even if it's only twenty-five a week. And when you get your week's pay, get out of this dump. The place is enough to drive a man to drink." He looked at the window. Then he rose abruptly and walked over to the opening, where he took up the paper-clad flask and deliberately dropped it down the courtway. A few seconds later, from the dark, trash-covered bottom, came the dull crash of splintering glass. "And cut out this stuff."

The other was fingering the bill eagerly. "Jason, old boy, you've saved my life! I tried not to write to you—until I had to; then I was worried sick for fear you might not come. If you hadn't I'd have had to get out and climb into the bread line, I guess. I'd never have got a job in these dilapidated togs. Jason, I owe you a debt——"

"Of exactly ten dollars," retorted the other firmly. "No more." He looked at his watch. Then he rose. "Well, old boy, I'm only stopping here while on a story over in this part of the city. Later, I'm going out on another story; hence I can't stay and gas with you. But I'll be over to-night, however, and we'll see what luck you've had, and also go over a few plans. And you'll stay off the moonshine, old man?"

The other stood up and wrung his hand fervently. "So help me, Jason, not another drop. Not—one— drop! I promise you." He held up his fingers again. They were like the fingers of a man with palsy. "So

help me, Jason, I'm off it for good. Never again."
He held up his right hand in mock solemnity.

Barton took his departure from Fawcett's room and
stumbled down the dark, musty-smelling stairway of
the Star Hotel to the sunny street. Outside he walked
briskly northward several blocks until he came to
Huron Street, a narrow thoroughfare lined on both
sides with cottages and lodging-houses of the cheaper
class, each bearing its drab sign in its parlor window.
There he turned eastward and proceeded a half-block
until he came upon a low store built out to the inner
edge of the sidewalk from the foundations of an old
tottering house. Its glass front had been covered with
cheap green paint up to a point just a little higher
than the level of a man's eyes, but above the opaque
coloring matter was painted in bright red the simple
announcement:

SAM TOY
Laundering.

The glass of the front door was hung with cheap
calico cloth, but through a long tear Barton spied the
figure of a bluecoat seated in a chair near the door,
and smoking away at a cigar. So he turned the door-
knob and walked in.

CHAPTER XXVI

A DISCOVERY

AT Barton's entrance the police officer looked up in surprise. The younger man quickly turned back his coat and displayed his reporter's badge.

"Heard a Chink got stabbed here last night," he said. "What is there to it, officer?"

The other spat contemptuously on the clean floor of the store. "Nothin' much to it. Tong stuff again. That's all. Wish the yellow heathens would murder each other all off and be done with it."

Barton gazed about the store curiously. The front had been boarded off from the rear by a crude partition of unpainted matchboards. The space near the store window was occupied by a trio of washtubs, a counter bearing a ball of string and a quaint inkpot, an ironing-board and a great compartmented rack filled with bundle after bundle of tied-up laundry, each ticketed with a red slip marked with a few undecipherable Chinese characters. A number of the red tickets were scattered over the floor of the shop. The one door through the partition was surmounted by a box-like transom, inside of which a piece of rusty screen had been tacked; the doorway appeared to lead in to a living-room at the rear.

"Yes," the bluecoat was saying, "Kelly seen the light

burning this morning and peered in over the green paint on the window. He found the Chink lyin' across the counter there." He flicked his thumb toward that worn article of store furniture. "The heathen's head was hangin' down and his pigtail was sweepin' the floor. Old-fashioned type of Chink, y' see: the kind that kept their pigtail to th' bitter end." He paused. "But as I was sayin', they'd run him in the ribs with a long knife. Same knife he cuts the string for the bundles with, accordin' to the man across the street." The bluecoat yawned. "He had his little paintbrush in his fingers just as if he'd tried to paint a farewell message on one of his blank laundry tickets; but Old Man Death got him too soon. Kelly 'phoned in to Chicago-Avenue, and me and one of the dicks came over and looked him over. Then we dragged him into the back room and flung him on the cot. There was a crowd outside boostin' each other up to the window, an' that's the only way we could get 'em away. Take a pike at him if you want. You're the first reporter that's got here. Most likely none of 'em'll take the trouble to run it down. They're all fed up on this On Leong Tong and Hip Sing Tong warfare."

Barton walked back into the rear room of the store. His sweeping glance showed him that the place was sparsely furnished, for it held only a kitchen range, a cheap wooden table bearing a cracked yellow bowl and a couple of chop-sticks, a cupboard of crude shelves containing a few teacups, a tin plate or so, and a teapot. On a rack back of the stove a few pots and pans hung, together with an American tea-kettle and an equally American coffee-pot. From the ceiling hung

a cheap coal-oil lamp, and in the corner of the room
was a wooden cot of the 79-cent variety, with a quilt
and blanket on it. And stretched out on the cot, his
yellow features rigid, was the victim of the Tong murder.

Barton, striding over to the cot, stared down at the
dead figure with some degree of interest. The queue
had been wound loosely about the forehead, apparently
by the officers, but they had not disturbed the knife,
the handle of which protruded from the Chinaman's
chest in a mass of clotted blood that had matted the
cheap cotton blouse into a hard lump. The loose blue
garments lay in folds over the gaunt figure, and the
blank yellow features had already shrunk into a grotesque death-mask. Tightly clasped in the Chinaman's
right hand was a thin brush with camel's hair tip;
and Barton, trying it roughly with his fingers, found
that the thing was held so rigidly that nothing less
than extreme force would have to be used to remove it.

For several more seconds he stared down at the shell
of the Chinese laundryman, and then, with a final cur-
sory glance about the living-room, he returned to the
front of the store where the officer was still tilted back
in his chair.

"So Kelly found him lying across the counter?" Barton queried curiously. "And with the paintbrush in his
hand?" He pondered for a moment. "Death couldn't
have come instantaneously then; he must have tried
to write something out—and fainted across the counter, eh?"

The other yawned. "I guess so," he assented wearily.
"I guess so." He unbuttoned his great blue coat and

looked at his watch. Then he turned to the younger man. "Say, Bud, can you stay here for a minute or two? I'd like to run into the saloon farther up the street and get a plug and a few cigars. I'm rooted here for the rest of the day, I'm afraid."

"Sure; go ahead," Barton acquiesced cheerfully. "I'll hold the fort while you're gone."

The bluecoat jumped up, buttoned his coat together and swung out of the door, forging eastward. Barton sat sidewise on the edge of the counter, pondering again over the brush in the dead Chinaman's hand, and reflecting on a city administration which made such things possible. "It's a shame," he commented to himself, "that in any big city a blackhander can kill an Italian and get away with it every time; and the Tongs can pot each other in the same way, and never get caught. If I had my way, I'd break up the Tongs and the blackhand if I had to swear in a thousand extra police."

His eyes fell on the blank red laundry tickets scattered about the floor of the store; then on the little pot of black ink on the counter. He leaned down and picked one of the tickets up. At the top had been crudely printed by a cheap handpress:

SAM TOY,
144 W. Huron Street,
Hand Laundry.

The rest of the ticket, however, was blank.

"I wonder," he thought, "if Sammy in the next room tried to write a scathing indictment of the Tong system before he kicked off." He paused. The opening of the door on the part of the officer, he saw, had dispersed the red tickets in a dozen directions. A sudden thought struck him. He went over to the door and held it wide open. The gust of wind that shot through the store and out of the cracked window of the rear living-room animated every one of the red squares. He propped open the door with a chair. Then he stepped to the doorway in the partition and wet his finger. With the moistened digit he could feel a most pronounced breeze.

"Now, I wonder," he said softly to himself, "if Sammy Toy did write something before he dropped across the counter—and it got blown away?" He was instantly on the alert. He looked down at the floor and under the counter. There was nothing there, however; but an idea struck him. He took one of the blank tickets, and holding it some distance from the floor, suddenly released it. Much to his surprise it sailed upward, caught in the flowing breeze through the store, and disappeared in the box-like, screened transom over the partition door. Quickly he got the chair, and, standing on it, raised himself up on tiptoe and peered over the edge of the transom.

His heart gave a peculiar little leap. There were two red slips there, the one he had just released, and one more.

He brought them hurriedly down. The one, of course, was blank; but the other, underneath Sam Toy's cheaply printed name, bore a wavering set of crudely splotched Chinese characters that ran in two vertical wobbly lines. The officer was just turning the knob of the door. Barton quickly stuffed the second red slip into his pocket.

"Maybe it's only a spare laundry ticket," he said to himself, "and on the other hand it may be Sam Toy's last message to the police. If it tells the name of the Tong that pulled the stunt—it means something more than a stickful. At any rate, my boy, we'll just hang on to it."

CHAPTER XXVII

OUTSIDE, Barton strolled leisurely away from Sam Toy's laundry, but a block away from the place he withdrew the ticket and studied it closely. There was nothing more to be seen than at first, however; only the crudely printed English words at the top, and below them the two vertical, wavering columns of Chinese hieroglyphics. There was the biggest possibility in the world, he realized, that a translation of those characters would reveal merely some banal facts about shirts and collars; or else the usual description by which Celestials manage to identify their customers. But there was the still more satisfying possibility that the characters presented the dying message of a man, who, even in the throes of death, had made one last great effort to get revenge on the enemy Tong which had terminated his own career. And in that was a story. Not a new story, perhaps; but something considerably more than a stick!

When he dismounted from a street car in the downtown section of the city it was ten minutes to ten. It was still too early to visit the Hotel Rydenour on Michigan Avenue and make the hopeless attempt to overwhelm Frangenac by securing an interview with the uninterviewable Princess O Lyra Seng; but, indeed,

203

the slip in his pocket suggested that he might yet present the *Dispatch* with something that would not grace the pages of any other evening paper. Already he had in mind the means of obtaining a translation, and so, after looking at his watch, he forged straight to the Illinois Central suburban station at the foot of Randolph Street.

He reached the platform just in time to board an express for Fifty-seventh Street, and sixteen minutes later he was walking over the campus of Chicago University. He entered the office of the world-famous college and strode straight to the desk of the registrar's clerk.

"How soon this morning can I get in touch with Professor Chan Fu—the exchange professor from the University of Peking?" He paused, and then explained: "Barton's my name. I'm the man who interviewed Professor Fu when he came to Chicago U. some months ago."

The clerk turned to a 'phone and rang a number. He talked for a minute, and then hung up the receiver. "Professor Fu left for the Field Museum in Grant Park some ten minutes ago. The board of directors there is holding a meeting regarding an exhibition of Chinese tapestries, and Professor Fu is to have charge. He's expected back at his rooms in the faculty building at three-thirty. Do you care to leave a message? If so"—he pointed at a desk in the corner of the office—"just write it out, and I'll see that he gets it on his return."

A little crestfallen, Barton turned from the desk. He had hoped from his slight acquaintanceship with the big professor from China to secure both a translation and some advice in the matter of the problem which centered in the Hotel Rydenour. He stepped over to the empty desk and sat down. Drawing over an empty sheet of paper, he wrote:

"DEAR PROFESSOR FU,
   "The undersigned interviewed you some months ago upon your joining; the university under the new exchange system with Peking University, and on the strength of that brief but pleasant acquaintanceship takes the liberty of asking you a favor. I am anxious to secure a literal translation of these few Chinese characters. I take the liberty of enclosing them, therefore, and will return at half-past three to-day."

He signed his name and drew out the laundry ticket. For a moment he gazed at it, and then, remembering with a feeling of disquiet that Chicago University boasted a whole corps of student journalists who sent in daily correspondence to every paper in the city, he decided not to do as the man in the fable—to place all his eggs in one basket. In fact, he dimly recalled at this juncture a woman friend of his who claimed to have a woman friend out in Ravenswood, who in turn had a Chinese servant—or who had had some months ago. And it struck him that the two egg-baskets for any possible scoop would admirably be that Chinese servant and the big professor, Chan Fu. So he deliberately tore the laundry ticket into two vertical strips, and proceeded to enclose only the right-hand row of characters in his letter. Then he sealed it up, and marking the Professor's name and the word "urgent" on it, left it with the registrar's clerk.

"Please see that the Professor gets this immediately on his return, and I'll call back later."

He took out an old black leather bill-fold and placed the left-hand strip of the ticket in one of its many empty compartments. Then, retracing his steps across the tree-dotted campus, he was soon back at the Fifty-seventh Street station of the Illinois Central. A quarter of an hour later he was emerging from the commuter's tunnel on busy Michigan Avenue, thronged now with stylishly dressed women and men of leisure swinging along with their silk hats and canes.

A brief walk brought him to the Hotel Rydenour. He knew it to some extent from having been there before, and recalled that it usually housed the visiting potentates and people of distinction from other lands; indeed, it consisted mostly of extensive suites rather than individual rooms.

He entered the big white-stone skyscraper, and strolling up to the desk, motioned the clerk to one side.

"On what floor is Princess O Lyra——?" he began.

"Suite 14B," interrupted the clerk. He grinned an irritating grin. "My dear sir, if you knew of the newspaper men that have been in here all morning, and filing out again, you wouldn't ask that question. Mr. Tsung has given me the Princess's instructions to tell all newspaper men that she does not care to give out any interviews."

Barton nodded carelessly, as though the matter were of little consequence to him one way or the other, and walked over to the cigar counter in order to get a cigar and consider the matter. It was just about as he had expected. He wondered if there were any subterfuge by which he could get a 'phone connection with suite 14B. But as he was nipping off the end of his purchase in the steel cutter, a short, stocky Asiatic with squat features, yet clad in an expensive suit of Scotch tweeds, stepped up to the counter, and in perfect English spoke to the clerk about a certain brand of cigar.

Barton scrutinized him carefully. He was about fifty years of age, as near as the newspaper man could guess. Dangling from his coat pocket was the ungainly metal shingle which is always attached to hotel keys. And when he strolled back to the lobby and rejoined a woman whose face, showing through the thick folds of her veil, was distinctly Chinese, and elderly at that, Barton whistled softly to himself.

"That's Li Hwei Tsung, the prime minister and his wife, all right." His eyes searched the lobby. "But where's the Princess?"

Chewing on his unlighted cigar, Barton watched the two, the yellow-faced Chinese dignitary and the veiled woman, step out of the foyer and into a taxicab drawn up to the curb. A second later they had driven off. Then he spoke again to himself, this time with some enthusiasm.

"Out on business or to see the city by themselves. And he keeps the key right on his person. That means that our haughty Princess and her maid are alone in their suite. By the Lord Harry, I'll try it!"

He made his way quickly over to the elevator shaft, and entered the waiting car. "Fifteenth floor," he said quietly.

The elevator stopped with a rush at the fifteenth

floor. Barton stepped out, and leaning over, fumbled with his shoe-lace until the car had descended. Then he hurried down the carpet-clad hall until he came to the stairway. Quickly he descended one story and, proceeding along the hall, studied carefully the gold-lettered wording on each of the four great oaken doors that clustered about the elevator shaft on that floor. He passed suite D, suite C, and finally found himself in front of suite B.

He lost no time. There was no telling when the elevator might return with a passenger; so he knocked three times. There was no sign of life. Again he knocked, this time louder. Again no answer.

He stooped over and, peering through the keyhole, found that the door opened only on an inner corridor, at the further end of which were several other oak doors and a half-opened window. He tried the knob and found, as he now half anticipated, that the door was locked. But the sight of the iron framework of a fire-escape on the window at the end of the corridor gave him an idea which he lost no time in putting into execution.

After some hesitancy as to whether to go up or down one flight, he hurried back again to the fifteenth floor. There he tried the door of suite 15B and found to his satisfaction that it was unlocked. He walked rapidly down the narrow corridor, passing several open rooms which showed by the condition of their bureau covers that the suite was untenanted. Reaching the window, he raised it part way, and clambered out on the fire-escape, which looked down upon a courtyard far below.

Down he went exactly one flight, until he came to the

half-opened window he had glimpsed through the key-hole. He tumbled inside quickly and, gazing along the corridor, identical in appearance with the one above, he saw with satisfaction that the big oaken door which separated the suite from the outer hallway now protected his operations as much as a few minutes before it had barred them.

He stepped along the corridor a few feet, straining his ears, his heart pounding a little forcibly at his unparalleled effrontery. Now, for the first time, matters had begun to dawn upon him; and over him rolled a sudden wave of resentment against Frangenac who had been the cause of his adopting such a sensational and obtrusive method of securing something exclusive for the *Evening Dispatch*. But suddenly Barton stopped. Behind the second door he detected faint feminine voices, one sibilant and strangely girlish, another speaking in a harsh tone words which were quite indistinguishable.

A second longer he listened, and then, with some trepidation, knocked firmly on the door three times. "Now to get ordered out like a dog," he remarked dolefully to himself. "Confound such a game, anyway!"

CHAPTER XXVIII

AT Barton's knock the voices stopped suddenly and a profound silence followed. A second later the door swung open a bare crack, revealing an obviously elderly Chinese woman in quaint Chinese costume. Even before she had a chance to open her mouth Barton spoke rapidly:

"Madam, Jason H. Barton is my name. I represent the American Press—the *Chicago Evening Dispatch*. The American people are more than anxious to——"

"No unlestan'," she said helplessly. She started to close the door in his face, but the movement seemed to be interrupted by a sudden command in unintelligible words. The maid, for such it must have been, looked back in indecision as though ordered not to close out the visitor. Then she swung the door wide open, and Barton, his heart beating rather wildly, stepped inside.

He found himself in the usual stuffy hotel parlor, furnished with red plush furniture of undoubted expensiveness, yet chilling from its very absence of any homelike aspect. And standing in the center of the floor, her back turned to a great pier glass, was a Chinese girl.

She was slender—as slender as any American girl.

210

Barton's keen appraising eye took in the jet-black hair, done on her head with a rose, exactly after a Harrison Fisher girl on a magazine cover which was pinned to the edge of the pier glass; and he could not but smile at the suggestion it gave of femininity being the same the world over. She was clad, however, in a most ornate Chinese costume, the pantaloons and blouse of which were covered with tapestry threads of gold and silver and multi-colored silk, with here and there a bit of carved jade hanging pendant. Her little feet were encased in slippers of gold thread, but they were not deformed, Barton noted at once, for the two steps that she took toward him were the steps of normal feet. The neck of the rich Chinese garment was cut low, revealing a soft, girlish throat that was in keeping with the slim, rounded form that might have done justice to any of her white sisters. Her cheek-bones were a trifle high, revealing the Celestial blood in her, but her complexion, soft and smooth, was a remarkable combination of cream and pink, with the pink blending at the mouth into a pair of the rosiest red lips. Long black eyelashes shaded the most alluring of violet-brown, almond-shaped eyes. And as Barton stepped forward uneasily, he could detect about her a sensuous, exotic perfume. For a second it seemed to him somehow that he was gazing upon a transplanted bud from a clime of sun and flowers.

"You—you are newspaper man?" she asked curiously, even timidly.

Barton bowed low and held out to her one of his cards. "Jason H. Barton is my name, Princess. I am with the *Dispatch* of this city."

The Princess studied the card closely, then looked up smilingly. "I think I like talk one of you newspaper men, Mr. Jason H. Barton. Everywhere I go I am cooped up and never get a chance to see or talk or live while I in this country. I speak English, you see. I educated in English in China, and I study much about it. Won't—won't you sit down?"

Rather bewildered, Barton sat down in the nearest chair, studying the girl across from him. The elderly Chinese woman had already closed the door and slipped over in one corner, where she sat like a graven image. Barton suddenly spoke:

"Princess O Lyra, your guardian, Mr. Tsung, has given to the Press a statement that you would furnish no interviews while in this country. But, this country is terribly interested in people of importance from other lands—and also in what they think of America. I should be highly honored if you would talk to me for a few short minutes upon subjects which I might write up and print in my paper. Is—is this asking too much?"

She pouted a delightful little pout. She dropped into one of the unfriendly plush chairs near her. "Honorable Tsung," she said slowly, "does not want me to see American Press. His words did not come from I. He thinks interviews not thing. Perhaps, though, that is command from my honorable father. I do not know. Yet I like talk to you. And if you not stop me, I tell you all I think and know. I am girl, you see." And she smiled sweetly at her feminine joke.

Barton laughed from sheer glee as much as from

the joke. He could scarcely realize yet that matters had turned out as they had. He had fully expected to be ordered out long since—yet here he was, sitting in the room with the only daughter of the Emperor of China. He reached into his pocket and drew forth his notebook and pencil. He paused undecidedly for a moment and then asked the old, old question that has been asked of every visiting dignitary who has ever crossed the city limits of Chicago.

"Princess, what did you think of our stockyards?"

She shivered a little. "I not like them. I cover my eyes with my hands when our carriage go by them." Suddenly she gave a delightful little giggle. "But the piggies—the cute little piggies!" Barton looked up startled from his notebook. "They are just same piggies I have seen thousands of times on roads out from Peking when I ride with my teachers. The same funny little fat stomachs, and same funny little curly tails. For once in my life, Mr. Jason H. Barton, I get what you call it—homesick!" Her face grew puzzled. "Why is it, Mr. Jason H. Barton, that while there are different races on face of earth, the piggies are just the same piggies the world over?"

He was rather busy with his pencil, taking down her quaint answer, but he looked up. "I'm sure I don't know," he replied, smiling openly. "Rather a silly little girl," was his inward comment, "in spite of the fact that she's an Emperor's daughter." He paused a moment. It suddenly struck him that Tsung might come back at any moment, and a sudden uneasiness seized him. So he drove straight to his interview.

"Princess O Lyra," he said, "what is your opinion as to the value to China of monarchy against republic?"

"Oh, I am very radical little girl," she replied promptly. "I read and study too much in China. I think, Mr. Jason H. Barton, that there must a day come when every country is republic. I am not in favor of monarchy anywhere." She made a sweeping gesture with her slender hand. "But my people—426,000,000 of them—are still for most part in ignorance and superstition. Everything they do is controlled by good and bad 'feng-shui,' or what you might call—might call—'aspects.' You, over here, hear of few thousand Chinese college graduates—a few hundred military generals—a diplomat or two—and you think China is at last come out of her shell of centuries. But no—it is not so. They to whom the light has come are but few thousand. There are millions—hundreds of millions in the great interior—that interior inaccessible even by oxen-cart—who have never even hear of other part of world—who do not know there is an America, or an England, or anything. Until great school system can be start that will educate, there is no hope for them to think for themselves. And creation of great school system with necessary tens of thousands of teachers will take decades yet—twenty—fifty years to accomplish. Until the masses in the interior can be educate away from their 'feng-shui,' I do not believe they can rule themselves. It is 'feng-shui'—and worship of honorable ancestors, yes, too—that has kept in China wooden railroads and wooden ploughs for all these years."

"But this condition," queried Barton, poising his pencil above the notebook and studying the delicate, dark, almond eyes of the girl wonderingly, finding she was a little deeper than he thought she was—"is it not due to their religion of Buddhism?"

"No, no, no!" she cried emphatically. "State religion of China is Confucianism—not Buddhism. We have some Buddhism—some Taoism—some Mohammedanism—but Confucianism is religion that permeates the bigger part of my people."

This set Barton on a new productive tack. "Then what are your opinions, Princess, on religion in general?"

"Oh, I have thought much—much about that subject. Confucianism is no barbaric religion you may think it is. You—most of you—do not know China. Confucianism is—is—highly ethical system of conduct. It is almost identical with Ten Commandments of Christianity. Its very key-words, Mr. Jason H. Barton, are Benevolence, Righteousness, Propriety, Wisdom and Generosity. It defines the relations between prince and minister, husband and wife, father and son, brother and brother, and friend and friend. It is mighty, spiritual—almost as much so as your Christianity. I think all time that, after all, Confucianism and Christianity are nearly identical at heart. I have study about your Christ. And His universal brotherhood is magnificent; His words, 'Do unto others' are greatest wisdom world will ever know. They would—they could—solve whole problem of racial strife. I, only Chinese girl, cannot exactly understand that the man Christ is—what you call it—divine. Yet, like

Renan, I believe His extreme sacrifice and his remarkable al—al—altruistic doctrines, even though He were
only ordinary man, did make Him divine, after His
death. You see, Mr. Jason H. Barton, it all rests upon
my inter—interpretation of divinity."

Barton heard her through, amazed, not forgetting,
however, to transfer every one of her words to his notebook. Open-mouthed, he looked toward her. "Good
Heavens, Princess, do you mean to tell me that you,
a Chinese girl, have read Renan?"

She smiled delightfully at the wonder on his face.
"Oh, Mr. Jason H. Barton, I what you call bookworm.
I not speak English or read English near so good like
I do German and French. I read Renan in French—
and I very interested."

"But, Princess," he ejaculated, almost forgetting on
account of her charming naïveté that he was talking to
an Emperor's daughter, "how do you get an opportunity to read such deep things—with court functions
to attend?"

"But I am only girl," she replied quietly. "I have
teachers to teach me—but no court functions. I practically cooped up in palace at Peking with nothing to
do—but read—read—read. I almost like Turkish
women like I see when honorable Tsung and we all of
us pass through Turkey. They live in—in—cocoon of
their own spinning. And I make for me a cocoon of
my thoughts—on things and the world."

He listened carefully. "Princess, you surprise me.
I did not expect, when I first began, to find our interview going into such channels as it has. Indeed, you
are quite a student." He paused. "Then may I ask

in all politeness what your opinion is of one of the biggest questions in the life of mankind—the race question? How do you think it will ever be solved?"

"Of that, too, have I thought much," she returned fervently. "Yes, the race question will be solved. It will not be ten years—nor hundred—nor thousand. It will be solved in but one way—not by science, by social laws, by partition, by world government, by universal disarmament, nor by international policing. Yes, Mr. Jason H. Barton, the race question, if solar system not destroyed through some ca—ca—cataclysm, will be solved one day through one process only."

"And the solution?" he asked eagerly, forgetting for a second even to wield his pencil. "What is your solution, Princess, of the race question—the biggest question in the history of civilization?"

CHAPTER XXIX

A FLOWER UNFOLDS

THE Princess O Lyra Seng dropped her eyes to the floor for one brief second. Then she raised them and faced the reporter bravely, a barely perceptible flush mounting to her cheeks.

"My solution is a radical one—but only one," she said simply. "And I think, Mr. Jason H. Barton, that you will agree with me. What is race? It is not color —although color is always one of visible characteristics. As to color—pigmentation—science will overcome that in less than few hundred years. Science will make us all of one shade. But race is something deeper —far deeper—than mere color. Racial distinctions date back thousands of years; they are rooted too deep to be outweeded by professors working in laboratories. And my solution is so—so simple. It is intermarriage! Intermarriage must take place between all races of earth until so-called racial distinctions are breeded out. Then, when in a thousand or five thousand years a great homo—homo—oh, dear, what is that terrible word in English?—homogeneous race shall people the earth, then shall there no longer be any race but human race. Then shall there be no race hatred—no war. You see, Mr. Jason H. Barton, so long as the desire for war may remain in hearts of men, even though war itself is made impossible, then humanity is not yet even on road to reach its—its capabilities. Race antagonism must go, you see. Hence race and pride of race must disappear!"

He studied her for a long time before he spoke. "Princess, you are what we know in this country as an idealist. You have stated a daring theory which would be scoffed at if broached in this present year. You astound me by the very depths of your thoughts. Yet I believe you have stated the problem and its solution." He paused. "May I ask, therefore, what are your views on love? One out of every two readers of the American newspaper is the American woman. She, Princess O Lyra Seng, will be greatly disappointed unless she learns the opinions on love from one of her own sex—from far across the seas."

The Princess smiled sweetly in his direction, and stared dreamily off into space. The maid still remained like a graven image of, perhaps, a female Buddha, never moving, never blinking an eye.

"Love!" said O Lyra Seng softly. "And if I speak on that, then will you say still more that O Lyra Seng is idealist. Love, Mr. Jason H. Barton, is a real, such a real thing in life. It is the biggest thing. I think I know what love should be—although it has never been satisfactorily defined. Plato try to define it—and come near it. He merely say it is attraction of opposites. But he not analyze it deeply, so like I. Love, I believe, is perception by a personality of its complementary personality. But personality—what is that? Is it not nothing but a great intricate bundle of simple characteristics in which one characteristic is complexion, another stature, another build, another physical energy, another physical courage, another mental courage; and so on through the diverse human attributes such as generosity, sta—sta—stamina, depth of thought, forethought, quickness of thought, idealism of thought, practicalness, and thousands of others, mental, spiritual and physical?"

She paused, then went on breathlessly: "In marriage—that free-choice sort which you American may enjoy—you do not always study and analyze the other's personality, hence you do not always secure your complementary personality. In China do we not even have any choice in the matter. Yet I believe in this heart of mine that in the whole, great, wide world is there but one personality that exactly supplies the opposite characteristics to our own personality. If we can find that—then have we love. If we marry that—then do we have real marriage, incidentally physical—but really the marriage of the soul. It is mutual understanding, mutual supplying of the opposite characteristics, mutual appreciation of human qualities in each other, Mr. Jason H. Barton, that makes this thing called love." The Princess paused again, quite carried away by her convictions. "And—and will that satisfy the American woman, Mr. Jason H. Barton?"

"That is a splendid, wonderful answer," he returned, raising his pencil from his pothook-strewn notebook. "You are indeed an idealist—a thinker—a poet. Please do not be angry when I make this remark; but I want to say to you that you should not have been the daughter of the Emperor of China. For your personality— your own unique personality—cannot find its complementary personality on account of your rank."

Her face grew sad. "Yes, I fear you have stated the tragedy, Mr. Jason H. Barton, in life of O Lyra Seng."

He changed the subject hastily, going back again to the race question. "It is said," he ventured, "that intermarriage between opposite races produces deterioration. I do not know this. I have only heard it from those not really qualified to discuss it. I——"

"Oh, it is not so," she broke in hurriedly. "You must not tear to pieces O Lyra Seng's theory. That is only superstition like our feng-shui—and just as bad. When first I began to think on this question, I heard of man Mendel who know all about heredity. And oh, how hard I tried to find this man Mendel's works! But his works were not in China. Finally I cry so much that my honorable father offer to give me three coolies and little palace and pond of goldfish for my birthday. But I cry and I want only Mendel. So he have consultation and he send way—way—to Germany for Mendel, and finally it arrive—a splendid big book. It is in German. It says that Mendel long since dead, but it tell of the men who make of his studies the science of Eugenics. I have to read slowly, and I find that your superstition not founded on fact. Mendel show many wonderful experiments with bean vines and sweet peas. For two long years I try them out myself in my garden—and I repeat them all. And I learn then that regardless of race, the result of the intercrossing of species is to produce descendants only according to certain laws concerning dominant and recessive characteristics. When this is done, why may not eugenics be as effective in breeding across the races as well as in one race? Why not make problem of life the perpetuation of good characteristics in the off-spring and the removal of bad, rather than the per-petuation of mere race, Mr. Jason H. Barton?"

At her last speech, Barton was more than amazed. "Studied and worked out the Mendelian theory of heredity with plants!" he ejaculated. "Heavens, if I could find a Caucasian girl with the personality of this Celestial flower, what wouldn't I give for her?" Lost for a moment, he regarded her in growing admiration, his eyes roving across her pink-tinged cheeks to the slanting eyes of dark velvet. Suddenly he collected himself and spoke—once more on business.

"What do you think of our hustle and bustle, Prin-cess?"

"I adore it," she returned quickly. "It is spirit of unrest, and unrest is creativeness. It is portrayal of—of—of smashing force, so unlike placidity of our coun-try." She clasped her hands together. "Oh, I like it so, Mr. Jason H. Barton. I long—I wish that I could be of this life—to act—to do—to think—to vote—to be one spoke in this great wheel of existence." Her face grew sad again. "Yet must O Lyra Seng enact the fate of her life. Just a girl of twenty—and she must follow road laid out for her."

Nothing was said for a moment. Then Barton asked curiously: "What did you think of London, Princess, when you passed through it?"

A shade passed over the Princess's face. "Ah—poor me! Fascinating London. I have vivid picture of the strange booses running like mad through the

streets. The houses—so close together; in no city in
world did I see houses from taxicab window—which is
only aperture out from where I ever see anything—
which did not have space between them. And oh—
how I wanted to ride in—they call them tubs—no,
tubes——" She broke off. "You—you have been in
London, Mr. Jason H. Barton?"

"Yes," he said briefly. "I spent many weeks there.
A good many of the chaps I was with called it Blighty,
however." He smiled at her puzzled face. "Well,
Princess, we have those same buses here in Chicago,
and had you ridden a hundred miles on those London
tubes you would not have seen a single piece of scenery.
But here in Chicago we have an entire subway system
with miles and miles of scenery on every side—most
bizarre scenery, to say the least."

"Scenery—in underground tube—in subway, which
means below ground? You maybe have beautiful
paintings and electric lights through tubes to amuse
passengers?"

He shook his head. "No, Princess. Our subway
system, due to our city being built on sand, and terra-
firma being so many hundreds of feet below, is built
on steel stilts high in the air. We call it an elevated
rapid transit system. From it you can gaze into perhaps one-fifth of the windows in Chicago—although
possibly I exaggerate that number a bit." He smiled.

"How fascinating," she replied naïvely. "I think
I should so like to gaze in people's windows—presum-
ing, of course, that they do not object."

"They never object," he laughed. He changed the
subject abruptly. "You are quite happy under Mr.

Li Hwei Tsung's guardianship, are you, Princess?"

She looked at him curiously. Then she shook her head slowly. "I not like honorable Tsung. And——"
She studied him closely. "Mr. Jason H. Barton, I am girl who trust everybody. Perhaps that why they don't let me see reporters. Yet I know by your eyes you are man to be trusted. If—if I make statements to you, you will promise not to put in your paper?"

He shut his notebook with a sharp snap and leaned forward. "Absolutely."

"Honorable Tsung," she said, "is not in heart like I. He hate America and Americans—he hate them bitterly. He hate England and Englishmen—just so bitterly. He hate all English-speaking white races and English-speaking countries. And I talk to him so much trying to get him to think different. But for reasons far, far back—reasons I know not—he not like the people I have just describe."

Barton restrained himself with difficulty from letting loose a whistle of astonishment. He recalled Li Hwei Tsung's sugared address to reporters at New York wherein the Chinese dignitary had pronounced the warmest and most cordial of sentiments for Americans. Almost a similar address had he given previously in London, which sentiments, somewhat condensed, had been duly printed on the American side of the Atlantic Ocean. Yet here the guileless Princess O Lyra Seng had given information quite to the contrary: that Mr. Tsung had his tongue in his cheek when he beamed gracious urbanities on either Uncle Sam or John Bull. But Barton knew one thing—and that was that not one word of her statement was going into the paper.

Indeed, he seemed to feel himself slipping under a spell that he could not understand—and the more he looked and talked with the girl across from him, the more deeply the magic of her grew upon him. Reluctantly he opened his notebook again and resumed the interview. He would have liked to talk with her of many things that could be of no interest to the world; but he was Jason H. Barton, a newspaper reporter, and he could not forget that he had a job to hold and a Frangenac to overwhelm.

"Such a student as you, Princess, has perhaps heard of psychotherapeutics—the most recent development in medicine. Two of the most prominent forms are Christian Science and Mental Healing. Do you account for the cures in any way?"

"Of them all I have read," she returned, her eyes brightening enthusiastically. "The Christian Science book I perused six times, trying to understand it. But it is very hard for Chinese girl, you know. This terrible English language! But while I do not yet fully grasp it, I think your Mary Baker Eddy and your Mental Healers and your psychotherapists, whether right or wrong, have uncovered great germic principle underlying all nature—that mind is more powerful than anything else in universe. I have vision of something back of it all—that what we want to be, we are. Does not the mind in its dreams assume the identities and the triumphs it wish to enjoy? In German I read Freud—also Jung and Adler—and I perceive then something that no one yet perceive—that the various phases of psychotherapy and the action of the subconscious mind, according to Freudian theories, are all connect by something—not apparently grasped by anyone. And so——" She stopped. "Mr. Jason H. Barton, I afraid I talk too much to you. I never get chance to talk of these things—of the things I feel and think. And it will be read by every one in Chicago?" she asked, awestricken.

He set aside his notebook. "By everyone in Chicago?" he echoed enthusiastically. "Why, Princess, this interview will be syndicated—it will be published in a paper in every city in the United States of America. It will be devoured by every man, woman and child. A new conception will rattle across the ocean about the daughter of the new Emperor of China. An ordinary interview would never have gone farther than Chicago; but this splendid exposition of yourself— why, it will be read by forty million people. It's a world-beater. Princess, you have made life very pleasant for one poor reporter."

CHAPTER XXX

B ARTON paused. A silence fell between him and the Princess O Lyra Seng. Finally he spoke again.

"And may I make a statement without offending you, Princess?" She nodded wonderingly. "I want to tell you—for you will never see Jason H. Barton again—that you are a very wonderful girl; that there are few such as you in the world. In you mingle femininity, beauty, youth, personality and insight into life and its grave questions. Princess, the man who gets you will be a very fortunate man. This is the verdict of the poor Chicago newspaper reporter who interviewed you!"

Her face was the picture of amazement. "And, Mr. Jason H. Barton, you think I am wonderful girl?" Her tone betrayed the utter incredulity in her.

"Indeed, yes," he said fervently.

She clasped her hands closer together. "And to me that is wonderful. All my life, Mr. Jason H. Barton, have I wanted to meet someone who did think I was wonderful—who could see me down to my soul. No one has ever said that to me before. Oh, but you cannot dream how I have wanted to be understood. Even my

227

honorable father does not know his O Lyra Seng. And you really think that, Mr. Jason H. Barton? That—this—is wonderful to me. Somebody—somebody at last understands O Lyra Seng." She paused. "I feel like I like to talk more to you—again to you. I think —I think I see way down in you, Mr. Jason H. Barton, that thing called personality; but you so anxious to put me down on paper that you all business and not Jason H. Barton at all."

A sudden daring idea shot into Barton's brain like a bolt from a clear sky. Over in the corner he saw a telephone. He quickly wrote a word and a number on the bottom of one of his notebook pages and tore it off. Then he leaned forward and handed it to the Princess.

"Princess, if in the next few days you feel that you would like to see Jason H. Barton again, and the honorable Tsung is not here, just raise that receiver over there, ask for this magic number in English, and ten seconds later you will be talking to me—or else to someone who can give you another magic number in place of it. And I'll be here. I'll——" He stopped short in trepidation at his own boldness.

She seized the fragment of paper and tucked it in a quaint blue-silk pocket of her Chinese costume. "I so lonely, Mr. Jason H. Barton, that minute honorable Tsung go—then I likely to do as you say. I like much to talk to those who understand me—but nobody ever quite understood O Lyra Seng yet. I am so young I live always in hope that man who marry me in China will understand me. I long to be of life, to do, to see, to think, to read, to act—yet I so unlucky as to be princess of royal blood, only daughter of my honorable father."

Barton glanced uneasily at his watch. It came suddenly to him with disturbing force that if Li Hwei Tsung should return during his visit it might lead to unfortunate—even embarrassing—complications. So he hurriedly opened his notebook to a blank page, and uncorked the end of his fountain-pen.

"Princess, will you sign this interview? Your signature, through what is known as a zinc cut, will be reproduced under your words, and you may feel sure that those words will be only those which you have given me. And, if you will, I should like you to sign further down again, so that I may keep your signature as a perpetual remembrance of a mighty pleasant meeting." He held it out to her.

Daintily she took the notebook and with the fountain-pen signed in great childish handwriting: "O Lyra Seng, Daughter of Seng Hoang-Ti of China." Beneath it she deftly made two intricate Chinese characters. Then, lower down on the same page, she duplicated the whole thing. "There," she said to him, smiling, as she handed it back to him, "I have made signature both in Chinese and American handwriting."

"You were telling me, Princess," Barton resumed, now that he had the most essential thing of the interview, "that you hoped to find in China someone who will understand you. But will you meet enough people in royal circles to give any degree of choice in marriage?"

"Well, there was once man," she explained, her face clouding up, "oh, much older as I, who say he love me. He was educated man; I know that, for he talk much with me. Then was I eleven years in age—and my honorable grandfather was on China's throne, just before China try being republic and fail. This man make serious mistake of going to my honorable grandfather with request for to marry me—we can marry so young we please in China, you know—and my honorable grandfather have him flogged. That make me very unhappy. And both my honorable father and honorable grandfather suffer for that, for this man Chu Li Yuan fled China with the Twelve Golden Coins of Confucius—and the work of centuries, of thousands of men, and millions of *taels* of silver was lost. And poor O Lyra Seng the innocent cause of it all."

"The Twelve Golden Coins of Confucius!" murmured Barton, interested. "I'm afraid I don't quite understand."

"I forgot," she said simply, "that you are not of China. You see," she explained, "when, in what in your calendar was year 478 B. C., the all-wise Confucius—in my land we call him Kong-Fu-Tse—die, he call to his bedside thirteen of his lifelong friends. To each of them did he give a golden coin hammered out by himself on his own gold-worker's anvil. He tell them, as he lay dying, that the owners of those coins shall enjoy good luck, health and prosperity to the thousandth generation—and that when those thirteen coins shall come again together in one ownership, shall China reach the highest state of which she is capable— in ethics, military prowess, civilization and wealth. These golden coins were handed down secretly from generation to generation; but two hundred years later an Emperor of the Wun dynasty constructed great spy system to ferret them out and bring them together into the coffers of the Emperor."

"And why was that?" Barton asked.

"Oh, they were so blind," the girl declared earnestly. "The rulers could not see—they cannot to-day—even my honorable father to-day does not see it any differently than his honorable fathers before him—nor do his present prime ministers nor his aids have even the proper interpretation yet—that Confucius meant it all figuratively; that if the owner of a coin believe it were able to bring luck and happiness, then the mental believe would bring that luck and happiness; that when individual superstition and individual greed had so far disappeared from mankind that the coins would be voluntarily given up to communistic ownership, then had mankind reached its highest state." She paused. "And so, during last twenty-one hundred years have thousands of spies been going through China trying to find who owns the coins of Confucius's original thirteen; millions of *taels* of silver have been spent in finding them. And one by one they have been located— their owners have been dragged into Emperor's court and forced under penalty of beheadment to give them up so that original thirteen might be brought together. After twenty-one hundred years twelve had been recovered. These were kept in great room in royal palace. And Chu Li Yuan was the keeper. It was one of highest honors in the Empire. But when my honorable grandfather have him flogged, he flee in the night; and next day most valuable thing in China's history was missing. Somewhere—perhaps between

Peking and the sea, perhaps in the mountains—did he bury them in his flight; but neither he nor they were ever seen since."

"Great Scott, Princess," commented Barton, "but that was some terrible revenge for a flogging—to undo the work of thousands of years." He paused and added jocularly: "Wouldn't it have been better if you had added your entreaties to the request of this royal Chinaman, and married him, young as you were, and helped to keep these coins which were priceless to the Emperor and the Empire?"

"But I not exactly like him," she said, with a little uneasy laugh. "I feel queer little shivers when I talk to him and look at the funny little patch of albino hair in his queue and the funny little scar on his nose. He make——"

She stopped, her eyes opening in surprise. Barton had stiffened up in his chair; there was a roaring in his ears and he felt a sudden dizziness of astonishment. He was thinking of the odd patch of white hair in the queue of Sam Toy, the dead laundryman—and the equally odd little scar across the latter's nose!

CHAPTER XXXI

THE Princess O Lyra Seng continued to gaze bewildered toward Barton. "You are ill, Mr. Jason H. Barton?" she cried apprehensively.

But for several seconds he found himself unable to make a reply. He was forcibly conjuring up again the mental picture he had of the dead Sam Toy back in the little darkened shop on Huron Street, wondering desperately if his imagination were playing tricks. But no; he seemed to recall most distinctly a short scar across the tip of the laundryman's lean yellow nose, and a wisp of white hair in the latter's queue. On top of this there occurred to him for the first time the complete isolation of the Huron Street shop, far away from Chinatown and the other Celestials in Chicago; hardly even in a good neighborhood for a laundry, since the district was poor and full of cheap lodging-houses in which the inmates did light housekeeping. Finally he collected himself and spoke hurriedly:

"Princess O Lyra Seng, will you do me a favor? Will you translate a few Chinese characters for me? I'll be greatly oblig——"

He stopped short. Outside of the stuffy hotel room he heard approaching footsteps. Then the door of the room opened slowly, and glancing over his shoul-

233

der Barton glimpsed the short, squat Asiatic whom he had last seen in the foyer of the Hotel Rydenour; and directly behind the latter was the heavily-veiled Chinese woman.

"Li Hwei Tsung!" Barton ejaculated to himself. He rose and bowed politely. "Wonder how he'll take it?"

The Chinese official stood in utter amazement in the doorway for a brief second; then he strode forward into the room, his face darkening. He looked Barton over from head to toe, then his eyes shot toward the Princess's maid, and finally toward the Princess herself. He spoke a few quick words in Chinese. The Princess replied immediately in the same tongue; and, as it seemed to Barton, rather spiritedly. At once Tsung turned to the newspaper man.

"You—you have been interviewing the Princess, sir?" he said, his voice dangerously near a snarl.

"I think," Barton reflected, to himself, "it's my move." Then aloud: "Why, yes, honorable Tsung, the Princess saw fit to talk to me of her life and her ideas. What she told me will be highly interesting to the American people." He tucked his notebook snugly into his back pocket.

"My man," stated Tsung slowly, "do you not know that you cannot publish any interview with her Highness? Those are the especial instructions from her honorable father, the sole ruler over the great Empire of China."

"But this is America, honorable Tsung," declared the younger man, nettled, "and America is a free country. So long as the Princess is of age and wished to talk to me, then I have a perfect right to take her words. It is my intention to publish it, signature and all, on the first page of my paper to-night. And when a paper gives its first page, you may be sure it highly appreciates the value of the news that covers that page."

The Chinaman moved toward him as if to strike him. He seemed to control himself by a mighty effort.

"How did you enter here?" he asked meaningly.

Barton smiled for the first time during the catechism. He knew that every hotel boasted a house detective— and he read the plan in the mind of the wily Oriental in an instant.

"I walked in, honorable Tsung, through the door. I suggest that when locking a door behind you, you try it carefully to see that the lock has not slipped back."

Tsung scratched his chin with his forefinger. A shade of annoyance flashed over his stolid features— a look that told plainer than words of self-recrimination for his own apparent carelessness. Finally he looked up.

"I do not wish to make threats," he announced, "but if you attempt to publish that interview, it will go bad with you in Chicago. The Chinese Empire has much power." He waved his hand in an impressive sweep. "It extends even to newspapers."

At this juncture Barton turned toward the Princess, who had stood motionless all the while, evidently cowed by the presence of her official guardian. "Princess O Lyra Seng, I have stenographic notes of all you have said. I prize those notes most highly. Yet if you say give them up, I shall do so. If not—may I use them?"

The Princess smiled reassuringly, and opened her mouth to speak. But even before her words came, Tsung snapped his fingers furiously toward the maid and spoke rapidly in Chinese, turning his head toward his wife and addressing a few words to her in the same tongue. A second later, both women had taken the Princess by the shoulders and were leading her almost forcibly into the next room. In the excitement Barton took up his hat and edged over until he was between the door of the stuffy plush parlor and the angry Tsung himself. And with the closing of the door of the adjacent room, he found himself quite alone with the Chinese official. Tsung came quickly to business.

"Fortunately," he said sneeringly, "I am long enough in your America to know how to talk in concrete American terms. Evidently, my dear sir, you realize that you hold the upper hand. Let us speak, then, in terms of the American dollar. Exactly how many of them, Mr. Reporter, do you ask for your notes and your forgetfulness of the Princess's words?" He fumbled in his back pocket and withdrew a fat tan leather wallet, burned over with intricate Chinese dragons.

Barton laughed contentedly. He waved a hand away from him. "Please—please don't attempt to talk money to me, honorable Tsung. You have evidently made a mistake in sizing me up. If a million dollars were flung on that table over there it wouldn't move me. I have a right to that interview and I intend to keep it. Unfortunately you are from another land, and therefore don't know American newspapers and newspaper men. News ranks just a little higher, you see, the world over, than mere money."

The Chinaman stood with his wallet in his hand and gazed at the newspaper man most carefully, evidently taking in the splendid physique and the clear eye of his opponent in the duel of words. Perhaps, as an official of a great empire, he had a due appreciation both of physical strength and psychology—of the strength of the human body and the strength of character—for he suddenly changed his tack entirely.

"What is the name of your paper?" he asked, not unfriendly.

"The *Chicago Evening Dispatch*," returned Barton coolly.

"And your editor?"

Barton surveyed him through half-closed eyes. "I imagine I see what he's driving at now," he thought. "Lord, if he only knew Frangenac as I know him! He could put a ten-thousand-dollar bill on Frangenac's desk, and old Frog-Eater would fling it back in his face." Then he answered the other's query: "Leon Raoul Frangenac."

"Very well," replied Tsung quietly. "You may go. I thank you." He stepped over to the door and held it open.

It was plain that the interview was at an end; so Barton backed rather ungracefully out of the room and into the narrow corridor. The stout oak door that barred the way to the elevator was now partly ajar on account of Tsung's entrance into the suite; the silver shingle of the key hung loosely from it on the outside. He stepped from the corridor into the outside hall and

pressed the button of the elevator. A moment later
he was travelling downward with the elevator boy staring rather suspiciously at him.

Outside on Michigan Avenue, in the bright noon
sunshine, Barton laughed aloud with sheer glee. "The
wily old devil—trying to buy me off with money. And
now he thinks he can buy Frangenac off. That's good.
That's even funny! Poor Princess O Lyra—to have
to take her trip round the world under the care of that
old codger and his wife!" He sighed a deep sigh.
"And—and what a wonderful girl she is!"

Instead of making his way back to the *Dispatch*
office, he boarded a State Street car in the Loop, and
shortly afterwards was back on the north side again,
walking rapidly westward toward the Huron Street
laundry of the dead Sam Toy. As he turned in at the
door of the shop, he glimpsed a sign in the window
which showed him pointedly that there was nothing
in the universe swifter than the American business instinct. The sign read simply:

"TO RENT.—Apply to PATRICK McGURK,
740 N. State St."

The same officer was still stationed grumpily in the
doorway, and he looked up with evident surprise as
Barton stepped in and closed the door behind him.

"Back again?" he grunted. "Few of your brothers
have been here, took a look, and blew out again. Body's
going to be taken to the police department morgue in
half an hour—then I lock up and send the key over to
the landlord."

"Guess I'm just in time, then," said Barton easily. "Want to have a second look at the Chink."

He strode into the back room and went over to the cot. The space at the back of the partition wasn't particularly light, so he struck a match in order to view the features of the dead Chinaman more accurately. A tiny scar was across the nose; and in the queue, lost at times among the bristling black hairs, was an undoubted strand of white albino hair weaving back and forth. Barton blew out the match and tossed it in the corner. The words of the Princess O Lyra came back to him with startling clarity: "Somewhere —perhaps between Peking and the sea, perhaps in the mountains, did he bury them in his flight. But neither he nor they were ever seen since."

"It's Yuan all right," he said incredulously. "Chu Li Yuan himself! I can hardly believe it, either." He turned from the body. "And now comes the big scoop when I get that half a translation from Professor Chan Fu at Chicago U. Will it say anything about the Twelve Golden Coins of Confucius, I'm wondering?"

CHAPTER XXXII

TSUNG MAKES A CALL

AFTER the newspaper man had left, Tsung paced angrily up and down the stuffy parlor of the suite. In the next room feminine voices, punctuated here and there by girlish voices, chattered excitedly; and an expert psychologist might have detected in the chattering the traces of sex sympathy rather than recrimination or discipline.

As for Tsung, he stopped finally and poked his head in the next room, addressing a few words to his wife. Then he jammed his hat on his head and left the room. A second later he had locked the great door that led into the suite and was in the elevator itself.

Down in the lobby he quickly had a taxicab summoned, and climbing in, gave the driver the instructions: "*Evening Dispatch* office, if you please."

From the Rydenour on Michigan Avenue to the *Dispatch* office on dark, dirty Market Street was only a drive of five minutes for a taxicab. In front of Newspaper Row the Chinaman dismounted, and bidding the chauffeur wait, ascended the worn steps of the *Dispatch* building.

Inside he inquired from a scurrying reporter the method of reaching "the honorable Mr. Leon Raoul Frangenac, editor," and, securing a list of hurried directions, made the climb up the wooden stairway, past long rooms in which batteries of linotype machines were clicking methodically away.

He paused undecidedly in the doorway of the city room, gazing curiously about at the reporters working feverishly away at the scattered typewriters, the floor covered with scraps of paper, the signs of indescribable confusion that seemed to permeate even the very atmosphere. Then, catching sight of the ground-glass cage that bore the words "City Editor," he strode down the long room and rapped politely on the door.

Frangenac, working inside with his collar and tie off, his sleeves rolled up, his desk covered with a great tangle of clippings, takes, 'phone numbers, books, telegrams and miscellaneous papers, growled an unwelcome "Come in," and went on working without even looking up. Yeah!" he snapped, as he heard the door open and close, and he proceeded to dive into a great dictionary for the spelling of a word of which he was not sure. "Whatchwant?"

"Honorable Frangenac—city editor of *Dispatch?*" he heard a polite voice inquire at his elbow.

Surprised, Frangenac glanced up. Some feet from him was a short, squat Chinaman dressed in a most stylish suit of imported Scotch tweeds. "Li Hwei Tsung is my name," he heard the visitor announce deferentially. "I am the prime minister of the new Chinese Empire."

"Glad to meet you, Mr. Tsung," said Frangenac, rising. He indicated a chair near his desk. "Have a seat. What may I do for you, Mr. Tsung?"

Tsung dropped into the chair indicated. He glanced

about the tiny room for a moment before he spoke. Then he drove straight to his subject.

"Mr. Frangenac, I am a man of few words—like most of my countrymen. I regret that I do not speak French, for I perceive that you are a Frenchman, and what few words I shall use might be more explicit in your mother tongue. But English it will have to be." He paused. "You undoubtedly know that the honorable Emperor has appointed me the official guardian of his daughter, the Princess O Lyra Seng of China, on her trip around the world?" Frangenac nodded wonderingly. "The Princess is not a diplomat, Mr. Frangenac. And for that reason her honorable father has given me the most strict instructions that no interviews from her shall get into your splendid American papers. I hope you understand."

Frangenac wrinkled his brows. "I'm afraid I don't just get it," he announced genially. "We should be glad to have an interview with the Princess—and would be willing to have you direct the channels in which that interview runs."

Tsung made a gesture of dissent. "It is not that of which I have come to speak. I am here to talk in concrete terms. One hour ago one of your reporters—I have not his name—forced his way into the Princess's apartment and secured an interview with her—a complete interview—and even took notes of her words. He——"

"The devil you say!" broke in Frangenac delightedly. "The devil!—and I didn't think Barton could do it."

Tsung's face darkened. "But that interview must

never see the light of American print," he announced
meaningly; "for if it should, I would never be able to
explain matters to her honorable father in Peking. So
I am here, honorable Frangenac, to talk to you of
methods of suppressing that interview in its entirety.
You Americans—and because you are in charge of an
American paper I include you under that category—
are a peculiar race—a race that measures everything
in terms of what you call the dollar. I therefore
frankly ask you, honorable Frangenac, exactly how
many of those dollars it will require to have the *Dispatch* go to the print-presses to-night without the
words of the Princess O Lyra Seng gracing its splendid front pages?"

Frangenac leaned back in his chair and, twirling his
waxed moustaches gleefully, gave a deep, hearty laugh.

"My dear Mr. Tsung," he said happily, "I couldn't
conceive of any number of dollars that might induce
me to forego such a scoop as that. Indeed, no! I'm
afraid you haven't a due appreciation of the Press."
He paused. "Why, good Lord, man, we're not going
to pound the Princess! I'll wager that it's the most
complimentary interview that you ever saw. We're not
scurrilous in what we write about people. I haven't
seen it myself yet, for Barton hasn't come back. But
I know his general line of news-writing."

Tsung leaned forward and pounded his fist angrily
on the other's desk. "You are blind, then, if you look
at it in that way. You have no possible conception of
the probable effect upon the destinies of the new empire for the Princess to go about foreign countries
spouting her idealistic theories of life and love and a

hundred other silly things." He paused. "Here," he said curtly, "I am a busy man. There is much in Chicago I must do before we go. Say that I pay over to you one thousand of your dollars—secured in any way you wish. You, in return, will see that that is the end of the interview."

Frangenac's face grew dark. His forehead crinkled up in a frown. "Did you make any such offer to Barton?"

Tsung replied curiously: "I intimated some such reward. I am a man of action and deeds. But the young fool is full of idealistic theories of news, as he calls it. So I decided to go to an older man—and 'from there, if necessary, to the owner of the *Dispatch*."

Frangenac gave a short, hard laugh. "Owner's travelling in California just now—and yours truly is fiscal agent, president, chief clerk, bottle-washer and editor of this rag." He paused. Then he spoke in the Oriental's direction. "Honorable Tsung, you are of another race—and you can't understand some of our ideas. If any other man but yourself had come in here with such an offer, I should have had him kicked downstairs by a dozen reporters, if necessary. But, as I say, you are not to blame—you do not grasp us. You are of another world. There was a time once in my life when money and the power of money seemed everything—but that time has passed with my youth. This sheet to me is like a precious toy to a child—it is my life—and this is a life job for me, in all probability. Your thousand dollars couldn't tempt me to strike out one word of an interview which might give the *Dispatch* the advantage over other papers. If you laid a cold hundred thousand on the desk, I should have to turn it back to you. But because you are from another land, I should do it politely. I am getting on in years, you see, and with respect to news have even more ideals than the youthful Barton." He tapped himself on the chest. "You were not talking. to Mr. Frangenac, Mr. Tsung. You were talking to the *Dispatch.* I—I am the *Dispatch.*"

CHAPTER XXXIII

"SAVEGEAU"

AS Frangenac talked, Tsung's face grew more and more wrathful. His lean fingers kneaded themselves into his palms until his long nails bit into the skin. Frangenac himself, at the end of his speech, leaned forward toward the Chinese potentate, emphasizing his every remark with his forefinger. And as he did so, the loose neck of his shirt, where he had removed the collar, fell away. Barely visible on the chest was the bearded head of some mythological figure, adroitly tattooed; and as he leaned forward still a degree further there was revealed, slightly foreshortened, to the ever-watchful Chinese observer, the figure of nothing less than a satyr with hairy goat's legs, its hands strumming on a six-stringed lyre, the whole done in red and blue and vari-colored inks that had faded considerably with the passing of years. At the sight of it the Oriental's jaw dropped with a strange emotion; apparently oblivious to the words of the other, his slant eyes widened first at the sight of the half-animal, half-human figure, and then, travelling from it, fastened themselves on Frangenac's countenance, searchingly, feelingly, as though groping far back in his memory for something he could not quite place.

"So there you have it, honorable Tsung," concluded

Frangenac, leaning back at length in his swivel chair.
"You must appreciate the position of the Press as being
higher than money or anything else."

Tsung made no retort. His face was a study. Suddenly he pointed to the one window of the city editor's
tiny office. "Did you see the enormous crowd on the
street below?" he inquired blandly.

"Crowd!" ejaculated Frangenac. "Crowd? No!
Something must have happened. Maybe a story right
in front of a newspaper office and nobody to cover it."
He rose quickly from his chair and hobbled over to the
window, where he looked out. Then he turned back
to the Chinaman. "There's no crowd down there now,"
he said, mystified.

He returned to the desk and stood looking down at
the Oriental. On both his trip to the window and his
trip back to the desk, the creak of his artificial leg
was evidently not lost on his visitor, for a casual spectator might have noticed the strangest of looks pass
over the Chinaman's face as the latter listened tensely
to each squeak in the city editor's stride.

"Sit down—honorable Frangenac," ordered Tsung.
"It seemed to me when first I entered this room that far
back in my memory was another Frenchman, with a
pair of beady black eyes like yours. But that figure
with the goat legs on your chest—and the squeak of
your leg! Ah, how it brings back strange memories
to me! Look at me, Savegeau. Do you remember
me?"

At his words, Frangenac's face flushed chalky white.
He stared down in horror at the Celestial and weakly
dropped down in his chair.

"You—you are mistaken," he choked nervously. "I—I do not know you."

"So you lost the leg?" said Tsung easily. "I never saw you after that last day—but I heard of it." He shook his head amusedly. "Don't try to deny it, Savegeau. Look at me. I am an old man—shrivelled and a little yellow—and becoming shrunken like a li-chee nut. Yet look at me carefully, Savegeau."

Frangenac hunched down in his chair, the picture of fright and dismay.

"You—you are—you are—Li Ling?" he said in a hoarse whisper.

"Yes, Li Ling himself," nodded Tsung cheerfully, rubbing his lean yellow hands together. "We Chinamen, friend Savegeau, as we rise in the world pass through what we might term an evolution of names. Then I was Li Ling—hoping some day to bear the great suffix Hoang-Ti. But Ling Hoang-Ti it was not to be. To-day I am Li Hwei Tsung. Perhaps it was for the best. And what have you got to say now, friend Savegeau?"

"My God, Ling!" murmured Frangenac weakly. "Not—not so loud. I—didn't dream—you—prime minister of the new Chinese Empire. I saw you drop that day—when hell broke loose. I—I always thought you were dead. I—I never dreamed."

"I am far from dead, honorable Savegeau." The Chinaman laid a sneering stress on the word "honorable." "Bullets do not always kill—although they sometimes cripple." He looked about the room. "Savegeau—city editor of an American newspaper. What a handy thing it is, is it not, to speak English?

H'm. Afraid, eh, to go back to France after—that?"
He laughed aloud. "Suppose we revert once more to
the subject of interviews. Will you offer me a thousand dollars, dear Savegeau, not to give a splendid
news story to the Chicago newspaper men this afternoon?"

Frangenac's voice was nothing but the shadow of a
voice. "A thousand dollars," he said faintly. "A thousand dollars—Ling? Oh, man, man, I—I can't get a
thousand dollars. Ling——" He leaned forward and
seized the other by the coat-lapel. "Ling, you don't—
you wouldn't call in the reporters," he pleaded. "Of
what use could it be to you? And it would mean for
me——"

"That you could not enjoy a peaceful night's sleep
in any white country on the globe," retorted Tsung
savagely. He shook off the other's grasp of his coat-
lapel. "Come, come, man; brace up. Tsung does not
need money. We were friends in a common cause
once. Now he needs a favor. He simply demands one
concession: that interview with the Princess O Lyra
Seng must not appear to-day or any other day. Is my
little favor granted or not? Remember—I am now
offering nothing."

"Yes—yes—Ling," mumbled Frangenac feverishly;
"it is granted. I promise you that, Ling. It is granted. It shall not appear. I promise you." He put his
head in his hands and thought intently for a moment.
Then, wide-eyed, he looked up at the other. His words
were more calm. "It is not a simple matter, Ling, to
kill it. But it will be killed—please be assured of that.
If he even suspects that I were going to suppress such

a big thing as that, he'd go straight to the office of the *Sun*—and they'd give him a bigger job than he's ever had a chance of having here." He thought hard again, chewing on his thin lips. Then he faced Tsung. "There's but one sure way to do it, Ling, and that way I'll follow. I can send him off post-haste to Washington this afternoon as soon as he writes it up—to help Carstairs with the developments on the impeachment of Speaker Farley. By the date the Chicago papers reach Washington—and he writes in hot-headed for an explanation—it'll be dead cold stuff; you and your party will be on your way back to your land. And then I'll—I'll convince him some way that—that Great Britain—the—the British consul—stepped in, pulled some international wires and prevented its publication. Ling—will that suffice?"

The Chinaman arose. "It will. But see that you follow it out in every detail, Savegeau," he warned. "We leave for 'Frisco in another forty-eight hours and go from there back to China. I shall say good-bye now for ever; but if that interview comes out in this or any other paper, I shall have an interview myself with the newspaper men—and it will astound your Chicago."

"I tell you, Ling, it will be killed—for good and all. I assure you of that." Frangenac rose. He passed one hand dazedly over his white forehead. Then he thrust out the other trembling hand. "Good—good-bye, Ling, and—and good luck to you. Good-bye."

The Chinaman looked down at the proffered hand, and a faint smile curved his lips as he noted how it shook.

"Li Hwei Tsung does not shake hands with such as you," he sneered. He turned on his heel and a moment later was gone.

With the closing of the office door, Frangenac slumped down into his chair again, the picture of shame, defeat and humiliation. *"Le Bon Dieu!"* he groaned softly to himself, lapsing unconsciously for a second into his own tongue. "But who would dream that the threads of life can weave as they do?" He dropped his head in his arms and remained thinking for ten long minutes. When he sat up, his face was more calm, his black eyes held a colder light than ever before, his lips were set in a hard line of determination. "Thank God, though, it wasn't too late! Now—now to fix Barton."

He raised the receiver of his desk instrument and a second later was telephoning downstairs to the cashier's office for transportation and expense money for one correspondent to go to Washington, D. C.

CHAPTER XXXIV

A CROSSING OF SWORDS

BARTON remained only long enough in Sam Toy's shop to make sure that the dead laundryman bore the peculiar physical disfigurement that the Princess had spoken of in regard to the missing Chu Li Yuan, keeper of the Confucian coins. Then, with a long, contemplative glance about the hopelessly bare room, he left the shop and sped to the nearest car line.

It was a quarter to one when he ran lightly up the steps of the *Dispatch*. Entering the city room, he saw that the door of Frangenac's office was closed; but he also noted by the silhouette on the ground-glass panels that the city editor was alone and hunched down at his desk. So, for once in his life, he walked in without knocking.

"Well, Mr. Frangenac, I got it," he announced triumphantly. "A most astounding full-page interview with the most astounding little piece of femininity the world will ever know." He tapped himself on the chest heroically. A man can indulge in a few antics when a man has achieved the impossible. "Jason H. Barton—mixed American and British—has interviewed the Princess O Lyra Seng."

A queer smile settled over Frangenac's lips. He rose from his chair and gingerly thrust out his hand.

252

"You're all right, Barton," he said abjectly. "I owe you an apology for all I said this morning. I am sorry, my boy; really sorry. As you Americans so aptly say: I take my hat off to you." He coughed nervously and glanced out through the tail of his eye at the few reporters in the city room. "The boys will tell you a Chinaman called on us a short while ago. It was Li Hwei Tsung. He's furious. He tried to get the Old Man's address, but I wouldn't give it to him. After making a few threats about seeing both the British consul and the Chinese consul as well, he sailed off to one or the other of the two offices. Says he'll stop that interview if it tangles up the whole foreign office." He laughed a short, hard laugh. "Of course it's all bluff. He can't do anything—I don't believe."

"Of course he can't," Barton snapped. "He's just bluffing. The British consul isn't going to interfere with a thing like that. And the Chinese consul can't do anything even if he wanted to."

Frangenac nodded absent-mindedly. Then he looked up. "All right, boy. Never mind telling me how you got it; jump to your machine and hammer it out. It'll be on the first page to-night and on the Associated Press wire for syndication. I'm holding space for it. So hop to it. Then I've got some interesting news for you."

Barton, much mollified by the city editor's unusually friendly attitude, walked back to his machine and tossed his hat on the hook near it. He nodded to one or two of the boys across the room, and jerked the rubber cover off his typewriter. Then he rolled in a sheet of white paper. He was just about to strike the keys when a sudden thought struck him instead. He reached into the drawer of his desk and took out a sheet of carbon paper. "Guess I'll make a copy to read in future years," he said to himself sadly, "in case they have to cut it anywhere to fit space. Inside of a month it'll all seem like a glorious dream."

He jerked out the sheet, inserted the carbon paper between two clean sheets of paper, and rolled them all back under the platen again. Then followed for three quarters of an hour a furious clicking, in which he jerked sheet after sheet from his typewriter, each written in the white heat of furious creative effort. Part of the interview he furnished from memory—part from the stenographic notes he always took. At times the sheets rolled out so fast that he almost forgot to insert his carbon paper, but he always caught himself in time and succeeded in making for his personal possession a pale-blue duplicate of every one.

At last he was finished. He mopped his forehead and gathered first the original sheets together, then the carbon copies. The latter he sealed in a long envelope with the duplicate of the Princess's signature, which he tore off the page in his notebook. After depositing the precious envelope in the breast pocket of his coat, he took in the loose originals to Frangenac.

"Read—and marvel," he said grandiloquently to the other. He opened his notebook and tore out the first signature the Princess had made. "And here's the name for a little zinc etching to put at the bottom of the whole blame thing."

Frangenac, glancing over the sheets, appeared entranced. "It's splendid, Barton; it's splendid. It's a remarkable interview—really—really—it's remarkable!" For several minutes he continued to shuffle the pages, commenting at every one. Then he looked up. "Splendid! Now let me take your notebook to file away in case of any possible complications in the matter. You know, my boy, a matter of safety first."

Barton, somewhat surprised at the request, tendered the other his notebook. The city editor, his leg squeaking at every step, hobbled over to the big iron safe in the corner and locked it carefully away.

"And now," remarked Barton cheerfully, "I don't want that thing changed very much in the editing. I'm going to leave that to you, Mr. Frangenac. Also, I'll have to tell you later all about how I got it; right now I'm going out on the biggest little story that's ever broken yet around this little old London of the West. And God knows when I'll get it or when I'll get back."

"Wait!" said Frangenac sharply. He raised a hand. "Wait! You forgot that good news. You're going to Washington, D. C., on the three o'clock Washington Flyer. You're appointed special correspondent of the *Dispatch* during the impeachment trial of Speaker Farley. If you've got a little story up your sleeve, you'll have to pass it over to some other man."

"To Washington!" ejaculated Barton, in a tone of dismay that surprised the other man. "To Washington?" he repeated. "But, Mr. Frangenac, I tell you I've got a story bigger than the *Dispatch* has printed in six months. To Washington—on the three o'clock train?" His voice trailed away in utter unbelief.

"Exactly," said the other calmly. "Carstairs has his hands full in Washington on the latest leak inquiry.

Now that the impeachment trial is to start, he's wired for another man. I've wired back that I'm sending the *Dispatch's* best man on the Washington Flyer. You'll get full instructions from Carstairs. Grab a taxi to your rooms and throw just the things you need into a suit-case. Trial begins at ten to-morrow morning. It'll mean a daily column from the Capitol—with hot interviews of all the Congressmen involved in the thing. Boy, it's the finger of Fate welcoming you to something big." Frangenac shot open the drawer of his desk. He took from it a paper and a sheaf of bills. "Here's your credential paper, filled in and stamped with our seal. Here's one hundred dollars for your fare and expense money. Sign here on this line. And I'm raising your salary fifteen dollars a week."

Barton, stupefied at the sudden turn of affairs, not quite certain whether to throw up his hat in joy or to stamp his foot in rage, stood silently staring at the other.

"But—but, Frangenac," he said feebly, "you don't understand. I—I can't go to Washington. I tell you, Frangenac, you'll—you'll have to send some-one else."

Across Frangenac's face flashed a sudden trace of anger at the recalcitrancy of one of his humble re-porters. He stroked his black pointed beard angrily, and gave a vicious twist to one of the points of his waxed moustache. "Come, come, Barton," he said sharply. "Forget it, please. We haven't time to waste this way. Unless you hop on the Washington job by way of the three o'clock train, you can sever your con-nection with the *Dispatch* right now. You brought me a splendid interview—a tremendous one—I compliment you—and now I offer you something that means about two weeks' work in the Capitol; it's a chance that any reporter in the country would jump at like a frog after a piece of red flannel. Yet there you stand, wailing about a two-by-four Chicago story—probably a fizzle at that. Don't care what's up your sleeve; here's something good staring you in the face. Wake up, Barton. Are you asleep, man?"

It was trembling on Barton's lips to pour out the whole strange story of the Twelve Golden Coins of Confucius, the dead Sam Toy, and the laundry ticket with the cryptic hieroglyphics, but something seemed to halt him. He didn't feel in the mood now for incurring the anger of a man who was in full control of the *Dispatch* on account of the owner's absence. Indeed, a change of heart had come about in him since learning that Fawcett had walked the streets without landing a job. So it might not be good policy to antagonize the one individual who governed his present berth.

But the thought of Fawcett, sitting jobless in his dim little room in the Star Hotel on the north side, gave Barton a sudden daring idea. If he should play a trick on Frangenac and then proceed to land the startling story that seemed trembling already above his head, he knew full well that he could appease the city editor. He thought harder than he ever had in his life. Fawcett, when sober, was a crack newspaper man. There was none better in the Middle West. True, the Capitol city of prohibition America was literally a river of whisky; and yet, Fawcett had given his promise. And as for Fawcett, when he was on the water wagon he had approached some of the biggest men in the country. Barton made up his mind in an instant.

"I'll go," he snapped out. He jerked out his old leather bill-fold and seized the credential paper, noting first that it was stamped correctly with the *Dispatch* seal and that his name had been filled in on the line left blank for that purpose. He jabbed it viciously in the bill-fold, and buttoned the latter article in his breast pocket. He leaned over and made a quick count of the money lying on Frangenac's desk, and scribbled his name to the receipt that appeared to be all in readiness. "I've got to make speedy time if I'm to throw my things together and catch the three o'clock train," he said quietly. "What am I to do when I get there."

"I'll send full telegraphic instructions to Carstairs to-night," returned Frangenac, drawing in a long breath between his thin lips. "He'll inform you on everything and start you out. He'll go ahead with the leak inquiry, and you'll handle the Speaker Farley trial. Give us all that looks good." He glanced toward the big wooden clock. Its hands pointed to 1.45. "Now go, man. Trial starts at ten to-morrow—and you must reach the Capitol at nine."

A moment later Barton stood on the steps of the *Dispatch*. "Of all the cursed blooming luck," he groaned aloud, "that ever hit a hound hot on the scent! It couldn't have happened any time but now. But, thank God, there's more than one way to skin a cat."

Frantically he hailed a yellow taxicab that was rolling aimlessly down Market Street, its metal flag reading "Vacant." The machine stopped at the curb. "Star Hotel, 550 Wells Street," he instructed the driver. "And make time, please. Got to catch a train."

The taxicab ran down Madison Street at a moderate rate of speed, but reaching Wells Street was soon shooting like an arrow over the bridge. Down below, a number of schooners, their sides plastered with gaudy circus bills, were tied up to the docks in the bright sunshine; a tug, belching black smoke, darted along the sea-green river. But Barton saw no schooners, no posters, no tug; his mind was far away.

Up Wells Street the machine shot, and with a whining and shrieking of the brakes, drew up sharply in front of the same dilapidated building which Barton had entered once before that day. He sprang out, and ordering the driver to wait, dived up the dark inside stairs three steps at a time. At the rear room on the third floor he didn't pause to knock, but flung open the door.

Fawcett stood in front of the mirror putting on a collar and tie. Barton's quick glance about the room showed that not a sign of a bottle or glass was visible. He noted also, as the man at the mirror turned in surprise, that the latter was shaved and clean; that his eye possessed a light of keenness and force, quite different from the sodden drunkard's eye that had characterized him during later years.

"What the—— Barton!" Fawcett ejaculated, staring.

Barton closing the door behind him, jumped quickly

to his proposition. "Charlie, do you still want a news-paperman's job? Speak quick, man—a temporary job in Washington?"

The other nodded dazedly, not comprehending.

"Then you're going to the Capitol with an A No. 1 credential paper and a fat wad of railroad fare and expenses, under the name of Jason H. Barton. You're going to send back a daily write-up of the Speaker Farley trial. And yours truly is going to be scooting *sub rosa* about town here, unearthing the biggest little story ever sprung in the State of Illinois!"

CHAPTER XXXV

WITH the ends of the loose tie trailing over his shoulders, Fawcett gazed blankly at his visitor. "Not—not kidding me, are you, Jason? Do you mean to say——"

"Exactly," retorted the younger man. "Tie up that tie and listen to me. First: do you know Reedy, Carstairs, McClintock, Hempfield or Van Slyke—the Washington correspondents for the Chicago papers?"

Fawcett shook his head vehemently. "No, Jason. Don't know any of 'em."

"Good," commented Barton hurriedly. "Neither do I." Hastily he related the brief facts of his interview with Frangenac, not wasting any time by going into details as to what his "story" was about. And he finished: "So you see, Charlie, that Fate sent you along just in time. You lope down to Washington with my credential paper, tell Carstairs that you're Jason H. Barton, write up whatever Carstairs tells you to take care of, and shoot the stuff back each day. When the Speaker Farley trial is over, back you come. If my story works out to anything like I hope it may, I'll go to Frangenac long before and confess my share of the deception; but if by some chance it should fizzle, I'll lie low till you come back to town. Then I'll march

261

into Frangenac's office—fresh from Washington! Sound good, old man?"

"But listen to me, boy," put in the older man uneasily. "You're a fool to chuck this chance for any story. It means an opportunity to meet some of the biggest senators in the Capitol. Don't know what you've got up your sleeve, but drop it. Never mind about me. God knows I'd like the chance—and under any conditions I'd turn back to you half of the salary money they send on. But——"

"But me no buts," returned Barton firmly. "And you'll send back no money—except perhaps the ten I loaned you. That's final." He stooped down and dragged from beneath the bed the other's leather suitcase; then an empty travelling bag with gaping mouth. "Do we pack in a hurry—or don't we?" he asked with his hand on it.

"We pack," said Fawcett quietly. "I won't let you back out now, Jason, even if you want to. That Washington job is mine—and I pay nothing for the use of your name. Nothing—remember that!"

While Fawcett finished his toilet, Barton packed the other's few belongings hurriedly into the two leather containers. His watch showed the time to be twenty minutes after two; so he gave his instructions while he packed. In ten minutes the room was bare and the suit-case and travelling bag stood in the middle of the floor.

Down in the office Fawcett handed in his key to the greasy-looking man in the shirt-sleeves, and together he and Barton entered the taxicab, still waiting at the curb. The drive to the Grand Central station took a full fifteen minutes on account of a traffic jam at Adams Street; so Barton himself carried the suit-case over to the baggage counter while Fawcett secured the ticket and Pullman berth. The Washington Flyer was drawn up on track six, the engine coupled to it, the smoke-stack smoking in the train-shed.

Rejoined by Fawcett, and the suit-case checked through, Barton passed through the iron gates with the older man and saw him on the smoker. Then he stood outside on the platform, talking up to the other in the window of the coach. It was eight minutes to three when Fawcett, evidently recollecting something he had forgotten to say, leaned out of the window still further and beckoned the young man close to the coach.

"I've got your business cards, Jason, but I mighty near forgot the credential paper," he said in a low voice. "Slip it to me. Also, you haven't told me what hotel I'm to find Carstairs at. I'll have a devil of a time locating him around the big Capitol building between the time the train gets in and the trial starts."

Barton scratched his head, struck by the fact of his own forgetfulness. "Charlie," he replied quickly, glancing again at his watch, "I didn't forget the matter of the credential paper. I slipped it in the suit-case —in the pocket back of the shirt straps. But I did forget about Carstairs' hotel, though." He wrinkled his brows, stepping aside as a baggage truck bearing Fawcett's suit-case bore down upon him and rolled up to the open door of the baggage car. He looked up. "Strange thing, too, that that matter didn't occur to

Frangenac." Watch in hand, he thought quickly for a moment. "Old man, we've got seven minutes till the train pulls out. I'll beat it back to the waiting-room, call up Frangenac, tell him I'm just ready to board the Flyer, and ask him about that matter. And it'll help to lend a bona-fide appearance to this stunt of mine." He spun quickly on his heel. "If I fail to get back in time, you'll have to connect with Carstairs around the Capitol building some way. But I'll do my best to be back here before the train pulls out. So long, old man."

With a final nod to the gloomy Fawcett, now lolling back in his seat with an unlighted cigar in his mouth, Barton hurried back along the platform and into the big waiting-room. There he found all six telephone booths filled with people, and he fumed angrily up and down for a minute, until the occupant of one came out. Whereupon he hurried into it, and closing the door on the heavy, foul air, he dropped a nickel in the slot and asked for Central 4444.

A clicking ensued. The voice that answered he recognized at once as that of the girl switchboard operator in the *Dispatch* office.

"Mr. Frangenac, please."

"Sorry," she said, "but Mr. Frangenac's line is busy. Will you call again, sir, or shall I hold the wire? Anyone else?"

"Listen, Nelly," put in Barton eagerly, "this is Jason Barton of the editorial rooms. I'm at the depot supposed to leave for Washington in seven minutes, and Frangenac's forgotten to give me all my instructions. I've got to talk to him. The baggage is on the train and the bells are ringing now. Please break him off, Nelly—quick."

The girl seemed in some indecision. "I'll tell you what I'll do," she returned quickly. "I can't cut him off—but I'll cut you into his conversation and you can get what you want and make your train. I'll——" She cut herself off as she made some change on the switchboard that threw Barton squarely into another connection.

He had just opened his mouth to shout: "Listen, Frangenac, it's me, Barton," when he stifled his words even as they trembled on his tongue. Frangenac was talking, but the startling thing about that fact was that he was talking of no one else but Barton himself.

"I fixed Barton, Ling," he was saying. "I got him off to Washington with a raise and a commission, and it will be several days before he will know that the interview is killed. Then it will be what we term old stuff. Also, I've got his notebook, all his copy and the Princess's signature. I shall be glad to give these all to you if you will come here—or shall I send a boy over to the Rydenour with them?"

Barton gasped when he heard the voice of Li Hwei Tsung in the receiver.

"That is very good, Savegeau. Li Hwei Tsung compliments you on your clever workmanship." The voice ceased for an instant. "But what will you tell him when he does learn the truth?"

Savegeau! Barton wondered dazedly if he had heard aright.

"I'll simply have to humor him—even if it means still more salary for a while. I intend, though, to tell him that international complications arose after you saw the Chinese consul, and that the thing had to be suppressed. Don't fear, Ling. I have hushed it up for good. It hurt me to do it—it was a remarkable interview—but I've done everything you asked. You —you are satisfied?"

"Quite satisfied," came back the voice of the Oriental in the 'phone. "As to the three articles you mentioned, I shall leave it to you to destroy them all. I think you understand the situation correctly. You have done very well. We leave the city day after to-morrow, and while I shall get the Chicago papers in San Francisco, I believe this is the end of it. Good-bye—Savegeau."

As the clicking sounded forth, Barton, too, hung up his receiver and strode from the booth, hot and perspiring. Far down the track the engine bell on number six was ringing, white-capped porters were pulling in their stools, brass-buttoned brakemen were shouting "All aboard!" But Barton was oblivious to it all.

"The sly devil of—of—of a Frangenac!" he choked in suppressed rage. "The sly devil! Shooting me off to Washington—and killing the whole interview." He stared dumbfoundedly into space. "Savegeau— Frangenac, Tsung—Ling!" The train on track six, with a screaming of axles, pulled out and rolled away over the sunlight-covered railroad yards. "But it's Fawcett that's on his way to Washington," Barton said grimly to himself, "and not little innocent Jason Barton. The latter's on his way to the offices of the

Chicago *Sun*—and he's thinking that that interview, signature and all, will be on the news stands to-morrow morning."

He jostled his way through the waiting-room of the depot, and, taking a taxicab out in front, drove straight to the offices of the *Sun.*

CHAPTER XXXVI

ARRIVING at the *Sun* offices, Barton went straight upstairs to the city room, and sent in his card to the city editor by an ink-smudged copy boy. The city editor, however, proved to be busy with a visitor. Nothing daunted, Barton left the city room, and, proceeding along the outer corridor, turned the handle of a ground-glass door which bore the words, "L. Britton, Proprietor and Editor-in-Chief." The room that he entered was filled with waiting people, held in submission by an office boy with a baleful glare in his eye. This time, however, Barton did not send in his plain card to the inner office, but wrote carefully on the back of it: "The man who interviewed the Princess O Lyra Seng." Then he dropped into the nearest chair and waited.

The office boy appeared a moment later and beckoned him in. "Mr. Britton seys 'e'll see yer," was the precious information which he vouchsafed, to the consternation of the other waiting occupants.

Barton walked in. The office boy closed the door behind him. At a desk near the window sat an elderly man with white hair; on his nose were a pair of gold-rimmed eyeglasses from which peered two of the keenest of grey eyes. Through a pair of great folding

268

doors at the side of the room Barton could hear the muffled click of the typewriters coming from the city room on the other side. Britton was holding the slip of white paste-board, and he scrutinized his visitor carefully.

"Do I understand, Mr. Barton," he said quietly, "that you have secured an interview with the Princess O Lyra Seng? I see by your card that you are with the *Dispatch*."

"Not any longer," explained Barton laconically. Whereupon, with a half-smile, he drew up a chair close to the other's desk, and proceeded to relate the whole happenings of the day, from the moment that Frangenac of the *Dispatch* had told him to give up his job if he could not achieve the unachievable, to the moment that he had heard the latter talking over the 'phone to the Chinese minister. This time, however, he did not omit to tell the whole bizarre story of the Twelve Golden Coins of Confucius, the dead Chinese laundryman, and the mysterious red ticket with the hieroglyphics—half of which was out at Chicago University.

Minute after minute rolled along, Britton leaving forward on his elbows, rapt. Outside in the ante-room people fidgeted and fidgeted and continued to send in cards. To every one Britton sent out word by the office boy that he could see no one. The clock ticked steadily, inexorably, on the wall. Its hands had pointed to three when Barton entered the inner office. It was 3.25 when the older man finally stood up and put his hand on Barton's shoulder. The envelope containing the carbon copy of the Princess's interview stood torn open on Britton's desk, the leaves strewn about where the *Sun* owner had run his trained eye over them. The duplicate of the Princess's signature which she had given Barton for his own personal possession was pinned under a glass paperweight near by.

"Of course you're part of the *Sun* machine after this," Britton was saying. "We need men like you, Barton. Unlike the *Dispatch*, with its narrow—I call it pusillanimous—Francophile policy of cancelling only France's debt to America, the *Sun* has fought a terrific battle for some years, both in the public mind and the minds of congressmen at Washington, to get America to see at least the economic wisdom of killing the whole fool foreign debt; and to fight that battle it has had to have one-hundred-per-cent. picked journalists in every department. Now, fortunately, the actual economic results of having money owed it by all the people with which it trades are beginning to bring about what the *Sun* has tried to put over from a standpoint of fairness alone, and America is beginning to see that the *Sun's* policies were not as crazy as it thought. But that doesn't mean that the *Sun* is not going on just as before, with the best journalists and the highest class journalism that money can buy. So we want you, of course. Your time starts from eight o'clock this morning. We'll simply waive our hidebound rule about employing only men who have been ten years in the newspaper game. After all, what the owner says goes, I believe." He smiled. "Sixty a week at once—and probably more if you can uncover this story you are on." Britton paused. "Now, boy, this is big stuff. Get out on this 'golden coin' end of it and bring in another such story. Don't delay. The

cashier will be putting you on the books while you're
gone." He opened one of the drawers of his desk, with-
drawing a packet of colored cards. From it he slipped
off a pink card. "Take this—it's a taxicab charge
card, good until midnight to-night. Use it and charge
everything to the *Sun*. And good luck."

When Barton left Britton's office he was treading on
air. Outside, he entered his taxicab once more and had
himself driven straight to the Illinois Central suburban
station at the foot of Van Buren Street. He charged
the whole thing by means of the pink ticket Britton
had given him, and inside of five minutes had boarded
a train for Fifty-seventh Street, wondering what sort
of results he was going to secure through the aid of
Profesor Chan Fu, now that the latter had returned
to the University.

He left the train and started across the grassy
campus toward the faculty building. Even before he
reached it he saw a closed carriage draw up in front of
it and a figure dismount. It was a tall figure, dressed
in a most gorgeous heavy gown that, flashing in the
afternoon sun, gave forth the rich colors of green and
red and gold. On his head was a quaint black cap,
and on his eyes great hornshell glasses that even at the
distance made him appear like some colored tropical
owl. From his upper lip two branches of a jet-black,
silky moustache hung clear below his chin, like trellised
moss.

Barton quickened his pace, for he recognized that
tall figure immediately. It was Chan Fu himself, the
eccentric and learned exchange professor from Peking
University, China.

It took him another minute to reach the faculty building. Fu had already ascended the steps and disappeared. After inquiring from a student clerk the whereabouts of Chan Fu's suite, Barton took the elevator to the third floor and knocked on the old-fashioned door. The Chinese professor himself answered it. Barton, peering through the opening into the cozy study, could see the latter had just finished reading his letter, for the envelope stood torn open on the table and the half of Sam Toy's red laundry ticket was grasped in the Professor's fingers.

Barton bowed. "Professor Fu, my name is Jason H. Barton. You perhaps remember me. I see, also, that you have received my short note—requesting a favor."

The Chinese threw open the door widely, exposing to Barton's gaze a small library fitted with a heavy student's table, an ornate lamp of hammered bronze, and easy chairs of dark leather, and a great bookcase whose volumes were shut off from view by a green silk curtain embroidered with a great gold dragon.

"Please to enter, Mr. Barton," he commanded in very precise language. "I have just returned from a fatiguing directors' meeting of the Field Museum, and am more than interested by your letter."

Barton stepped inside and dropped into an easy chair by the table. Somehow, he felt a little nervous. Chan Fu closed the door and, returning to the table, dropped into a chair across from the reporter, where he studied the younger man curiously. Then he took up the red slip.

"Honorable Barton, if I may ask without seeming

unduly curious, may I inquire as to where this came from?"

"Well," rejoined Barton pleasantly, "I may say that I found it while out on some newspaper work."

The Chinaman smiled, and stirred slightly in his gold robes. "I see," he remarked politely at the vague answer. "Then may I ask if you have already had a translation of it—and have perhaps come to me to corroborate what you have received?"

Barton shook his head. "No, Professor. I have plenty of means by which to secure a translation, but none so convenient as you. I remembered our pleasant interview of some months back and so ran out on the Illinois Central." He paused. He glanced meaningly at his watch. "And you will assist me in the matter?"

"Indeed, yes," said Chan Fu. "But may I ask but one more question—without offending you. The other half—where is that?"

Barton stirred uneasily in his chair. "The two halves, Professor, came into my possession while working on a newspaper story. At the time I brought this out to you, the remaining half"—he paused, and then went on, lying resolutely—"the other half hadn't come into my possession. It's now at my rooms. Had I felt sure of finding you I would have brought it along— but I decided to come out and regain the one I had left, and secure a translation somewhere else."

Fu nodded. "I see," he said casually. His eyes roved over the slip of red paper. "The words themselves are of little interest," he pronounced. "They appear to be only a part of a poem. But the characters are characters used only by an educated man. And I doubt whether you could have secured a translation, honorable Barton, through ordinary channels. They read merely, translated, idiomatically, 'The Twelve Coins of Confucius are——' and there they stop." He looked at the man across from him, but ventured nothing further.

"So it seems to be part of a poem, Professor?" Barton meditated. " 'The Twelve Coins of Confucius are——' That's rather odd. What are the Twelve Coins of Confucius?"

Chan Fu tossed over the red slip to him and stifled a perceptible yawn. "I could tell you much of Kong-Fu-Tse," he said, shrugging his shoulders, "but the Twelve Coins of Kong-Fu-Tse sounds rather puzzling even to me." He glanced up at the onyx clock on the bookcase. "Tell you what you do, Mr. Barton. Suppose you bring in that other half, and we'll run over it together and see what this Chinese schoolboy of yours is driving at. I am curious—and so are you. Also, the characters are 'feng' characters—they are of a special alphabet used only by learned men in our country. I am more than glad to give you my poor services." He paused. "There might be something of interest there."

Barton rose hastily. He tucked the half-ticket carelessly in his coat pocket. He was trembling with eagerness, but carefully refrained from showing it. "I'll be glad to do that, Professor Fu. I'll be back later inside of an hour with the other half, if you'll help me out."

"Indeed I shall," said the other, rising. "I am very grateful to you for your splendid write-up of me some months ago." He glanced again at the clock. "I shall see you in an hour?" he asked.

Barton nodded. A moment later he had bowed himself out of the professor's rooms and was making his way across the campus in as dignified a manner as he could. He wanted to shout and throw up his hat, but he knew that he dared not betray his feelings within sight of those old, austere buildings.

As for Chan Fu—the moment his visitor got out of the rooms and the latter's footsteps were echoing down the wooden stairs, he stepped quickly to a telephone on the wall and raised the receiver. "Give me Harrison 2428," he directed in perfect English.

A clicking followed; then: "This is Professor Chan Fu, Chinese exchange professor at Chicago University, speaking. Put me at once on the wire of Mr. Li Hwei Tsung, if you please."

Another clicking, a man's voice, and Fu spoke quickly, excitedly, hastily, into the 'phone, using the Chinese language.

"Tsung? This is Chan Fu of the university. Tsung, I have most astounding news for you. A newspaper reporter just visited me with a paper which he wished translated. He claims to have found it in some peculiar manner. It appears to describe the location of the missing Coins of Confucius, but goes no further than to mention the coins and there it stops. It reads: 'The Twelve Coins of Confucius are——' It is written on the face of a red slip, bearing at the top in English the letters: O-Y; then R-O-N-space-S-T; then D-R-Y. There is another half—the left half—containing the last half of the message and the first half of the Eng-

lish words. And this reporter is to bring this other
half back in an hour. He———"

"You believe, then," broke in Tsung's voice excitedly, in the same tongue, "that it could possibly be connected with the missing Yuan?"

"I do absolutely," affirmed Fu. "I have always held
the theory that Yuan fled to America by way of Mexico. Likewise, one of the characters is a 'feng' letter.
Honorable Tsung," he went on breathlessly, the gut-
turals tumbling over themselves, "do not underestimate
the importance of this discovery—or the seriousness of
it. If this man in any way suspects—if he learns the
location of those Coins, he is likely to have power beyond all description in the empire. You know the
value which Hoang-Ti attaches to them. He considers
them priceless—absolutely the biggest treasure in the
history of China. One more—and he believes China
shall be the most powerful country on the face of the
globe. He has told me this in his own words—years
ago. And if this reporter succeeds even in locating
them, there is no telling what Hoang-Ti might do for
him. What steps shall I take?"

"Give him an erroneous translation of the other half
when he returns," snapped the Chinese prime minister. "Do—do anything to steer him away from the
truth. In the meantime I shall be searching city di-
rectories for the names of all Chinese tradesmen ending
in O-Y. Professor Fu, do not let this man get away
from you. I believe there is something in it. If so,
then you and I have the Emperor by the nose. This
means the biggest stroke ever put over in court circles
—and you and I shall share it together, Fu. Keep me

in touch every half-hour with developments. I shall call you, also. And keep to your rooms."

"I will do that," said Fu grimly. "I shall play this end correctly, Tsung. Never fear."

He hung up and, dropping back into the big chair, took down a great Chinese water-pipe which he proceeded to smoke, drawing in great draughts from the heavy Chinese tobacco, and drumming nervously on the table with his long fingers.

Barton, in the meantime, was boarding a city-bound express at the Fifty-seventh Street platform.

"The Professor seemed more than interested," he ruminated as he dropped into an empty seat. "There seemed to be a most eager gleam in his slant eyes; even his long black moustache seemed to quiver. And he lied even worse than I did when he disclaimed all knowledge of the Twelve Coins." He paused in his reflections. "I'm thinking I'd better get a translation of that other half just as far away from Chicago U. as I can. But where in the name of Jupiter can I find an educated Chinaman? Perhaps he lied—perhaps they're ordinary characters, after all. If so, there's Mrs. O'Malley's friend's Chink servant in Ravenswood and——"

He fumbled in his breast pocket, but suddenly stopped short in his search. His hands fell helplessly to his side, his breath left him in a great gasp, the bottom seemed to fall out of the universe.

For the first time that afternoon he recalled that he had placed the other half of the laundry ticket in his old black leather bill-fold—that he had also placed Frangenac's credential paper in that same bill-fold—and that in the hurry and excitement of packing he had

slipped the bill-fold in Fawcett's suit-case without removing the torn red slip.

"Oh Lord, oh Lord!" he groaned to himself, slump-
ing down in his seat. "And now—now—the rest of
Yuan's message is on its way to Washington in Fawcett's luggage!"

CHAPTER XXXVII

B ARTON didn't go back to the Loop. Instead, he got off at the Twenty-sixth Street station and went home to his rooms, to indulge in a few self-recriminations at his stupidity in letting the vital half of Sam Toy's laundry ticket get into Fawcett's suit-case. He was tired, disgusted, disheartened at the unexpected turn of affairs, and he felt in the mood for condemning himself as all sorts and manners of an idiot.

Reaching his rooms, he flung himself on the bed and, staring vacantly out at the late afternoon sunshine that lighted up the white-stone steps of Prairie Avenue, fell to thinking of what his next move must be. There seemed no way to get in touch with Fawcett before the latter should reach Washington, unless he telegraphed ahead and had the message delivered by the conductor on the Washington Flyer. But that was not going to bring back the vital half of Sam Toy's message.

"The Twelve Coins of Confucius are——" It was maddening to know that he had perhaps stumbled on the greatest secret of the Chinese Empire—if not on the biggest story of the day—but that he was hopelessly checkmated for the next twenty-four hours.

But his concentration evolved a plan. He would have

279

a telegram dispatched long before Fawcett should reach Washington, addressed to one, Jason H. Barton, in care of the correspondents' rooms in the Capitol building. And at the thought of sending a telegram to himself he smiled whimsically as he lay back on his bed. In that telegram he would apprise Fawcett of the latter's accidental possession of a piece of Chinese writing, and tell him to drop everything—even the Speaker Farley trial if necessary—secure a translation of those few characters, and then to wire that translation back to Chicago.

With this problem solved for the time being, although unsatisfactorily, to be sure, he began to think about the Princess O Lyra Seng. Somehow, since he had seen her, a strange unrest, a feeling of unhappiness, a sense of profound mental disquiet had filled his being; and he was dimly conscious of the fact that something had come into his active life that was going to constitute a psychical disturbance for a long time to come. He closed his eyes and fell to thinking of her slim figure, of her cheeks with their creamy tint and their pink tinge, of the silky black hair with the rose in it, of the peculiar personality that radiated from her in her every word and gesture. And tired from working late the night before, he dropped away into sleep.

He awoke suddenly, rubbing his eyes. The sun was gone. Outside the street was dusky—almost dark. Long purple shadows filled the room. And by the cuckoo of the Swiss clock on his wall, he knew that it was half-past six—that he had slept for two hours. He wondered, as he sat up and blinked his eyelids into some semblance of winkability, why he had awakened so suddenly, and then—he found the reason. The telephone bell was ringing violently.

With a strange leap in his heart, all sleep gone from his being, he jumped from the disarranged bed and flew over to the instrument. He raised the receiver and uttered the customary "Hello?"

"I am talking to Mr. Jason H. Barton?" tinkled a voice that had been echoing in his ears the livelong day.

"Princess!" he ejaculated, "I—I knew you at once. This is Jason H. Barton—at his rooms."

"Mr. Jason H. Barton," she said, "I used the magic words because—because—I think as I like to see you once more. You so busy to-day—but you say that you come again if I call you on telephone."

"Indeed I'll come, Princess O Lyra Seng," he responded quickly. "Indeed I'll come. But where is honorable Li Hwei Tsung—and Mrs. Tsung?"

"Mrs. Tsung at Chinese consul's home for rest of evening," the girl said clearly into the transmitter, "and honorable Tsung leave hotel few minutes ago in big hurry. He tell not where he go, but say he be gone good while. My maid belong to me—she say nothing if I command. And—and so—Jason H. Barton, I want to talk to you. You will come so like you did to-day and you will tap on door. Then we have nice long talk—nicer than ever we had this morning. Princess O Lyra Seng commands that from Jason H. Barton."

"Princess, I'll be there in three-quarters of an hour," he said gaily. "I've wanted much to see you again— but I should never have tried to come unless you had asked me first. I have due appreciation of your rank, you see."

"Then I wait," she said happily. "And you come sure."

He hung up the receiver in a daze. "My God! One more chance to see her and talk with her," he started to say aloud. He snapped on the lights and looked at himself in the mirror. "You fool, hold your horses! Don't go dippy. That girl, idiot, is the daughter of one of the biggest men in the world—and a member of another race. Don't go and lose your head. Keep your balance. Keep——"

But before he realized it he was madly flinging his working clothes off and dragging from his wardrobe a splendid dress-suit that he had worn at a newspaper men's banquet two days before. He was stripping himself to the skin, plunging into his shower bath and out again like a meteorite; he bruised his thumbs trying to jam studs into a stiff white shirt; half-clad, he walked around in a circle trying to locate a silk opera hat which he suddenly found on a shelf in the closet and in front of his very eyes.

"You crazy fool!" he kept muttering to himself under his breath as he dressed with lightning rapidity; "you crazy fool. From the way you're primping up you act as though you think you're calling on your best girl."

In less than no time he was surveying himself in the glass with some slight degree of pride. "There, Jason H. Barton," he commented, "you look like something half fit to touch the hem of a princess's garment and talk—not like the wild-eyed newspaper man that you were this morning. Now for a taxi."

Outside, he stepped to the curbing, and looking up and down the two rows of frosted-globe street lights that illumined that quiet thoroughfare, spied a lone yellow taxicab bearing down on him. He hailed it and climbed in. "Stop at the first florist's shop you come to," he ordered the driver. "Then go to the Hotel Rydenour." And with the sudden forward lurch of the machine he settled back on to the cushions, his face burning with a strange excitement.

On Sixteenth Street near Michigan Avenue, the cab stopped in front of a florist's shop. Out he jumped, returning a few minutes later with a great bunch of "American Beauties." Again he climbed back in and finished his journey up Michigan Avenue, lighted from this point on with hundreds of brilliant shops whose store fronts reflected even in the oiled macadam pavement. The cab stopped finally in front of the Rydenour, where Barton dismounted and paid the driver. Then, a bare trifle uneasy, he walked boldly into the hotel through the small side entrance, and made the elevator without having to pass through the throngs in the lobby. "Fifteenth floor," he said nonchalantly to the operator, and essayed an artificial yawn as he said it.

He was whisked like an arrow to the fifteenth floor. Again he made a pretense of fumbling in his pockets until the car had descended; then he stepped hurriedly up the deserted hall, lighted only by a few shaded electric bulbs, and slipped like a shadow through the door of vacant Suite 15 B. Down the dark corridor he proceeded, and finding the window whose fire-escape led to the interior of the suite below, descended it carefully, and within sixty seconds was inside the royal suite. He tiptoed down the corridor, wiping his hands on his handkerchief, and tapped three times on the door.

When it opened, he gasped. The room was lighted only by the soft rays of an electric lamp. In the opening stood a slender girl, clad in a filmy black dress that bore the unmistabable marks of the latest Parisian fashion. It was covered with a gauzy stuff that showed beneath it the sheen of black silk; it was full, yet did not quite come to her ankles. The slim ankles themselves were encased in black silk, with two black silk slippers bearing buckles of jet and gold. But it was the Princess, for her peculiar dark eyes with their slightest of obliquity gazed out at him in welcome, and her silky black hair was done on one side of her head into a cluster of curls so bewitching as to have excited the envy of the most vain of American girls. There was but one Chinese note in her startling transformation: that was the gold and green tip of a peacock feather she had daintily woven into her hair.

"I am so glad you come," she said, holding out one slim hand. "You see—Mr. Jason H. Barton—I fix myself up just so like American girl—so you like me a little more. And we have time to talk now."

She spied the great bunch of "American Beauties," and he held them out to her. "'American Beauties' to the most beautiful girl in both China and America," he said with a bow.

CHAPTER XXXVIII

SHE hugged the flowers to her with a little cry of delight. She led him inside the room and closed the door. The maid sat over in the corner again like a graven image, and Barton felt an almost irresistible impulse to go over and touch her with his finger to see whether she were living or graven from wax.

O Lyra Seng surveyed him from head to toe with her eyes beaming. Then she pointed to a chair and drew up another one very close to it. "Now we talk," she ordered. "Honorable Tsung say he not be back for long, long time—and we not ever get another such chance."

Settled across from her, Barton endeavored to get her to tell him what had happened after he had been forced to leave there that morning. But she dismissed the subject in a few words. "Honorable Tsung all happy now," she averred. "He go away from here directly after, and then come back. He say: 'Princess, you've been bad girl, but you all forgiven now. Everything is all right—and your honorable father will understand.' "

Barton gave a short, hard laugh. "I'm glad of that. I'm glad that honorable Tsung is pleased with the outcome. He may be a little hasty, though." He

285

looked at the splendid young form across from him. "Princess, in Chinese costume you were what we call stunning—but in these French garments you are ten times as much so."

"I have it made for me at Monsieur Paquin's in Paris," she announced, "on our trip through. I never wear it though, until tonight. But I feel you rather have me in American costume."

Barton swallowed rather hard. He felt for the first time a disquieting suspicion that he was being coquetted with a little; and he didn't like this trait in the personality which he had discovered that morning.

"Princess," he said, to change the subject, "tell me more of your life in China as you were doing when we were interrupted this morning."

She raised a hand. "No, Mr. Jason H. Barton, you have it all. Just lonely little girl—some day to rule over Chinese Empire, since she have no brothers—who was always cooped up with her books to dream and think. I bring you over here to have you talk about you. Tell me where you were born—and how you happen to become writer of news. And about your honorable papa and illustrious mama. All that interests me much."

So, seeing that she was intent upon learning more of him, Barton drew his chair nearer to her and told of his early days on the Texas farm where he had been left an orphan: that Texas farm which had proved the happy refuge for his grandmother, one English girl of many who had journeyed in a covered wagon half across the Indian-infested plains and burning deserts in response to Brigham Young's lying London proselytizers. He told how the farm had been lost, at his parents' death, through the mortgages caused by a succession of terrific Texas droughts; how he had been put into the care of an old farmer whose only desire was to make him earn far more than his keep; how he had milked the cows and worked early and late, often fourteen hours a day; how he had finally run away at the age of thirteen, and made a two-thousand-mile trip on freight cars to the city of New York, where he had become a newsboy on the streets of that big metropolis. He described vividly to her how his heart had ached when he saw other children tripping to school every day; and how finally a big-hearted Wall Street broker had taken pity on him and helped him through grammar school.

He went on to describe how he had finally gone to college in Nebraska, finishing the preparatory school in two years, and supporting himself the whole six years by working in the Nebraska wheatfields during the torrid summers; he described the struggle he had had in his impecunious condition, and how he had ultimately met big Fawcett, the one man who had befriended him and helped him; the day he had graduated with the consciousness that the big struggle was ended.

He told her briefly of his trip to France with a Canadian contingent, of how their ship was torpedoed in mid-ocean, of how the entire force were transferred safely to a Standard Oil tanker, of the bit of shrapnel in his shoulder, of London, of home again. Then he told her of how the second great gold strike had been made in the northern tip of Alaska, and how he had given up a promising clerkship in a Montreal broker's office to join the searchers after the golden treasure of a second Klondike. He described the silent trips through the long Northern nights on dog sleds, and told of the expensive prices of food up in the snowy wilderness.

He showed her the bullet mark on his wrist where the lead had passed through in the great bar-room fight at Kinikanik City, the night that big Red Bransom, the bully of the camp, had been killed by the town preacher, a mild man with his glasses and Bible in one hand and his six-shooter in the other. He told how the preacher had grimly read the funeral sermon over the man he had killed, and how even the Indians had cheered lustily. He told her of how the fabulous vein had petered out; and of the wreck of his ship when he was coming back from the North to civilization; how the crew and passengers had lived in life-boats for two interminable days and nights on the cold seas.

He related how he had landed penniless and broken in spirit in Seattle; how he had tried to get his first newspaper berth; how he had secured only a space-writer's job; how he had stumbled accidentally on the whereabouts of Emerich, the missing cashier of the Seattle State Bank; and how he had written up the scoop and landed the position that was to throw his life into new channels. And he described briefly how he had drifted from city to city, finally winding up at Chicago.

All the while he talked the Princess listened open-mouthed, her even white teeth gleaming, her little red lips parted in utter amazement at his vivid portrayal of phases of life of which she had only dimly heard.

She shivered perceptibly during his recital of the great bar-room fight in Kinikanik City, and of his dramatic visualization for her of the horrors of two days and nights in an open boat on the Arctic seas.

At the end of it he looked down at her and smiled whimsically. "So you see, Princess, it's not a particularly illuminating recital. Pretty sordid—and hard. Nothing in it in the way of poetry. All fight and tough struggle—the whole way through. And not a thing really accomplished after all."

"Oh, but it is the life you have lived!" she breathed enthusiastically. "It—it was all accomplishment. You—have seen and done—while O Lyra has been chained in with her dreams." She looked curiously up at him. "And you never marry?" she asked with a peculiar wistfulness in her voice.

He shook his head.

"Why?"

He wrinkled up his forehead. "Well, Princess, the reason is connected with those dreams you spoke of. Likewise with that elusive thing you have called personality. In all these years I have been searching hopefully for that companion personality—the one who might understand Jason H. Barton—and never have found her. I knew partly what she was to be like, for she had been in my mind for years; I knew always that when I met her I would recognize her at once." He looked down at her. "And does that answer your question?"

Her face was very serious. "But you never yet have found the personality you—you might love?"

He swallowed with difficulty. Something seemed to

rush into his being.   A sudden mad impulse came over him to seize the dainty hand of this Celestial flower and tell her fiercely that it was a personality exactly like hers he had been seeking for.   But he knew that he dared not; that she had invited him there as a friend— not to break rudely all the conventions of friendship.

"Princess, I cannot answer that question exactly," he fenced quietly.   "As I said, I knew I could recognize that personality when I met it, and——"

"And so you have been only as I," she put in hurriedly.   "I, too, Jason H. Barton, have waited dreaming all these days for such a personality that I might love.   When I was little—so little—I did not know that empire could be complicating influence in my dreams; but later I began to realize it—and a sadness seemed to come into me.   Oh, I want so to tell you— for I afraid you never know it.   But this morning— when you come—when you come—something seem to tell O Lyra—that you—that you the man—the personality—the kind of man—the——"

His jaw fell open.   "Princess," he exclaimed in alarm, "you can't mean what you say.   You——"

She snapped her fingers toward the maid and spoke a few quick words in Chinese.   The woman, suddenly galvanized into action, rose and passed noiselessly out of the room.

"I am not girl who pretend.   My heart speaks— like heart should always.   Love is not something for— for—dissimulation.   The heart that first recognizes should speak—and the heart of O Lyra Seng—sees— speaks——" She stopped.   A tear rolled down from one of her brown eyes.

"My God, Princess!" Barton said dazedly. "I—
I never dreamed, I never dreamed!" He leaned forward
in his chair and closed his big hand on one of her
smaller ones. "And you could love me? You—a Princess of the great Chinese Empire? And you are sure
it is not a girlish——"

He did not know how it happened. In after years it
was all confused in his mind in a maze of delirous
thoughts and actions. The slim form was in his arms,
her moist red lips were close to his, and he was kissing
the daughter of the Emperor of China!

CHAPTER XXXIX

BARTON pulled himself together finally, and leaning back in his chair, stroked the silky black curls of the girl who nestled in his arms.

"But, Princess, what happiness can all this bring to you and me? I love you—I knew it this morning—I have known it all day—and I think that you love me. If you are sure of yourself, then it would seem that we are two peculiar idealists who have found each other after a dozen years of searching—over half the world. I think that you and I could always be happy together —that we are companion personalities." She nodded vehemently in his arms. "But of what use is it all? It can only mean bitterness. You are the daughter of the Emperor of China, and I am just a plain newspaper-man compounded of a pair of like races which are yet most highly differentiated from yours." He paused, looking down at her. "If only you were not Princess O Lyra Seng, I should ask a question that I shall only ask of but one girl in this world. But it is not to be."

She nodded her head. "No, it is not to be. That I must make myself realize. But I am so happy to be here in your arms—that I like to forget the big world revolving outside—the great empire with its millions of people—and just think there is only you and me in universe." She sighed a long sigh. "Life is all so—so a tangle. Oh, how I wish I had never studied, nor thought, nor read! Then would I be only ordinary Chinese girl—not in mind such as I am. But it is all what East Indians call Ki—Ki—Kismet."

He sat for a long time, stroking her dark hair. He knew down in his heart that the whole thing was merely a wonderful, fantastic dream, and that any moment the alarm clock on his bureau was going to ring; that he would arise, wash, dress, and go down to the *Dispatch* office, enter the grind, and that he would hear the sneering voice of Frangenac with his eternal contemptuous comparison: "A Frenchman is worth two Poles, three Swedes, four Englishman or four Yankees!" But he hoped desperately that dawn was still far away and that the dream might last longer.

They talked. Psychology, science, philosophy were shelved—as always psychology, science and philosophy will be shelved before the more engrossing little nothings that have been talked even by the cave man and his mate-to-be in the far distant Paleolithic Age. It was 8.30 before Barton pulled himself together and looked down at the girl who seemed so content to be cuddled in his arms. The threatening alarm clock had not yet jangled; and he realized suddenly that he himself must terminate the dream.

"Princess," he queried meaningfully, "do you see the time? Do you realize it means that honorable Tsung may be back at any moment? He can do no harm to me but there is your own precious self to be considered. This has been the happiest hour of my life—and it has sped by on wings of quicksilver. But you must not be jeopardized by my staying any longer. And so—it means that we'll have to say good-bye!"

She nodded unhappily and looked up at him. "Yes, Jason H. Barton, it means good-bye; I know it too well. But oh, how happy I am, so glad, that I have make you see what I see when first I meet you—that I make you realize that race, religion, rank, all these shrink for time in face of biggest thing in the world! But now you see—and some day when you think of little O Lyra Seng far over the Pacific, perhaps you will feel little sad—and yet little glad that you knew O Lyra once in your life." She arose and with true feminine instinct smoothed out her disarranged dress.

He swallowed hard and arose also. "I wish I didn't have to think of that, Princess. It will mean unhappiness—not happiness." He looked toward his silk hat. Oh, why, oh why couldn't Tsung be detained for hours, days, for ever?

He held out his arms. "Good-bye, O Lyra Seng," he said.

"Is there not another word," she asked, "that—that goes before my name?"

"Dear O Lyra——" he began.

"But still ending on adjective?" she asked.

He smiled as he understood. "Good-bye, dearest O Lyra Seng."

She smiled up at him, and standing on tiptoe threw her arms about his neck. She kissed him—a long, tingling, lingering kiss; then, with a sudden frightened little cry, unloosed her arms and fled from the

room. He stood bewilderedly alone, feeling the warm
pressure of her lips. Then, realizing that the dream
was over for good, he seized his silk hat and tiptoed out
of the room into the silent corridor. He went up the
fire-escape into the night, rocking with the dizziness of
the past hours. He found himself finally descending in
the elevator, then out on the street staring stupidly
along the rows of brilliant street lamps. And suddenly
thoughts began to pour into his cranium with lightning
rapidity.

"I wonder if—if there isn't more than a story for
poor me in those Coins of Confucius? I wonder—I
wonder if the man who locates those twelve coins isn't
going to stand pretty pat with the emperor of a country
which has spent thousands of years and money to get
them together? I wonder what the other half of that
red ticket in Fawcett's suit-case is going to say? God,
what a wonderful little creature she is! And she—she
loves me. It's all a crazy nightmare. I wonder——"

His chaotic reflections ceased abruptly. A newsboy
was going by the Michigan Avenue corner crying out
his extras. The words were garbled, but Barton
caught his breath as he seemed to hear in them the
phrase "Washt'nin Fly'r."

"Here—boy—here, a paper!" He tossed the boy a
nickel.

The urchin shoved a damp paper into his outstretched hand and moved on up the street to where an
elderly gentleman was beckoning. Oblivious to the traffic on the sidewalk, Barton stood under one of the flaming street lamps and devoured the contents. For him,
indeed, the news that the big black headlines screamed

forth was startling news—yet so meagre that it filled less than two hundred ems of type. It ran:

"WASHINGTON FLYER GOES INTO THE DITCH. SENATOR AND TWO CONGRESSMEN AMONG THE INJURED.

"At 7 o'clock to-night the Washington Flyer struck a defective switch just outside of Bentleyville, Ohio. The front half of the train ran into the ditch and overturned completely. All of the injured passengers were rescued from the overturned cars before the sparks from the engine set fire to the coaches. The baggage car, mail car, smoker and first coach are burned to a cinder, and the inhabitants of Bentleyville are fighting the flames which bid fair to consume the rest of the train. Among the most seriously injured of the passengers are Senator Fealy, Congressman Opp, Congressman Rann—all of Illinois—and Jason H. Barton, a Chicago newspaper man. A relief train is on the way from Dayton, Ohio."

With the knowledge of the trained newspaper man, Barton scarcely comprehending as yet, ran his eye across the page to what is known as the drum paragraph. There, printed in cheap red ink, not even proof read, were a few further details which had come in by telegraph while the edition was on the press. They read:

"DYING PASSENGER CLEARS UP CHICAGO TONG MURDER.

("Special telegram to the News)

"Among the passengers injured in the overturning of the Washington Flyer to-night was one Charles Fawcett, an Omaha newspaper man. On account of cards found on his person his name was erroneously reported as Jason H. Barton. He was removed to a temporary hospital in Bentleyville, but lived only an hour. Before he died he made a brief statement in which he declared that he stabbed a Chinese laundryman late last night in the Central West metropolis, during a struggle which followed an attempt on his part to take out his laundry on credit. He stated also that the weapon he used was one which was lying on the counter, and that he feared he had mortally injured his opponent. The stabbed Celestial, according to Chicago police headquarters, is the man Sam Toy of 144 West Huron Street, whose death was supposed to be the result of a Chicago Tong war."

That was all there was to the news thus far. Barton, completely stupefied, stood staring down at the paper trying to realize that it was all true. "Poor, poor Charley!" he found himself saying mechanically again and again. "Poor poor Charley. Poor old boy." He thought dazedly of the clean linen which he had helped the other pack into the suit-case, and now in a flash everything seemed to fly together with devilish accuracy: the clean shirt and collars themselves; Fawcett's drinking that morning; the location of the Chinaman's laundry not three blocks from the Star Hotel; the newspaper man's great physical strength in former days; his trembling fingers that morning; his mood of utter depression . . .

But as Barton read the two paragraphs for perhaps the fifth time, a sudden deathly sickness seemed to seize him in the pit of the stomach, and a wave of frigid cold seemed to sweep over his whole nervous system. For the first time one sentence stood out at him as though printed in 100-point type instead of agate: "The baggage car, mail car, smoker and first coach are burned to a cinder." In that baggage car was Fawcett's suit-case, and in that suit-case was the leather bill-fold containing the other half of Yuan's dying message.

"Good-night, Coins of Confucius!" groaned Barton softly to himself. "Good-night, dreams! Good-night, love! Good-night, everything! Oh, why—oh, why, does everything in life go wrong?"

CHAPTER XL

FOR ten long minutes Barton stood on that Michigan Avenue corner, oblivious to the passers-by, oblivious to the time, oblivious to the fact that he was in evening clothes, oblivious to everything, lost in the deepest of blue funks. The clue, if ever there had been a clue to the Twelve Coins of Confucius, was gone now. Of that there was no doubt. Mentally he berated himself as all kinds of an idiot for ever letting the other half of the Sam Toy message get out of his possession. But the thing was done now; and all that remained was to go back to his rooms and think of the most wonderful girl in the world—the girl he couldn't have—the girl from whom he was now farther away than ever.

But instead of going home he decided to make one last hopeless effort from the wreckage of his plans; so he turned disconsolately to the drug store back of him, and entering the telephone booth, riffled over the directory till he came upon a certain name. Then he dropped his coin and rang his party.

A man's voice—terse and businesslike—answered.

"Am I speaking to Mr. McGurk, renting agent for the laundry at 144 West Huron Street?" Barton was appalled at the dullness, the lifelessness of his own voice.

"Yes, sir."

"Barton is my name," the newspaper man went on. "I'd like to look over the store you have for rent there. Could I drop into your place in the next twenty minutes and get the key? I think I may find a party to take the place."

The renting agent laughed. "Indeed, you could, my friend; but a prospective renter is looking it over now. A Chinaman just came in and got the key from me; says he wants to open up a Chinese laundry there for his brother."

"Was he——" Barton began. But he stopped. "Thank you," he said. And he hung up.

He stood in the booth for a moment, thinking. He held a faint suspicion that that Chinaman might be a Chinaman he knew, yet he could conceive of no manner in which Li Hwei Tsung might have become involved in the Sam Toy affair, since he, Barton, had not even had a chance to mention it to the Princess. But he decided then and there to verify or disprove his suspicions.

He hurried from Michigan Avenue and over west, where he boarded a North State street car. A number of rowdies grinned and nudged each other at the sight of a man in a dress-suit and an opera hat on that plebian branch of the traction system, but Barton saw nothing and heard nothing. He arrived at Huron Street within eight minutes. He walked westward on the dirty, dark, narrow thoroughfare, and passing La Salle Avenue caught sight of a taxicab stationed up the street a short distance in front of a saloon, and as he passed the saloon he saw the chauffeur's cap bobbing over the green baize doors.

"A taxi on Huron Street," commented Barton curiously. "And a hundred feet from Number 144." He hurried on a short distance, and came to Sam Toy's laundry. It was lighted up both front and rear by the hanging coal-oil lamps; but the space in front of the pine partition appeared to be quite devoid of any inspecting renter. The key, however, was in the door, and on the outside; so Barton stepped in off the sidewalk, and closing the door noiselessly behind him strode into the room back of the partition.

There he stopped dumfounded. The whole place had been torn up till it presented a picture of indescribable confusion. The cheap wooden cot had been ripped apart; the thin mattress had been torn up and its hairy contents scattered over the whole room. On the floor along the wall were ranged the kitchen utensils, the yellow bowl and chop-sticks, the cups and saucers; the tiny pantry had been ripped out from the wall, and the kitchen table stood upside down. The gas range, pulled partly out from the wall, showed how forcibly the rigid pipe connections had been twisted. A number of loose boards in the floor had been bodily ripped up, and a great patch of loose plaster had been dislodged by a well-directed kick. And in the midst of all the confusion stood Li Hwei Tsung in his American clothes, and Chan Fu of the University of Chicago, his gorgeous robes producing the most emphatic contrast to the sordid surroundings.

Barton stopped in surprise, dubiously surveying the two Orientals; but almost before he had time to say Jack Robinson, Tsung, with a few quick words in Chinese to Fu, whipped out a great foreign-looking military revolver and pointed it straight at him.

"Honorable Barton, you will thrust your hands far above your head. You are just in time."

Barton bewildered by this unexpected display of hostility, hesitated, then suddenly shot his hands ceilingward. Both hands in the air, he turned and gazed toward the gloriously clad Chan Fu; and his voice was vibrant with scorn.

"Well, you crooked Chinese traitor!" he ripped out. "So—so you were trying to double-cross me on that red ticket, eh? That's really funny."

Fu, obviously ill at ease, made no retort, only speaking in Chinese to Tsung. Whereupon Tsung turned furiously toward the reporter.

"Out with it now!" he snarled. "Out with it, sir, and be quick about it! The other half of that red ticket you brought up to Professor Fu's."

Barton smiled bitterly. "I'm not just ready to give up that half-ticket," he announced coolly. "It contains half of a poem that interested me. Something about some coins of Confucius."

The very mention of the words seemed to work Tsung into a fury. "Search him, Fu," he commanded the other. "Take it from him at once."

"Wait, gentlemen," Barton cautioned suddenly, as Fu started reluctantly toward him. "You have the upper hand of me. I can't stand out against you. If that half-poem"—it was doubtful whether they could detect the sneer in his voice as he spoke—"is of any value to you, you are welcome to it. But it's not on my person. And only on one condition will I tell you exactly where it is. Is that a fair bargain?"

The Chinese professor spoke up eagerly. "Where —where is it?"

Barton ignored him utterly. He continued to address his words toward the squat Oriental who kept the military revolver trained on him. "How about it, honorable Tsung?"

"What is your condition?" the other bit out savagely.

"Simply this," insisted Barton, flicking away with his toe a tuft of the hair from the mattress. "My curiosity is aroused to such an extent as to how you succeeded in killing that interview with Frangenac to-day, that I'd give anything to know just how it was done. I only want to know what is the meaning of Ling, Frangenac, Savegeau and Tsung." He paused. "I am no longer with the *Dispatch*. I am now with the *Sun*."

The Chinese prime minister bit his lip eagerly. "You will tell me where the other half of that poem is, if I answer your simple question?"

Barton nodded emphatically. "Absolutely."

Tsung, without even allowing the barrel of his revolver to waver by a second of arc, spoke quickly to Fu in Chinese. The Chinese professor answered him quickly in the same tongue, evidently urging him to do something, for he nodded his head energetically toward Barton and swept his long-sleeved arm about the room.

Tsung at once turned his attention to the newspaper reporter. "That—that is all you wish to know?" he asked cautiously. "And you will immediately disclose the whereabouts of that other half of the poem?"

"I'll tell you exactly to a dot where it is." And Barton looked him straight in the eyes.

"Very well then, my friend," the Chinese minister remarked quietly, "you shall have the little information you want. But remember—you are to return the favor. That is understood?"

CHAPTER XLI

B ARTON, hands upraised, nodded, whereupon Tsung spoke, scratching his chin doubtfully.

"You are a young man," he observed sagely. "Yet you have heard, perhaps, of the—the—Boxer uprising in China in 1900?"

"The great uprising against the white foreigners?" Barton replied. He nodded slowly. "Indeed, yes."

"But you are young, as I say," continued the other, biting his lip, "and you do not know all the things of that day. In fact, my friend, there was a white man— a man of your own race—who trained and led those people of my country who endeavored to throw off the hateful foreign yoke. This man was a deserter from the guard around the French legation at Peking. He was a man who had served in the English army, the Belgian army—Buddha alone knows how many white men's armies. He hated them all, evidently, because he was only a captain, even in the army of his own country. His desertion to the Boxer forces brought invaluable technical military secrets that helped that uprising tremendously. If that Boxer movement had gone through successfully, he would have held a great office in China; but it would have been at the expense of the blood of hundreds of his own race." Tsung

305

paused. "But when Peking fell before the combined forces of your English, French, Russian and German, troops, and the Boxers were driven into the mountains, this Captain Napoleon Savegeau was carried with them with a dum-dum bullet in his knee. And that renegade to his race, that traitor to his color, was——"

"Frangenac, city editor of the *Dispatch*," put in Barton, with a long-drawn-out whistle. "Good God! but I always wondered who he was and where he had come from." He looked the other over admiringly. "No wonder you had the goods on him, honorable Tsung. He couldn't have found a spot on the globe to lay his head in peace, if the world knew that he led the Boxers against his own people. The dog! He——"

"Allow me to interrupt," said Professor Fu quietly. "You were, I believe, to establish for us the location of that half-ticket. We are now patiently waiting for you to fulfil your end of the agreement."

"Gladly," Barton acquiesced, with a free-and-easy laugh. "The other half of that paper, dear Professor Fu, is out in Bentleyville, Ohio, in the smoking ruins of a baggage car. It has been reduced to a delicate black ash in the wreck of the Washington Flyer. I refer you to the late extras, now on the streets." He watched the others with curiosity, wondering what effect this bombshell would have upon them.

Its effect was magical. Both men started as though struck with the lash of a whip. Tsung stared at him, his face for a moment the picture of defeat. "You lie, you dog!" he snarled. He turned angrily to Fu. "Fu, search him. This play has gone far enough. It was a trick—nothing more. I was a fool to have listened to him in the first place. Go through every pocket, Fu."

The tall Chinese professor shuffled forward as though not particularly liking his job. He approached Barton, whose hands were still upraised, and inserted his long, lean, yellow talons first into the latter's breast pocket. Barton submitted meekly to it until Fu began to unbotton his vest; then he suddenly lowered his hands, and with a mighty shove sent the Chinese professor spinning across the room straight into the stomach of Tsung, who was watching operations with the revolver tilted slightly downward.

The latter, his equilibrium upset by the hurtling weight of his companion, staggered back against the wall, putting out one hand wildly to steady himself. But like a flash Barton cleared the room in three great leaps, one of which was over the body of Fu, who lay flat on his stomach trying to get up, and shot out his clenched fist straight to the prime minister's jaw. A second later his fingers closed about the barrel of the gun—and the tables began to turn.

Tsung, with a mighty oath in English, strange to say, lurched at the young man with his yellow fist, still keeping his grip on the handle of the revolver. Barton dodged and wrenched and tugged at the barrel, trying to wrest the weapon from the hand of the Chinaman. Together they reeled around the floor, tugging, panting, sweating, cursing; and all the while Fu was trying, groaning, to get to his feet. Suddenly, in the struggle, the revolver went off. Barton, his opponent's wrist pinioned under his own elbow, pushing out with his other hand, heard the ping of the bullet and a faint clattering noise; but all his attention was riveted on the work in hand. With a last mighty twist, in which the Chinese prime minister cried out in pain, the revolver came away in Barton's hand, barrel first, and he sprang to the clear just in time to dodge the infuriated Fu, who had struggled to his feet and was coming wildly at him, his blackened teeth gleaming in the lamplight.

In a jiffy Barton inverted the gun. "Stop, gentlemen!" he puffed. "Stop—or I'll shoot—as sure as there's a heaven—for Christians."

Fu stopped dead in his tracks. His knees seemed to quaver under him. His long arms gesticulated wildly. "See, I have stopped!" he squealed, panic-stricken. "I have stopped! I have stopped! I have stopped!"

Tsung, at the back of him, thrust his own hands to the ceiling. It was plain that he knew the game had completely turned, and saw that further resistance was useless. He spoke to the other sparingly in Chinese, and Fu ceased his excited snivelling.

"Right about face—both of you," snapped Barton. "Quick—faces toward the rear wall." He pointed at the wall with his free hand.

Tsung, bitterness in his face, turned with hands upraised. Fu, apparently too scared to act on his own initiative, turned too, following the example of the short, squat Chinese minister. Then Barton found himself master of the situation, both Celestials with their backs to him, their hands in full sight.

"Oh, gentlemen, gentlemen," he said, laughing hysterically, "but I would love to play a certain game we boys used to play on the farm! It's played with the human toe, and——" He stopped, his words trailing away, his lower jaw falling open.

He was looking down at the floor, near the wall. He recalled, as he stared downward, the metallic ping of the bullet which had escaped from the weapon during the struggle, and now for the first time he saw what that bullet's mark had been. The lead missile had pierced the yellow bowl on the floor, and had splintered it into a dozen jagged pieces. But a peculiar condition of that bowl now showed up under the smoking light from the oil lamp above his head.

Protruding from the rough edge of almost every one of the jagged fragments was a coin, round and massive. Some stuck all the way out; on others, only the tips peeped forth from the clayish composition. But the portions that were exposed showed the glint of gold—old gold, greenish gold, Chinese gold! For a long minute Barton remained staring downward, his eyes popping out of his head. Then he suddenly pulled himself together.

"Forward march, gentlemen, clear to the wall," he ordered hurriedly. He stooped down and began loading the jagged fragments into his pockets. "I'll have to bid farewell to you both in a minute, but when I go I'm thinking I'll be pulling out with the Twelve Golden Coins of Confucius!"

CHAPTER XLII

A MATTER OF HIGH SPEED

WITH the pockets of his newly-pressed dress-suit bulging almost to bursting with the fragments of the yellow bowl, Barton, never allowing the revolver to waver from the backs of the two stolid Orientals, backed slowly from the place. Reaching the front door of the shop he swung it open, and in a flash slammed it shut, snapping the key in the lock. He jerked the key from the key hole and ran swiftly and happily down the dark street toward the waiting taxi.

Passing a sewer inlet, he ran out to the curb and dropped the key down the broad mouth. As he flew on toward the stationary vehicle, he heard back of him at Sam Toy's shop a furious pounding on the doors and windows, but he ran on.

The taxicab driver was just emerging from the door of the saloon, wiping his mouth with the back of his hand.

"Taxi!" panted Barton. "*Sun* office—Market Street—drive like hell!"

The driver hesitated. "But—but I just brought two gents to that there laundry back there. They ain't paid their bill yet. And they told me to wait."

Nervously Barton jerked out his roll of money. He tore off a crisp five. "There's their money," he lied

310

gracefully. "They told me they weren't coming. Now hop up and put me at the *Sun* office as fast as your old tank can go."

The driver at the sight of the bill smiled a broad Irish smile. He grabbed it, and with one curious look back toward the shop from which came sounds like the beating of fists on the windows and door panels, he grinned and climbed into the seat of his machine. And as Barton closed the door with a slam he shot off with a lurch that threw his lone passenger flat against the cold cushions.

Around to Wells Street he flew, over the bridge that covered a dark gap through which spat numberless red and green lights from the masts of moored vessels, and on to Madison Street he turned sharply, and with a grinding and shrieking of the brakes stopped dead in front of the *Sun* office.

Barton was out on the running-board before it had come to a stop. "Wait here," he told the chauffeur, and with a bound was up the outer steps of the newspaper office. Up the inside stairs he went four at a time, and racing past the open door of the city room, hurled himself against the ground-glass panels of Britton's office, through which a light showed. He jerked open the door and shot through the tiny anteroom, empty at this hour of night, and flung open the door of the private office inside.

Britton, his finger on the electric switch, stood near the wall with his hat and gloves on. His cane lay across the table, and his flat-top desk was all in order. It was plain that he was just leaving for home.

"I got 'em, Mr. Britton!" shouted Barton excitedly.

"The whole twelve of 'em—the Coins of Confucius."
He pointed to the big vault in the corner of the room.
"But for God's sake, man, lock 'em up at once—without delay! They're the biggest thing in the history of China. They——"

He stopped. One by one he hurriedly turned the pockets of his suit inside out, dumping forth the jagged fragments of heavy yellow pottery. From one of the pieces a coin dislodged itself and rolled off the table to Britton's feet. The older man stooped dumbly down and picked it up, studying it bewilderedly under the bright light above his head.

"Man, man!" he ejaculated slowly. "How—how did you do it? Where did you get 'em? What was——"

"Never mind now, Mr. Britton," broke in the other hastily. "Don't stop to examine 'em—or anything. Get every one into that vault with three inches of cold steel on the outside of them. I'm off now." He broke one of the fragments on the table with a sharp rap, and slipped the freed disc of gold into his vest pocket. "I'll keep this one for the time being."

Britton, galvanized into sudden action at the younger man's tense attitude, peeled off his tan gloves, tossed his brown derby hat in the corner, and a second later was standing in front of the big vault, with the massive doors swung open, depositing the jagged fragments of pottery in a steel drawer at the rear. Barton was already at the door.

"Wait for me until I come back," he shot out. "Can't stop now. Things are breaking fast. But don't open that vault for anyone in God's kingdom—whatever you do." And he was gone.

Down the stairs he ran, leaving the dumbfounded Britton standing in front of the vault scratching his head. Into the waiting taxicab Barton bounded. "Hotel Rydenour," he snapped. "And speed—speed—make speed."

The cab shot eastward and was soon on Michigan Avenue. In front of the Rydenour Barton climbed out. He gazed down Congress Street, and a short distance off spied the opening of an alley-way that led into the back of the building. So he leaned over close to the driver's ear.

"Run your machine over to that alley-way," he instructed, "and be ready to make the quickest journey of your life. Never mind expense. You're getting double pay, my man. And I pay the fines."

And he was in the hotel and scurrying through the lobby.

He entered the elevator. A new elevator boy—evidently the night man—had come on duty. That was fortunate, Barton reflected, for too many times that day had he made the trip to the fifteenth floor.

The elevator boy whisked him to the fifteenth floor, and the moment the car descended, Barton dived through the door that marked Suite 15 B, and reaching the dark window that led out to the fire-escape, was down it and into Suite 14 B before twenty seconds had elapsed. He ran lightly down the corridor and pounded wildly on the door that marked Suite 14 B. The maid answered it, but he shoved her aside and pushed his way into the room.

Over in the great chair under the lamp, her chin in her hands, sat the Princess O Lyra Seng, the picture of unhappiness. The moment Barton appeared in front of her she sprang up, her eyes glowing with a strange light—the light of surprise, of welcome.

"You—you—came back?" she breathed. "And why——"

Barton strode quickly over to her. He took her two slim hands in his.

"Princess, I must say quickly what I am going to say. When last I saw honorable Tsung, I left him locked in a Chinese laundry, where he was trying to get his fingers on the Twelve Coins of Confucius. Any second he will arrive here. But I have those coins—all of them. Think of it, Princess. It sounds unbelievable, but I cannot stop now to explain. You must just believe me, that's all.

"Today I told you I loved you. I love you more as every minute passes. Your every action has shown me that you care for me in the one way that really counts. So shall we make a grotesque mistake by parting to-night, never to meet again? Or shall we do what God intended those to do—who—who have discovered each other? Perhaps my words sound as though I am crazy. Perhaps I am dreaming it all. But I am going ahead with my question—no matter what happens. I want to marry you—not to-morrow—not next week—not some day when it will be hopelessly impossible—but to-night—right now—when it *is* possible. An hour from now and it will be too late. You must think quickly, Princess. Remember—I have the Twelve Coins of Confucius."

He drew from his vest pocket the one greenish disc he had kept possession of, and held it in front of her eyes. "No matter what happens, this—the other eleven, too—will go back to the Emperor of China—to the nation itself. But I want something bigger and better than those. I—I want to steal the Emperor's daughter." He looked down at her. "What is your answer, O Lyra? It must come quick—or never!"

Her eyes wide with astonishment, perhaps instinctive awe, she gazed at the greenish gold coin in his fingers. "It—it—it is of the Twelve!" she breathed. "Oh, I can't comprehend—as yet! But it is one of them—that I have seen so often with my own eyes in the palace." She turned her face up to his, and her eyes beamed with pride—pride of him. "I am so—so glad you came back. When you go, then I realize suddenly that O Lyra Seng have make mistake of her life. I know then that I like more than to love—I like to marry with you. I do not know how you get these twelve historical coins, and I do not ask; I only believe you.

"Yes, Jason H. Barton, I know with sadness in my heart after you go that love is biggest thing in the world—and that I am coward—afraid to put to test all my fine-spun theories. But now the true vision come to me. I do not care what my honorable father, or the Chinese officials of my country, or anybody in whole world say—I shall fulfil O Lyra Seng's destiny to find her own happiness—in the way the Great Spirit behind the universe desires—and dictates. There is but one question—and I ask it again. You will love me always? I want you—but perhaps to get you I give up everything in the world. I do not know now. But O Lyra is willing to take chance—if you will tell

her only that you will always, always take care of her
—and care for her."

He bent down and kissed her. "Always, O Lyra. I
only wish that I were the one who was perhaps giving
up everything—and you nothing. But conditions are
the reverse. It will be the dream of my life, though,
to make you feel that you received more than you
gave up, providing such a thing results from what we
are contemplating; but the choice must come from
you."

"I marry you," she said simply. " I marry you
now this minute—anywhere—anyway."

"Then listen carefully to me," he cautioned hurriedly. "We can never go by way of the lobby of
the hotel. We would be stopped instantly by the house
detective. Are you a brave girl? There is only one
way to get out. That is by way of the fire-escape.
And remember—Tsung will arrive any minute."

She stepped into the bedroom and emerged a second
later with a quaint little picture hat tied under her
chin with pink ribbons. On her arm was an expensive
cloak of Persian camel's hair, dyed a rich purple. "I
am ready," she said quietly. "Lead—and O Lyra will
follow."

He held the cloak for her, and she crept into it.
He buttoned it carefully about her, for he knew that
the air of the evening was going to become chilly during a certain swift drive. He didn't quite want to
realize what he was doing lest he lose his courage; so
he worked quickly at the buttons to keep his mind
busy on details.

When he was finished she stepped over to the maid, and patting her on the cheek, addressed a few words in Chinese to her. The woman smiled back at her—rather wistfully, as it seemed to Barton. Then the Princess turned to him.

"I am ready, Jason H. Barton."

CHAPTER XLIII

BARTON flung open the door of the room and led the way to the fire-escape. Out he climbed on the little iron platform, lighted dimly by an arc light far below in the alley and put forth his hand to help the Princess out. She shivered a little and hesitated.

"Do you wish to go back, Princess?" he asked kindly. "It is not too late."

She smiled to him in the half-light. "I tell my maid to tell honorable Tsung that I go marry with most wonderful man I know—and now I never go back till I make marry with him. Lead—and I follow."

"Then don't look down," he advised. With his hand on her arm, he led the way down the first flight of the clinging stairway. She clutched at him fearfully at first, but as they covered flight after flight, she seemed to get back her courage, and several times gave a delighted little laugh. At the bottom landing he ran out on the great swinging arm a few steps, and with a ponderous groaning it dropped to the ground and after a bump or two lay stationary.

Down the flight they sped, like two children on an escapade. Through the dark alleys, past boxes and barrels they threaded their way, guided only by the brilliant lights at the alley opening on Congress Street.

Out they came on the sidewalk, and Barton breathed a long sigh of relief. The taxicab was waiting, the driver posted in the seat smoking a cigarette.

They dived across the pavement, a few pedestrians stopping point-blank in their tracks at the strange performance. "Down Michigan Avenue—quick—and turn off at Eleventh Street," said Barton, as he helped the girl in and slammed the door.

When they had covered a few blocks and were off the brightly lighted boulevard, he thrust out his head from the half-opened door. "Where's the nearest Indiana town to the State line," he queried, "that a marriage can be performed without legal residence and without a town license?"

Was ever a taxi driver who was not encyclopædic in his knowledge of customs, geography and topography for miles and miles around? "Whiting," the young Irishman responded, grinning. "Can get ye to a minister's house in Whiting inside of an hour and a half. Just the other side of the South Chicago steel mills."

"Shoot!" directed Barton, and settled back on the cushions again.

The girl nestled in his arms. "I am so glad we make up our minds," she said simply, looking up at him as a rapidly receding arc-light flashed into their faces for a bare instant. "China—the Empire—the life of my youth seems to be far away—something unreal. But this is real, so real—and to-night I know I am living life."

So, leaning back on the cushions, his arm about her, Barton told her fully of his two experiences in Sam

Toy's shop; one earlier in the day, and one that evening with her "honorable guardian," as he termed him; and of the finally astounding discovery of the coins, fashioned into the crude bowl of yellow pottery. And discussing the matter, their machine rolled before they knew it into South Chicago, with its rickety gas lamps, its sunbaked cottages, its pink-tinged sky from the great blast furnaces and converters. Rapidly the dull "boom-boom-boom" from the plate mills grew fainter and fainter in their rear; soon they passed two great concrete posts bearing the sign "State Line." And fifteen minutes later they shot into a quiet little town with dirt-paved streets and great green trees lined along the roadway.

The machine stopped in front of a tiny vine-covered cottage. The driver looked in and nodded. "We're there," he announced.

Barton sprang from the taxi and helped the Princess out. He beckoned to the driver. "Come," he said; "we'll need you for a witness."

The marriage was performed by a white-haired old clergyman, in a quaint little parlor which held an old-fashioned organ quite in keeping with the hand-worked Bible quotations about the walls. For a ring, Barton placed on the Princess's slim finger the ring he had received from his mother—the ring which he had always carried; for witnesses, the clergyman's wife, bedecked in a huge gingham apron, and the chauffeur sufficed. Fifteen minutes later all three emerged, in Barton's pocket a crisp white certificate bearing the information that one O Lyra Seng, twenty years of age, and Jason H. Barton had been made man and wife.

Back over the State Line, through Steeltown, and to the *Sun* building the taxicab went by Barton's direction. Long before they reached the city proper the streets began to be deserted. In front of the dingy building on Market Street he helped out the smiling Chinese girl. On glancing up, he could see that Britton's office was brilliantly lighted, the rays piercing the dark gorge of Newspaper Row.

Up the stairs he conducted her and into the office without the formality of knocking. But there, seated against the folding doors that shut off the city room, were two men with Britton. Each of them had stout, strong jaws; each was smoking a big black cigar; each wore a shiny Federal badge on his vest. The moment that Barton and the girl entered the office, she standing timidly at his elbow, the taller of the two men arose and came straight over to him.

"Your name Jason H. Barton?" he asked.

Barton's face showed his puzzlement. "It is."

The man gave a searching glance toward the Princess, then faced Barton again.

"I am sorry to say that one Li Hwei Tsung made a technical affidavit two hours ago before the commanding official of the Federal Immigration Bureau. His affidavit declares that he and his party entered the United States for commercial purposes, and he requests immediate deportation back to China—including Princess O Lyra Seng." He paused. "You know the law. You've heard of the Asiatic Exclusion Act. This girl must go with me to the Federal Bureau and be put under the charge of the matron—and from there be sent back to China."

Suddenly the officer's words seemed to pierce the Princess's consciousness. She clung to Barton, shrinking. "Oh," she wailed, looking up helplessly at him, "you—you won't let them——"

But she did not finish, for Barton strode forward a step and looked the other man straight in the eye.

"It was a brilliantly clever move on Li Hwei Tsung's part," he stated quietly, "to make that affidavit, but I'm afraid he's hoist by his own petard, and that he's the jolly little boy who'll have to take the toboggan chute out of the U.S.A. Indeed, sir, I have due respect for the Chinese Exclusion Act. It rules that no member of that empire may permanently enter the United States after the year 1908. But I will call your attention to a peculiar modification or so. First, however, I have the honor to inform you that this lady became my wife two hours ago in Whiting, Indiana" —he dug down into his pocket and whipped out the crisp marriage certificate—"and by the completion of that ceremony automatically placed herself under the invariable immigration ruling that wives and husbands, when the husband is an American citizen and the wife a native of a country which has no quota, cannot be separated by all the immigration laws there are. So let me introduce you all to Mrs. Jason H. Barton, who may now pass back and forth from this country to China just as often as she pleases, and may reside, likewise, as long as she pleases in either land, and whenever she pleases. She cannot be barred now by ten thousand exclusion acts."

The tense silence following his words was broken by Britton clapping his hands and pounding on the table.

Over the face of the Federal officer a broad smile came. He thrust out his hand. "Bully for you, old man! I really hoped you had done it. It was your only chance." He made a careful examination of the marriage certificate and handed it back. Then he motioned to his companion. "Come, Jimmy; we're not needed around here."

Already Britton was swinging open the great doors that led from his office into the city room of the *Sun*. At the raising of his hand the fearful clatter ceased and a score of reporters and sub-editors sat stiffly in their chairs. A profound silence filled both rooms.

"Gentlemen," said Britton in the doorway, "attention, all of you—if you please! The Fates that govern news have unduly honored the *Sun* to-night. A *Sun* reporter, descended on one side from British stock, and on the other side a Yankee, has married the only daughter of the Emperor of China, and recovered the biggest treasure in the history of that peculiar empire. It means many things, gentlemen, many strange things—for a Chinese empress does not surrender her rule when she marries. It means, for one thing, the end of pernicious, embarassing Japanese influence in China, for three countries are now involved instead of one. And God knows how many other changes it is going to mean in the ultimate political history of Europe and Asia. Gentlemen, our paper—all of us—hold in our hands to-night the biggest, strangest, most exclusive and most unbelievable story of the year. This way, every mother's son of you—and bring your chairs and note-books!"

CHAPTER XLIV

AND THE CLOCK STRUCK FOUR!

A MOST dramatic pause followed Krenwicz's swiftly-moving narrative, with its strangest of all love stories. The mission clock on the wall, suddenly striking four times, seemed to bring to each man the realization that it was four in the morning, that there remained but one hundred and twenty minutes more of life for part of the little group. Each waited curiously to hear the decision of the Irishman. The latter knocked out the ashes of his clay pipe into the bolted cuspidor.

"Well, by gorry," he exclaimed, exactly as he had after McCaigh's story, "but that there wur a swift-movin' yarn. It hild me from start to finish. 'Tis thinkin' I'll be goin' out mesilf, afther hearin' that, an' marry me a Chinese girl." He paused. "An' Misther Krenwicz, you be another Misther McCaigh, with yer clockwir-rk—wheels within wheels and little wheels still inside o' the little wheels!" He gazed curiously toward Eastwood. "'Tis not yet, though, that I'll be sayin' which were the bistest story, Mister McCaigh's or Mister Krenwicz's, but they was diff'runt from each other—both like good booze, but like two kinds—say Scotch an' Irish." He smiled a broad, genial Irish smile. "W'at beats me, Misther Krenwicz, is how

324

you git started on wan of these here things, ye calls
plots. How do ye do ut?"

"Yes," put in Eastwood, leaning back wearily
against the stone wall, "how do you accomplish that,
Krenwicz? I have written, I daresay, and had published, well over a thousand stories in my day, some
short and many practically of novelette length. But
I have always worked from a central idea, rather than
tried to accomplish that peculiar co-ordination of motive and incident we call plot. I believe I should be
lost entirely should I try and deliberately create a plot.
And your story was admirably plotted, let me assure
you."

"I thank you," replied the Russian writer. "That
was my swan song. And the swan song is the sweetest song that the swan sings." He paused a moment,
contemplating the floor. "The art of creating a plot,
at the expense once more of disillusioning our estimable
friend Shanahan, consists of a psychological manipu-
lation of initial ideas, which even McCaigh, who has
never perhaps analyzed his own mental reactions, will
probably concede is infallible. Hundreds of professional writers, and thousands of amateurs in all countries to-day, are vainly striving to create plots, and are
being forced to give up that satisfactory mode of at-
taining a rounded-out story or play, because ignorant
of this basic principle which has never been stated
mathematically. The preliminary structure of the
amateur plot-maker in all instances—perhaps with
you, too, Eastwood, who work out from a pivotal idea—
invariably collapses because of a paucity of threads
with which to weave the web; because, in other words,

the plot-builder gets up a blind alley." He paused. "And so because but one of us, after all, may carry this little secret back to the outside world, I think I may state it here to-night."

He was silent for a bare moment. The other two men looked curiously, McCaigh, himself a plot-builder, leaning forward in his chair.

"The author," declared Krenwicz, "must first get clear in his mind that, in that web we call a plot, any character or vital inanimate object such as a letter, or a weapon, or a photograph, will constitute a thread. He must therefore first conceive of a thread which we may call the viewpoint thread, or thread representing the eyes of the character through whom most of the story is to be seen, and which we may term thread 'A.' This thread 'A' must figure with another thread 'B' in an opening incident which we will term incident 'n,' since its chronological order relative to the very earliest incident in the entire plot structure depends solely upon what revelations shall subsequently be made as to vital happenings occurring prior to the actual opening of the story. Very well. After inventing incident 'n' between thread 'A' and thread 'B,' there must be invented immediately an incident of numerical order 'n +1' involving thread 'A' with still another thread 'C'; then an incident 'n + 2' involving the same thread 'A' with one 'D'; then an incident 'n + 3' comprising an incident between thread 'A' and still a further thread 'E'; and this, to avoid an impasse, must be carried on as a rule to not less than an incident of order 'n + 4' or even 'n + 5'; and now mark well the essential desideratum of this preliminary invention. Here it is: Incident 'n' must produce incident 'n + 1': 'n + 2' must be the result of incident 'n + 1'; 'n + 3' must be the result of 'n + 2'; and so on. This much correctly done, any writer—no matter who he be— will have a real set of threads with which to weave, as well as the nucleus—if we may use such a term—of the web itself." He turned to McCaigh. "Is my rule right?"

McCaigh nodded slowly. "I grant you are, Krenwicz. For it is only, after all, by the method you express mathematically that the plot inventor will secure sufficient materials with which to work." He went on nodding. "Yes, Krenwicz, you have stated the very method by which I developed my Strange Adventure of the Giant Moth. Indeed, you have stated a psychological truth in an admirable form."

Eastwood, however, shook his head. "I still maintain," he said, quietly, "that having done a thousand stories in which I proceeded out from a central idea, I can get along without that mathematical law."

But here the Iron Man put in a succinct observation. "I do believe, Eastwood, that your mental processes in making up your story follow that law subconsciously, as mine have for years until Krenwicz bluntly stated it."

Eastwood made no retort. Instead, he spoke to Krenwicz. "I was struck, Krenwicz, by your theory —for does not a writer invariably express his own theories in his own stories?—is not all art merely life viewed through a temperament?—that the one solution of the ever-antagonistic feeling between races and nations lies in the complete homogeneizing—if I may coin the word—of the human race through interbreeding? Do you yourself hold that view?"

Krenwicz leaned forward, the enthusiast, his eyes now full of fire, lighting a new cigarette in the lamp light.

"Yes, although the accomplishment depends to a considerable extent upon modifications of conditions which science is already beginning to give us. In the first place, the ultimate creation of a universal language which will take place and be taught in every school in the world within a century, some hundred years minus two hours after we—or part of us—have become clay—will be the first step toward bringing about a better *rapprochement* of the races. The creation of giant air-liners which will bring India closer to the United States than St. Louis from Chicago, and England, France, Russia and Italy as close to New York as Philadelphia is to Washington, means a greater intermingling of human folks than the world has ever dreamed. A hundred nationalities will then be seen any afternoon on any boulevard of any big city."

"But, Krenwicz," put in Eastwood, "how are we going to expect to see the various black tribes of Africa with their flat noses and kinky hair mix with, say, the blond races of Saxony with their golden hair and blue eyes; or who thinks he will see a flat, squat Malay of Asia with his enormously high cheek-bones and almond eyes, mated harmoniously as well as biologically with a delicate English or American girl? Granting that all else furthering a mixing of the races is accomplished?"

"That," said Krenwicz, "will be accomplished in the physiological laboratory instead of the shop or the printed glossaries of the etymologist. Remember that no occult causes lie back of the negro's hair being kinky or his skin being black. That spiralling hair of his is but a hair with an oval cross-section, while the cross-section of a white man's hair is a circle. Remember that pigmentation is after all only skin deep, a distribution merely between the derma and the epidermis of a simple organic matter known as mellanin, and containing almost invariably sulphur. Nothing mystic about that, I think you will concede. And we know now that the endocrinologist, with his new science of the ductless glands, is opening up possibilities for very radical changes in the human body, both physical as well as psychological. By the little weapon known as the hormone, or the proper combination of hormones, man may ultimately become pigmented or depigmented within a few days; his hair may change its cross-section between two visits to the tonsorial artist—in other words, as fast as Nature allows it to emerge from his scalp, and he may thus become straight-haired instead of kinky-haired. Need a white girl of America or England feel compunctions against marrying with a de-negroized native of Africa, educated in an African university, speaking her language, familiar with her city, possessing straight hair—yellow, if you wish it— with body slim or muscular as is desired, with aquiline nose, normal lips—and last, but not least, courteous deportment?"

McCaigh, the American, laughed a hard, mirthless laugh. "You issue a radical theory, Krenwicz. There

is a bit of the Southerner in my heredity, however. I
find myself unable to conceive of a de-negroized nigger
as being a white man, no matter how many physical
attributes he may have snatched from the white man;
or moreover of a Chink whose yellow color has been
taken out of his face and been transferred to his hair,
figuratively speaking, as being a white man. I am
not medically read up as you are, nor have I hob-
nobbed with so many great surgeons as Eastwood over
there."

"It took," warned Eastwood wearily, in Krenwicz's
direction, "many billions of years, Krenwicz, for the
Pithecanthropus man to evolve into the Piltdown man,
thence into the Neanderthal, and further many more
millions of years to become the Cro-Magnon. And Cro-
Magnon man, with those countless eras between them,
resembles more nearly the Pithecanthropus than does
Negro resemble Chinese, or Chinese resemble Caucasian."

"It does not matter," said the Russian kindly. "A
white family—let us say a white Welsh family—living
in the year 1928 give birth to one of those medical
anomalies, a Mongolian idiot, with slant eyes, high
cheek-bones, and all the other characteristics of the
Mongol. Now if we accept the theory that the Mon-
golic, Ethiopic and Caucasic races descended from
definitely differentiated Simian precursors of our present differentiated species of large apes, there has trans-
pired backwards in the period of nine short months
a complete evolution—or de-evolution—over trillions
of years to the original ancestor of even these Simian
precursors, and thence down some more trillions of

years along another evolutionary branch altogether. Or, if this be a little too fantastic for you, then at the very least a backwards evolution of some thousands of years has taken place to that time when the Mongols invaded and settled in Wales. Now take that Mongolian idiot, treat him with endocrines for his mental and psychological deficiencies—particularly thyroid, thymus, suprarenal and pituitary gland extracts—and you have to all intents and purposes a speaking, thinking Chinaman out of white parents. Where are your billions of years?"

But no answer came forth. Conversation seemed suddenly to have ebbed—and ebbed ominously. As for Shanahan, who in the meantime had sat stupidly staring at the propounders of these scientific questions, Shanahan long used to death hysterics, to the breaking down of strong men at the last moment, the Irishman evidently decided to press on with that entertaining game which had thus far made his unpleasant watch so simple and easy. He glanced at the clock. It was now after four in the morning. In the square window of the death cell, however, the velvety black sky still showed its scintillating star points. Morning, chronologically speaking, was still in the offing. He glanced toward Eastwood. "An' now, Misther Eastwood, won't yeze tell me *your* story? You fellies is certainly entertainin' a poor prison guard as he's never been entertained before."

"Yes," said Eastwood, as a man speaks who is far away in mind and emotion, "so we are; so we are." He paused. "McCaigh admits he plots his stories, and Krenwicz here even puts his rationalizations into a sort of system or mathematical law. I shall endeavor to entertain you all with a story developed by my own technique—a story which shall evolve such plot as it may have out of an idea, instead of gathering up ideas by its own structure." He paused. He poured himself out a stiff drink from the decanter. He lighted a cigarette with fingers that now showed the faintest sign of a tremble, then he dropped into a chair and leaned back in the rays of the prison lamp.

"I shall not attempt to lay my story in that dubious millennium when the ductless glands shall have accomplished so much—for they never may—but will lay it now, when our skilful surgeons do much that Krenwicz expects from the powers of the hormone; these days, a little more than ten years after the Great War, with its shrapnel-ripped crania, its destruction of brain lobes, its replacement of muscles by golden springs and of bones by silver plates, these days which teach us that man is after all a mighty intricate machine at the best. And thanks to what McCaigh calls my association with a few great surgeons here and over across the waters, I shall ask you to step with me into a little room fitted up with scarcely more than an iron bed, a little room in the heart of London, where you will meet Eustice Annesly—who, thanks to a bit of our modern scientific surgical knowledge, faces a dilemma unlike that any other man ever faced before. I shall term my little tale 'The Strange Adventure of the Missing Link.'" With which curious introduction Eastwood, in his quiet, soothing voice, began the narration of:

THE STRANGE ADVENTURE OF THE
MISSING LINK

CHAPTER XLV

A LONG shuddering sigh broke from Eustice Annesly's lips. Out of a welter of pain, searing knife-edged agonies, his tortured mind slowly reasserted its sway. It was as if he were just wakened from some ghastly nightmare in which every conceivable torment had joined to lacerate nerve and tissue, and leave his aching body raw and quivering with intolerable anguish—a nightmare of physical horrors giving way gradually to a foggy torpor broken by white-robed silent figures who came, ministered to him and departed, with every departure leaving him a blissful interval of comfort and forgetfulness. Of late these healing respites had lengthened, the tormenting pangs had been allayed, and the black fog which bound his brain had paled to a thick white mist in whose enveloping folds his eyes served only to reveal a blank wall of opaque light.

With an effort Annesley roused his sluggish body. His hands groped for the bedclothes and threw them aside as he rose with an unwieldy movement and stood uncertainly erect at the bedside. Lifting his hand he tore the gauzy bandage from his eyes and blinked at the unfamiliar room. Around him he saw white distempered walls, a wheeled table whose glass-covered top was laden with a gleaming array of instruments and medicine phials, a large white wardrobe with full-length mirror door.

But what he saw reflected in the mirror sent a thrill of horror, of revulsion, of fear, sweeping over him, a thrill of such staggering intensity that a cry of surprise slipped involuntarily from him.

For, staring at Eustice Annesly from the polished surface of the glass, was a huge, shaggy, monkey-like creature, with squat body and long, hairy arms that reached far below its knees. Its enormous cranium, sloping as it did into a pair of shoulders twice as broad as those of a human being, its total lack of any forehead, its tightly drawn-back lips from which protruded four sharp, yellow teeth, its little, close-set eyes, its deep nostrils, its hairy paunch—all filled him with such fear for his safety that he reached out toward the wall to keep from falling. And, as he did so, the creature behind him performed the same action. So he spun quickly around and looked at the back of him.

But, with the exception of himself, the room was quite empty. And as he stood there, trembling and shivering in every fibre at the strange illusion that he had just seen, the door of the room opened quietly and a white-capped nurse thrust her head in the opening. For only the briefest second, however, did she remain there, staring. Her lower jaw dropped open. Her face blanched as white as her cap. Then, as

Eustice Annesly stepped toward her with the intention of learning what peculiar illness could have caused him to see such an apparition or hallucination in the mirror, the nurse disappeared like a flash. A second later he heard her feet pattering wildly down the corridor. And now he knew that he was in London, for her terror-stricken scream was followed by words with the suggestion of a Cockney accent:

"Gawd 'elp us—the monk is loose!"

The monk! Very odd, reflected Eustice Annesly, that Eustice Annesly, electrical engineer of the Lots Road generating station for the Underground Electric Railways, graduate of the Imperial College of Science and Technology, should be referred to by such a term. But, on the other hand, what was the reason for that reflection in the mirror? Again he turned bewilderedly to it, and for the second time beheld that hideous squat body with its little, beady, malevolent eyes. Oh, it was all too—too incomprehensible, he told himself uneasily.

But as he stood in that one spot debating with himself as to whether he should go down the corridor and seek someone who could throw some light on the nature of his illness, the door of the room was flung violently open and three stalwart young men—evidently janitors or porters, since two of them carried mops—burst into the room and threw themselves ferociously upon him. Only for a bare second did he stand motionless. Then, seeing that the intentions of the newcomers toward him were nothing less than hostile, he fought back with all the energy at his command.

And Eustice Annesly was surprised at his own strength. Twice he struck out with his right arm.

Each time his blow sent a victim hurtling clear across the room. Then he caught himself sinking his teeth in the arm of the third fellow. But, just as he found himself, strangely, getting the better of the whole three, one of them circled quietly behind him, and a second later two hands were gripping his throat like a vise, and his breath—his precious breath—was cut completely off. Rapidly his struggles grew weaker and weaker. The room got darker and darker. And the last thing he remembered was a dizzy blur in which two of his opponents were clutching his kicking legs. Then his knowledge of things external passed away in a swirling blackness.

When he opened his eyes for the second time he saw that he was in the same room, empty as before; the same walls, the same simple, enameled bed were visible. But to his consternation he found himself unable to move. By dint of twisting his neck around he discovered that he was held fast by four great thick, leather straps which ran tightly across his body and terminated in shining metal clasps at the sides of the bed.

What a strange, strange hallucination it all was, he told himself miserably—for hallucination it surely must be! Why in the name of all that was logical should Eustice Annesly, electrical engineer for the Lots Road generating station, be clad in a tightly-buttoned monkey skin and struggling with three strangers? It seemed more like a dream—a horrible nightmare. But then, as he kicked impatiently at the coverlid with a leg that was partly free, he realized with a pang that the illusion was returning: that leg was muscular and hairy, and the toes were long and more prehensile even than fingers.

When, in the name of heaven, he wondered, would someone come and explain how this error of vision—or perhaps of belief—had entered into his prosiac existence? Was it possible, he reflected, by running hastily over the recent events of his life, to arrive at some sort of an explanation of this dumbfounding situation? And acting on his self-suggested idea, he struggled back in the dim recesses of memory, desperately trying to find where and when the thread of consciousness had been snapped off.

CHAPTER XLVI

HE was Eustice Annesly. That much was certain. He had been employed in the engineering department of the huge generating station which supplied the Underground Electric Railways. That, too, was a fact beyond doubt. He had lived at Scarborough House, a private hostel in Guilford Street, W.C.1. That was plainly rememberable. And if he had lived in a hostel, he must have been a bachelor. Suddenly a girl's face flashed across his memory—a face which embraced that unusual combination, yellow-gold hair and brown eyes. And the eyes of tender and yet unfathomable brown were those of Sybil Mainwaring!

With this much fixed in mind, everything else seemed to come back with a rush. With a wave of disappointment and pain, he found himself recalling the last night he had seen her—the night when he had called at her home in Tavistock Square and told her that to him she represented all that was worth having in life. And then, then—ah!—that was the cause of the pain, for her answer had told him that he was too late.

"Eustice, dear boy," she had said. "I'm truly, truly sorry that you've cared for me in the way that you say you have. We have found ourselves to be the same in tastes, likes and dislikes, education—and what-not

338

else. But, dear boy, I don't love you in the way I should to marry you—because—because—the real one has come into my life—and it is too late."

"Too late!" he had ejaculated, while a feeling of bitterness had gripped him fast. "Too late? Some-one else has asked you already, Sybil? You care for him? You've promised him?"

She had nodded slowly. "Yes, Eustice. You will be surprised when I tell you. I met him first at the Claridge ball in Grosvenor Square. It—it was love at first sight. He is——" She had paused, radiantly beautiful at that moment. "He is of the nobility, Eustice. He—he is Geoffrey—Lord Olford."

Lord Geoffrey Olford! Perhaps, then, Eustice An-nesly reflected bitterly, that was the cause of his being where he was, for the mental shock he had received when he learned that the girl whom he loved with all his heart and soul was to marry into the nobility, was stag-gering, to say the least. Geoffrey—Lord Olford! True, he did not personally know the man—nor had he even ever seen him. But he had heard and read of the Eleventh Earl of Olford a great many times. Young and handsome the earl was said to be, a man democratic to the highest degree, a man who was to be seen about London either driving his own car or else walking afoot from his town house to his offices in Leadenhall Street, a man who, though democratic, was yet a member of most of London's most fashionable clubs, sportsman, and, last, but not least, the possessor of a fortune in-herited from his father, the old earl, of over a million pounds sterling. Surely the information that this distin-guished, much blessed and much liked young Earl of

Olford had captured Sybil Mainwaring's heart had been a big reverse for one Eustice Annesly, commoner, in the game of life. But there had remained no alternative but to bear the blow stoically, for one thing was certain: he knew Sybil Mainwaring too well to believe that she had been influenced in any way by either Geoffrey Lord Olford's title, or even Geoffrey Lord Olford's fortune of a million pounds. She loved the young nobleman—and that fact alone must shatter any hopes on the part of Eustice Annesly.

He caught himself up with a start from this sentimental mind-roving. This would never bring to light the peculiar causes that had led up to his being where he was—and encased in this monkey-skin garment. And so, then, what had followed his departure from Sybil Mainwaring's home in Tavistock Square? He thought hard for a moment, and then remembered. A sleepless night, a night of tossing until dawn, a night of misery and soul anguish. And the same thing the next night. And the night following. And then over and over for several more nights—until he had found himself becoming haggard and worn from loss of sleep and continuous brooding.

Here he paused in his reflections. Had he gone insane in that week of mental torture after he learned that Sybil was to become Lady Olford? If so—and it seemed reasonable—then this room was the private room of a workhouse observation ward—or even a lunatic asylum—instead of a room in a hospital. And furthermore, the queer hallucination of shaggy body and hairy limbs was explained.

But he must find out more definitely than that. He had no remembrance of any court trial for alleged insanity. In fact, he had not reached the break in consciousness yet. So what had happened after that week of brooding and insomnia, that week when he had even thrown over his berth with the electric company that fed the tubes, with a half thought of going out to the colonies? He strained his mind on this point, for he realized that it was important. Had he gone to Australia—to Canada? No, he held no recollection of boarding a passenger liner, at least at this juncture. But suddenly it flashed upon him: Scarnum's American Circus! That was it! The hoardings of London had been plastered with lithographs announcing that Scarnum's American Circus and Collection of International Freaks would open at the big new Aldwich Hippodrome, just off the Strand, the week of April 3rd. April 3rd, then, was a date to use as a starting-point. And he—he—yes, of course,—that was it exactly—he had decided to take in Scarnum's show on the opening night in a desperate attempt to get his mind off the loss on which it was dwelling so fixedly; to forget the one fact that was slowly undermining his happiness and spoiling his life.

And so, on the night of April 3rd, he had found himself among the crowds threading their way back and forth between the platforms of Scarnum's side-show of freaks, distracted to some extent from his own woes. In turn he had viewed the American curiosities known as the rubber-skinned man and the tattooed woman; and then—then—the petrified mermaid, the albino negro, the glass eater, the three-legged man. And then—what? Ah—he had stopped in front of a stout cage which bore a sign reading:

GRILLO, THE MISSING LINK
THE ALMOST HUMAN GORILLA
Has Every Function of Man but Speech.
Habitat: West African Coast.

Now that was really odd. It was the first thing, Eustice Annesly decided, that he had been able to bring to mind which could be connected in any way with his hallucination. The recollection of that grotesque, man-like creature, skulking in one corner of the cage, was very distinct. Its long, hairy arms, its yellow-fanged, red-gummed, leering face, its huge, hairy chest were identical in appearance with the apparition he had just seen in the mirror. In his mind's eye he could still see it, just as it had appeared when it walked to the bars of the cage and stood erect on its hind legs, looking vacantly out at the gaping crowd.

But what had taken place after that? Again he concentrated on the past. There had been a swarthy, black-moustached Italian sweeping that portion of the floor which lay between the platforms and the railing which kept back the spectators. The latter had —he had—yes, he had carefully deposited his coat on the railing near Eustice Annesly while he prepared to work underneath the cage with his long brush. In his eagerness and curiosity to catch a better glimpse

of that African simian Annesly had pressed forward to
the railing. Accidentally he had dislodged the coat.
It had slipped to the floor. And then——

A blinding flash. A roar. Thousands of twinkling
lights, followed by darkness—black, utter, impalpable
—which closed quickly in on him. And that, therefore,
had been the point where the thread of consciousness
had parted.

But how—how—how in the name of all that was
sensible, all that was coherent, all that was rational,
had he come to find himself in such a weird situation as
this? Oh, it was all so absurd, so impossible! He must
have an enormously high temperature, he concluded,
and therefore be delirious. But would no one ever
come and explain matters? Was there no doctor in
the place that could——

The door of the room swung open and an elderly
man entered. He was somewhat stooped. His chin
was covered by a bushy black beard, flecked here and
there with gray, and his twinkling black eyes were
framed in heavy gold-rimmed eye-glasses. It was plain
that he was a doctor or a surgeon, for he wore a surgeon's long white apron and carried a shining stetho-
scope hanging loosely around his neck. At his heels
trotted a younger man, with sleek black hair deftly
parted in the middle, and with features strongly resem-
bling those of the older man. Like the first, he, too,
wore a long white apron.

Quickly he closed the door and turned the key in
the lock. At once Annesly burst out:

"In the name of God, doctor—if you *are* a doctor
instead of the keeper of a madhouse—what is the mean-

ing of all this? Where am I? What is the explanation of this monkey skin that I am buttoned in? Why am I strapped here in bed?"

The older man looked toward the younger one.

"You see, Boris," he said. "Your father's theories were correct. It *can* be done. The hypoglossal nerve was the last to join. He speaks."

"Ah, father," replied the man addressed as Boris, speaking with a faint accent, "I have done you a gross injustice all along. I apologize. I salute you, father, as the greatest brain surgeon of the twentieth century. At last you have——"

"Stop this infernal palavering," Annesly shouted, "and loosen these straps. What have I done that I should be fastened to my bed like a raving maniac? Am I——"

The older man raised his hand. "Do you solemnly promise that you will be sensible—and quiet—and that you will attempt no violence whatever if I release you?"

"Promise?" Annesly retorted angrily. "Certainly I promise. But there is no need of your exacting such a promise from me. I am Eustice Annesly, an electrical engineer of the Underground Railways power station. I am——"

"No," interrupted the younger man. "Eustice Annesly—or nearly all that was mortal of Eustice Annesly—was buried in Brompton Cemetery just seven weeks ago to-day."

CHAPTER XLVII

"BURIED?" stammered the individual who had just informed the doctor that he was one Eustice Annesly. "Eustice Annesly—buried? Myself—buried?" He laughed loudly. "Come, come, my dear sir. You're a poor joker. But tell me the truth; I'm waiting for it."

"I told you once," the younger of the white-aproned figures returned coolly, "that Eustice Annesly was——"

"Hush, Boris," broke in the bearded man. "He is our patient—do not lose sight of that fact. You must not excite him. Bring up two chairs." He glanced down at the bed and its occupant. "I will try to explain, Mr.—er—ah—well, my friend, I am going to address you as Eustice Annesly, for after all, a man is indisputably that which thinks for him. And I want *you* at all times to consider yourself Eustice Annesly, for if you allow yourself to think otherwise, Heaven alone knows what disastrous effect it would have on the integrity of that vital part of you which is, after all, Eustice Annesly. Remember that, my friend, after you have heard all you are to hear; never allow yourself for a moment to consider yourself other than

345

he, for that way lies madness." He paused. "You see—Eustice Annesly, so far as all bodily intents and purposes go, is dead. And you—well—you are, in body at least, one Grillo."

"In body—Grillo?" gasped the patient in the bed, listening to this strange, half-explanatory, half-apologetic peroration. "Good God, doctor, you are not trying to tell me that—that I am Grillo, the monkey-man? Surely not that—not that. Oh, how could such a thing—— You must explain. You must! And release me," he begged.

The older medical man strode quickly to the bedside, and, with three sharp snaps of the steel buckles, flung the straps off the body there held down. Annesly—or at least he who had just received the dumbfounding advice that he should continue so to consider himself— drew himself stiffly up to a sitting posture in the bed, involuntarily shuddering as he caught sight of his arms —long and shaggy. Then he gazed, wide-eyed and fearful, toward the man who was to tell him something that he dreaded; dreaded and yet did not understand. The two medical men dropped into the chairs. Then the elder asked:

"Do you remember where you were when you lost consciousness?"

"Yes, Dr.—Dr.——"

"Michaelovitch," the bearded man put in. "Dr. Andrev Michaelovitch."

"Yes, Dr. Michaelovitch. I had attended Scarnum's American Circus at the big new Aldwich Hippodrome in the attempt to forget an unhappy love affair that was spoiling all my days and nights. I was standing

in front of a cage which held a great hairy gorilla."
Annesly paused and fell to weeping. "Oh, doctor,
doctor," he broke forth, "don't tell me that in some
unaccountable way I have—have become that beast.
It's all a horrible delusion on my part, isn't it?"

The bearded man made no denial or affirmation of
this statement. So Annesly wiped his eyes on the
corner of the sheet and went on desperately: "And,
doctor, I was standing near the cage, watching the—
the—thing. A black-moustached fellow—evidently an
Italian—was sweeping in front of the cage. He placed
his coat on the railing. Accidentally I dislodged it.
As it fell to the floor a blinding flash took place, a
fearful roaring noise began in my ears—and that's all
I can remember."

"Poor, poor fellow!" the bearded man commented,
looking at his patient with eyes in which kindness and
pity were plainly visible. "Poor, poor fellow!" he repeated. "You have stated things exactly as they
occurred. I know that you cannot realize the pity I
have for you—how I feel for you. And I am afraid,
too, that after I have finished you will hate me instead
of admitting that I saved your life. But the explanation you must have, for it is due to you. Now pay
close attention.

"Boris here, my son, and I are surgeons, both graduates from the University of Moscow, Russia—although
thirty years apart. You will note that we speak
English—almost perfectly. In regard to that it is
only necessary for me to say that all scientific men on
the Continent, all men who aspire to any position in
their respective professions, learn English. So much

for that. For thirty long years I have made a specialty
of the technique and theory of brain operations; Boris
here is already following in my footsteps. But what,
you wonder, are we doing in your country? That is a
question which must surely appear to you. In answer
to that let me say merely—present political conditions
in Russia. No man who has given his life to the mastery
of a field of knowledge and the perfection of a technique
can tolerate a Communism which rates the lowest
laborer as the highest productive factor in the nation's
economic existence, and ranks a specialist with the non-
essential classes. No, my friend. For that is Russia,
at least at the present. And that, I think, will explain
sufficiently why Boris and I left that country just two
years ago. We came to your Liverpool. And from
your great throbbing city of Liverpool we travelled on
to London.

"My friend, to a man, or to two men, in fact, who
have made their living for a number of years either by
being called into consultation on serious brain injuries,
or by operating on the human cranium for such, as
well as brain tumors, it proved no easy matter to gain
a foothold in London. Securing permission to remain
in your country was but an infinitesimal part of the
battle. We had no professional reputation, no ac-
quaintances, no hospital connections. Brain injuries,
brain tumors likewise, are comparatively rare, and
Harley Street seems to have a monopoly of those which
do occur. So had we endeavored to remain in our
special field only, either starvation or the reduction
of our capital to zero would have resulted. And so
finally after talking it over, we used our capital to build

and equip this tiny emergency hospital off Trafalgar Square. We——"

"Oh," Annesley broke in, a light suddenly dawning on him, "this is the Charing Cross Emergency Hospital, then?"

"Yes," answered the medical man quietly. "Not the Charing Cross Hospital in King William Street, but the Charing Cross Emergency Hospital in the Strand —a private institution depending for its upkeep solely upon the chance accidents that happen in the busy down-town section of London. We take care of many surgical cases here, for they come in to us at the rate of four or five a week. People whom we help at a critical moment for them, as a rule pay us. A few, of course, are not able. At any rate, ethically—and financially— we have made good. So much for that. And now let me return to my explanation.

"On the night of April 3rd we received a 'hurry call' to the Aldwich Hippodrome by telephone; some sort of an explosion had taken place. Although Boris usually acts as ambulance surgeon, I, too, sprang into the ambulance that night, for I realized that we were perhaps confronted with an unusually shocking situation. In less than four minutes we had reached Aldwich, and a moment later the Hippodrome itself. There we were excitedly informed by Mr. Scarnum, the American manager of the circus which had opened there, what had occurred. A terrific explosion—according to the testimony of a number of spectators—had taken place barely an instant after a young man had dislodged a coat from a railing. The owner of that coat, an Italian porter employed by the circus, was fatally injured.

"So at this point," Dr. Andrev Michaelovitch went on, "I shall interrupt my narrative in order to tell you briefly of that Italian's dying confession, made through an interpreter and in this very hospital two days later. In that confession he declared that he had joined the show at New York for the express purpose of killing or injuring Scarnum, the wealthy American owner and manager, against whom he had a personal grudge. And for this reason he had carried a dynamite bomb with him for days, clear across the ocean, in fact, awaiting his chance. He knew that his chance would come on the opening night in London, for Scarnum always personally inspected his exhibition on each opening night. And this night the fanatical Italian was all in readiness, the bomb with its delicate triggers in his right-hand coat pocket. But in the excitement of affairs he had thoughtlessly removed that coat. A spectator in front of the cage of Grillo, the 'missing link,' had accidentally knocked it off the railing where it hung. It exploded—with fearful effects.

"Most of the onlookers fortunately suffered only minor injuries. But the man who had dislodged the coat, as we later discovered by letters in his pocket, was a Mr. Eustice Annesly, an employe of a plant of this city which supplied current to the Tubes. Oh, my friend, he was fearfully, terribly mutilated. Both arms and a leg were blown completely off. Had it not been for the fact that a level-headed doctor in the audience had immediately stepped in and ligated the opened arteries of the poor injured body, the man, Eustice Annesly would not have lived even long enough to be brought to our Charing Cross Emergency Hospital.

But now let me describe the effects of the explosion on the cage containing Grillo, erroneously known as 'the missing link.' That cage was splintered into matchwood. The iron bars were distorted and twisted in every direction. And one of these bars, broken in the middle, had pierced the skull of Grillo, with the result that the animal, although absolutely unscathed so far as its body was concerned, was injured in a vital spot, the brain. It was an exceedingly valuable animal, you may be sure, and its American owner, eager to save its life, begged us to take it to the hospital in the ambulance. Knowing that I would be interested in the case, Boris needed no urging. Thus it fell out that poor Eustice Annesly, trembling on the brink of death, along with the gorilla in the same condition was put in the ambulance and driven as swiftly as possible up the Strand to this hospital.

"Now, my friend, Eustice Annesly was doomed. Had he lived, his life would have been nothing less than a hell to him, crippled and deformed beyond all description. As for the gorilla it was sinking rapidly; if it died, however, it meant merely the loss of a valuable animal to Scarnum, the American Circus owner. So here was a chance, a Heaven-sent opportunity, to make an experiment the making of which had long been the dream of my life. I am going to describe that experiment to you—but I fear that it will be exceptionally difficult for me to make it comprehensible to one not versed in surgery. So if I use scientific terms which are not wholly understandable, then you must pardon me. I will do my best to render it plain to an unscientific mind."

CHAPTER XLVIII

"BEFORE I proceed," the doctor said, "may I ask if you have ever read of how Dr. Alexis Carrell, of France, during the Great War, ten years ago, transposed the arm of a French private to the stump of a French general?"

The man in the bed nodded wearily.

"Then you are, of course, aware that by careful technique, in stitching together the blood-vessels and the nerves of an organ to a body in which that organ never grew, Nature causes a complete reunion of the tissue. In fact, long before Carrell's experiment in France, this was amply demonstrated by a surgeon in America's mid-west, Dr. Victor Lespinasse, who had succeeded in amputating the hind leg of a dog and replacing it with the hind leg of an altogether different dog. That case is fully set forth in the surgical bulletins of those years. Both the *Journal* of the American Medical Association and the London *Lancet*, I believe, hold detailed accounts of the experiment. But if, however, not being a reader of the medical Press, you have any doubt about the verity of the foregoing accomplishments, you doubtlessly recollect a case which was described all over America and England some years ago: a case in which a young New York millionaire, shot by a chorus girl

352

whom he had wronged, was ultimately forced to go on the operating-table and have the kidney of a St. Bernard dog put in place of his injured one. The operation, I may add, was a complete success."

Again the man in the bed nodded weakly. "Yes, I read of that case."

"Well, having recounted the foregoing cases." Michaelovitch went on, "let me proceed to describe in brief, certain salient and basic anatomical facts about the human brain. That organ, as you may know, governs the different muscular systems of the human body—and likewise takes impressions from the various impression localities—by a simple system of a single spinal cord and twelve pairs of nerves known as the cranial nerves. The superficial origins of all these cranial nerves and that one great nerve, the spinal cord—in other words, their points of emergence from the brain—are found in the ventral surface of that organ; and by an intricate process of branching and re-branching they ultimately form the great nervous system.

"Now some of the fibers of these cranial nerves and this cord, these trunk lines, as I might call them, are purely sensory; that is to say, they receive impressions only. Others are motor, which means that they actuate with motion the different muscular systems of the body by means of their infinite branches. And some of them are even both motor and sensory. Running quickly over the twelve pairs of cranial nerves, they are respectively: the olfactory, the optic, the oculomotor, the trochlear, the trigeminal, the abducens, the facial, the auditory, the glossopharyngeal, the pneumogastric, the spinal accessory, and the hypoglossal.

"Now, regarding the blood supply of the brain: suffice to say that the large arteries of the neck and of the spinal cord unite at the base of the brain to form a complete arterial circle which surrounds the pituitary body and the optic chiasm. In other words, the blood supply of the brain is connected to the blood supply of the body by a close group of vessels, all of which enter in company with each other at the tiny lower orifice of the skull known as the occipital foramen. So much for that. I daresay I weary and confuse you.

"Why not, I have always asked myself, could not a human brain be transposed from the body of one man to that of another? True, the great specialists of the last century in brain surgery—Sir Victor Horsley, Krause, Cushing, Frazer, Hartley, Kenyon, Keen, Buchardt, Kocher—would have laughed at such a project. But I, Dr. Andrev Michaelovitch, have for years maintained that the thing was possible under the following conditions: first, that a substitute for the cerebro-spinal fluid could be found and injected below the brain membrane, the dura and pia mater, immediately after the operation. Only with the proper substitute could the anastomosis, or joining up of blood-vessels and nerve trunks, be furthered by Nature. Second, that the optic nerves of the new brain were joined to the optic nerves leading to the retina of the eyes; the auditory nerves to the nerves leading to the tympani of the ears, and so forth all through the twelve pairs of cranial nerves. And third, that the blood-vessels of the transposed brain were connected without error to the blood-vessels leaving the spinal cord of the body, which was to constitute its new abode, artery to artery, vein to vein. Under these conditions why would not all-wonderful Nature permit the healing, the union, to take place? Ah, my friend, I, Andrev Michaelovitch, have absolutely demonstrated the truth of my theory. But I digress. Let me continue:

"Coming back in the ambulance that night, I made a quick examination of the mutilated body of Eustice Annesly and the body of the simian. I found, as I already told you, that the brain of Eustice Annesly was uninjured—while the body was fearfully mangled; that the brain of the simian was mutilated—and its body was unharmed. Quickly I disclosed my plan to Boris.

"While the bodies were placed on the double operating-table I quickly killed a pair of white rabbits which I had been keeping for experimental purposes; then I withdrew in a sterile syringe the spinal fluid which I had counted upon to further the union of nerves and blood-vessels. But, ah!—that is the secret of my success—I mixed with that spinal fluid a certain organic compound. When the name of that compound and its proportions in the mixture are published in my book a year from to-day, cranial surgery will become revolutionized. Completely so. But again I digress.

"With the two bodies in our tiny operating-room, we drew down the shades and locked the doors. Both of the victims were unconscious; hence we required no prying nurse to administer an anesthetic. Now, my friend, had it been twenty years ago, the operation would have been utterly impossible. In those days the old operation of craniectomy was exceptionally slow and tedious, consisting as it did of the Gigli process. This process comprised a preliminary boring of holes in the skull a short distance apart, with the cranial drill, the passing through these holes of a threaded probe, the drawing through of the Gigli wire saw, the cutting away of the bone from within outward, and the final trimming with the Rongeur's forceps. In this way an opening was made for trephining operations an inch at a time.

"But to-day we have what is known as the electric trephine saw—a circular blade revolving many thousand times per minute by means of a tiny motor attached to the handle, and provided with an adjustable guard which allows the saw blade to cut only through the bone and not to cleave the brain membrane lying directly below. So much for that.

"In less time than it takes to tell it, Boris was working upon Eustice Annesly, I upon the gorilla. I first made a number of radiating incisions in the scalp, and laid it back in long strips, each strip pinched at the base with a steel clamp to prevent undue hemorrhage. Then, by means of one of our electric trephine saws, I cut quickly through the skull, traveling along a line which crossed the forehead and dropped down and around the base of the head. I was then able to remove the dome of the cranium, together with the entire rear almost to the spinal column, all in one piece. It remained a comparatively simple matter to remove the terribly mutilated brain, although I was forced, of course, to ligate the blood-vessels of the spinal cord to prevent hemorrhage from that source.

"And by this time, Boris, with the use of another trephine saw, had rather clumsily exposed the brain of the man, Eustice Annesly. I then stepped in and removed it, using the most extreme care in detaching it from its connections with Eustice Annesly's eye sockets, spinal cord, and other points. From that time on I had no assistance. In fact, I was forced to work in such close quarters that I greatly feared my technique would prove ultimately to be a waste of time.

"My friend, I cannot go into details about that transposition. You could not understand the difficulties which I encountered. Enough to tell you that within exactly one hour I had joined the brain of Eustice Annesly to the body of Grillo, the monkey-man—at every main nerve and blood-vessel. Below the dura mater I had injected a quantity of my combination of rabbits' spinal fluid and—— But—ah!— that, of course, is my own secret. I had replaced the huge, irregular cup of bone—now trepanned by Boris at the point where it had been fractured by the cage bar—on the remaining portion of the skull, fastening it securely in place by four silver plates and their tiny silver screws, all of which had been first sterilized by boiling and then kept in a solution of boric acid. And, lastly, I had drawn back the strips of scalp and sewn them together, with drains between each strip. It now remained to be seen what the result would be.

"You—a combination of the body of Grillo, the monkey-man, and the brain of Eustice Annesly—lived. You lay motionless for days and days. With the exception of Boris and myself, not an employee of the hospital knew but that you were merely Grillo—for to this moment neither of us has ever breathed a word of that operation. After a few days of coma, and then a further week of artificial feeding, you ate automatically from a spoon. A day after that you opened your eyelids. Came a later time when you moved your limbs in response to the stimuli of pinpricks. We perceived with astonishment that, one by one, the muscles were gradually falling under control of the new brain; that the brain center governing each muscle had an unimpeded path for its energy currents; that, in other words, the human cerebrum and cerebellum were able to govern perfectly the body of the creature most nearly human anatomically. You are aware, no doubt, that the gorilla has no tail. It would be interesting, a very interesting experiment, to see whether the brain of Eustice Annesly were able to govern or control an entirely new organ. But that we cannot ascertain.

"And so, day by day, we watched your recovery to health and strength with painstaking minuteness. But as you grew stronger and stronger you seemed to be in a daze mentally. Could it be possible, I asked myself again and again, that the monkey tongue was not susceptible to the impulses from the speech centers of the human brain? Or had the hypoglossal nerve, governing the tongue muscles, failed to unite? Or had I, in the course of the operation, in some way damaged the speech center, that region including the cortical area of all the convolutions which enter the formation of the fossa of Sylvius? I tell you we were puzzled.

"And to-day, as Boris and I entered the hospital together, we were informed that our strange patient, Scarnum's monkey, had risen from bed and attempted to wander away—and that three of our porters had been compelled to choke it into insensibility and strap it down. Immediately we entered the room, with the result that at last we heard speech from your lips— speech which we had looked for so long and so hope- lessly. That is all."

CHAPTER XLIX

THE doctor had finished. A thousand thoughts whirled through the mind of Eustice Annesly—that mind now imprisoned in the body of a simian. Unable for a minute to utter any sort of a reply, he lay there dimly wondering what life could mean to him now that he was no longer in human form. But the more he tried to think on the matter the more strange, terrible, overwhelming it all became. During that short space of time, which seemed like ages to him, he feared that he would go mad.

He pressed the palms of his hairy hands to his equally hairy head and struggled to think—to gain some conception of this new order of things which must persist until his death. Dr. Michaelovitch had saved his brain—the brain of Eustice Annesly—yes. But he had imprisoned it hopelessly for life in the hideous body of a gorilla.

So what had he gained? Life? Yes. But life—life—what must such a life be to the personality, the mentality, the psychical side of Eustice Annesly? How could he ever adjust himself to it? As to that, however, time alone could tell. So after what seemed hours of soul agony, he answered the man who had explained matters so painstakingly to him:

"Dr. Michaelovitch, I cannot thank you for saving my life. I cannot grasp the situation as yet. I cannot realize it all in this short space that I have had time to think about it. All I know is that it would have been far kinder to Eustice Annesly to have allowed him to die in entirety that night of April 3rd." He stopped, overcome by his own feelings. Then he raised himself up in bed. "In your own scientific enthusiasm you believe that you have saved a life, but"—and his voice raised to a high pitch—"you are a murderer, Dr. Michaelovitch, a man who has murdered another man's soul!"

To his surprise, however, two great tears welled up in the medical man's eyes, and in a low voice the latter replied to his accusation:

"You are wrong—totally, totally wrong. Above all else, it is the surgeon's duty to save life—or to prolong it. Grillo, the monkey-man, and Eustice Annesly, the engineer, were sinking rapidly to death, one with an uninjured body, the other with an uninjured brain. It was my duty to save one life from the two—and that was what I did. To any man with a fair, rational mind, I did the right thing. And I feel that some day you will think the same. But, apart from all consideration of medical ethics, you forget, my friend, my duty as a surgeon to science itself. Within a year from to-day I shall have in the Press a book that will cause nothing less than a tumult among the surgeons in your country and America. And I shall then ask you to come forward with your testimony and substantiate my claims. That book, containing an exposition of my own peculiar variations in operative technique, as well as the secret formula for my artificial cerebro-spinal fluid, will make possible operations never dreamed of at the present day." He paused and then added: "Will you not try to look at the matter from my point of view?"

For several long minutes Eustice Annesly—for so he had just been advised to consider himself, and so he intended to do as long as sanity held out—pondered. After all, he reflected, why harbor resentment and hate against this surgeon? In the medical man's estimation he had done what was best. And surely there would be some niche in the world that the new Eustice Annesly could occupy with happiness to himself and use to his fellow-beings. So he thrust out a hairy paw. A look of relief came over Michaelovitch's face as he seized it and grasped it firmly.

"I'll try," said the patient. "But I have an instinctive fear that I shall fail to be in accord with life from now on."

And Eustice Annesly was right. For his existence, through many long months to come, proved to be only a burden, a miserable, unhappy one for him.

His recovery to health and strength was rapid after his interview with old Dr. Michaelovitch and the latter's son, Boris Michaelovitch. Each day the former visited his bedside and talked long and earnestly, trying to reconcile him to the fate to which he had been doomed by the act of a fanatic Italian. But he noticed, however, that on the second day the medical man ordered the mirror removed.

Often during the long, tedious afternoons he lay back in his bed and studied his condition from the strict viewpoint of cause and effect, trying to convince himself that Sybil Mainwaring was wholly to blame. For had it not been on account of her refusal to marry him that he had attended Scarnum's American Circus? And was it not at Scarnum's Circus that he had met with such a horrible accident? But try as he might he could not blame her dear self for his present situation. All he could associate with his mental picture of her was longing, deep, heartfelt yearning, unceasing tenderness and love. And thus, by the peculiar mental action which causes each individual in life to blame someone for the calamities that disturb his life, he began to hate a man whom he had never seen, never known: Geoffrey Olford, Lord Olford—the Earl of Olford!— the one person to whose arms Sybil Mainwaring had turned.

But one brief gleam there was to illumine his dark and gloomy thoughts: there was no one, neither mother nor father, brother nor sister, to bemoan the supposed death of Eustice Annesly in the explosion at the Aldwich Hippodrome. Thank God at least for that. No one need feel grief at his going, unless it be a cold, hard-faced spinster who kept a hostel in the West End, and she no doubt had long ago sold the last of his belongings that sat in the big front room on the second floor overlooking Guilford Street and the morning flow of Royal Mail vans.

As for Scarnum, he was to have more to do with that paradoxical individual before he left the hospital. Three days after his first interview with old Dr. Andrev Michaelovitch, a tall, flashily dressed man, radiating in every sartorial detail the atmosphere of America, wearing gray spats, a gray vest, a diamond pin of at least five carats in size, and a suit containing the most striking checks, was ushered into his tiny hospital room. After insolently staring down at Eustice Annesly for several minutes, he finally burst out:

"Won'erful, won'erful, won'erful! Beyond my understandin', that's what it is! Old Dr. Mike, downstairs, has told me all about your case. I tell you our fortunes are made." He jerked out a typewritten sheet of paper and a fountain-pen. "Here's a contrack connectin' you with the Scarnum shows at ten pounds a week. How does that strike you?"

"No money could tempt me," Eustice Annesly retorted from an easy-chair where he was convalescing, "to go on exhibition before a crowd of jostling, staring curiosity-seekers. So it will be quite useless for you to make any offers."

"Won'erful, won'erful!" the check-suited man replied, apparently undisturbed by the curt refusal of his offer. "That body—and hooman speech! Grillo—the talkin' ape! With that advertisement we'll take Amurrica by storm. My friend, I meant guineas instead o' pounds. Is it a go?"

Eustice Annesly's only answer was a derisive, bitter laugh. "You raise me ten shillings, eh, my good friend?"

The peripatetic human cross-word puzzle from the other side of the Atlantic Ocean was nonplussed. "My friend, I was slightly in error when I mentioned the sum of ten guineas a week. In reality I meant twenty guineas."

"Absolutely useless," returned Annesly angrily, for

the self-confidence of the American showman in believing that he could induce him, Annesly, to sign his contract, grated on the very monkey ears that heard the offer.

And so, by degrees, Scarnum worked up to fifty guineas a week. And when Annesly sneeringly refused that last offer, a cold, hard look came on the showman's face. He thrust one forefinger at his hearer and snarled:

"You forget, my friend of the anymule kingdom, that, while your brain is your own, you're usin' a body which formerly belonged to me—the body of the original Grillo, for which I paid two thousand five hundred cold dollars from an African hunter. And, furthermore, the body is worth exactly that amount to me. Either deliver it over or pay me the cash. I've got you just where——"

"That will be enough from you, Scarnum!" calmly interrupted the elder Michaelovitch, who had entered the hospital room at that second. "I have the names of witnesses who heard you say, directly after the explosion, that if the monkey died his body would not be worth even one hundred dollars to you for taxidermic purposes. And since on the poor multilated body of Eustice Annesly there was a wallet containing nearly thirty pounds, I herewith tender you twenty-one pounds of it—and I give you exactly three minutes to accept!"

And Scarnum, old and wise to the devious ways of law, accepted the money without further dispute and wrote out a bill of sale giving to one Eustice Annesly full and unqualified possesion of the body of Grillo, known as the "missing link." But as he picked up his hat and cane and turned to leave the room, he looked toward Annesly and remarked, in a surprisingly friendly tone of voice:

"Always remember, my friend, that the offer of fifty guineas a week in England or two hundred and fifty dollars a week in Amurrica stands good. I'll warrant that you'll not find the world so pleasant a place to live in—now that you've got the outward semblance of an anymule. And so I leave you, f'r the present. But I think you'll come round to my views before many moons. Wire me collect when you're ready to join. Our route's in the *English Carnival Review*—an' in Amurrica any telegraph office can locate Scarnum's Show. Awr revore!" And he walked from the room.

As time proved, Scarnum was right.

On the day Eustice Annesly left the hospital, he departed in perfect friendliness with old Dr. Michaelovitch, but with a fixed determination not to return to that starting-point of his new life, no matter what befell. And although plans he had none, hopes beat high in his heart that he would surely find some work in the world, some congenial occupation by which he could prove his use to mankind in spite of his dreadful handicap. But the events of the first day only turned that hope into a feeling of profound despondency.

CHAPTER L

WHEN Eustice Annesly left the Charing Cross Emergency Hospital, he carried in his pocket eight pounds, eleven shillings, and three pence, an amount sufficient to sustain an ordinary man in London for a month. He was completely clad in human apparel, wearing a black suit, ill fitting, to be sure, considering the grotesquely proportioned gorilla body which it had to cover, huge black shoes of the largest size that a Strand bootmaker could make, shoes which clumped and thumped at every step; a soft hat, and an immense pair of tan kid gloves. He also carried a light cane. But there was unfortunately no way by which he could conceal his hideous face with its tufts of coarse fur, its sharp, protruding yellow teeth, its tightly-drawn red lips, and its tiny, piercing black eyes.

As a result of this, no doubt, no sooner had he traversed a half-block along the Strand than a horse, drawing a baker's cart, caught sight of him, reared up on its hind legs, snorted, and dashed madly down the street, overturning the light cart and throwing out the driver. And in getting quickly away from that spot lest he be held responsible for the accident, he came around a bend into full view of another horse,

367

which reared on its hind legs and then dashed madly up on the pavement, sliding down, light cart and all, the steps of the yawning entrance of a Tube station, from which the people poured out panic-stricken. Immediately, a tall bobby, helmet on righteous head, stepped over to him and brandishing his truncheon cried angrily:

"Keep h'out of this district, you H'American side-show freak, you! You'll 'ave h'ev'ry 'orse in Lunnon a-runnin' aw'y. H'if the traffic gets tangled up on h'account of you, I'll be takin' you in, and you'll be gettin' a month in gaol 'er fined ten pun's. Now—out with you!"

So, without any argument, Eustice Annesly turned sadly away, beckoning a staring cabby, who listened wide-eyed at the curb to the conversation: for he had seen enough of London police to know that traffic in the heart of the city was their God. "Drive me to the East End—anywhere—set me down somewhere on—on a side street off—off Commercial Road."

The cabby scratching his head, drove off with his strange fare just as a large crowd almost swamped the taxi. And seated back on its cushions, Eustice Annesly bowled through the City, out through Aldgate, and over to that part of London where a shabby, ill-dressed, horrible monstrosity such as himself would surely fit—the East End—the slums! As the cab at last came to a whining halt, he climbed out, tendering the cabby a pound-note and waving away the change. The latter, staring at the note and then at his fare, was off in an instant, probably lest the latter suffer a change of heart.

And now Eustice Annesly walked slowly along Commercial Road, where bobbies there were none, and horses not in sight, at least at this point. He turned quickly down the first cross-street, which was obviously thickly populated by people of the poorer class, with small dun-colored brick houses crowding each other, and each with shutters that hung for the most part by one hinge. A group of children played in the street. Dogs frisked about them. All was peace and tranquillity. Then a child looked up. He beckoned to his little companion. Then the entire group looked up. Terror! Panic! Every child in the group ran screaming and terror-stricken into the closest houses! And people stuck heads out of windows from all directions.

The dogs were the only creatures that did not run. While a few backed off yelping with tails between their legs, a number of others growled deeply at Annesly. Then, as he stepped back in alarm, they tried to attack him, fangs bared; and it was only by beating viciously at them with his cane that he was able to drive them off, to set them one and all in terrified flight. A cat, standing on a front gate which he passed slowly by, puffed up its fur and spat fiercely at him. And now the East End side street became suddenly filled with adults instead of children. They ringed themselves about him with, however, a generous allowance of space between themselves and him—and as he walked straightway right through the ring, it broke, melted, and the occupants thereof turned like cattle and joined the enormous throng that now formed itself in his wake.

"Wot in 'ell is it?"

"Blimey, Ned, wot does you fink it is?"

"H'it's a h'animal, that's wot it is?"

"Dahn't you fool yourself. Hit's a dirty nigger with 'air glued on 'is fyce."

"H'it's a bloody griller, like wot's in the Zoo. An' 'e's wearin' pants an' a cowt, that's wot."

"Griller me h'eye! H'I've been abaht meself a bit. Looky th' owld lydy. She aren't tykin' no chawnces. She's got a bloomin' brick in 'er 'and. Throw it, ol' lydy, throw it 'ard."

"Drive th' stinkin' thing off the street. Thinks it's a toff, do it? Gettin' a dole, I bet you, w'en it art to be in a cyge."

"Hi! you—wot you lookin' fer? They ain't no pub in this street. Lumme!"

Exclamations, hoots, jeers, discussions—Annesly heard them all. And then suddenly someone threw with vicious force a brick, the sharp corner of which struck him squarely in the ribs. Only the padded fur beneath his ill-fitting coat saved him from injury, and the force of the blow sent him staggering forward. Goaded to desperation, he turned and rushed at them. And they fell away from his onslaught like leaves before a gust of autumn wind, fighting, tumbling, tripping over one another to escape. And in that instant Eustice Annesly began to see plainly that he was a thing outcast.

And thus it was, therefore, that he walked aimlessly, hopelessly, up and down the side streets that led off Commercial Road, till noontime, with always that immense mob dogging his every footstep, a mob that attained an increment of a new human member for every one who, satiated with the strange sight, dropped

off and went back to his home. But at twelve o'clock
Eustice Annesly began to feel the pangs of hunger, an
overwhelming desire for a bun and a pot of tea at the
least, and with a backward glance at that ever-follow-
ing rabble he stepped into a spruce little restaurant
with white tables and an inviting cold joint in the window. But no sooner had he opened the door than a
woman, who had evidently been watching all the time
from within, flew at him with a broom, like a veritable
wildcat.

"Get h'out o' 'ere, ye 'orrible beast, ye freak!" she
shrilled. "Do I be feedin' the likes of ye' with yer
dirty red tongue, an' I'll never 'ave a customer again
for a year."

The rabble behind him sent up a mighty jeer. He
slunk wretchedly away. The mob followed. After a
short while he conjured up enough courage to try
another restaurant which advertised "skate and chips"
for tenpence. But the result was the same: he was
driven away, the very doors locked on him, the mob
hooting derisively in his rear, before he had even a
chance to speak. And he kept trying all the afternoon,
this time boldly up and down the whole length of Commercial Road itself. But invariably he met with only
one of two receptions—either terror or utter hostility—
and in almost every case doors that were locked before
he even put a hairy, gloved paw on their polished knobs.

By nightfall, consequently, he was so faint from
hunger that he could scarcely stand upright. So he
changed his tactics and, after slipping into the friendly
opening of a mews, made his way round to the rear of
a cheap eating-house whose only provender appeared,

from its Commercial Road front, to be "hot jellied eels" at sixpence the bowl. The proprietor, a black, greasy-looking man, came out to the rear door, but in his free hand he held a protecting meat-cleaver threateningly upraised.

"For God's sake," cried the man trapped for life in a monkey body, "give me food! I'll pay anything. I'll eat out here in the rear. I—I won't hurt you. Give me food."

Evidently seeing a glorious opportunity to mulct a queer being who had strayed from some traveling sideshow, the proprietor kindly offered, cleaver still upraised, to provide all the bowls of hot jellied eels that would be desired—at four shillings the bowl! Without any hesitation or discussion whatever, Eustice Annesly reached down into his pocket and handed over four shining shillings from his capital of eight pounds odd. A moment later he was gratefully seated on an old, battered ashpail, devouring the tin pie-dishful of jellied eels that was handed him at the door in exchange for his money.

Wherever he walked that night, the crowds still continued to follow him up and down the streets. And at every place he tried to negotiate for a bed he was met by a reception similar to those he had met with in his effort to secure food. The doors of a very decent hostelry in York Road were locked with alacrity as he ascended the steps—to open no more. A Chinaman with club studded with sharpened iron spikes drove him menacingly away from an Asiatic sailors' boarding-house in Pennyfields. He was cursed at—through the upper windows only—of the cheapest lodging-house in the cheapest part of the Limehouse Basin.

He thought desperately of going to the other extreme—of trying his luck at the Cecil, at the Savoy; then he looked down at himself and thought desperately of his scant eight pounds capital, already dwindling; for a moment, too, he held thoughts of going back to that little haven of refuge in Guilford Street—but his remembrance of those dignified individuals who inhabited it caused him to shake his head, for he realized but too well that that step was now impossible. And so he continued walking, walking.

Thus nine o'clock, ten o'clock, eleven o'clock came. Then the crowds that had been following him since early that day began to melt away. By midnight he was walking the East End alone. At twelve-thirty he was fortunate enough, by ringing door-bell after door-bell, to stumble on a sympathetic female lodging-house keeper who, at least listening to his plea through the barred door, gave him permission to sleep on a dirty mattress in her wood shed—for five shillings, cash in advance.

And thus ended his first day, huddled on a damp mattress, his fur under his ill-fitting suit the chief protection against the cold night air of London.

Followed more days, days like the first, days of sixpenny meals at four shillings—nights of rest on that foul mattress—at five shillings a night! And thus, naturally, at this rate of expenditure, his capital melted away. After seven days had passed—seven hideous days of barking dogs, gaping crowds, rearing horses, and threatening police—he realized, with a sinking heart, that he had reached the jumping-off place, for his money was reduced to a lone one-pound note. Scarnum was right, after all.

The circus, with its people of freakdom and its side-show platforms, was the only life left for him—his last refuge. So he made his way boldly in a cab to High Holborn, walked quickly into a large periodical store that he had patronized in days that were now gone for ever, and purchased a copy of the *English Carnival Review*, the publication that Scarnum had claimed was devoted entirely to the interests of shows and outdoor exhibitions. In the department set aside for routes and dates, he found that Scarnum's American Circus was playing in the town of Marseilles, France. And with this information in his possession he bade his waiting cab carry him to the Western Union telegraph office off Trafalgar Square, which he resolutely entered and over whose polished counter he sent the brief wire:

"Scarnum, Marseilles, France.
"Will join. How about transportation?
"Grillo."

Not thirty minutes later the answer to his wire came clicking back:

"Grillo, Western Union Office, Trafalgar Square, London.
"Position and salary O.K. Am wiring ticket and Channel passage. Show goes back to America next week. "Scarnum."

It was the most welcome message Eustice Annesly had ever received. The outcast was to be taken in, to be made a peer of his fellows.

CHAPTER LI

TO Eustice Annesly's dismay, life with the circus proved scarcely better than life on the outside. Not one of the freaks—every one of which at least possessed a human body, even though deformed, diseased or abnormal—evinced a desire to have anything more to do with him than was absolutely necessary. So far as actual association with him went, it appeared to them to be unthinkable, even to such a monstrous thing as the Human Spider, a poor, ignorant, illiterate creature from the Kentucky hills, whose legs and trunk, due to a childhood attack of untreated anterior poliomyelitis, a spinal cord disease, had withered away so completely that, by means of his powerfully muscled arms, he walked inverted on his hands. And because of this kingly isolation which he had literally thrust upon him, Annesly suffered a loneliness endurable only because of an occasional chat with Scarnum.

As for Scarnum, he was radiantly happy now that Annesly had demonstrated his willingness to become a permanent fixture of the Scarnum shows. After they began to strike the American towns where Annesly, under the professional cognomen assigned to him, had been billed in advance, the crowds became enormous. In many of the larger cities Scarnum was forced to

375

turn people away from the tents on account of the inability of the guards to keep the throng moving.

Packed shoulder to shoulder, the spectators stood their ground in front of Eustice Annesly's platform and showed no desire to leave. They stared at him, open-mouthed. Men held up their little sons, and women their little daughters, that the children might have a better view of him. University professors of anthropology brought their classes in a body to his tent. And for enduring all this he received two hundred and fifty dollars at the end of every week.

His duties, fortunately, were very simple. By the terms of his contract, all he was compelled to do was to remain seated on the platform, rising every twenty minutes to give a short two-minute talk. In this talk, which was written by Scarnum's Press agent, he related briefly how he had been captured in an African jungle when he was only a small monkey; how he had been traded to a missionary living on the West African coast; how the latter had slowly educated him and taught him human speech, syllable by syllable; how he had finally come to America following the death of the missionary from sleeping sickness caused by the bite of a tsetse fly.

On account of the gigantic crowds, he realized that he could easily have coerced Scarnum into paying him five hundred dollars a week for his simple and easily performed work. But he was too heartsick, too unhappy, too full of misery to care for money itself. For of what use was money to him? Eustice Annesly —his body at least—was dead and buried. And he— or Eustice Annesly's brain—had been imprisoned by

the devilish technique of a too skilful surgeon in the
body of a gorilla. What, then, could life hold out for
him? Nothing—for hopes, visions, aspirations were
dead, too.

Often and often he thought of Sybil Mainwaring.
Many and many a night he awoke in his tiny bunk
in the animal car of the circus and saw her charming,
girlish face floating in the ill-smelling darkness that
surrounded him. And sometimes, too, he thought of
one who was a stranger to him, Geoffrey, the young
Earl of Olford, the man who had won her—and he
cursed so long and fervently that even the beasts
awoke and with low growls commenced pacing up and
down in their cages.

Now and then he wondered whether the marriage had
taken place between Sybil and Lord Olford. Always,
for some reason, a tiny spark of hope burned in him
that she had not married the nobleman—that she had
suddenly come to the realization that it was Eustice
Annesly whom she loved. But, after all, he realized
how futile was such a hope on his part, for Eustice
Annesly was dead—and he was now only a black ape-
man who could never expect to have any woman for
a wife.

The show, heading ever westward across the United
States, was exhibiting in a huge tent pitched on the
bank of the Mississippi River, at Burlington, Iowa,
when Annesly's last spark of hope was cruelly snuffed
out. The crowds these days and nights were even
heavier than heretofore, for far to the south of this
small city a farcical trial was being concluded in a
tiny Tennessee country town, a trial attended by

journalists from all over the world, a trial in which
a young teacher of Evolution was being held to punish-
ment for teaching that man and monkey were in some
way related.   Scarnum had long since added to his
flamboyant lithographs taunting signs against Tennessee, and the crowds that now came to see the talking
gorilla were heavier than ever before.   On the night
in question Annesly had just finished his last weary
speech for the night.   A hundred feet from the open
tent door a Mississippi steamboat, with huge paddle-
wheel at stern, rose and fell on the broad bosom of
the river.   Negroes laughed and rolled ivory dice on
the broad, sloping, cobble-stoned levee, using the very
light that filtered freely from the ticket-taker's stand
for their gleeful gambling.   The crowds were being
shoved and driven out by the guards.   One by one
the flickering gasoline lamps were being extinguished.
An elderly man, carrying a valise, a portable typewriter and a cane, a man who had arrived too late
to do more than get in for a brief glimpse of the
curiosity and hear its closing words, a man whom
Annesly was afterwards to learn from the ticket-taker
was an English journalist who had been sent clear
to Dayton, Tennessee, to cover the Scopes trial, and
who on the way back to his boat at New York had made
this roundabout journey merely to add to his copy a
few words about the talking monkey, dropped a newspaper from his coat pocket as he left the tent uneasily
consulting his time-table.   From where Annesly sat
he could see that it was a *London Mercury;* so he
hopped down on all-fours from his platform to the saw-
dust-covered floor and rescued it.   He opened it

eagerly, anxious to see some news from the city where he had spent his life as Eustice Annesly, and almost the first article that caught his eye, in the two-weeks-old newspaper, was one whose headlines ran:

"THE EARL OF OLFORD TAKES A WIFE

"Geoffrey, the Youthful 14th Earl of Olford, Weds Miss Sybil Mainwaring at Noon To-Day

"Society turns out in full to attend the brilliant ceremony held in St. George's, Hanover Square.

"London's democratic young Earl adds a rare beauty to his private fortune of a million pounds sterling."

That night, in his bunk in the animal car, Eustice Annesly's eyes, animal orbs as they were, little and beady and black, demonstrated for the first time that they could supply a copious flow of tears. In fact, it was not until next morning that he had composed himself even to the point where he could finish the article.

From that time on he sank into deeper and deeper gloom. An idea, at first not to be considered for a second, began to recur to him with greater and greater persistency. And on the last day of October, the date on which Scarnum's Circus always disbanded and went into winter quarters, he arrived at a definite decision regarding his plans for the future.

With his accumulated salary strapped in a chamois-skin belt around his waist, he traveled to the nearest railroad division point. There he hired a private car for four hundred dollars and rode dejectedly across America's mid-west to New York. As soon as the train

reached its destination he engaged a taxicab at the
very door of the Grand Central Station and ordered
the driver to carry him to the main offices of the
Cunard Steamship Line. From here he emerged a
few moments later, minus another four hundred dollars, but in the breast-pocket of his coat a fully-paid
first-class passage, via private suite, from New York
to Southampton, England. Within ten minutes he
was at the Cunard Pier at the foot of Sixteenth Street,
where three giant funnels, reaching high above the pier
itself, and belching black smoke, marked the imminent
departure of another leviathan of the seas. One hour
later as the ship, now out of the river, threw off its
tug lines and headed into the open sea on its own
steam, he sat alone and dejected in his private suite,
staring unseeingly out at the dancing blue waves
through the porthole.

Followed six days in which he never even went on
deck—six days in which his meals were brought to him
by a very nervous steward. Then Southampton. A
special train, wirelessed for by him when his ship was
but one day out from England, awaited him in the
huge train-shed, puffing alongside the very boat-train
itself. Almost an hour and a half later, a full twenty
minutes before the arrival of the actual boat-train
which followed him, he was threading his way hurriedly
through Waterloo station—dear familiar sights were
meeting his eyes—and climbing once more into an
English taxi. And still ten minutes later he was being
whirled up to the tiny door of the little Charing Cross
Emergency Hospital which had turned the channel of
his existence into a path that he had never dreamed of

in years gone by. And when at last he stepped into the tiny reception-room, no less a person than old Dr. Michaelovitch himself stepped forward to greet him.

"Why, why," the old surgeon began, surprised, "is it really——"

"Yes," Annesly interrupted bitterly, "it's the man whose life you ruined by your damnable surgical ingenuity. I promised you five months ago that I would try life under the new conditions. I've done so—and failed to find it anything but a living hell." He snapped open his money belt and flung it on Michaelovitch's desk. "There—that belt contains nearly four thousand American dollars. It's yours to use for charity—or for medical research—as you see fit."

"But—but—yourself?" Michaelovitch asked.

"I've determined to end it all, to kill myself."

For a long time the medical man stared gravely at him. Finally he spoke: "I can plainly see by your tone that you are desperate; that you mean what you say. And I realize now that any arguments on my part will be useless. You may not have known it, but for a good many months I have been thinking of you —and of your case—and of how you were 'making out' over there in America. There was an article about the Scopes evolution case—in the *London Mercury*, I think it was—and the writer of it who had been over there mentioned the existence of a talking ape he had seen for a few minutes in a traveling show somewhere in the State of Iowa—an ape similar to the one which lived in the East End here for a week last spring. So I realized full well, of course, that that was you." Michaelovitch paused gravely. "But now let me ask

you a question—and think well, mighty well, before
you reply. Are you willing to take a chance of losing
your life entirely in order to regain your position in
a human body?"

"Willing?" responded Eustice Annesly. "Willing?
Is a man trembling on the brink of self-destruction
willing to take a chance to remove the cause of his
unhappiness? But I beg of you not to tantalize me
with false hopes. How—how can it—— Tell me what
you mean by your question?"

"Simply this," Andrev Michaelovitch replied, beckoning his visitor into a chair, and dropping into one
himself. "Every now and then we see a patient—in
most instances a man—brought into the hospital here,
injured in such a way that he ultimately dies. A few
of these cases are due to tram accidents; others are
due to bus and car accidents in London's narrow
streets; and still others are head and brain injuries,
resulting from objects being carelessly dropped by
workmen from the roofs of buildings; and, in one case,
we had a skull concussion due to a piece of metal dropping from a plane headed for Croydon Aerodrome.
However, as to the rate at which these accident cases
are brought in, it varies greatly. Sometimes they
arrive as fast as three a week. At other times we do not
see one for a month or more."

"Yes," Annesly broke in eagerly, "and what bearing
can this have on my case?"

"As follows," Michaelovitch went on: "Suppose that
some time in the future we receive a case of a fatal brain
injury. Suppose that you have held yourself in readiness here at the hospital for an immediate ascension to

the operating table. Suppose that I remove your brain—the brain of Eustice Annesly—from your body —the body of Grillo, 'the missing link'—and attempt to transpose it for a second time to the brain cavity of that victim, whoever he may be. I might fail. The operation is dangerous—highly so. It demands the most skilful technique. The chances are against its being a success—and I verily believe that without the injection of my artificial cerebro-spinal fluid, of which the formula is still known to me alone, it would be an absolute impossibility. At any rate, there is the proposition. Are you willing to submit to it? It rests entirely with you."

CHAPTER LII

FOR a moment Eustice Annesly gasped. Then for
the first time did he realize what the sensations
of a spirit doomed to the lower regions might be on
seeing a chance of Heaven held forth to him. Finally
he collected his wits.

"Oh, Dr. Michaelovitch," he implored, "I'll do anything—absolutely anything—to get even a chance to
gain my freedom from the body of a gorilla. Even
if you could transfer my brain to the body of a cripple
—or an East Indian—that would be a thousand times
preferable to my present condition."

"I am willing to risk it for your sake," Michaelovitch
said. "We are taking a big chance. If I fail to join
up the optic nerves properly, you will be blind. If
the auditory nerves do not unite, you will be deaf. If
the cells of the spinal cord fail to cohere to those of
the brain matter, you may be worse than deaf or blind;
in other words, you may be paralyzed. Are you still
willing?"

"Absolutely," the monkey-man affirmed. "Anything, anything but this——" And with a gesture
Eustice Annesly indicated his grotesque monkey body.

So that night he entered a bed in the Charing Cross
Emergency Hospital—to begin the indefinite wait for

a fatal accident which would provide him with an uninjured body. At times he was gripped by the desire to live, by the fear of risking his life on the skill and knowledge of one man alone—but always, when he thought of the circus days in America and his complete isolation from human-kind, he steadfastly determined to proceed with the project at all hazards.

One afternoon the telephone bell in the downstairs office rang loudly. A minute later he detected the clang of the electric ambulance as it whirled from the hospital. Not a quarter of an hour afterwards he heard the return of the same vehicle; and, shortly after, the shuffling of feet on the floor below—the shuffling noise always made by men carrying a stretcher. And as he lay there in bed, wondering what it was all about, young Dr. Boris Michaelovitch hurried into his room, wheeling the rolling platform that was used to carry patients to the operating-room.

"Quick!" he whispered. "Roll on! No time to explain. Every second is precious."

Tremblingly, Annesly mounted the flat carriage and found himself, amid a chaos of conflicting thoughts, being rolled from the room on rubber-tired wheels. A quarter of a minute later he was being wheeled into a tiny room, enameled all in white, and with hundreds of glittering instruments in glass cases around the walls. Then he caught a glimpse of old Dr. Michaelovitch bustling about a table on which lay the body of a man partially covered with a sheet.

"Hurry!" the latter grunted to his son. "The ether cone—on your patient! Work fast!"

And, as young Dr. Boris Michaelovitch placed the

ether cone to Eustice Annesly's face, the man with the body of a simian dropped away into blissful unconsciousness.

Followed an eternity of blackness, punctuated at irregular intervals by faint glimpses of light, by ill-defined impressions of moving figures, and by the peculiar buzz-buzz of voices talking in subdued tones. And then after what seemed thousands of years of this half-consciousness, he opened his eyes one sunny morning and found himself in a narrow, white-enameled bed, placed in a small room not greatly unlike the one where he had first awakened to a new life as Grillo, the 'missing link.' He blinked his eyes dazedly for a few seconds; then he became aware of the fact that Dr. Boris Michaelovitch was standing at the foot of the bed, looking sadly down at him.

He stared about himself, blinked for a few more seconds, and suddenly asked:

"How—how—how did the operation fare? Did it fail? Were we too late? Did——"

Dr. Boris Michaelovitch crossed the floor swiftly, and presently returned, bearing a large hand-mirror which he thrust into the fingers of his questioner.

"Look!" he commanded. "Does it seem as though the operation had failed?"

Eustice Annesly stared at the mirror unbelievingly. Then a cry of delight broke from him, for he saw the face of a man—an actual human being—instead of the dreadful, hairy countenance of the gorilla. The face in the mirror had light yellow hair and clear blue eyes, and the skin was white and smooth and without a blemish. Although he had never personally fancied the extreme type of blondness in men, he lay back in the bed and fervently breathed the comment:

"Doctor, it seems too good to be true."

The latter brought up a chair to the bedside.

"But it is true, nevertheless," the young medical man said simply. "You will be shocked at what I have to tell you, though. My father is dead!"

"Dead!" ejaculated Annesly, rising on one elbow.

The physician raised his hand. "Yes, dead. But don't excite yourself for you are still convalescing from the last operation, which occurred just six weeks ago to-day. I'll try to explain what happened, to the best of my ability. It seems that on that last afternoon—the afternoon on which, you'll remember, I wheeled you to the operating room myself— an unusual accident took place in Shaftsbury Avenue. The driver of a motor truck which carried an assortment of twisted and round steel rods intended for use in reinforcing concrete work in a new structure ascending there, lost control of his machine—with the result that it unexpectedly backed on the pavement. One of the projecting rods, however, squarely caught a passer-by. It forced his head tightly against the wall of a building, piercing his skull for a bare half-inch.

"A near-by chemist telephoned to us here, and we immediately sent for the victim. Father found, on examination, that it was a fatal case, for the brain was badly mutilated by the impingement of the steel rod. At his command I brought you speedily to the operating-room and put you under ether. While I was doing this, father was laying back the scalp of the injured man in long strips, and using the electric trephine saw in such a way that he could remove the upper and rear portion of the skull in one piece. This accomplished, he took out the injured brain entirely, preventing hemorrhage in the blood-vessels that were left by ligating them, exactly as in the previous operation. Then he directed his energies to your own person—which at that time, of course, was the person of Grillo. Fortunately he did not have to delay matters in opening the cranial cavity of the gorilla, for as soon as the scalp was laid completely back the only procedure necessary was the removal of the tiny silver connecting-plates placed there seven or more months ago. Anticipating the possibility of having to do much work in a short space of time, father had had for several days a quantity of his artificial cerebro-spinal fluid in readiness refrigerated and sterilized. So the only difficulty that confronted him was the actual transposition itself of the brain of Eustice Annesly to the cavity of the unfortunate victim of the accident.

"It would only weary you, I am sure, if I were to describe the finer points of the operation. So I shall pass over them by telling you that after father had joined up artery to artery, vein to vein, nerve to nerve, and had injected a quantity of his compound, he merely followed the usual procedure: first, trepanning the hole in the skull caused by the impact of the steel rod; secondly, replacing the bone cup and fastening it to its base by the usual silver plates and inset silver screws; and thirdly, drawing back the strips of scalp and stitching them together, with tiny pieces of gauze between to act as drains. If you will raise your hand to your scalp you can feel under the hair a number of hard ridges where those strips have grown together again. Now is everything clear to you so far?"

"Absolutely," Annesly assured him. "But—but the death—the death of your father. I don't understand that."

"I am coming to that. The nervous strain of that last operation was so severe on him that he took a walk that night along the Embankment in order to breathe in the fresh, cool air off the Thames and quiet himself down for a restful sleep. A piercing, sleety rain came up—a rain such as only London can provide! He was insufficiently clad to withstand the effects of it. Pneumonia, the nemesis of the older generation, set in. Within seventy-two hours he was dead. From that time on I took care of your case myself. One of the deplorable features of the whole thing, however, is that with father's death there passed a secret of medicine that would have brought about world-wide changes in the art of brain surgery—for not a scrap of paper, not a line of writing, not a final word did he leave by which the formula of his artificial cerebro-spinal fluid could have been given over to the profession." He rose from his chair. "And now for a few simple tests, that we may determine the degree of success of the operation."

CHAPTER LIII

THE doctor passed out of the room, but presently returned to the bedside, carrying a small glass tray on which stood a number of test tubes, each holding a glass stirring-rod. After opening what seemed to be a clinical notebook, he withdrew one of the glass rods and placed it directly beneath the nostrils of the patient.

"Sniff this," he ordered, "and tell me what odor it gives forth."

"Peppermint," Annesly said, without any hesitation.

After making an entry in his notebook, the young doctor withdrew another rod and placed it between the patient's lips. "What flavor?" he asked.

"Cinnamon."

He then opened his surgeon's white apron and held up the end of his necktie. "What color is this?"

"Lavender," replied Annesly.

"Good!" the physician commented. "The union of the cranial nerves, so far, is all satisfactory."

Dr. Boris Michaelovitch then withdrew from his pocket his watch, which he held in turn to each of his patient's ears. After their owner had assured him that he could distinctly hear its ticking, the medical man ordered his patient to roll his eyes, to raise his eyelids,

390

to frown, to open and close his lower jaw, and to perform a host of other odd, muscular actions. When each test· had been passed in an apparently satisfactory manner, Boris Michaelovitch smiled for the first time.

"An absolutely perfect transposition," he announced. "Except for those long ridges on your scalp, no one could ever know that such a strange operation had been performed. It is remarkable—highly remarkable!"

"But how," asked the man in bed finally, "am I going to assume the position in life which belonged to this man—this man whose body I now have? His name, his profession, his degree of education, his past, his friends will all be unknown to me. I shall get inextricably tangled up if I try to pretend that I am he. So what am I to do?"

"I have taken care of all that," replied Boris Michaelovitch. "While you were still in the post-operative coma, his friends and relatives were allowed to see you only for a moment or so each. As you commenced to emerge from it, these visits have been cut down even to his closest family connections. And in the meantime I have not been idle." Boris Michaelovitch withdrew a packet of papers from an inside pocket and held it up in full view. "I have here data which I have been collecting for several weeks. That data, which I shall place immediately in your hands so that you can study and familiarize yourself with it down to the finest detail, contains this man's age, his name, the descriptions of his friends' appearances, his connections, and dozens and dozens of facts and happenings of his past life. Fortified with that—and a reasonable amount of what the Americans call 'bluff'—you should be able to step from the hospital back to his position in life with but very few slips. Those slips, however, which are bound to crop up now and then in the future, will be overlooked by those who knew him and attributed to the effects of a supposedly simple trepanning operation. Now take these papers and commence to study——"

The young physician paused, listening. A woman's voice was plainly audible in the corridor, just outside the door of the room. Her words came in to the two occupants with startling distinctness:

"But you shall not keep me from him any longer," she was saying tearfully. "For an entire week now I have been denied. I will—I tell you I *will* see him."

Dr. Boris Michaelovitch immediately dropped the packet of papers to the floor and rushed quickly to the doorway. But he was too late. The door flew open. A woman swept swiftly across the room and dropped on her knees by Eustice Annesly's bedside, flinging her arm around his neck and pressing her cheek snug up against his own.

"My dearest one, my dearest one," she said, smiling through her tears, "they have saved you for me."

For a few chaotic seconds he stared at the face which rested so close to his own—the face of a girl who had meant so much to him—the face of Sybil herself. Then he folded her joyfully into his arms, as the glorious, overwhelming truth burst upon him.

In that second brain-transposing operation he had

secured the body of no other than Geoffrey, Earl of Olford—with the result that Lord Geoffrey Olford's fortune of a million pounds sterling, Lord Geoffrey Olford's title, and Lord Geoffrey Olford's wife were now his for the years to come.

CHAPTER LIV

SOME time before Eastwood had reached the astounding end of his unusual story, the square open window of the death cell had changed its curtain from point-flecked black velvet to gray—shroud gray! Now, as he stopped speaking entirely, the gray began to be pierced by rays of orange-red. Krenwicz arose silently, stepped forward and snapped out the one bulb of the prison lamp. Now the four men sat in the semi-light, neither darkness nor day, like gray figures. The clock on the wall ironically struck the hour of five-thirty. Thirty minutes more to live? Far down the corridor could be indistinctly heard the sound of several voices, the muffled blow of a hammer, the clank of a wrench, the voice of a man saying: "Try and throw . . . that switch . . . in backward . . . tighten up the knee-pad connection."

Not a word had been spoken in the square cell, and it was Krenwicz who, gazing fascinatedly at McCaigh, the Iron Man, who sat in the gray light immobile, unmoved, unshaken at the imminence of the fate which was now rushing with the speed of an express train upon two of them, broke the silence. His voice was forced, ghastly, shaky. His eyes no longer shone with

394

the dancing devils of nine hours ago. They were now hollow, dead.

"Eastwood, your story—your story—was a most remarkable piece of fiction. I am glad that I—I—had the privilege of being your auditor, for you succeeded in carrying me completely out of myself in these—our last horrible hours." He paused, passing a hand over his white forehead. "God, what a night it has been! Romance, Fantasy——" He gazed across from him at the emotionless Iron Man who coolly tossed the smoldering stub of his cigarette into the cuspidor. Then, swallowing hard, the Russian added: "And now, I— I think you will all agree with me, we—we must ask Shanahan which of the three stories appealed to him most."

Even as he had spoken, the white light of morning had spread itself through the tiny window, filling the lone room with a weird radiance. A chill feeling—a feeling as of being enveloped in semi-fog—seemed to wrap itself around the men assembled there. A beam of sunlight clambered over the sill and threw itself defiantly against the gray rugosities of the opposite wall. Shanahan opened his lips to speak, but stopped short. Voices, this time louder, more distinct, more authoritative, sounded down the corridor. Many feet. A second later the oaken door swung open, and in the opening, the gray-haired warden of Sing Sing at one side, a fresh-faced turnkey at the other, stood the same elderly man who had appeared there the night before. He stepped in. He beckoned Shanahan out. He waited a moment. The warden, with a courteous nod, and the turnkey with a jingle of his keys, departed up the corridor. The visitor was now quite alone. He advanced slowly into the center of the open cell, and stood leaning against Shanahan's chair. The three men noted his bloodshot eyes, his dishevelled hair, the lines of worry and age that had crept into his austere face.

"Gentlemen," he said, and his voice was old and quavering, "pity me—pity me because I am now man instead of official. Pity the governor of the State of New York who resigns at noon to-day." He paused. "The woman who was with Creynell the night you saw him in the foyer of the New Amsterdam Theater—the woman whom he had prepared to ruin the night after two of you killed him—the mere girl as she was—has told me all." He fumbled in his breast pocket. He flung on the table three crisp documents, each bearing on its face in staring black type the one significant word "PARDON." "Gentlemen, it is right that you three should know the truth, bitter as it is." His voice rose. "By God, he *was* a snake! A cruel, despicable snake. That woman—that girl—told me all before dawn this morning. She—she——" his voice broke, "she was my—my daughter."

He swung suddenly on his heel and with head bowed down walked from the cell. And only the three gleaming white documents and the sound of his dragging footsteps were left to prove the reality of his visit. As for the three men, they rose stiffly, dazedly from their chairs, and each from his corner moved toward the table as if in a dream.

"The governor's daughter!" murmured McCaigh, the Iron Man, brokenly. Then, with an inarticulate sob, he collapsed into the quick-reaching arms of his two companions. And the sun, now generously pouring the cool liquid gold of life itself over the sill of the stone room, filled the entire space.

THE END